A WEDD   ANY

SANDY BARKER

One More Chapter
a division of HarperCollins*Publishers* Ltd
1 London Bridge Street
London SE1 9GF
www.harpercollins.co.uk
HarperCollins*Publishers*
1st Floor, Watermarque Building, Ringsend Road
Dublin 4, Ireland

This paperback edition 2022
1
First published in Great Britain in ebook format
by HarperCollins*Publishers* 2022

A catalogue record of this book is available from the British Library

ISBN: 978-0-00-853678-7

Printed and bound in the UK using 100% Renewable Electricity
by CPI Group (UK) Ltd

For my sister, Vic
Thank you for inspiring such a fun character to write – I love you

Prologue

*O*h, my god! How could I have been so stupid?

    Because getting married is stressful! And travel is stressful! And when you put those two things together …

    Argh! I cannot believe this. How did I let this happen?

    The others whiz around me, checking every nook and cranny of our Tuscan castle apartment. Josh has even checked the car——no luck. As they look under furniture and rifle through the wardrobes——again!——I mentally scour every step of our journey here, trying to remember when I had it last and where I could have left it.

    Oh, god, I'm going to be sick. Breathe … breathe … breathe …

    Minutes pass, then everyone stills, silently coming to the same conclusion. My sister locks eyes with me. Concern, confirmation, commiseration——they all play out on her face.

    'It's not here,' her eyes tell me.

    IT'S NOT HERE!

    Oh, my god! Where the fuck is my fucking wedding dress?

Chapter One

CAT

London

I climb onto a stool at the breakfast bar and watch as my scrummy French boyfriend potters about the kitchen, his tall frame moving with practised ease. After being together for more than two years, he knows my kitchen better than I do, though to be honest, that isn't hard. Tonight, he's making *coq au vin*, one of his specialties, and it smells delicious in here. He's an amazing cook. He says he's *'comme ci comme ça'*—just all right—but that's him being modest.

I love having Jean-Luc here in London, especially during the week—coming home to him after a long day of teaching, spending our evenings together talking or listening to music or watching television. It makes me feel like part of a normal couple. Well, a normal couple who share a flat with someone else. Thank god my flatmate, Jane, is so understanding—she adores Jean-Luc, and she certainly loves his cooking.

He's not here all the time, mind you—just a couple of

times a month for four or five days, sometimes longer. This time, it's a short visit. He arrived today—Thursday—and can only stay until Monday morning, as he's doing an interview in Bern on Tuesday. My boyfriend—International Journalist Extraordinaire. I'm so proud.

I definitely prefer his visits to London than mine to Paris, which are usually just for a weekend. That means an evening train there on a Friday and a late-afternoon train home on a Sunday. Hardly ideal—expensive too—but I'm just not ready to move. To Paris. With my hot boyfriend.

Yes, really.

He's asked about a million times. All right, it's six—a number I'm sure of because I'm counting.

I do love him. As in head-over-heels-he's-my-soulmate love. In actual fact, I've loved him most of my life—first as my best friend in high school, then as a young woman exchanging letters across the world. But at nineteen I'd put an end to it. Stupidly. Because of a jealous boyfriend. A decade and a half later, chance brought us together again—in Paris—and I finally realised that I'd always been in love with him, that he was my *person*. I am not going to let him go again.

But London is home. And as much as I (mostly) enjoy my time in Paris, it isn't. I'm not sure it ever will be.

And even if Jean-Luc started talking about moving here—which he hasn't—well, I'm not sure I'm ready for that either—living together full time, I mean. What if we run out of things to say to each other? What if cohabitating obliterates the romance? Or worse! What if he gets bored with me? He used to be married to a supermodel anthropologist and I'm just a schoolteacher who hails from Sydney.

Now I sound like my sister.

'Wine?' he asks.

'Hello, Cat Parsons, pleased to meet you,' I deadpan. He tuts good naturedly, then pours me a glass of the red he brought with him from France. That's another thing to love about him—he always shows up with wine. JK!

'*Salut*,' he says, clinking his glass against mine. We sip our wine, watching each other over the rims of our glasses.

See? Isn't this lovely, just as it is? Why mess with perfection?

Lizzo starts belting out from my phone as it vibrates on the countertop and when I pick it up, it's my sister's boyfriend, Josh.

'Hello, you,' I say, accepting the video call.

'Hey. So, I think I've figured it out.' Josh is planning a surprise for Sarah's fortieth birthday. My thinking is that turning forty is surprise enough—oh, my god, where did my thirties go?—and that she hates surprises.

'And?'

'Tuscany,' he says. One word, but he drags it out like he's pitching a film location. 'Tussscannnyyy.'

'That sounds good,' I say. 'Sarah likes Italy.'

'That's it? I've been working on this for weeks and that's all you've got?'

'Sorry. How about this? Oh, my god! That's brilliant and she will absolutely love it!' She won't. I mean, she *will* like a trip to Tuscany, but a *surprise* trip? Uh, no. My sister likes to organise everything down to the last paperclip, especially travel.

Josh rolls his eyes at me. 'Hey, man,' he says to Jean-Luc who's just appeared at my shoulder.

'*Salut, mon frère*.' I love that these two get along—they really are like brothers. Sarah even said that Josh feels closer

5

to Jean-Luc than he does to his actual brother. 'So, Tuscany? I think this is a good plan, a good present,' says Jean-Luc.

'Thank you!' Josh makes a face at me, like he's been vindicated or something.

'It's not that it's a bad idea——Italy, I mean——but how are you going to make the trip a surprise? Drug her, then carry her onto the plane and she wakes up in Italy? Surprise!'

'Of course not. I just want to figure everything out before I tell her. Part of the present is that she doesn't have to organise any of it.'

'That's the other thing. Have you met my sister? The one who organises her friends' pantries for fun, who loves sticky notes, and lives and dies by her calendar? You sure you want to take that away from her? She may never forgive you.'

He laughs again. 'I'm sure. She's turning forty. I want this to be *big* and I don't want her worrying about any of the details.'

I shrug. 'It's your funeral.'

'*Anyway*, I also wanna double-check the dates——I'm still looking at late October. I know you only have a week off around then, Cat, but do you think you can get some extra time off?'

'Already on it. I've talked to the Head of School and it's looking likely that she'll let me go on half-term a few days early.'

'Oh, cool.'

'And even if Catherine cannot be there, I will.' I throw Jean-Luc a stern look which he rebuts with a grin.

'Awesome,' says Josh. 'Shit, she's out of the shower. Talk to you guys later.' He ends the call abruptly.

'A trip to Tuscany will be nice, *n'est-ce pas?*' asks Jean-Luc.

'Yes,' I concede, 'it will. I've only been there for a minute-and-a-half on that bus trip.'

'I am not sure that counts,' he says, spinning my stool so I'm facing him.

'It definitely doesn't. I think we had all of six hours in Florence and I barely remember the surrounding countryside.'

'That is the best part, the countryside——the fields of sunflowers, the towns, the *castles*. It is a beautiful part of the world,' he says. 'Romantic.' Honestly, the public loos at Waterloo Station would be romantic with Jean-Luc. He's like romance personified. He proves my point by leaning down to nuzzle my neck with his soft lips, peppering it with tiny kisses that send shivers down my spine.

'Hello, loves,' Jane calls from the hallway. Jean-Luc steps back, blows me a kiss, and returns to his spot at the cooker as Jane bundles in, laden with cloth carry bags. She dumps them on the floor.

'Salut,' says Jean-Luc, now wiping down the countertop——he's a clean-as-you-go cook, another reason to love him——and that's me *and* Jane.

I leap off my stool to help Jane unpack. 'Bought out most of Sainsbury's I see.' I start pawing through the bags and extracting items of interest. Ooh, brie!

'Honestly! What is wrong with me? Every sodding time! It's all very well when I'm *in* the sodding shop, lugging the basket around, but when will I learn? It's a stuffed-to-the-gills bus ride and a long walk back to the flat, *Jane*,' she chastises herself.

I look up from the shopping and her cheeks are pink with frustration——or maybe it's exertion. 'Right, leave all this to me. Go and change and when you come back, there's

7

wine!' I say brightly. She steps out of her ridiculously high heels—really, they must be at least five inches tall—and sighs. Sending an air kiss my way, she retreats to her room. 'Thank you, lovely,' echoes back down the hallway.

I do love living with Jane. When our former flatmate, Alex, moved out—because I may or may not have accidentally and drunkenly shagged him only to discover that he'd been madly in love with me for ages and thought we were going to be boyfriend and girlfriend but I didn't feel the same way—Jane and I had planned on getting a new flatmate. But weeks turned into months and even though we'd both gone from paying a third of the rent to half, we actually preferred it being just the two of us. And of course, when Jean-Luc became a semi-regular fixture, I was glad we didn't have another flatmate. That and being able to turn Alex's bedroom into a guestroom-cum-study.

'We are close, *chérie*,' says Jean-Luc. 'Set the table?'

'*Absolument*, as soon as I've finished here,' I say, moving things about in our too tiny fridge and shoving things in where they can fit. I close it and glance at Jean-Luc, his proud Gallic brow creased in concentration as he sprinkles fresh parsley over three plates of *coq au vin*. I may just have the most perfect boyfriend in the world. Why would I want to mess this up by moving in together?

'Catherine. *Catherine*.' Jean-Luc's voice wakes me from a deep sleep and my eyes flutter open to see him perched on the edge of the bed, doubled over. It's a jolt to my brain and I sit upright and scramble over to him.

'Are you all right?' I reach for the switch on the lamp

next to the bed and turn it on. He recoils, squinting and turning his head away. 'Sorry, darling.' I rub his back as he groans, grimacing. 'Are you going to be sick?' He doesn't answer but bolts for the bedroom door and disappears into the darkness of the flat. The door to the loo slams and I listen uncomfortably to my love being sick. Eventually, there's a flush and he returns to the room, pale-faced, almost greenish.

He leans against the doorframe and runs his hands through his hair. 'Food poisoning, I think,' he says quietly. 'Oh.' He dashes back to the loo. Oh, god, the poor guy—now it's coming out both ends. I slip out into the hallway and retrieve a bucket from under the kitchen sink and a wet flannel from the bathroom. When I get back to my room, he's prone on his side of the bed panting slightly, his brow slick with sweat.

'Here, darling,' I say, laying the flannel across his forehead. His hand clasps mine as a thank you. 'And I'll put this here in case you need to be sick and can't make it to the toilet, all right?' I show him the bucket and he squints at it through the slits of his eyes, then gives a slight nod of his head.

'Everything okay?' asks Jane from my doorway. I see her eyes flick to Jean-Luc's near naked body—he only sleeps in his briefs and the covers have spilled onto the floor—then they meet mine, concerned.

'He's sick. Food poisoning, he thinks.'

'The chicken?' she asks, her eyes widening.

'*Non, non, pas de poulet.* A baguette from Gare du Nord, I think,' says a weary voice from the bed. Jane looks visibly relieved and I have to say that I am too. Jean-Luc is the best cook in the flat and I'd hate to have to ban him from the kitchen.

'All right. I hope you're feeling better in the morning,' she says. She offers a wan smile and leaves. It's only now that I look at the time. 2:13am.

'Do you want some water?' I ask. 'You're probably very dehydrated. You should at least take some sips if you can.' My mother's voice echoes in my mind—for all her foibles, she's always been an excellent nursemaid.

'*Oui*, yes, thank you, *chérie*.'

By the time I get back from the kitchen, he's asleep. I set the water on the bedside table next to him and carefully climb over him to my side of the bed. When I'm situated, he groans softly and rolls onto his side, turning away from me. My poor, poor love. In all this time together, I've never seen him sick—not even a head cold. It's like he's been impervious to illness—until now.

As I drift off to sleep, I realise with a start that I will need to take the day off tomorrow. I can't leave him on his own in my flat, sick and miserable. He needs me. Besides, I may have limited culinary skills but I am a master at making toast and tea—the perfect elixir for the infirm.

I took today off claiming the food poisoning as my own, because I'm not sure where my (very posh) inner London school stands on taking sick leave to look after one's French boyfriend because he ate a dodgy baguette from a train station.

Jean-Luc has been a stoic as ever, never once complaining as he's spent the day shuffling back and forth between bed and the loo. He's the total opposite to me, and everyone else in my family, who love to moan long and loudly if we have so much as a headache. I even managed to convince him to nibble on a slice of my perfectly made toast around lunchtime—dry, of course, as Mum would insist on—and sip some tea.

He's now sort-of upright on the sofa and chuckling intermittently at *FRIENDS*. 'Can I get you anything?' I ask, sitting next to him and tucking my feet under me. I reach over and smooth the hair from his forehead. He's getting some colour back—or rather, normal colour now that he's not chartreuse.

He turns towards me, his intense greens eyes creasing at the edges. 'I am fine for now. Thank you for looking after me.'

'Of course!'

'And for lying for me.'

'What sort of girlfriend am I if I can't chuck a sickie to look after my sick boyfriend?' I say, bunging on a broad Aussie accent.

'You are adorable.'

'Accurate.' He smiles, but his expression suddenly turns serious. 'What? Do you feel sick again?' It's been ages since I had food poisoning—the culprit, a kebab from a food truck in Camden on a particularly big night out with Mich, my bestie—so I'm not sure how long he'll be unwell.

'*Non.*'

There's a small stab of doubt in my gut.

'Jean-Luc?'

He expels a long sigh and the stabbing sensation intensifies. I really hope he's not going to bring up me moving to Paris again. There are only so many ways to deflect a propo-

SANDY BARKER

sition like that before a man decides he wants out of a relationship. But I'm just not ready. I'm not sure I ever will be.

'This is not what I had hoped for the weekend is all.'

'Oh!' I say, adding, *Is that all?* in my mind. 'That's all
right. We'll just have a quiet weekend in. It's fine. And Jane's
going to some festival tomorrow—she's staying overnight so
we'll have the place to ourselves. We can Netflix and chill,' I
add, although I'm positive Millennials abandoned that term
ages ago.

'That's not …' The stabbing sensation is back. 'I had
something special planned—a special restaurant for tonight
… a surprise …' Unlike my sister, I *do* like surprises and I
feel a momentary twinge of disappointment—even though
this isn't his fault and I have no right to be disappointed
about something I didn't even know about two minutes ago.

I reach up and run my fingers down his stubbly jawline.
He really seems upset about our ruined plans and I still feel
a little uneasy. 'We can go another time—next time you
visit.'

He looks at me again. 'Wait here.' He heaves himself off
the sofa and I watch him disappear down the hallway. Even
not-quite-well and wearing baggy sweatpants and a creased
T-shirt, he's sexy. Though sexy thoughts are highly inappropriate at the moment and I give myself a mental slap.
Instead, I stand and start tidying the remnants of our pop-
up infirmary, taking dirty dishes to the kitchen.

'Catherine,' he says from the doorway. 'Please, come and
sit.' He indicates the sofa and as I cross the room, I swallow
the hard lump that's lodged in my throat.

I sit.

He kneels in front of me and retrieves a small velvet box
from the pocket of his sweatpants. His serious expression

softens as he breaks into a sweet smile and looks into my eyes. I want to stare at that box, but there is something about his gaze that draws me in like a tractor beam.

'I had wanted to do this in a beautiful restaurant after a perfect meal and with champagne but, *alors*, the fates conspire. And as I sit here today, I go backwards and forwards—wait for a better time or ask you now? But what better time? I needed you today. I needed you to look after me and you did—you were here for me.'

Oh, my god.

His eyes are brimming with tears now—so are mine, I realise.

'Catherine, I have loved you since I was a boy, I love you more today than I ever have, and I will love you even more tomorrow. You are my most favourite, most special person, my love, my life. Will you, Catherine Louise Parsons, do me the incredible honour of marrying me?'

He opens the box and sitting inside is an elegant gold ring with a filigree band and a solitaire diamond. It's beautiful.

'It was my *grand-mère's*, *Grand-mère* Ellie. She would have loved you. You would have loved her. If anything makes me sad *maintenant* it is that you didn't meet.' A tear spills, running down his cheek and he smiles.

I still haven't uttered a word. What words are there? What words can possibly encapsulate how much I am in love with this wonderful man, how beautiful his heart is, and how his proposal has made me feel?

Before my mind catches up with my heart, before I can rationalise and fret about implications, about work visas and addresses or the fact that before he and I reconnected I'd been single—on purpose—for more than a decade, I finally am able to say the one word that *does* capture everything I'm feeling.

'Yes.'

He grins now and I beam back at him and his hand shakes as he slides the ring onto my ring finger. It's a perfect fit and I caress it gently—it's *so* beautiful. When I look back at Jean-Luc, he takes my face gently between his hands, presses his lips to my forehead, then to each cheek, and finally against mine.

'*Je t'aime*,' he whispers in between kisses.

'*Je t'aime aussi*,' I whisper back, then pull him closer.

Oh, my god, I'm engaged!

Chapter Two

SARAH

Sydney

The melodic sound of Caribbean music intrudes on my dream and for an instant, I exist in that state between (blissful) sleep and awake. I drag my sleep mask down to my chin, pick up my phone and squint at it. It's 6:01am and my sister's profile pic is grinning up at me.

Cat!

I sit up and scramble to answer the video call. 'Hey,' I say quietly, hoping not to wake Josh, 'everything okay?' Now the real Cat is grinning at me and I shake my head. *Wake up, Sarah*, I command myself.

'Everything's brilliant.' Well, at least it's not bad news. Josh stirs beside me, then scooches closer and rests his head beside mine on my pillow.

'You do know what time it is, right?' I say, succumbing to a yawn.

'Six o'clock, Cat,' Josh mutters. 'And it's Saturday.' Now Jean-Luc appears on the screen next to Cat, also grinning.

'It's not too early is it? I——sorry, *we*——waited as long as we could. We have news.'

I push myself into a seated position and Josh does the same, rearranging the pillows behind us to prop us up. 'Okay, we're up. What gives?' I ask.

'We're getting married!' they say in unison. Now I am properly awake.

'What? Oh, my god!' I look at Josh and he's as surprised as I am. 'You're engaged?'

'Yes!' and '*Oui*!' Two more grins.

'What? How?' I sputter.

'Congratulations!' says Josh. Oh, yes, that's what you're supposed to say.

'Congratulations!' I add, a moment later.

'Thank you!' Cat is positively beaming and Jean-Luc lands a kiss on the side of her head. God, I love these two together.

'So, like … this just happened today?' asks Josh.

'Well, yes … our today——your middle of the night. And I know it's early there, but *we're engaged!*' Oh, I *so* wish I could share this with them in person. A sob takes hold and in seconds I am boo-hooing like a total dag. 'Sez? Those are happy tears, right?' asks my sister.

I nod, but my face onscreen looks miserable. 'Here.' Josh takes the phone from me while I snatch tissues from the box by the bed and sop up my tears. 'So,' he says to them, 'have you had any thoughts about when——and where? I'm guessing with you guys, the "where" will be trickiest, right?'

'Well … yes, uh … actually, that's something we wanted to talk to *you* about.' Something about Cat's tone catches my attention and I grab the phone back from Josh.

'What's wrong?'

'Nothing,' she says unconvincingly. Her lips disappear between her teeth and her eyes flick towards Josh, who's suspiciously squirming next to me. *Something* is going on.

'So, what ... you guys thinking somewhere on your side of the world?' asks Josh. Cat's expression shifts and my eyes home in on Jean-Luc's hand squeezing her shoulder. Why is everyone being so cagey?

'Uh ...' Cat and Jean-Luc exchange a look. 'Well ...'

'Oh!' I say, 'are you're getting married here? Oh, my god, that's amazing!' I grin at Josh.

'Uh, no, Sez,' Cat says and my grin dissipates.

'Oh. Well, what then? Why are you all acting weird?' May as well call it like I see it.

'We're not,' Cat says brightly. 'We're just ... you know ... we were thinking——'

'Somewhere in Europe,' interjects Jean-Luc.

'You mean like *France*? You know, where you *live*?' I ask pointedly.

'*Peut-être, oui*, France would be nice,' he replies.

'And it's just that we know it's a big ask—coming all this way for a wedding ...' adds Cat.

'What? How is that a big ask? You could get married on the International Space Station and I'd be there.'

'Of course! I didn't mean ... We're just not sure where we'll get married, is all,' says Cat.

'They've barely gotten engaged, Sarah. Let's give them a bit of time to figure out the details,' Josh cajoles. *But he was the one who asked the question!* I think, flummoxed.

'But autumn—definitely,' says Jean-Luc.

'Right, autumn sounds nice,' I say vaguely.

What is wrong with me? These are two of my favourite people in the world and they're betrothed and I'm ruining the moment. I push my suspicions aside and right my emotional state. 'I am *so* happy for you guys,' I say. They must be the magic words, as Cat's shoulders drop a centimetre and the tension between us dissipates. 'I wish I could be there to celebrate with you, but no matter *where* you decide to get married—or when—I'll be there. For sure.'

'We both will,' says Josh.

The beaming smiles are back. 'Brilliant,' says my sister. 'And … uh … we'll keep you posted. Oh, and you're the first people we've told so …'

'Of course! I promise not to ruin your surprise with Mum and Dad. Actually, they'll be up by now, you know.'

'Golf,' we say at the same time. Cat and I joke that we were golf orphans growing up.

'All right, loves, we'll let you go. Sorry again about waking you,' she says.

'No, no, it's okay. We really are happy for you. Definitely worth getting woken up for,' I say.

'Yeah, totally. Congratulations, you guys.'

'Thank you!' and 'Merci,' then a swap of sisterly 'I love you's and the call ends.

I sit with the phone in my hands, smiling. My little sis is getting married—to her childhood sweetheart. The tears come again and Josh holds me while I sob with joy.

'Do you think we need more cheese?' asks my best friend, Lindsey.

I look at the assortment of cured meats, three kinds of olives, four varieties of cheese, and three kinds of artisanal crackers, then back at Lins. 'I think we're good. It's just the four of us. And there's all that,' I say, indicating the preparations for a barbecue dinner. Even though it's mid-winter, it's been mild today and Lins called this afternoon with the impromptu invitation.

Her gaze roams the platter again, then she nods with satisfaction. 'Right. You grab the wine and I'll grab this.' She's entrusting me with a tray laden with four wine glasses and a full bottle. Me—the walking disaster.

'Actually, wait …' I say and she does. Josh and Nick are outside on the patio, drinking beer and talking about whatever it is that men talk about when they're alone and I want my bestie's ear for a moment. 'There's something else. When Cat and Jean-Luc called this morning and we started talking about where and when they're getting married … well, they said autumn and somewhere in Europe, but everyone was being weird—all three of them.'

'What do you mean?'

'I mean, it was like that scene in a murder mystery where one of the characters is in the dark and all the other characters are acting suspicious. Well, that was me this morning—I'm the one in the dark. Something's going on.'

She nods at me with an 'Mmm', which is the correct way to show someone you're actively listening, but also how you indicate that you know more about what's going on than they do.

'You know, don't you?'

'Know what?'

'Hey, do you need a hand with that?' Josh. Perfect timing—for Lins, that is.

She smiles brightly at him. 'Thanks, Josh.' He takes the heavy board and returns to the patio. Through the window, I watch him set it on the low table between the two outdoor couches. Lins now has the tray with the wine. 'Probably best if I carry this, anyway,' she says.

'It was one time!' I reply, slightly miffed.

'It was one time but a whole *tray* of glasses.'

'I bought you new ones!' She laughs at me as I follow her outside. 'I am not letting this go, you know,' I say. 'I'm going to bug you all until someone tells me what's going on.' I sit, then lean forward and help myself to a generous wedge of gooey camembert.

'Letting what go?' asks Josh.

He and Lins share a loaded look and now I am positive. '*What?* What is the big secret that everyone seems to know but me?' I ask through a mouthful of cheese.

'There's a big secret?' asks Nick, playing dumb. He's the worst liar of the lot and now I feel like they're all ganging up on me.

'Just tell her,' says Lindsey.

Josh sets his near-empty beer bottle on the table and sits beside me, taking my hands in his. Oh, god, is he dying or something? My stomach lurches and I instantly regret the cheese. 'Tell me,' I say quietly.

He laughs softly. 'Hey, it's nothing bad.'

'Really?'

'No, I … it's just that I wanted everything to be perfect but it's still a little in flux, and I was hoping to have more of it figured out before I told you. I wanted to surprise you.'

'There's a surprise?'

'Yes.'

'But I hate surprises.'

He grins. 'You hate *bad* surprises.'

'So, it's a good one?'

'Yes. It's for your birthday.'

'Oh.'

'I'm taking you to Tuscany. Actually, we're all going to Tuscany.'

'All of us?' I look at Lins and Nick and they're grinning at me. 'You guys too?'

'Yep! Surprise!' says Nick. Lins grins.

I look back at Josh. 'So, my surprise is that we're all going to Italy for my birthday?'

'*Yes.*'

'I love Italy. I love Tuscany!'

'I know,' says Josh, humouring me.

'Oh, my god, that's … that's … I love it so much!' I throw my arms around his neck and I'm laughing and crying at the same time—so much crying today.

I sit back and wipe the happy tears from my cheeks. 'And you all knew—you all knew!'

'Yep,' says Lins.

I sigh contentedly. Josh is not sick and there's no big conspiracy. He's just the best boyfriend in the world. Then the penny drops. 'Oh, so Cat and Jean-Luc … they know too, right.'

'Yeah. They're gonna come.'

I frown. 'So, this morning … do you think …?' I ask him.

'Yeah, I do … That seemed to be what they were getting at.'

'What were they getting at?' asks Nick.

'I think they're hoping to combine their wedding with Sarah's fortieth,' says Josh. *Forty*, I realise with a start. Yikes.

'That makes sense,' says Lins, always the practical one. 'You'll all be together anyway—one trip instead of two.'

'But how do you feel about it, Sarah?' asks Josh. 'I don't

21

want anything to take away from your day, from our celebration of *you*.' It's so sweet that he's asking, that he cares this much about making it a special birthday for me, but I feel a little queasy.

'I'm turning forty,' I say aloud to myself.

'Yeah, Sez, it comes after thirty-nine. I know you're not a Maths teacher but ...' Nick jokes. It's not funny.

'You okay?' Josh asks, his thumb stroking the back of my hand. Crap. Now I'm dangerously close to ruining another big moment for someone I love—first Cat's news and now this.

I smile at him. 'I'm okay. It's just ... I guess part of me thought I'd be thirty-nine forever. Most of the time, I still feel like I did in my twenties and now I'm gonna be *forty*. That's like ... proper grown-up age.'

'Well, you're way hotter than most twenty-somethings, so ...' Josh waggles his eyebrows at me, making me laugh.

'It's an amazing surprise, babe. I ... I can't believe we're all going on a trip together, to one of my favourite places ... it's so, *so* thoughtful. Thank you.'

Josh grins at me and I can tell he's relieved. 'You know, Cat said I was daring to organise something like this without you—that you'd hate it.'

'Oh, yeah, she was right about that. You're not organising one more detail without me.'

'Ahh, okay, I see how it is.' Josh's eyes narrow jokingly.

'And now there's a wedding to plan as well!'

'You sound more excited about that than the trip, Sez,' teases Lindsey.

'They're kind of on par,' I retort.

'Hey, can you swap out the wine for champers?' she asks Nick. 'I think we should be celebrating.'

'Too bloody right! Back in a tick.' Nick takes the tray away and Lins settles into the couch opposite Josh and me, and I nestle into the crook of his arm.

'How long have you known about all this?' I ask her.

She looks at Josh. 'What, maybe three or four months?'

'*What?!*' I ask, sitting upright.

'That sounds about right.'

I look over at Josh. 'I'm impressed, Joshua.'

'You are?'

'*Yeah*. You're sneaky.' He laughs. 'In a good way, I mean.'

'Yeah, yeah.'

'Here we go.' Nick has returned with a different bottle and four champagne flutes. He makes quick work of the foil, then the cage and when he pops the cork, I shout, 'Hooray!' I just love bubbles. And I love these wonderful, beautiful people. And in four months, we're all going to Italy together. *Italy!*

———

'Hello. You're saving me from a pile of marking, so thank you.'

'I know now,' I say to my sis.

'Hi, Cat, how are you?' I poke my tongue out and she sniggers. 'Anyway, I'm glad you know *and* …?'

'And let's plan a destination wedding-slash-birthday.'

'Really?'

'Of course!'

'We weren't sure how you'd feel about sharing your big day.'

I shrug. 'It's just a birthday.'

'It's *forty*, Sez.'

'So people keep reminding me.'

'You're not upset about it, are you?'

'No, I'm good with it—we'll just have the birthday party and the wedding on different days. It's all good.'

'No, I mean—well, yay, that's fab—but I'm asking if you're upset about turning forty?'

'I don't know. I don't want to think about that right now.'

'All right.' She pauses, obviously deciding whether to press me on it. She lets it go. 'Now, you do realise that if we combine these events, Mum and Dad will be in Italy with us, right?'

'*Oh*, right.' Cat laughs. 'Yeah, that makes sense,' I say with a shrug. 'It's okay—a minor inconvenience.'

'Um, it may be a bit more than "minor". Mum's going to want to help plan the wedding. When we told them the news, and I mean *literally* right afterwards, she started getting excited about flowers and dresses and then babbled on about readings, which we're not even sure we're having. I'm worried she'll go full Mumzilla.'

'Hmm, I can see that happening—and *you* hate planning things. How are you going to manage planning a *wedding* with *Mum*?'

'Umm …' She grins at me hopefully—raised eyebrows and all.

'*Really?*'

'You're the most organised person I know!'

'You just don't want to spend the next few months arguing with our mother.'

'Accurate … *Please*, Sez. It'll be a really simple wedding, I promise—just, you know, rustic Tuscan chic.' *Whatever the hell that is*, I think.

24

'Pfft. *Fine*.'

'Thank you! And, I promise, once we get to Italy, I'll take over,' she offers. 'Run interference—focus all Mum's energies on the wedding so you can just enjoy yourself. How does that sound?'

'It sounds like a fantasy.' Cat laughs again. 'It's okay, though. We'll figure it out.' What I *don't* say is that she's actually doing me a favour—planning a wedding is the perfect distraction from the whole 'turning forty' thing.

'Oh!' she says suddenly. 'I'm such a muppet—I totally forgot.'

'What?'

'Will you be my Maid of Honour?'

'Really? You're not asking Mich? Or what about Jane?' Like me, Cat only has a handful of close friends, but they're almost like sisters to her and I don't want her to feel obligated to choose me.

'Sarah Jane, I only want you. You're my sister. *And* my best friend in the whole world.'

'Well, in that case,' I say, feeling the sting of tears in my eyes, 'I humbly accept.'

'Brilliant.' She grins at me.

'And I guess if I'm also the wedding planner, I can choose my own dress, right?'

'Of course! And, like I said, it will just be a small wedding. We won't go overboard with guests or anything … Actually, I suppose some of them will overlap—besides Mum and Dad, I mean.'

'Did you hear that Josh has invited Siobhan?' I ask with a smile.

'Oh, I just *love* Siobhan.' Siobhan is the Irish friend Josh and I met during our trip to Hawaii. And later that year, she came sailing with me and Josh, and Cat and Jean-Luc off the coast of Croatia.

'Oh, we should invite Duncan and Gerry!' says Cat—more mutual friends. When Josh and I met on our sailing trip in the Greek Islands, Duncan was skippering the boat with Gerry by his side. And by the time he skippered our sailing trip in Croatia, they'd got married. They're living in Queensland now and have a son.

'Hmm. We'll definitely ask them, but Jave is only one. Not sure they'll want to travel all that way with a baby. And you know that Lindsey and Nick are coming to Italy, right?' I ask. 'Josh told you?'

'Of course! And they're welcome to come to the wedding.' Cat has only met them a few times over the years but she knows Lins and I are close—*and* how much I adore 'Big Brother' Nick. He can be a pain in the arse some-times—okay, it's a lot of the time—but I still love him to bits.

'And we'll be asking Jane. And Mich, of course—though her mum's *really* unwell now and I don't know that she wants to leave the country anytime soon.' She frowns and I know we're both thinking the worst. Poor Mich.

'And the dates line up?' I ask, changing the subject to something cheerier.

'Yes!' She's definitely as relieved about the change of subject as me. 'It's half-term the last week of October but I've already talked to my Head about taking some family leave a couple of days either side.'

'She said yes? Really?'

'She did. She has a soft spot for me,' Cat says with a shrug. 'It's because *I* always say yes whenever she needs someone to fill in last minute—you know, someone has a sick child and needs to collect them, that sort of thing.'

'And it *is* your wedding.'

'Well, yes, but I asked her ages ago—for your birthday trip. What?' she asks in response to my shaking head.

'It's just … I can't believe how many people were conspiring behind my back.' I'm not upset by this, just baffled by the level of subterfuge. Seriously, how did they pull it off? I'm usually more astute about this kind of thing.

Cat smiles. 'Well, you're very hard to buy for and it's your *fortieth*.' There's that reminder again. It doesn't sting any less this time, either. What the hell is that about?

It's not that my life is lacking in any way. I mean, it was a few years ago, before I went to Greece and met Josh. He'd been experiencing something similar back then. 'I want my life to be bigger,' he'd said, summing up that feeling so succinctly, so elegantly, that the words had thrummed inside me. Then something had clicked.

And after that trip I'd sought—and built—my bigger life.

So it's not that—none of the usual impetuses for a midlife meltdown. But something feels 'off', as though this milestone birthday is happening to someone else and I am standing outside of myself, watching it approach.

Of course, I know in my heart that forty isn't *old*. But it will definitely cement my status as 'middle-aged'. I halfexpect someone to pull me aside and give me a new to-do list, like take out life insurance and get breast scans and start reading those emails from my retirement fund instead of filing them away, unread, and forgetting about them. Those are all things that middle-aged people are expected to do, right? You know, proper adulting?

And am I supposed to get my (mad) curls cut into a sensible style, swap my heels for flats, and take up golf? Although Sarah Jessica Parker didn't do any of that in her forties—well, at least not the hair and the heels—I have no idea if she took up golf—so maybe that's the 'brand' of middle age I can subscribe to. It will certainly make all the proper adulting more palatable if I can maintain my youthful fabulousness.

All this flies through my head as Cat continues. 'The poor guy had to come up with something *spectacular* and we were all sworn to secrecy. *Tuscany*, Sez!'

It's only now that I see how excited she is and her enthusiasm is enough to pull me from my introspective funk. I return her smile. 'Oh, Cat, I just *love* that part of the world. It's going to be amazing.'

'I know!' We grin at each other maniacally, like sisters do.

'Anyone else you want to invite?' I ask. 'What about your friends from the Europe trip?

'Well, *Lou*, of course, but I'm not sure about Dani—we're more like Facebook friends now. And definitely Jae and Alistair. They should be back in Edinburgh around then, so Italy won't be such a big ask, and the guys have become really good friends.'

'They still splitting their time between the US, the UK, and Bali?'

'Uh-huh. I would hate that,' she adds after a moment's pause.

'Me too.' This is the understatement of the century. As much as I love travelling—taking trips—I was very close to a lifetime of constant travel a few years ago. Not wanting that lifestyle was one of two reasons I realised the older man

I was seeing—James—wasn't the one for me. The other reason? I was in love with Josh.

'What about Jean-Luc's family?' Cat scrunches her nose, then gets up to close the door. 'So, the in-laws didn't take it well?' I ask.

'We haven't told them yet,' she says quietly.

'What? But …'

'Look, his parents … well, you know how he's closest to his mum?' I only know what Cat has told me but I nod. 'Well, she's been even more clingy with him lately. The last time I was there visiting … I don't know, it's *odd*, how she is around him—how she is with me. It's almost like we're in competition. I think she's afraid I'm going to steal him away to England and she'll never see him again.'

'Oh, god.'

'Mmm-hmm. And she's the *nice* one in the family.'

'Not the sister?'

'Cécile? Uh, no. She's still close friends with Vanessa.'

'What?!' Vanessa is Jean-Luc's ex-wife.

'Yes, exactly.'

'You never told me that.'

'I haven't wanted to bother you with it.'

'It's not a bother—'

'Anyway … Jean-Luc's going to tell them tonight after dinner, but I won't be on the call.'

'Oh, Cat, I'm so sorry.' She shrugs, but it's clear how much it hurts. 'At least you have us. No matter how intense Mum gets about wedding stuff … we've got the best parents.' It's true. Sure, Mum can drive me around the bend sometimes but she always means well. Cat nods, her smile unconvincing.

'And, I mean, Jean-Luc was practically part of the family

when you guys were at school together and now, he'll be *official*.' I just need her to see how our family, and all the love that comes with it, can make up for what's lacking in Jean-Luc's.

'I know. It's just …'

'What?'

'What if she's right?'

'Who?'

'Jean-Luc's mum.'

'About you? She's wrong. You're wonderful.'

'Thank you, but I mean the part about me stealing him away to London.'

'Is that where you're going to live?'

'I'm not sure where we're going to live.'

'What? You haven't talked about that?'

'No. I mean, we have, sort of … I mean, he's asked me to move to Paris a million times, but …'

'That's not home.' I get it—I really do. Sydney is home for me and I would never want to give that up.

'Exactly.'

'And?'

'And what?' she asks.

'There's something else.' She shakes her head slightly. 'You can tell me, Cat.'

She gulps and this odd look transforms her from happy bride-to-be to someone about to face the gallows. 'I'm worried about us living together,' she says, her voice barely audible. 'I'm not sure it's what I want.'

Now this I *don't* get. I love living with Josh. I love our home, the one we've made together. I could probably go the rest of my life without another trip to IKEA, however—that place is a nightmare. Regardless, Cat has accepted Jean-

Luc's marriage proposal and my guess is that he thinks living together was implied.

'You're not saying anything. It's strange, isn't it, not wanting to cohabitate?' she asks.

'Yeah, it is. I don't know many couples who are married and live in different cities, Cat. Not on purpose, anyway.'

'But what if …? What if living together fucks up everything we have?'

'I don't know. But, Cat, if this is how you feel, then why did you say yes when he proposed?'

'Because I love him so much, Sez. And I got all caught up in the moment but … ever since we got off the call with Mum and Dad, it became real and …' She shrugs, then huffs out a breath through her nose.

'Cat, you have to tell him how you feel.'

'Really?'

'Um, yes! I think he will notice if you maintain different addresses after the wedding!'

'Shhh.' She looks at the door to the study, worried.

'Sorry,' I say, though it's unlikely he heard me all the way from the kitchen—the two rooms are at opposite ends of the flat. 'Look, all I can say is that living with Josh makes me happier than I ever thought possible. Just give it some time, okay, and if you still feel this way in a few weeks, then you have to tell him.'

'Maybe.'

'Cat.'

'*All right.* I should go. Dinner will be ready soon.'

'Okay.' Now I'm the one letting her off the hook.

'Let's talk next weekend—discuss plans and such,' she says.

''Kay. Love you.'

31

'Love you too.' She ends the call.

When Josh comes into the lounge room, he catches me staring off into space, pondering why my sister accepted Jean-Luc's proposal when it seems that she doesn't want to *be* married. 'You okay?' Josh asks.

I smile brightly at him. 'Yep. Just about to jump in the shower.'

'Cool, I'm heading out. Steaks on the barbie tonight?' he asks. It's so cute how he's adopted these Aussie-isms.

'Sounds great.'

He lands a soft, lingering kiss on my lips and leaves for work. I just love our life together.

Chapter Three

CAT

London

'I will see you in twelve days,' says my sexy boyfriend—no, sorry, fiancé! I'm still not used to it, but I suppose it has only been three days. Three wonderful (and terrifying) days.

'I'll miss you,' I say, standing on my tippy toes to kiss him. One hand holds his overnight bag and one hand holds me by the small of my back. He pulls me closer and kisses me softly but longingly and when the kiss ends, he presses his lips to my forehead, his signature move that tells me how cherished I am.

It would be very easy to grab his hand and drag him back to bed, but then he'll miss his flight to Switzerland. 'I will meet you at Gare du Nord,' he says.

'You don't have to.' I've made the trek from the train station to his apartment on my own so many times now I've lost count. I hardly need an escort.

'For the first time my fiancée arrives in Paris? I will be there.'

Swoon. Like I said, Jean-Luc could turn the simplest task or the worst location into a romantic moment. Twelve days apart suddenly feels like forever.

'Go, or you'll miss your flight and I'll be late for school.'

A cheeky, lopsided grin, another kiss and he's out the door calling, '*Je t'aime*,' over his shoulder. Jane bustles past me in the hallway—she must have been waiting for us to finish our goodbyes. 'See you tonight, lovely,' she says, also not waiting for an answer before the front door closes behind her.

We told her our news last night after she returned from her festival. She was excited for us and she's going to ask for time off to come to the wedding, but later, when Jean-Luc was making dinner, she asked what our plans are. And she meant our living arrangements. But we've only been engaged three days, so nothing has to be decided right away—even Jane said that.

Shelving my worries about where to live has freed up enough emotional real estate to obsess about the other elephant in the room—Jean-Luc's family. As expected, his parents reacted to our news with lukewarm enthusiasm—at least, that's my interpretation of his recount.

And his sister was downright rude. But what did I expect? Since Jean-Luc and I reunited a couple of years ago, Cécile has actively thwarted all my attempts to get to know her, creating this icy discordance between us. So while most people find me loveable, there's no winning over Cécile. No doubt, it's because I pale in comparison with Jean-Luc's ex, *Vanessa*—Cécile's perfect, beloved former sister-in-law.

Thank goodness her husband, Louis, and their daughters, Alice and Abigail, seem to like me. Actually, the girls *adore* me—they even call me '*Tante* Catherine' and always greet me with tight hugs and a plethora of cheek kisses. Perhaps another reason Cécile can't stand me. It's possible her daughters like me more than they like her.

Jean-Luc doesn't know that I know this, by the way—how she reacted to the engagement. He couched his retelling like the darling he is, but I was listening at the door. And my French may only be conversational, but I know what *'femme anglaise'* followed by *'simplette'* means. She'd also called me *'aiguë'* which I had to look up on my phone. After spelling it wrong three times, I figured it out—'shrill'. I'm guessing she didn't mean it as a compliment.

The rest of the weekend ... well, Jean-Luc came good from his bout of food poisoning by Saturday afternoon—thank goodness—and, as I kept my hurt feelings to myself, we were able to celebrate our engagement. In lieu of a fancy restaurant dinner, we ordered in (a respite from the kitchen for Jean-Luc) and opened a bottle of bubbles and then he made love to me for hours. Gentler than our usual (quite rigorous) lovemaking, but still, *hours*.

Yesterday was more of the same until we dragged ourselves out of bed *and* the flat for a jaunt into Central London. It was a glorious day—twenty-three degrees and sunny—so the perfect reason to escape our love nest.

Our love nest.

As I gather my belongings for school, the marked assignments and my laptop, I look about at my bedroom. Would it be strange to live in a flat-share with my husband? It would only be part of the time, I suppose, if he kept his apartment in Paris. We could be like Helena Bonham-Carter and Tim Burton. They live in different houses, don't they? Oh wait. I think they're divorced now.

Hmm.

So, I'm engaged (hooray), I'm perfectly happy being in a long-distance relationship (what could go wrong there?), and my fiancé's sister hates me (bollocks). Hence, both a wonderful and terrifying weekend.

'Hellooo!' At the sight of Lou's face on the screen, I break into a broad smile.

'Hey, so good to see you!' she says.

'It feels like it's been ages.'

'Too long, for sure. So sorry—I've just been unbelievably busy with work.' Lou is a counsellor for troubled teens and she's recently been promoted to team manager.

'And with *Anders*,' I tease. Her new boyfriend is a veterinarian from Toronto who moved to Vancouver late last year.

She giggles, then leans her face close to the screen and whispers, 'He is *so* wonderful, Cat.'

'Why are you whispering? Is he there?' She nods. 'Well, can I meet him?' I can't believe after several months, I am finally going to meet the famous Anders. Lou has been keeping their relationship close to her chest—not even posting photographs on social media—but she's been gushing to me about him for ages. It seems very likely that Anders is her *person* and I want to meet him properly.

'Hey, hon, there's someone I'd like you to meet.'

Lou is looking offscreen and I can tell the exact moment he comes into view because her face lights up like it's been illuminated by a thousand candles. Anders steps behind her and lowers his head so he's in frame.

'Hey.'

'Hello, Anders.'

'You must be the famous Cat.'

'I was just thinking the same about you—the famous Anders, I mean.' We grin at each other.

'What are you up to?' he asks.

'Actually, I have news,' I say excitedly.

'Oooh,' says Lou, bouncing in her chair.

I let the moment build, just for a few seconds, then blurt, 'Jean-Luc and I are getting married!'

Lou leaps from her chair and all I can see is her mid-section while she jumps up and down and squeals. Anders chuckles good-naturedly in the background and eventually Lou settles back onto the chair, her face flushed.

'Oh, my goodness! Oh my *goodness*!'

'I know. It's very exciting.' I will not ruin this moment by revealing that my excitement is accompanied by a hefty dose of terror.

'Oh, Cat …' she sighs, blinking back tears. 'Who would have thought it, huh? Jaelee accosts a guy on a street in Paris, he turns out to be your high-school sweetheart, and now you're getting married!'

That's the dustcover version, but she's essentially correct. I was on a bus trip in Europe—booked hastily in the aftermath of the 'sleeping with my flatmate' debacle—and I met Lou, Jaelee, and Dani, forming a firm foursome on the first day. And one night in Paris, we did (indeed) randomly run into Jean-Luc on the street—well, Jaelee stopped him to ask for recommendations on somewhere to go, assuming someone as hot as him would be in the know.

And call it kismet or fate or whatever, we were reunited—French exchange student and the bookish Sydney schoolgirl who were best friends for years, then estranged, reunited on a Paris street on a Monday night. The stuff of romcoms.

And now we're getting married.

'I know. I can hardly believe it myself.'

'Lou says that even a few seconds either way—if you were walking down the street a little faster or slower—you would have missed him,' says Anders. I've thought the exact thing a thousand times since that night and it always leaves me feeling slightly queasy. It must show because he quickly backpedals. 'Sorry,' he drawls in that sweet Canadian way. 'I didn't mean to put a dampener on your news. It's just an amazing story, is all.'

'No, it's all right. And it's not unlike you two. If you hadn't been the vet on duty that night …'

'Or if Mr Snuffles hadn't decided to eat my *yarn* …' adds Lou, turning her head to smile up at Anders.

'Exactly!' I declare. Mr Snuffles is Lou's neighbour's wayward feline who she was minding at the time—apparently, he has a propensity to eat things that aren't edible. That was his third trip to the vet in a year.

'Anyway, I'll let you two talk but so nice to finally meet you, Cat.'

'And you, Anders.' His broad shoulders and handsome face disappear from frame. 'He's so lovely,' I say softly to Lou.

'Yeah.' She shrugs—slightly self-satisfied but also humble, the way that only Lou can be.

'And you're going to think I'm an idiot, but I was sort of picturing Chris Hemsworth as Thor … you know, the Nordic Viking look.'

She chuckles. 'It's the name. You probably won't meet many black men named Anders Eriksen. But his dad's got the Viking look down pat—broad shoulders, like Anders, but blue eyes … he even has long hair, though it's silver now. He was born in Norway—came here for college in his twenties and never left. He met Anders' mum, they fell in love, the usual story …'

'*You're* in love, Lou,' I say.

She shrugs, pressing her lips together, then breaks into a broad smile. 'Maybe.'

'Have you met them yet, his parents?'

She nods. 'We flew back east last month for a long weekend and I met the whole family—siblings, cousins, aunts, uncles—everyone. They're amazing, Cat and …' She hesitates.

'What?'

She sighs. 'I just wish … my parents are still so close with Jackson's parents and …' Jackson is her ex-husband. 'It's *time*, you know. I want them to meet Anders and I know they'll love him, because he's a total sweetheart, but I also think it will be hard on them. Even now, Mum still holds out hope that Jackson and I …'

'But you're divorced.'

'I know.'

'Oh, Lou. That sounds like a right pickle.'

'Yeah.'

'Well, I'm always here to listen if you need me.'

'Thanks, Cat.'

'And I do have more news.'

'Oh! Of course—the wedding. Sorry, I didn't even ask. Where and when? I'll be there!'

I grin. 'Tuscany, this autumn.' Her eyes widen. 'I know! I promise we'll have the exact date soon, but we're looking at late October.'

'Oh, wow, that's coming up fast!' I hadn't thought of it that way, but I suppose she's right—it is only four months away and some people take a lot longer to plan their wedding.

'Sarah is helping us organise it—actually, it's her fortieth around the same time, so we're having a joint celebration.'

'Oh, that's awesome. I'll finally get to meet her!'

'Yes. We'll all be together. That's what Jean-Luc and I want—all our loved ones with us. So, you can definitely come?'

'Yes! No matter what,' she says.

'And bring Anders too,' I say quietly.

'Oh, thank you. I definitely will.' She leans in close to the screen. 'And you're right, I do love him. I'm working up the courage to tell him, but … it's true.'

'Oh, Lou, that makes my heart sing. And do tell him—it's obvious he's in love with you too.' She smiles and looks off camera again. God, this is wonderful news. When I met Lou, her marriage to Jackson was rocky and she's endured a rough couple of years—the separation, the divorce. I am definitely Team Anders.

'And Tuscany!' Lou adds. 'Gosh, our trip through that part of Italy is a *total* blur—even *Florence*.'

'You mean you don't have vivid memories of getting caught up in a police raid and missing the bus back to the campsite?'

She chuckles. 'Traumatic flashbacks, more like.'

'It was a good trip,' I say.

'Oh, yeah, for sure.' She lowers her voice again. 'I don't know that I could have made my big decision if I hadn't been on that trip with you girls.' She's referring to the decision to leave Jackson.

40

'I know. Oh, Lou, I cannot wait to see you—properly, I mean.'

'Me too.'

'Hey, hon?' Anders calls.

Lou looks over her shoulder. 'Yeah, hon?' Oh, my god, they are so adorable together.

'We've got that brunch reservation. We should probably get going.'

She turns back to me. 'Sorry. I need to go, but I'm *ecstatic* for you, Cat.'

'Thank you.'

'And you give Jean-Luc a big hug for me and let us know about the wedding, 'cause we'll be there.' The 'we' makes my heart sing. No one deserves happiness more than our Lou.

'I promise.'

'Love you, Cat.'

'Love you too.'

'Hey, what's up?' Jaelee is looking off to the left and I can hear her typing.

'I'm getting married.'

She stops typing and gawps at me. 'No shit.'

'Absolutely no excrement at all.'

'That's awesome. To Jean-Luc or …?' She breaks into a cheeky double-dimpled grin.

'Or. Actually, I'm running off with the dustman.'

'I have no idea who or what a dustman is, but I hope he's hot.'

'He isn't. He's also old and mean and his name is Frank.'

'Wow. I can see why you dumped your hot, sexy Frenchman for him. But, really, that's awesome, Cat.' For Jaelee, that's practically gushing.

'Thank you!' I reply. 'So, remind me, where are you now?'

'At home.'

'Are you being obstreperous on purpose?'

'Always. We're back in Bali.'

'Again?'

She shrugs. 'We're kind of in love with the place.'

'Perhaps I'll come visit you one day. I'm definitely due for a do-over,' I say, referring to my one and only trip to Bali—a rite of passage for many Australians only most of mine was spent on the toilet.

'Oh, yeah, you were sick.'

'Yep, the dreaded Bali belly.'

'So, you gonna bring Frank the mean old dustman?'

'If he behaves himself.' She chuckles.

'So, I'm guessing I'm invited to this shindig?'

'Yes. You both are. Unless Alistair wants to come alone.'

She pays my quip with a half-raised eyebrow. 'So, London?'

'No, a destination wedding.'

'Okay, so where are we going and when do we need to be there?'

'Italy. In autumn.' She writes something down on a pad next to her.

'Date?'

'No date yet. But we're combining the wedding with my sister's fortieth, so it will definitely be late October.'

'Oh, cool. We're heading back to Edinburgh soon and I

think we'll still be in the UK then. If not, we'll head there from Bali.'

'Brilliant.' I was hoping she'd say that.

'And who's your planner?' she asks.

'My planner?'

'Your wedding planner.'

'Oh, uh, my sister?' Jaelee—PR consultant and event organiser extraordinaire—makes a face. She's clearly dubious about Sarah's abilities in this area, so I quickly add, 'Sarah's very organised—*very*.' This results in a head tilt and narrowed eyes. 'She also seems pleased that the wedding will take some of the focus off her. I don't think she's particularly keen on turning forty. It's a good distraction for her—the planning.'

'Mmm.'

'I can put you in touch with her if you like. How about that?' I do not want to get in Jae's bad books—*no one* does.

'Acceptable,' she says, one of her dimples making an appearance. Phew. Jaelee is the type of friend who would give you the shirt off her back—even if it cost a mint—but you might have to psych yourself up to ask for it.

'And how are you?' I ask, redirecting the conversation.

'Busy. But good busy, you know. I think I'll have to hire another person soon.' Jaelee started her own PR company last year and she's well on her way to building an empire. She's incredible.

'That's brilliant, Jae.'

'Actually, I need to get this proposal ready so I can send it off first thing tomorrow.'

'I'll let you go. Say hi to Alistair for me.'

'I will. And Cat?' Her mouth widens into a smile, both dimples appearing again. 'It really is awesome news.'

'Thank you, lovely. Talk soon.'

'Bye.' We end the call and I set my phone on the kitchen counter.

So, that's four more for the guest list. I add them then regard the list.

Mum & Dad
Sarah & Josh
Lindsey & Nick
Jane
Mich (?)
Siobhan
Cécile (bleh) & Louis (maybe Alice & Abigail)
Lou & Anders
Jae & Alistair

Jean-Luc called last night. It turns out that his dad will be recovering from knee surgery at the time of our wedding, so Cécile and Louis are 'representing the family'. Cécile, the one who calls me shrill. At least I get along with Louis. And there are enough people on my side of the aisle, so to speak, to dilute the presence of my soon-to-be (horrid) sister-in-law. And if she's particularly awful, I'll sic Jaelee onto her—or Sarah. Hell, maybe Lou can smother her with kindness until she can't *help* but behave like a human being.

And maybe purple elephants will fly out of my arse.

Chapter Four

SARAH

Sydney

I may have gone a little overboard.

I'm seated in our lounge room literally surrounded by magazines— bridal and travel—all with Italy on the covers. And I *may* have stopped at the stationery shop to stock up on new folders and dividers and sticky notes. And coloured pens. And they had the most adorable wedding stickers—how was I supposed to resist those?

But it looks like Instagram exploded in here and when Josh walks in the door after work, his first words are, 'Should I be worried?' He crosses the room and deposits his laptop bag on the dining table, then leans down for a kiss.

A magazine falls from my lap onto the floor with a thud so loud it scares our cat, Domino, and he takes off down the hallway—Domino, that is, not Josh. 'Why that's, Joshua? There are people all over Sydney arriving home precisely at this moment to this exact scene.'

He sniggers and plops onto one of our armchairs,

running his hands over his face then breaking into a loud yawn. 'Sorry. Is it Friday yet?'

'Tomorrow it is,' I say brightly. 'So, how's the new team coming together?' Josh is a software guy—he, well … you know … works on software stuff. His company has brought together a team from all over the world and Josh is now their manager. It's a big deal, this promotion, and he deserved it but he's looking a little peaky after only a fortnight.

'Good. They're a cool bunch of people, but lots of different personalities and skillsets and experience and … honestly?'

'Always.'

'I'm feeling a little … like I'm in over my head. I mean there are fifteen of them and one of me.' I stack the magazines that are in my immediate proximity and set them on the table—which is also covered in magazines—then cross the room and crawl onto his lap.

This is less sexy than it may sound as I am an athletic (i.e. solid) woman of five-foot-six-inches and it's not that big a chair. Those ballet-dancing hippopotamuses in *Fantasia*? They have *way* more grace than I do. Eventually I manage it and when I am ensconced in Josh's arms (the best place in the world to be, in my totally biased opinion), I look deep into his eyes and say, 'Cut the crap, Walker. You're a bloody genius and they're bloody lucky to have you. Okay?'

He laughs—full on 'ha-ha-ha' laughing, then stills and kisses me properly. 'What do you say we call in sick tomorrow and stay in bed all day?' he asks, his gravelly voice tinged with lust.

'Hmm. Tempting, but my students have their practice exam tomorrow and most of them are freaking out enough as it is without me being absent.'

'You love them more than you love me.'

'What do you think the bridal magazines are for? Once they pass their exams—with flying colours because, like you, they are all brilliant and also because *I* am their teacher and I'm also brilliant—then I will be the first secondary teacher to officially marry her job.' He shifts in the chair. 'Oh, am I squashing you?'

'You're not squashing me—well, maybe a small part of me.'

'How small?' I ask, waggling my eyebrows cheekily.

'Not that small—and growing by the minute.' I lean in for a kiss and just as Josh's hands find their way inside my waistband, a loud 'meow' interrupts us. We break the kiss as Domino decides this is now a family meeting and that there is room on the armchair for three.

'For fuck's sake, Domino. You're so heavy!' I pluck him off the chair and deposit him on the floor which earns me a disdainful look over his furry shoulder. Sexy moment ruined. I climb off Josh's lap as inelegantly as I climbed onto it but before I can leave for the kitchen to feed Domino, he grasps my hand.

'Leave him. He won't starve.'

'He won't because he's a total boombalada.'

Josh chuckles. 'Exactly my point.' He stands and snakes his arms around my waist, then leans down and kisses me softly. 'How about I take a shower, wash the day away, and I meet you in the bedroom?'

His grey eyes are stormy with desire and when I lean into him, I can feel his erection straining against his jeans. 'How about I join you in the shower and we see what happens from there?'

'Better.'

'Meow.'

'Quiet, Domino,' we say together. A miffed 'maw' follows, but I barely register it as Josh takes my hand and leads me to our en suite.

'Seh-rah!' Lindsey's voice echoes through the house.

'In here!' I call.

She appears in the doorway of our spare bedroom. 'Hey. You're not dressed.' I look down at my jeans and T-shirt. 'For yoga,' she adds.

'Oh shit.' I flick my wrist, my watch telling me I've been at this for way longer than I thought. 'Sorry.'

'What *is* all this?' she asks, surveying the detritus of my morning's task. I've been rifling through my boxes—the ones that contain everything from my Year 1 reports to dried (and crumbling) roses from my high school boyfriend to movie ticket stubs from the 90s.

'I'm looking for a letter.'

'From who?'

'From me.'

'Right.' She leans against the doorframe and gives me a funny look.

'It's this letter I wrote to my future self when I was around nineteen. You know, "Dear Future Sarah … This is who I want to be when I grow up … blah, blah, blah …".'

'Ahh.'

'It was during the first year of uni—for a creative writing class,' I add, ever-so-slightly defensive. I go back to rooting through a box filled with journals, letters (from other people), and greeting cards that date back to my first birthday.

'So why are you looking for it now?'

'Well, I'd totally forgotten about it, then last night I woke up around two—like, *wide* awake—' I snap my fingers for emphasis '—and I remembered it. Hang on, shouldn't you go? You'll be late for class.'

'Eh, wasn't really feeling it anyway.' She comes into the room and makes some space on the bed so she can sit. 'So, this letter?'

'Yeah, well, you know how Josh has planned this whole trip to Tuscany for my birthday?'

'I'm familiar, yes. I was there yesterday when he told you.'

'Right. So, it's *forty*.' I leave the word hanging in the air, my eyes boring into hers. There's a flicker of a frown—she's confused. 'Well, I think my subconscious was chewing on that while I was asleep, so I woke up, remembered the letter and now I want to find it so I can see where I thought I'd be by now. You know, in life.'

'You're exactly where you should be, Sarah,' she says patiently.

'I *know* that—in here,' I say, tapping on the side of my head. 'It's just that … look, this might sound weird but yesterday, when I heard that number—in relation to *me*—I felt this …' I wave may hands as though I can pluck the word from the air.

'Slight twinge?'

'More like a tsunami of panic.'

She blinks at me. 'Well, shit.'

'Yeah.'

'Kudos, 'cause you hid it well,' she says.

'I often do.' I reply quietly.

'Mmm,' she murmurs. 'So, why panic do you think?'

I thumb through a glitter-covered journal, flecks of pink littering the carpet. 'I can't tell if it's fear of what's to come or that I've missed something I *should* have done.'

'You know how I feel about that word.'

I stop searching. 'Should?' I ask rhetorically. 'Yeah, I know. It's a *bad word*.' I abandon the glittery journal and pick up the next one.

'"Shoulds" come from other people's expectations of us,' she says. This is one of her well-established philosophies and not the first time she's uttered those exact words. 'So, even though you wrote this letter, it's not from you. Young Sarah is someone else——remember that.'

'That may be too existential for me, Lins.'

She shrugs. 'Eh, I tried.'

Just then, I come across a folded A4 sheet, the creases still sharp and the paper almost pristine. 'Booyah.'

'Booyah?' she teases.

I poke my tongue out at her, dropping the journal back into the box and unfolding the page. 'I wanna see,' she says.

I lift my gaze, having only read 'Dear Sarah'. 'Okay, scoot over.' I sit next to Lins and read aloud.

'Dear Sarah,
  Congratulations, you made it. You are OLD.'

Lins laughs while I mentally slap my former self——how rude! 'I guess when you're nineteen, forty *is* old,' she says.

'You're not helping. Besides, I was supposed to read it when I turned thirty.'

'Keep going,' she prompts through more laughter.

'This letter is to remind you of all the things you wanted to do when you were young. Your bucket list! Hopefully by now, you've done them all but if you haven't, you still have time before you die.'

'Oh, my god! You were hilarious,' says my soon-to-be-replaced best friend. I silence her with a withering look—well, I try but she continues to laugh at me, her body shaking. 'Honestly, this is the most fun I've had in ages.'

'So! Where to start. First, (I think) I want us to get married.'

I show Lins the parenthesis and they even make me smile.

'Mum and Dad have this incredible marriage and if you can find someone like Dad who puts up with all the weird things about us, then DO IT! And if you're reading this for the first time at thirty and you're still not married, then you either got weirder or you haven't been looking hard enough.'

I drop the letter into my lap. 'Was I really this much of a cow when you met me?' I ask Lins. We've been best friends since the second year of uni but now I'm starting to wonder what she saw in me.

'Hardly. But I'm guessing this is "inner voice Sarah" —she's always been kind of a bitch to you.'

'Hmm. Very astute,' I acknowledge. As usual, Lins is bang on.

'Are you gonna keep reading? At this rate, we'll be planning your fiftieth before you finish.'

'Ha-ha.'

'I hope we follow in Mum's footsteps and become a teacher. English, in case you didn't already know. ;) We can shape young minds and make them fall in love with words! And I want us to travel to every continent and do and see all the things. I want us to have adventures – go skydiving and white-water rafting and hiking and sailing – just like Aunty Tessa.'

'Aunty Tessa?' asks Lins. 'Have I met her?'

In an instant, tears prick my eyes.

My (honorary) Aunty Tessa had been one of Dad's closest friends from his university days back in the UK. From the moment I met her when I was fifteen, I knew she was the person I wanted to be when I grew up. She was 'bolshie', as Dad would say, and so full of life. She inspired me to be adventurous and brave—me, the timid-at-heart scaredy cat who'd suffered from anxiety since childhood.

She stayed with us a few times when Cat and I were in our teens—stops on her epic trips—but the visit that impacted me most was during that first year of uni. I was all wide-eyed and soaking up knowledge—simultaneously confronted with my naivety and thinking I knew it all—and she was about to embark on a year-long trip to help establish a school in a Cape Town township.

We wrote letters during that time—hers newsy and full of the setbacks and triumphs as they battled bureaucracy and bias to get the school built and ready for the students, but tragically, she didn't make it back to the UK. Five months into her quest, she was diagnosed with stage four breast cancer. She died not long after in a Cape Town hospice. She'd only been forty-three.

'Um, she was one of my dad's best friends. She was …' Words fail me. How to sum up Tessa and who she was to me? 'She inspired me,' I say, battling the lump in my throat. I look at Lins, my lips pressed together as I try to steady my breath and she lifts a hand to rub my back. 'She died. Not long after I wrote this, actually,' I say, holding up the letter.

'You've never mentioned her before,' she says gently.

'I know,' I say, suddenly flooded with shame. It's not that I'd *forgotten* as much as …

'Too painful?' she asks, understanding immediately. I nod. 'So, what else does young Sarah have to say?' She gently takes the letter from me and starts to read.

'And maybe, just maybe, think about writing a book. We are brilliantly creative and clever——'

'Aww, that's sweet,' Lins says and I smile, dragging the back of my hand under my nose.

'… and by the time we're thirty, hopefully you'll have a lot of adventures to write about. And to keep this short and sweet, one final thing. Be amazing.
   Love,
   Sarah'

'I like that last bit—and you are amazing.' Lins jostles me with her shoulder.

'Thanks.'

'And you've already ticked off most of it,' she says, folding the letter and handing it back to me. 'No glaring "shoulds".'

'Just a trip to Antarctica,' I reply, smiling brightly. 'Oh, and I'm not married, either.'

'You and Josh may not have the piece of paper, but

you're in a marriage, Sez.' I nod—I guess she's right. And I did find the perfect guy for me. I think younger Sarah would be happy about that.

Lins leaps up. 'You're off?' I ask.

'Yeah, I think I will go to class.'

'You're gonna get in trouble,' I sing-song. Our yoga instructor does *not* like latecomers.

Lins shrugs it off. 'Eh, I'll try and sneak in the back.' We both know that's not going to fly with the always-Zen-except-when-you-disrupt-her-class Paula. Lins kisses the top of my head. 'Call you later.'

'Okay. Bye.'

'And forty's not old!' she calls out from the front door. I guess she'd know—her fortieth was three months ago.

———

'Need a hand?' calls my dad from the front steps of my parents' house.

'Um, yes, please, Dad.' He jogs down the steps and across the lawn to meet us at the car.

'What on earth?' he says, taking in the contents of the boot.

'Do you mind taking one of these, Ron?' asks Josh. He hands my dad one of two stacking cubes filled with magazines and folders—portable wedding planning for the sister on the go!

'I thought it was just going to be a *small* wedding,' says Dad, leading the way inside. Josh follows with the second cube, and I bring my laptop bag and a two-bottle wine carrier.

'I'm discovering that destination weddings are the opposite of "small", no matter how many guests are invited,' I tell him. 'Hi, Mum,' I call out as soon as we're inside.

'Hello, Sarah.' She emerges from her study to kiss me on the cheek and relieve me of the wine. 'Just put all that in there,' she says to Josh and my dad, indicating her study. 'Glass of wine before lunch?' she asks me.

'Yes, please,' I reply.

'Josh, wine?' Mum calls out, making her way into the kitchen.

'Sure, Karen, thanks.'

'Or I've got beer?' Dad offers.

'Actually, a beer would be good. And I'm driving, so …'

'Light beer coming up,' says Dad.

Every time we come here, it hits me that Josh is not just my partner, he's part of the family—even though he's only lived in Sydney a couple of years. Not long ago, I even heard Mum refer to him as her son-in-law to my aunty. I loved that and I love seeing how at ease he is here, chatting with Dad and doing Mum's bidding without complaint (as we all do).

And as far as in-laws go, I've hit the jackpot. Josh has taken me to Chicago twice since he moved to Sydney and I've met his brother and his parents, some extended family. His parents are *lovely*—we chat with them online at least once a month and they've even mentioned coming for Christmas this year, which would be amazing. I feel for Cat not having that relationship with her in-laws. It must be horrible being on the out like that—with *family*.

Mum hands me a glass of wine. 'Here's to your sister.' It's a sweet toast and I clink my glass against hers and take a sip. A riesling from Western Australia, it's flinty and minerally—delicious.

'Ron, Josh, the lamb's just gone in the oven and when

the timer goes, pop the veggies in, then re-set the timer for thirty-five minutes and when *that* timer goes, get the peas on. Then take the meat out and rest it before you carve, okay?' They both nod, though Dad has been sous chef to Mum for forty-two years, so it's doubtful he needs such explicit instructions. To me, she says, 'Shall we?'

'Let's do it.' Bravado at its best. It occurred to me not long after she asked that by agreeing to help Cat plan an Italian wedding, I've bitten off way more than I can chew. I'm actually grateful Mum insinuated herself onto the planning committee.

'Better bring this,' she says, taking the bottle from the counter. Maybe she's feeling it too. Minutes later, we're settled on the floor of Mum's study, surrounded by stacks of magazines with sticky notes marking specific pages, folders open, and pens at the ready. Sure, there are online wedding planning sites and Pinterest boards and e-magazines, but Mum and I like *paper*—the tactility, the indescribable pleasure of flicking through a magazine and finding that just-so inspiration and marking the spot with a sticky note.

'Right … now that you and Josh have settled on Montespertoli and he's booked accommodation at the castle—'

'You mean the two-bedroom apartment in one of the outbuildings.'

'Yes, Sarah, that's what I mean,' she says impatiently—Mum doesn't like to be interrupted. 'I'm wondering if you've looked closely at the rest of it?'

'The castle? Well … yes … sort of. What do you mean?'

'I mean that it's the perfect place for the wedding! It's a thousand years old, it has a beautiful aspect, *and* it's a working winery. Just imagine wedding photos in the cellar surrounded by barrels or out amongst the vines at sunset.'

'Oh, I hadn't thought of that.' It's not a bad idea.

'And look.' She flips open her laptop and angles it so we can both see the screen. 'I was thinking perhaps this large room … *perfect* for the ceremony, then straight into the reception.' She scrolls through image after image of an ornate room filled with paintings and sculptures and antique furniture. 'Can you imagine?' Her eyes are alight with excitement, but I can foresee is Cat scrunching up her nose at the ostentatiousness.

'Um, yeah, that's cool, I guess.'

'Honestly, Sarah, it sometimes baffles me how you can be an English teacher *and* so ineloquent.'

I love my mother, I love my mother, I love my mother, I chant in my head.

'How about this? I'll send the link to Jaelee and she can check on their availability and the cost.'

Mum sighs——one of her 'why is the world the way it is?' sighs. 'I'm sure she's lovely, but I can't understand why your sister's letting her friend help with the planning when she's got us.'

I know *exactly* why. Because, just like Karen Parsons, Jaelee doesn't take no for an answer. And Cat has asked me to be intermediary——with Jaelee on her behalf *and* between Jaelee and Mum. It was only a few weeks ago that Cat was promising to run interference between me and Mum and now look at me. A human buffer.

'Jaelee's a pro, Mum. Organising is *literally* her job——or a big part of it, anyway, especially the communications aspect *and* she works globally. Besides, if we leave the logistics to Jaelee——like all the bookings and the wedding license and the officiant——then we can do all the fun stuff.'

I am actually *delighted* Jaelee is helping us plan, as getting married in Italy is mired in red tape—particularly as, between my sister and her betrothed, they are citizens of three countries. And they want the marriage to be legal in all three!

That's why Cat and Jean-Luc are travelling to Milan immediately before meeting us in Tuscany. She has to take the '*Atto Notorio*' she will acquire at the Italian Embassy in London to the Australian Consulate in Milan to get the '*Nulla Osta*'. Then they'll have to present those, along with a translated 'Certificate of No Impediment' and a bi-lingual Statutory Declaration, both notarised in the UK, to the local authorities in Montespertoli, where we're all staying and where they will get married. And that's just for Cat! Jean-Luc needs his own '*Nulla Osta*' from France. Exhausting!

'Hmm, I suppose,' Mum admits reluctantly. She takes a large sip of wine. 'Why don't we start with the flowers, then?'

'Oh, perfect. This is what will be in season in Autumn.' I open a travel magazine to a special feature on Tuscany and cross reference that—colour-coded sticky notes really are the best—with a 'Weddings in Italy' feature from one of the bridal magazines. We 'hum' and 'ha' over several ideas, Mum peppering her commentary with desktop research into Tuscan wildflowers.

'What about sunflowers?' When I was a tour manager in Europe a decade-and-a-half ago, one of my favourite parts of every tour was driving through western Italy past acres and acres of those stunning, vibrant-yellow flowers.

'Won't it be too late in the year?' asks Mum.

'There *are* perennial sunflowers that bloom as late as October.'

She scrunches her nose—a staple in the Parsons

women's arsenal of expressions. 'They're kind of simple, aren't they? A bit too peasanty?'

'Mum, don't say "peasanty".'

'Why? Isn't it PC enough?' she challenges.

'I have no idea. It just doesn't sound very nice. How about "rustic" instead?'

'Fine, but is that the type of wedding your sister wants? *Rustic*? I mean, I have *no* idea!' It seems Mum *is* feeling overwhelmed.

Now I take a sip of wine, if only to give me time to think. Every time I've asked Cat what she wants—actually, every time any of us have asked—me, Mum, and Jaelee—Cat replies with something vague and if we *can* pin her down on anything, it usually contradicts something she said earlier.

In the past three weeks, I've shared a seventeen-email exchange with Jaelee on this very topic. Apparently, Cat wants her wedding to be chic *and* simple, quintessentially rustic Italian but super caz and kinda Aussie, yet beautiful and memorable. And very *Tuscany*.

None of that makes sense and when you put it all together, you end up with a sister, a mother, and a close friend going around in endless circles. I'm beginning to see why Jaelee raised her hand for logistics and legalities. More fool me! I thought I was getting off lightly with flowers!

Still, this is *way* better than succumbing to the dread of my approaching milestone birthday. Even after reading that letter to myself—on the surface, a very reassuring letter—I feel like something is off, missing even. I doubt it's that I've yet to travel to Antarctica.

And all that aside, if we leave it to Cat, there may not be a ceremony, let alone a reception.

'Honestly, I am thrilled to bits that Catherine is marrying Jean-Luc,' says Mum, 'and as confusing as all this is—*and* overwhelming, I might add' —I was right!— 'if we leave it to her, she'll end up getting married in an airport lounge.'

I chuckle. 'I was just thinking the same thing.'

'I love your sister …'

'So do I …'

'And this is her special day, so let's just start deciding things then move on to the next. How does that sound?'

'Sounds good, Mum.'

By the time Dad calls us to sit down to a roast lamb lunch, Mum and I have decided on an aesthetic for the wedding that sits somewhere between 'peasanty rusticity' and 'high-end chic'. Actually, I'm quite proud of how much we've accomplished today. Before packing up, I send an email off to Jaelee with links to the castle's website, a local florist, and a local bakery—all with clear instructions about what she's to inquire about.

Our plan is to give my sister the wedding she never knew she always wanted.

Chapter Five

SARAH

Tuscany, Autumn

Three legs, two stopovers, and thirty hours after leaving Sydney, we are *finally* in Tuscany.

Whose idea was a destination birthday-slash-wedding anyway? If I didn't love Josh and Cat as much as I do, I'd be cursing them both. Kidding! Well, mostly.

At least the flight from San Francisco to Zurich was in business class. Josh cashed in some frequent flyer points—thank you, babe!—and we got five-star treatment and a decent night's sleep. But after this long in transit, I am desperate to get out of these stinky clothes and take a shower.

International travel is so glamorous! Hah! I stand by my long-held belief that travelling is fantastic but transiting sucks.

Cat and Jean-Luc should have arrived in Florence an hour ago and will be meeting us on the other side of Customs and Immigration. 'You okay?' asks Josh as we shuffle along in line to show our passports. I smile up at him, only allowing the kiss that comes because I'm still chewing my 'landing gum' and at least my breath is fresh.

Eventually, we are at the front of the line and, as always happens when you are 'next', all the frustration and stress of waiting dissipates and soon I've been welcomed to Italy and have another stamp in my passport. I meet Josh on the other side of the Immigration booths and we grin at each other. Our first time in Italy together—actually, his first time here at all.

Our bags don't take too long and when our luggage tumbles onto the carousel intact and unscathed—surprising after being routed through two other international airports—I feel awash with relief. *Many* of my flights over the years have ended far less successfully. Josh collects our bags and we load up the trolley, adding our garment bag and two carry-ons. Trolley first, we emerge into the throng of people awaiting the arrival of loved ones, scanning the crowd for ours.

'Sez!' For a little person, as she likes to call herself, my sister has a big voice. We grin at each other across the expanse and Josh manocuvres our trolley through the throng to Cat and Jean-Luc. Cat and I hug tightly and I'm vaguely aware that the men are greeting each other with chatter and back slaps. Cat and I finally pull apart, her smiling up at me and me smiling down at her.

'How was your flight?' she asks.

'Long. How was yours?'

'Short, but the side trip to Milan … Oh my, g—'

'Hello, Sarah.'

'Hello, you. Happy wedding week,' I say, getting a hug from my soon-to-be brother-in-law.

'And happy birthday week.'

'Don't remind me.'

When we let go, Josh and my sister are hugging. He's even taller than Jean-Luc and she looks absolutely tiny in his arms. The four of us share excited grins, momentarily oblivious to the people bustling past us. We're sort of in the middle of things.

Reunion over, Cat hooks her arm through mine. 'Come on, let's get the rental car sorted and I'll fill you in.'

Cat leads the way out of the terminal, practically dragging me by my elbow, and Jean-Luc and Josh follow, each pushing a luggage trolley. Outside, the sky is brilliant blue and after being inside for a day-and-a-half, I squint against the bright light. 'So, where to?' I ask my sister.

'We're catching a bus to the rental car company—there.' She points towards a bus stop that's crowded with people all vying for a spot on one of the shuttle buses. I look at the enormous amount of luggage we have between us—even an intimate wedding requires a plethora of accoutrements—and at the 'queue'—a.k.a. the swarming mass of impatient travellers.

If we get to the rental car place inside of an hour, I will eat my hat. Of course, I will have to dig it out of my suitcase first.

'Are we having fun yet?' I ask with false cheer. Cat throws me a look that tells me my attempt at humour has failed.

'Come on. The sooner we get sorted, the sooner we'll be in Montespertoli and then we can *relax*.' Now may not be the time to point out that they've only travelled here from London—with a brief stop in Milan—and that if anyone deserves to relax, it's me and Josh.

Three buses fill up and move on before we're able to

board one——and *that* is a feat of speed, agility, and outright rudeness as we pass our luggage between us and stake a claim on enough floorspace to accommodate it and us. It's a relief when we get to the other end and decant onto the pavement outside the rental car place. Jean-Luc disappears inside while the three of us bake in the autumn sun, an unspoken agreement between us that we won't properly have arrived in Italy until we're en route to our home-away-from-home in a Tuscan castle.

Three hours after landing, I rest my head against the back seat of the four-wheel-drive, grateful that Jean-Luc is driving and Cat is navigating and Josh and I have been relegated to 'passenger status'. It allows me to watch out the window with growing glee as we leave behind generic motorways and fast-food restaurants and head southeast to Montespertoli.

Soon enough, the countryside I've been dreaming of for months surrounds us. As though the entirety of the Tuscan landscape has been painted by a giant artist, we pass patchwork fields of emerald-green, dusty-sage, and tawny-yellow blanketing the rolling hills, their borders lined with Italian Cypresses——tall slim conifers——as well as the much-anticipated fields of sunflowers. They may not be as abundant here as they are further south but even the occasional sight of those yellow 'faces' all tipping towards the sun is enough lift my spirits.

It's silent in the car——the others must feel it too, the reverence at being in such a beautiful location——and I grasp Josh's hand across the back seat. When he turns to smile at me, his eyes are alive with delight.

Montespertoli, as the name suggests, sits atop a sprawling hill——not quite as impressive as the Tuscan walled cities, but still a beautiful town with its pastel buildings and terracotta rooftops and clumps of bushy dark-green trees. A castle tower stands above the other structures. 'I wonder if that's our castle,' says Cat, pointing to the mottled stone structure.

The road gets windier and our view is swallowed up by greenery, the afternoon sun breaking through and dappling the road and our car with spotted sunlight.

At the top of a rise, we arrive almost unexpectedly at our destination and Jean-Luc makes a sharp left off the main road into the driveway of Castello Tranquillo, parking next to a two-storey, pale-coloured building with a terracotta roof.

As soon as I open the car door, I smell fragrant lavender and rosemary permeating the air and all the travel weariness seeps from my body. I climb out and stretch skyward, taking in deep breaths and sighing them out in a state of sheer bliss.

As Josh booked our accommodation, he searches his carry-on bag for the reservation. I made him print it out because I'd read multiple times that many Italians prefer 'old-school ways', such as reservations printed on paper in lieu of digital PDFs and QR codes, and you never can be too prepared.

Paper in hand, Josh disappears around the front of the building while the rest of us stretch our legs and start unloading the boot. When Josh returns, he's carrying a four-inch-long old-fashioned key and he's wearing a broad grin.

'Guys, this place is unbelievable and wait till you see the view out the back.' He walks over to a pair of tall painted wooden doors, one of which bears a brass '1'. 'This is us,' he says jiggling the key in the lock. *Why number one when it's the only accommodation in the castle?* I think. There's a click of the latch and he swings open the left side of the door and disappears inside. I grab our carry-on bags from the gravel driveway and follow him inside where the air is cool and the ceilings are high.

The hallway extends in both directions. 'Where are you?' I call out.

'Turn left.' I do, following the sound of his voice.

'Oh, wow,' I say entering a large, airy bedroom. I join Josh at the double glass doors that lead to a long, wide balcony running the length of the apartment. 'This is gorgeous.'

Josh's gaze remains fixed on the view. 'I know, right?'

'Hey, Sez!' calls Cat from the other end of the apartment.

I drop our bags on the Italian tile floor and head towards Cat's voice, passing a large bathroom on the left—our en suite. In the middle of the hallway, just across from the front door is a kitchen and dinette—by the look of it, renovated sometime in the mid-twentieth century—and when I get to the second bedroom, the doors to the balcony are wide open. I step out and join Cat at the railing.

'Well, this doesn't suck,' I say, taking in the view.

'It definitely doesn't.'

We are on one side of a shallow valley and our view looks like something out of a travel brochure. 'One Tuscany, please.' 'Here you are madam, just as you've ordered.' In between us and a row of houses that are perched on top of the next hill, are irregular parcels of land—a grove of olive trees, rows of grapevines, low scrub, clumps of bushy shrubs, and the ubiquitous Italian Cypresses that we'd seen dotting the countryside on the drive in.

It's breathtaking.

'Are you sure you don't mind if we take this room?' asks Cat. The room at this end of the apartment is slightly larger than ours but its distinguishing feature is the much larger bed. Ours has what I'd call a 'small double'.

'Of course not! You're the ones getting married—you get the bigger room.'

'I know, but we've split the costs and …'

'Cat, you're taking the room. Consider it a wedding gift.'

'You mean on top of letting me gate-crash your fortieth *and* doing most of the planning?'

'Yes.'

We regard each other affectionately. It has been far too long since we've seen each other in person—close to three years now—our longest stint apart in more than a decade. 'I've missed you,' we say at the same time.

We both smile through tears and I hug her tightly. My little sis is getting married this week. And we're here in Italy with our beautiful men, soon to be joined by our loved ones and everything feels right in the world. She lets go and goes inside, leaving me to gaze at the view and chew over my thoughts.

Everything is right in the world, as long as I don't dwell on my looming birthday.

Bleh. If it were up to me, I'd skip my birthday—arrive in Italy aged thirty-nine and (magically) leave aged forty. But Cat tells me Josh has gone to a lot of effort—everything from where my birthday celebration will be held to what it entails—and I don't want to hurt him by begging off.

Surely, if I can just breathe and enjoy where I am and who's here with me, then this will be less about a number and more about what makes me happy—Josh, my family and friends, being in a beautiful part of the world. Not to mention good food, good wine (presumably, as I do *love* a Chianti), and good times to come.

Perfect! I just need to get out of my own frigging way and all *will* be right with the world. Hah! Easier said than done.

―――――――

'What do you think?' I ask Josh.

After getting settled――which for me and Josh included a shower and a change of clothes and (okay) we may have had that shower together and taken a little longer than was absolutely necessary――the four of us have walked up the hill, away from our castle and towards the town centre, two-by-two as the footpaths are narrow here. And with Josh by my side and seeing Italy through his eyes as he gawps at even the tiniest details, it's almost as though *I'm* here for the first time too.

'It's a really pretty town,' says Josh, 'even if everything seems to be closed.'

'Siesta,' says Cat.

'Right, of course!' he replies. 'Other than daytime, my internal clock has no idea what time it is.'

'I'm *starving*,' I whine. Cat turns around and tuts at me. 'All very well for you――having lunch in *Milan*.'

'At the *airport*,' she retorts.

'Still counts,' I mutter, aware that I'm being bratty. It's just that travel weariness has hit hard and even though my outside feels refreshed――and recently ravished――I am dangerously close to a low blood sugar episode. I'm already lightheaded. I check my watch, which I set to Italian time just before we landed. 3:38pm. Twenty-two minutes until siesta officially ends. I can wait that long—I'll have to.

'Let's just explore the town, then stop for something to eat,' says my sister sensibly.

'Sounds good.' Josh is being diplomatic, I'm sure of it—his stomach just growled.

Just ahead, off to the left, is a wide street—almost a square of sorts and it screams, 'I am in Tuscany!' There's an unspoken agreement to stop and take it all in—the red-bricked monument in the middle of the street, surrounded by park benches; the double clock tower on one of the buildings, one clock set to the correct time and the other, well, not; the cream and white facades of the buildings, most with painted window shutters and some with Juliet balconies; and that pristine-looking church that's tucked away just off the road. It's a 'pinch me' moment and my hunger is instantly forgotten.

I've travelled to Italy many times before and all bar one of those trips was while leading coach tours. A 'simple walk into town' took precision planning and a vigilant eye on my tour group. Fifty people—even adults—can get themselves into all sorts of trouble while travelling through Europe, particularly 18–35s from the UK, Australia, and the US. I would spend most of my time corralling them off the roads and shushing them so the locals didn't get pissed off.

But this? This is me and my favourite people soaking it all in. I am in ITALY! We keep walking, now descending further into the town, the street getting narrower.

'Hey, Sez?'

'Mmm?' I tear my eyes from the buildings surrounding us and Cat is pointing to Pizzico, a *trattoria* and *enoteca* across the way, just past the next crossroad. I look before crossing the streets and run up to the front door which is gated. It's a tiny establishment but from what I can see, *this* is the place where we will eat—so many most exquisite wares pack the shelves. I turn to the others, who've caught up, and grin.

'And it opens in twenty minutes,' says Josh pointing to the sign, a sandwich board written in chalk.

'Let's explore some more, then come back,' I say excitedly.

Our exploration reveals a large town square—actually, more of a town *oval*—with shaded park benches around the outside facing inwards and one side blocked off to traffic. There is a gelato stand but it's shuttered at the moment. Mmm, gelato—maybe after we eat proper food. We do a circuit of the town oval, take a short detour down a side street, finding the supermarket, then meander back to our *trattoria*.

We arrive five minutes before opening, but a smiling woman sees us through the window and unlocks the door, then the large gate, swinging it open. '*Buonasera, signori,*' she says beckoning us in. When the four of us step inside, joining her and a man who I'm guessing is her husband, the tiny place is now chockers.

As I'd seen through the window earlier, so are the shelves and display cases. I could happily live off the contents of this shop for months. Cat and I immediately start exchanging exclamations. 'Oh, my god, Sarah, look at this—how good does this look?' 'Yeah but look at *this*.' 'Oh, we have to get some of that! And some of that.' It occurs to me that the guys are watching us amused and this time, it's *my* stomach that rumbles loudly.

Right—shopping for treats to take back to the castle can

wait. 'Can you ask about the menu?' I say to Jean-Luc, our appointed linguist, in a loud whisper. He nods at me.

'*Buonasera, signora. Un tavolo per quattro, per favore?*' he asks. Now, it could be because his Italian accent is so good or that Jean-Luc looks like a French film star, but our hostess bats her eyelashes at him, grins, then hands over a single sheet of heavy stock paper and indicates the small seating area outside. And in the nicest way possible, she shoos us out of the shop just as an older couple appears at the door. We situate ourselves around a tiny metal table and Jean-Luc graciously lets me and Josh read the menu first—except it's written in Italian and I only understand every fifth word—well, *tenth*.

Josh sits back in his seat, defeated. 'I can read it to you,' says our linguist.

'Please,' replies Josh. 'You'd think that four years of high-school Spanish would at least *help*,' he adds.

'The Latin language thing?' I ask.

'Yeah.'

'It is my pleasure.' Jean-Luc reads the short menu to us and by the time the *signora* comes to the table to take our order, he rattles it off and adds a large bottle of *acqua frizzante*. Ooh, I know that one!

'You know Jaelee, my friend who's coming to the wedding?' Cat says to Josh. I don't correct her by adding that Jaelee has actually helped *plan* it.

'Yeah. She's dating Alistair, the Scottish guy, and they're flying in from Edinburgh, right?'

'That's the one—well, when we were on our trip together, that bus trip a few years ago—all the way through Italy, she just spoke Spanish to everyone. Unapologetically.'

'Hah!' laughs Josh. 'That's awesome.'

'And that worked?' I asked.

'It worked. They'd speak Italian back to her and she'd have whole conversations with people.'

'That's impressive,' says Josh, though Jean-Luc is shaking his head and smiling. 'Well, not as impressive as speaking eight languages,' he says to Jean-Luc.

'It is only four—fluently, that is.'

'Yeah, yeah.' They share smiles across the table and I love this so much. I must savour these moments—especially the moments with just the four of us. In two days, wedding guests will start arriving and by the end of the week, we will be a party of sixteen—including our mum, who can be a little intense sometimes, and Jean-Luc's nasty sister, Cécile. I'm positive that Cat and I will be running interference for each other so intensely and intently, we'll be ready for our rugby jerseys by the time we return to our respective homes.

And that's another thing … I *really* need to get my sister alone at some point, because she and Jean-Luc still haven't told us where the matrimonial home will be. Yes, really. There's dating long distance and there's being married and living in different countries.

But every time I've brought it up—and I mean *every single time*—Cat gets cagey. Is she just letting Jean-Luc think they're going to live in his flat in Paris? Because she's told *me* that's a no-go—though she's never explained why. I mean, who doesn't want to live in Paris? Well, okay, there's visiting Paris and soaking up all the gorgeousness, and *moving* there. I'll admit, those two experiences are probably quite different. And Cat's French language skills are, well, *rudimentaire* at best, even now. Or maybe they've decided on London and are going to announce it at the wedding as a surprise. Who knows?! (And she knows I hate surprises.)

Cat's flatmate, Jane, may know. If I can't get Cat to tell me soon, I'll corner Jane when she arrives and weasel it out of her.

Signora appears with our plates of food, and my sardines and crusty bread and fresh salad look and smell so amazing, I think I may cry (again). Serious life discussions can—and must—wait when there is good food to be had. In *Italy*!

Chapter Six

CAT

Tuscany

We arrive back at the castle just before six, Sarah and Josh having eaten three plates of food between them, and Sarah insisting on stocking up on late-night snacks—just in case—wine, and several days' worth of breakfasts before making our way back. That meant buying out most of the enoteca and then heading back through the town to the supermarket—*away* from the castle.

By the time we unload the shopping, I am starting to feel the exhaustion of the day's travel, though I say nothing, as Sarah will likely give me a serve, *having been in transit for thirty hours*.

It was quite a day, however—an early morning flight from Heathrow to Milan, which meant up and out of the flat by 5:00am, collect our luggage in Milan, store our luggage at the airport, then a cab to the consulate for my appointment—thank goodness they weren't running too far behind, so it took less than an hour—then a cab back to the airport, collect and recheck the luggage, grab a quick lunch from the Milanese equivalent of Pret, and back on an aeroplane.

But I have all my paperwork now and this marriage will be legal in the UK, Australia, and France. At that last thought, my stomach clenches. Being married to a Frenchman makes it a *lot* easier to move to Paris than not being married to a Frenchman, and one of my reasons for not moving there will vanish in a week's time.

Hello, my name is Catherine Parsons and I am about to marry the love of my life and we still don't live in the same country.

Pathetic. No doubt there are hundreds—no, *thousands*—of women and men who, given the chance to live in a beautiful apartment in the eighteenth arrondisse-ment of Paris with *Jean-Luc*, possibly the most perfect man ever born, would leap at it. But Paris, with all its beauty and culture and the incredible *food* … it's not home. And I know deep within my heart that it never will be. I will never belong, I will never feel at ease as I traipse about Paris doing normal, everyday things, and Jean-Luc's family …

Well, that's a whole other thing.

I'm now *convinced* they hate me—well except Louis, Jean-Luc's brother-in-law and his nieces, Abigail and Alice. Only, two of my allies aren't coming to the wedding. *Cécile* didn't want the girls to miss any school, which is ridicu-lous—they're five and seven, not about to sit their A-levels, for crying out loud. And I doubt her decision had anything to do with their schooling. She just wants to punish me.

Beware Cat Parsons—shrill Englishwoman, poor second to perfect Vanessa, and evil thief of precious son and brother, Jean-Luc. She'll steal him away and make him sever all ties with us forever!

His family has become a firm mark in the '*Please*, can we not move to France?' column.

And even though I continue to (outwardly) extoll the virtues of London—it *is* my home—I don't feel any less anxious when I think of Jean-Luc moving there to be with me. I've never lived with my significant other before—I've barely even had a significant other before Jean-Luc—and I am fairly certain I will make a mess of it and be divorced within a year. That's *if* he'd even agree to live in London. Any time our marital home comes up it's Paris, Paris, Paris.

So, even though my fiancé has broached the topic numerous times, I've (barely just) managed to put him off. Even poor Jane still doesn't know if she is going to live with a married couple or whether she'll need to find a new flatmate.

What the fuck is wrong with me?

These thoughts consume me as I watch Sarah and Josh assemble a platter of food—*how* are they still hungry? —uncork some wine, and set up on the balcony to watch the sunset with Jean-Luc.

Actually, that could be rather nice—sipping wine while watching a Tuscan sunset. *And* a good distraction. But first, I need to shake off this fatigue. 'Lovelies,' I say, slipping past them and heading towards our room, 'do you mind if I freshen up a bit before joining you?' Perhaps a shower will rejuvenate my waning energy. There's an array of affirmative responses and I disappear inside.

Now, as soon as Sarah arrives at her destination, she likes to nest—unpacking and arranging everything just so. I am the opposite, the type of traveller who literally lives out of her suitcase. On the few occasions we've travelled together—and every time I've visited her in Sydney—it drives my sister bonkers. But I stand firm that a little chaos when you travel is one of the best parts—who wants everything to be as orderly as it is back home?

Tonight, however, as I rifle through my luggage seeking out my toiletries bag and something more casual to wear than my travel clothes, I make a sickening discovery.

'Sarah!' My sister comes in from the balcony, swatting at the gauzy curtains before emerging fully into the room.

'What's up?'

'Did you see a garment bag when we unloaded the car?' *Do not panic—it's here somewhere,* I tell myself. My stomach ignores the instruction, spasming.

'Um, there's the one we brought with us—with Josh's suit and my dress.'

'Jean-Luc!'

'*Oui, chérie.*' He appears at the doorway, followed closely by Josh.

'My garment bag.' The way the thoughts flicker across his face is almost comical. Only this is not a comical moment. He starts looking about the room.

'I'll check the car,' says Josh, rushing past me. I'm vaguely cognisant of the front door opening, so intense is the roaring in my ears. Jean-Luc is looking under the bed now and I want to snap at him to stop, because why would we slide a garment bag under the bed? Sarah does a cursory look about the room, then steps close and rubs my arm, the universal sign for 'everything's gone to shit, poor you'. Oh, god.

'Not in the car,' says Josh, returning slightly out of breath. Oh, god. Oh, god. Oh, god.

'Do you remember us having it at Heathrow or on the aeroplane?' I ask Jean-Luc, rising panic strangling my voice. His face is blank and so are my thoughts. Did we have it with us when we checked in? Bugger! I can't remember—it was far too early in the morning.

Maybe I left it at home—that's it! It's got to be. 'Jane!' I say so suddenly that the others start. I delve into my handbag for my phone, sit on the bed and, fingers shaking, call her. She's coming for the wedding and can bring it with her. As I wait for her to pick up, relief and anxiousness fight for dominance.

'Hi, love,' she says.

'Hello! Um, are you are the flat?'

'Yes, just got home. What's up?'

'We've gone and left my bloody wedding dress in London!' Jean-Luc sits next to me and our eyes meet, his hopeful.

'Oh, not to worry, I'll bring it with me. Where is it? In your wardrobe.'

'Yes,' I say, sounding more convinced than I am.

'So, how is it?'

'How's what?'

'Italy?'

'Um, yes, lovely.' I could be on the *moon* right now and not want to talk about how amazing it is that I'm here.

'Right, I'm in your room …' she says commentating as I hear her moving hangers about in the wardrobe. 'Hmm.'

'Hmm? That doesn't sound good.'

'Um, Cat, I've checked all the way through the wardrobe—twice—and the back of the door. Hang on, you didn't put it in Alex's old room, did you?'

'I don't think so,' I say, my voice steeped in panic.

'I'll check.' She's on the move again and moments later, she says, 'I'm so sorry, love, it's not here.' Oh, fuck, fuck, fuck. 'Did you leave it on the plane?'

'Um, not sure … I'll let you know. I've got to go.' I hang up on Jane and look at the three stricken faces watching me, Sarah's eyes filled with sympathy.

Oh, my god. Where the fuck is my fucking wedding dress?

Things you cannot do of an evening in Italy: contact an Italian airline's baggage department, an Italian airport's luggage storage department, an Italian shuttle bus service, or an Italian rental car company's service desk.

I know this because we tried.

Sarah and Josh scoured websites—mostly written in Italian—for the phone number of a customer service team, then I'd dial and hand the phone to Jean-Luc so as not to torture the Italians with my extremely poor Italian. Another thing to chastise myself about. I have known for *months* that I would be here and did I learn more than the basics? No, I did not!

Each time Jean-Luc made his way through the automated menus—'Press one for panicky brides who may or may not have left their wedding dress at our place of business'—he would hang up and say we had to call in the morning.

Four phone calls, zero progress. '*Mon amour*, we will call first thing tomorrow and find your dress, *d'accord?*'

I sit heavily on the bed, having worn myself out entirely with thirty frantic minutes of pacing. '*D'accord*,' I say.

'Why don't you have that shower, then come join us on the balcony?' asks Sarah.

They're all looking at me, practically *willing* me to adopt a stiff upper lip approach, which makes sense as I can do nothing about this situation. However, I may have lived in England for fifteen years and I may *sound* like an English-woman, but my upper lip is decidedly limp and all I want to do is crawl into bed and cry.

Tuscany, Tuscany, Tuscany, I remind myself.

'All right,' I say instead. The relief in the room is so palpable, it's like watching the air release from a bouncy castle.

Sarah disappears outside then immediately returns with a bright blue can of Aerogard, which she tosses onto the bed. 'And you'll need that,' she says, 'the mozzies are brutal.'

'What?' Josh and Jean-Luc have made themselves scarce—probably desperate to get away from the emerging Bridezilla—and Sarah just smiles at me pityingly.

'Yeah. It's beautiful here, but the mozzies are so big, they need landing gear. I read it on Trip Advisor.' As my mind struggles to grasp what this will mean for the rest of our stay, including my *wedding*, she adds, 'Don't worry I brought four cans. We'll be right.'

We may very well 'be right', but it looks like I may be walking down the aisle—if there is one, as that is another detail I have left to my sister and mother—wearing nothing more than fancy undergarments and heels and smelling like citronella!

Wonderful. And by that, I mean bollocks.

―――――――

Two hours and twenty-seven minutes after the Italian call centres open for business, we locate my garment bag. It's in Milan at the baggage storage place in the airport. And it will cost €320 to have it sent to us—in a fortnight. Maths is not particularly my strong suit, but I do know that a fortnight from now will be after the wedding *and* after we have returned home.

Meanwhile—just in case that's where it ended up being—Josh has been searching for round-trip tickets to Milan—fly up today, get the dress, fly back today—and at each result, he grimaces. The last-minute flights are either exorbitant or we can't get there and back in less than four days. We can't be stuck in Milan while our family and friends arrive and Sarah and Jaelee finalise the details of the wedding. Besides, I'd miss my hen's.

'How much to send it to London via slow boat?' I quip to Jean-Luc. If I can't wear my dress, then at least I can sell it to someone who can.

Jean-Luc presses his lips together in sympathy and asks the cost of sending it to London if it's *'non c'è fretta'*—meaning there's no rush. He covers the handset and says, 'One-hundred-and-twenty euros and it will take …' he shrugs, indicating that there is no clear indication of how soon I will receive my dress.

My dress! My perfect, *perfect* dress—the one Mich and I found after an exhaustive search comprising four full-day outings, nipping in and out of every bridal shop in Greater London, wearily wondering by the end of each day if I should settle for something 'close enough' and have it altered. When we finally found it, late afternoon on an unseasonably warm September Saturday—and at forty per cent off because it was last season's design—I actually cried.

Cream-coloured silk, lace overlay, plunging neckline to show off the girls, nipped at the waist, A-line to my ankles, and an exact fit for my petite frame, no alterations needed.

Utter perfection—if it wasn't in *Milan*.

I nod at Jean-Luc and he gives them my name and address in London, then rattles off his credit card number by heart. *I always have to look mine up*, I think. Focusing on banal details is easier than admitting to myself that I only have a week to find a suitable replacement—and potentially get it altered—in a foreign country. Jean-Luc wraps up the call. 'Ready?' he asks.

'I suppose. I'll just text Sarah.' She and Josh went on a walk around the castle grounds about an hour ago—no doubt a far more interesting pursuit than eavesdropping on our conversations with Italian call centres.

Our plan for the day, now that my dress has been located, is to head to San Gimignano, a walled city forty minutes from here that Sarah has been raving about. Once a tour manager, always a tour manager, I suppose. And, as it's our last day with just the four of us before the hordes arrive, I'm more than happy to 'mooch about', as Sarah says, have what will undoubtably be a delicious lunch, and just soak up the 'Italianness'.

I've also been promised gelato and I am *so* looking forward to drowning my sorrows in chocolaty goodness. 'Catherine,' says my soon-to-be-husband, head cocked in concern, 'I would marry you even if you only wore a bedsheet.'

'Is that an option?' I ask, eyeing the bed linens.

He smiles before kissing my forehead. '*Andiamo, chérie.*' He's so clever, he can placate me in two languages.

'This place … it's sublime,' I say as we emerge from a narrow street into a piazza. We've been wandering for more than half-an-hour now, accompanied by Sarah's impressive tour manager-style commentary, and she was right—it is lovely just soaking up the Italianness. *A thousand-year-old Italianness*, I remind myself. I feel a bit like I did when I was in Rome on that bus trip, suddenly struck by how much history surrounds me.

This place is practically *drenched* in it—the cobblestones, the irregular brickwork facades of some buildings, the (often patchy) rendering of others, plaster breaking away in places to reveal the bricks below, the arched doorways, and succinct rectangular windows, many with dark brown shutters that look almost painted on.

But I think I love the towers most of all. According to Sarah, they weren't built until the 1300s—medieval skyscrapers built by rival families in a feudal race to assert their importance, surprisingly straight and true, a stark contrast to the brilliant blue sky and the wispy fluff of the clouds. She says there used to be more than seventy of them—they must have blocked out the sun!—but there are only fourteen now. Still, they make this town distinctive and sightseeing is just what I've needed to take my mind off *THE DRAMA OF THE MISSING WEDDING DRESS.*

Well, mostly, as it's still there lurking behind the 'ooh's and 'ahh's—probably because Sarah has spent the past hour interspersing her commentary with intense gazes into shop windows—extremely unsubtle wedding dress shopping. Fruitless too, as you'd be hard pressed to find *any* kind of dress here. Leather handbags, absolutely. Ceramics, art,

SANDY BARKER

cured wild boar, definitely. But this town is hardly the epicentre of Italian couture.

'Sarah, I love you,' I say as she pauses in front of another shopfront, 'but if you don't stop that, I'm asking Mum to be my Maid of Honour.'

'How very dare you!' she says with mock indignation and we indulge a 'we love all things Catherine Tate' giggle. 'Besides, it would be *Matron* of Honour. Hey …' She grabs my hand and stops walking, letting the guys go on ahead. 'What *do* you want to do about a dress?'

'To be honest, I'm still a little numb, but Jae arrives tomorrow—and Mum and Dad. Maybe the four of us can go shopping the day after tomorrow.'

'You want to take Dad shopping for a wedding dress?' she deadpans. I roll my eyes and start walking again and she falls into step behind me. 'You *could* wear mine if you wanted—it's not exactly bridal but it *could* work. Maybe we can get someone in town to take it in.'

'That's sweet, Sez, but then what would you wear?'

'How about that?' she asks pointing to an apron hanging out the front of a tourist shop. It's white with red piping and has a panorama of the town screen-printed across the bottom.

'Right.'

'No, hear me out. I buy *two*, and wear one in the front and one in the back. Very festive.'

'Thanks for trying to make me feel better.'

'We'll find something, Cat, I promise. Something *beautiful*. Siena's not far and they have some *really* nice clothing stores.'

'Thank you. I'm sure you're right,' I say. Inside, I am less than confident. Just in case we don't find anything suitable in

84

the next six days, I texted Jaelee this morning. She and I wear the same size and she's promised to bring a few of her dresses for me to try on. Jaelee's clothes do lean towards 'Miami clubwear' but I suppose a sexy nightclub dress would be preferable to a homemade toga.

Ahead, in the centre of the piazza, Josh is taking photographs and Jean-Luc is looking about, just soaking it all in, his face tipped to the sun and a slight smile on his face. I know right in this moment that I would marry *him* if *he* were dressed in nothing but a bedsheet.

Perhaps that's the solution—homemade togas all around. Come, one and all, dressed in your best bedsheet! Jane would think it a laugh, no doubt Cécile would find a way to look chic and sophisticated, just so she could rub my nose in how superior she is to me in every way, and Mum would pass out from the shock.

Jean-Luc wanders back to me as Sarah jogs over to Josh and they line up a selfie. 'Hungry, *chérie*?'

'*Oui, j'ai très faim.*' He smiles the special smile that's just for me, one I get to see often but always after answering him in French—even if my accent is *très mal*.

'*Bien*. Josh, Sarah?' They come over to us. 'We have great hunger. Should we have lunch?'

'Oh, yeah! Actually, I know just the place if it's still there. They have the *best* wild boar *pappardelle* in San Gimignano!'

I'm doubtful that a restaurant Sarah frequented in her touring days—a dozen years ago—will still be there, let alone still serve the best pasta in the town, but she seems confident. She scans the piazza—getting her bearings, I imagine—then strides off, calling, 'This way.'

Not only is the restaurant still there, but she was right about the wild boar pasta. It's without a doubt the best pasta I've ever had and I am now utterly ruined for Prezzo.

After an epic lunch and more mooching—the guys did climb the tower, Josh returning to us energised, like he'd just had a good workout, and Jean-Luc flushed and wearing a sheen of sweat—we finally called it a day and drove back to the castle in the late afternoon. None of us were particularly hungry, so we doused ourselves in Aerogard, opened a bottle of Chianti, and sat out on the balcony to watch the sky turn from blue to pink to orange and finally settle into an inky darkness dotted by pinpricks of light.

Glorious.

Tomorrow, the others will start to arrive and if that folder Sarah brought with her is any indication, we'll all be assigned tasks and given deadlines. I hope she's scheduled in some fun—outings and such—though I suspect that her organisational efforts are as much about avoiding thoughts of the 'BIG 4-0' as they are about Sarah being Sarah—freakishly organised and a little bit bossy.

I need to get some time with her—proper sister-to-sister time. Perhaps she can help me with my thing. I mean, *where* are my husband and I going to live and *why* hasn't he asked me about it? Are we going to still be living in different countries in thirty years and then one day, one of us will say, 'Why didn't we ever live together?' and the other will reply, 'Well, you never brought it up'?

Around nine, I stretch my hands above my head and yawn loudly. 'We boring you?' Sarah asks.

'No, just shattered. Bedtime, methinks.' I stand and drop

a kiss on Josh's cheek, then hug my sister from behind. She squeezes my arms tightly as I rest my chin on her head. God, I love her. I can't believe we're *here*—*together*. Best wedding present ever.

I release her and reach out for Jean-Luc's hand. He clasps mine, then kisses it. 'I will be in soon, *chérie*.' I open the double doors leading to our room and push aside the gauzy curtains, and I'm just inside the doorway when I realise that I'm not alone. A loud buzzing draws my eye upward and the biggest wasp I have ever seen is doing laps of the room.

'Um … um … hello? Help!' I call, my eyes fixed on the beast invading our bedroom. It must be at least two inches long. And how the hell did it get in here? I sense the others behind me, bottlenecked in the doorway.

'Oh, shit,' says Josh. 'How fucking huge is that?'

'Oh, my god,' says Sarah.

Jean-Luc is silent beside me, his mouth agape—almost in wonder. '*Une guêpe*,' he says quietly.

'Sorry?'

'*En français*, it is *une guêpe*.'

'That's wonderful, darling, but I hardly think this is the time for a vocabulary lesson. Do you know how to get the bloody *guêpe* out of our room?'

'*Cat*,' warns Sarah, chastising me for being rude.

'Sorry, darling.' Jean-Luc shrugs—I'm forgiven—but while we've been conversing, I've lost track of the wasp. 'Crap, where did it go?' I am not sleeping in here with a wasp that may or may not want to kill me.

'There,' says Josh, pointing to the air-conditioning unit.

'He looks like he's doing a dance,' says Sarah.

'Maybe he's calling for the other wasps——"Hey, you guys! Fresh meat in here!",' jokes Josh.

'He'd better bloody not be,' I growl, glaring up him. 'We have to get it out of here. What about the Aerogard?' I ask Sarah.

'It'd probably just piss it off——and we need that for the mozzies. Oh, speaking of which.' She shepherds us further into the room and closes the doors behind us. Now we're locked in the room with the wasp-beast.

'Why on earth are all the insects in Tuscany so bloody huge?' I screech.

'I'm going to get a broom,' says Josh. He bravely passes directly under the wasp-beast on his way out, while the rest of us just stare at it, watching it do its evil little dance. Josh is back in moments with one of those old-fashioned straw brooms, passing under it for a second time and joining us in the middle of the room.

'What are you thinking?' Jean-Luc asks.

'Maybe we can swat it?' he replies. They throw each other a look.

'What? What does that mean? That look?' I ask, frantically. 'Is that secret men's code for, "I have no bloody idea what I'm doing"?'

'Pretty much,' says Josh.

'Wonderful.' Just then, the wasp leaves the air-conditioning unit and flies directly at us. We scatter and there's unbearably loud shrieking——all right, that may have come from me.

We are now congregated in a tight clump, backs to the wall and watching the bloody wasp-beast, who appears to be having a lovely time wandering about the gauzy net curtains. If it weren't so terrifying, I'd be laughing at how pathetic we are—four humans versus one (freakishly large) insect and all of us paralysed with fear. All right—again, that may just be me.

Sarah breaks away from us and starts creeping towards it. Oh, god. 'Sez, *what* are you doing?' I ask.

'I have an idea.' She moves slowly, deliberately, gathering the bottom of the curtain in her fist. Then in a flurry of movement, she rapidly twirls the curtain, trapping the wasp inside the folds. 'Right, Josh, you go outside and open the door.'

He runs out of the room, down the hallway, and out to the balcony, and is soon at the double glass doors, peering in. He opens the one on the right. 'Okay.'

'I'm going to pass you this,' she says, indicating the fistful of curtain, 'then we're going to close the door, trapping the wasp outside.' Brilliant. My sister is a genius. There's a brief moment where the wasp tries to escape the gauze and its buzzing is so loud, it startles Josh and he nearly drops the curtain. But the plan works and soon our bedroom is wasp-beast free.

'Oh, my god,' I say. I expel an enormous sigh then perch on the edge of the bed, catching my breath.

Josh returns to the room, passing Sarah on her way out. 'Where are you going?' I call.

'Not finished yet,' she calls back.

We exchange curious looks and moments later, Sarah untwists the curtain and flicks it until the wasp buzzes off into the night. Jean-Luc opens the door and Josh scoops her up into an embrace. 'You're a bad-ass, babe,' Josh declares proudly. She beams at him.

'*Now* we can go to bed,' she says.

Chapter Seven

SARAH

Tuscany

'Saving everyone from a killer wasp goes down as an Adventure Chick escapade, don't ya reckon?' I say, alluding to my alter ego at breakfast the next morning. Adventure Chick went into hiding a few years back, eradicated by a dead-end relationship. She re-emerged right around the time I met Josh, which was not coincidental and one of the reasons he's the love of my life.

Josh swallows his bite of muesli and yoghurt—our go-to, even when we're travelling. 'Oh definitely. Right up there with white-water rafting, abseiling, rock climbing ...'

'I should add it to my resumé.'

'Add what to your resume?' asks Cat. She's carrying tea and a plate piled high with toast. I am *so* having some of that after I finish my muesli—two days into our trip and I've already reignited my love affair with Italian bread.

'Sarah's just bragging about her exploits in pest removal.'

'Oh, right. Well, thank you for that—and I mean it. All I could come up with was locking up the room and moving to a pensione.'

'Good morning!' Jean-Luc joins us on the balcony with a brimming cafetière and a mug. Black coffee will be the entirety of his breakfast. It's his only fault—almost enough to ban him from my family for life—but we love him regardless, so we're keeping him.

'Right,' I say, snagging one of Cat's pieces of toast. She tries to slap my hand but misses—I'm too quick, probably remnants of my Adventure Chick powers. 'We all have assignments today …' Cat groans. 'And our parents will be arriving just after lunch.' Cat groans again. 'Hey, that's not nice.'

'At least they're not staying here.'

'Also not nice.'

She makes a face and goes back to her breakfast.

'What's on the list?' asks Josh.

'Excellent question. I'll just go and get it so I don't forget anything.' This is merely a security measure, as I essentially have our plans memorised, but you never can be too careful. I return to the balcony laden with a three-ring folder and my pencil case.

'You mean you didn't pack a whiteboard?' Cat jibes.

'I had to talk her out of it,' says Josh, piling on.

'Just give them all the unfun tasks, Sarah,' says Jean-Luc.

'Hah!' I laugh. 'Jean-Luc, *you* are my favourite.'

'Hey,' says Cat, indignant.

'Also, hey!' adds Josh. I chuckle. God, I love being here with them, just us. Maybe we can tell everyone else to bugger off so we can spend the next week celebrating by ourselves. I'm sure Mum would be delighted. Hah!

'Right,' I say again, consulting the schedule. 'We are touring the castle at ten' —I check my watch— 'just over an hour from now and you'll be making the final decision on where to have the ceremony. If it's in the great hall—essentially the main room of the castle—that will be transformed for the reception while you're having your wedding photographs taken. If not, when it's time for the reception, we'll simply move from your chosen room to the hall. Jaelee negotiated the same price either way, so it just comes down to your preferences.'

They nod along so I continue. 'Jean-Luc, you and I will then meet with the vintner and finalise the wine selection.' I've assigned this task to us, as Cat will essentially drink anything (don't tell her I said that) and Josh is more of a cocktails and beer guy.

'Cat and Jean-Luc, you're due at the Civil Status Office with your paperwork at 12:00pm. And after Mum and Dad arrive around two, we'll say hello, then take them to their accommodation and make sure they're settled.' Jaelee, bless her, recommended a resort for Mum and Dad on the opposite end of town to the castle.

Granted, Montespertoli is not that large, but the resort is far enough away that we won't be expecting any impromptu visits from Mum. Besides, I've seen the website and the place is *gorgeous*—total luxury. I can only hope Mum would rather lounge by the pool and stare out at the Tuscan countryside than hang around here driving Cat batty.

'And I have a few last-minute arrangements for your birthday party, too,' says Josh.

'I'm not sure there's ti—' I start to say.

'Jean-Luc, wanna come with me to the … uh … place? We can go after Ron and Karen get here.'

'Ah, *oui*, sounds good. I will come with you to the place.' Dual manly nods and it is decided. They are going to 'the place'. The others start gathering up the remnants of breakfast and under the guise of reviewing our plans, I sit, folder open and stare out across the valley.

My birthday celebration is the only aspect of the trip that Josh has managed to keep as a surprise. I still don't know what it is or even *where* it is. For some reason, Jean-Luc is involved, which has added to the intrigue. And there have been a number of times that Josh has come close to revealing a pertinent detail— he's so excited about it, he can barely contain himself.

At least one of us is.

Ironic, really, as when I turned thirty, I practically threw a parade. I was so convinced that all the angst and worry of my twenties—not really knowing what I wanted from life or who I was or wanted to be—would dissipate into the air at the stroke of midnight. I'd turn thirty and everything would click into place and I'd know for sure what I wanted from life.

Hah! Pop culture has a lot to answer for. Wasn't thirty supposed to be when you became a fully-fledged adult? But (probably not surprisingly) I was just as messed-up, insecure, and anxious about life in my early thirties as I'd been since birth.

Even a few years ago when I met Josh, I was all tangled in knots, insecure and unsure of what I wanted. But in retrospect—and believe me, there has been a *lot* of emotional dissection since then—that had more to do with the year-long relationship with my ex, Neil the cheating bastard, than my age.

Infidelity can crush your very soul and make you feel like

nothing. It's nearly impossible to bounce back from that, even when a cute American tells you how wonderful you are—and sexy and fun and clever. Those things can only sink in when you've healed enough to let them. Thank god I healed in time and didn't lose him. Although he had his own stuff going on and we *were* two sides of a love triangle—but that's another story.

Oh, Josh. He's been so thoughtful. He knew exactly how to make this occasion special, bringing me here to a place where beauty is abundant, where *la vita è bella*, and gathering my closest people to share it with us.

What is wrong with me? Shouldn't I be rejoicing? Isn't forty the new thirty or some shit like that? Maybe *this* is when I get my proper adulting badge, when feeling wise and competent far outweighs (far too frequent) bouts of self-doubt and existential befuddlement.

Because as much as I love my life—and I *do*, especially the life that Josh and I have built together—I *still* have this niggling feeling that something is off, like I've left the oven on or forgotten to lock the front door—only more intense, because accompanying this feeling is an acute sense of urgency. As though there's a timer ticking down—a non-reproductive biological clock.

It's becoming exhausting.

'This room is the library, so one of your options for the ceremony,' says our host, a dour-faced woman in her thirties named Bianca. I look about at the ornate ceiling, tall bookshelves along three walls, each shelf crammed with old leatherbound books and exotic-looking artefacts, and various stuffed armchairs, which somehow, despite the vastly different fabrics, complement each other. Beside each chair is an antique side table—again, all completely different—and on those are more artefacts. One table holds a collection of small animal skulls—fascinating, but a little creepy.

I glance at Cat and by the look of it, she's just spied the skulls. Her mouth contorts momentarily before reverting to a smile. 'Lovely,' she says to Bianca. It's convincing enough, even though I'm sure she hates this room.

'It is an interesting room,' says Jean-Luc.

'Interesting' is right, but I'm with Cat—I wouldn't want to get married in here. With all those bookshelves there's not even any natural light and the dim lamps only enhance the spookiness.

'You said fourteen guests?' asks Bianca.

'That's right,' says Cat. 'And us.' She waves her forefinger between her and Jean-Luc.

'*And* the celebrant,' I add.

'Mmm, seventeen people should fit comfortably. We move the chairs and the tables, of course, to make room.'

'Wonderful,' says Cat. If she keeps being so agreeable, she could end up with an Indiana Jones themed wedding. At least if the tables are going, the skulls will too—well, hopefully.

'And next door is the sitting room. Follow me, please.' Bianca exits through a large wooden door and we follow her into the next room. Unlike the library, this room has natural light and is much larger but the artefacts have ratcheted up a few notches to outright horrifying.

There are stuffed and mounted animal heads on the wall, a rug made from the skin of what appears to be a leopard——with the head still intact——and sitting atop a large wooden desk inlaid with green leather is an enormous animal skull——likely a rhinoceros but if I were being more fantastical, it could easily have belonged to a dinosaur.

Another 'interesting' room but definitely not what I would call romantic and Cat's face says everything I'm thinking——her beautiful English manners ebbing away before my eyes. 'Is your sister going to survive this tour?' whispers Josh in my ear. I look up at him, widening my eyes in mock horror and he laughs. It echoes around the room and Jean-Luc, Cat, *and* Bianca stop talking about moving furniture to accommodate a wedding and look at us.

'Sorry,' Josh and I say together.

I need to come to Cat's rescue——I can no longer stand by, watching her growing terror. Or is it gross disappointment? Likely both. 'Uh, Bianca, I think you had discussed with Jaelee Tan, our friend, that Cat and Jean-Luc could just do the lot in the great hall?'

We've already seen the great hall. We passed through it on the way to the library and the sitting room, and it is a *much* better choice for the wedding. Although it's markedly different from the (heavily edited) photo collection they've posted online. Mum would *never* have suggested it if she'd seen what it actually looks like. The décor is extremely over the top, including a twenty-foot mural, enormous paintings in gilded frames, faux Roman columns at intervals along the walls, and a domed ceiling painted to look like the sky, but at least there aren't any spoils from hunting excursions affixed to the walls.

'The lot?' Bianca asks.

'Yeah, have the ceremony in there, then … you know——'

I move my hands to demonstrate lots of activity '—set up for the reception. The lot.'

'*Mi dispiace, no.*' No? Does 'no' mean that she doesn't understand me or that I'm wrong?

'So … we just use the same space for both parts of the wedding—the ceremony *and* the reception.'

'*Sì,* but *no.*'

Yes but no? What the hell is that supposed to mean? Jean-Luc must be as confused as I am because he starts speaking to Bianca in Italian. She tuts and shakes her head and the more he talks—even though he is speaking in his usual gentle tone—the more vigorously she shakes her head. She speaks, he replies, then, she says, 'Is not possible,' in English.

'What's not possible?' asks Cat right as I say, 'What?'

'*Chérie,* there has been a misunderstanding. We cannot have the wedding in the great hall.'

'What?' I say again. 'But Jaelee said—'

'A mistake,' he says with a slight shrug.

'Shit,' says Josh quietly.

'So, we have to choose between the library and the sitting room?' asks Cat slowly, as though her mind is only just catching up to the words coming from her mouth.

'*Sì,*' says Bianca.

'Can we get back to you?' I ask, walking over to Cat and wrapping a protective arm around her shoulders.

'Of course. Is no problem.' Oh, so *now* there's no problem. I know exactly how much Cat and Jean-Luc spent on this venue for their wedding, and I can only imagine how queasy they're both feeling. I glance at Jean-Luc, who's frowning, and back at Cat, who appears dazed.

'We should head out,' says Josh brightly.

'Uh, yes!' I reply. 'Thank you, Bianca, *grazie*. We will …'

Josh bundles me and Cat out of the room and into the great hall. 'We'll let you know asap,' he says over his shoulder as we head outside.

Behind us, Jean-Luc says something to Bianca in Italian and she replies with, 'Something, something *giovedì*.' That means Thursday—two days before they get married, so we only have a few days to figure this out. '*Sì, grazie mille,*' he adds, then joins us in the courtyard.

'Catherine?' He peers at her, concerned. I'm concerned too, as I've never seen this exact expression on her face. She's also mesmerised by a potted geranium.

'So,' she says numbly, as if to herself, 'dusty old books or stuffed endangered animals? I suppose not everyone gets married standing on top of a leopard.' She's still staring at the pot plant and the three of us exchange worried looks.

'Cat, don't worry—we'll figure it out, okay? Jaelee and Alistair will be here tonight and she can sort everything out first thing in the morning.'

'Yeah, it's probably just some minor misunderstanding,' says Josh.

Cat nods. 'Right.' Mmm—she's definitely not convinced.

I look at Jean-Luc and his lips are pressed into a straight line. He's usually so easy going and I hate seeing them both so discombobulated. 'Hey, do you want to come with me and Jean-Luc to talk to the vintner?' I offer.

Cat's head snaps in my direction. 'Will we be tasting the wine?' she asks hopefully.

'I think so, yes.' If we're choosing what wine to serve at the reception, it makes sense that we'll be tasting it.

'Then I'm coming.'

She turns and walks back towards our apartment and the three of us follow. 'Sarah, I am troubled,' says Jean-Luc quietly.

'I know, but it will all work out, I promise.' I plaster on a massive smile which he returns wanly before jogging ahead to catch up to Cat.

'Is Cat superstitious?' asks Josh. 'Does she believe in signs from the universe or anything like that?'

'No, I don't think so.' She and I may be close, but no one knows *everything* about another person, even their sister and best friend.

'You don't, do you?'

'Eh, sorta … when it suits me,' I reply, smiling up at him. 'You know … when my horoscope says I'm going to have a windfall …'

'Or meet a talk, dark, handsome man.'

'I'm going to meet a talk, dark, handsome man? When?!'

'Ha-ha.' He nudges me with his shoulder.

We're at the front door of the apartment now and I pause before going inside. 'You thinking the same thing as me?'

'Not sure. What are you thinking?' he asks.

'That there's mounting evidence that *something* is fucking with my sister's wedding.'

'Oh, that? Yeah, definitely.'

'Jaelee *will* fix it, right—the venue?' I ask hopefully.

'Sure! I've never met the woman, but I am one hundred per cent positive that she will fix it,' he says.

'I wish I could do more.'

'Hey, you're doing everything you can to make this a special time for Cat—for both of them. And don't forget, you're supposed to be enjoying this too—this is *your* special time as well. Hey, what's wrong?'

'Nothing, I … It's nothing.'

'You sure?' I nod.

'Look, tomorrow we'll get the venue figured out, and you and your mom and Cat will get her a new dress. These are just blips, okay?'

'Okay,' I say, wanting to convince myself that it will all fall into place, even though some things are completely out of my control no matter how organised I am. Still, it's my sister's wedding and I absolutely will *not* be defeated by a missing wedding dress and a bizarre wedding venue.

'They're here, Cat,' I call out as I exit the apartment and cross the crunchy gravel. Hopefully, that was loud enough to rouse her. Last time I saw my sister, she was prone on her bed snoring softly.

A white taxi covered in decals idles in the castle's driveway, Mum emerging from one of the back doors. 'Hi, Mum.' It's only been a couple of weeks since I've seen her, but I am so glad she's here—a reinforcement for addressing current and future catastrophes. Everything I know about organisation, troubleshooting, and reining in wayward plans, I've learnt from my mum.

'Hello, Sarah,' she says. Despite being in transit a day-and-a-half, she looks pristine and when she falls wearily into my hug, smells only of her signature scent, Lancôme's Tresor. Karen Parsons, Travel Maven.

I release her and she starts stretching in that delicate way she has, like an ageing ballerina. Dad is handing over a wad of cash to the driver and I glance at the metre on the dash. Good god——€85! 'Dad,' I say as he climbs out of the car, 'that's a fortune. You should have let us pick you up from the airport. We've got the four-wheel-drive.' I nod my head towards our rental car.

'Hello, love,' he says, giving me a quick tight hug.

'Sorry, hello.'

'And don't worry about the cab. We're on holiday!'

'Well, yes okay, but promise we can take you to the airport when you leave.'

'Hmm, maybe.' He waggles his eyebrows at me.

'Honestly, Sarah, we've only just arrived and you're already talking about us leaving.'

'Sorry, Mum.' The driver has unloaded the boot by now, setting the luggage next to the car, and he gives us a wave and backs out of the driveway.

Dad and I each lift a suitcase while Mum collects her carry-on. 'How's it been the last couple of days, just the four of you?' Dad asks.

'Perfect, Dad. Thanks.' There had been a bit of discussion about when our parents should arrive but Dad had been the one to convince Mum that their girls needed some time together——other halves in tow——before everyone else arrived. He'd been right, as he often is when it came to matters of the heart.

'Mum! Dad!' Cat emerges from our castle apartment, crossing the driveway and flinging herself at Dad. He sets down the suitcase and wraps his arms around her. 'How's my girl?' he says, his voice cracking with emotion. So sweet.

Mum waits patiently and when Cat is free of Dad's embrace, she goes to Mum and reaches up for a hug. 'Hello, Mum, you look beautiful.'

Their embrace ends and Mum looks down at Cat and strokes the side of her face, then blinks back uncharacteristic tears. 'Hello, darling,' she says and they just smile at each other for a moment.

As much as Cat moans about Mum, there is clearly an abundance of love between them. I sometimes forget how lucky I am to live so close to our parents but this moment is a reminder. It's also the first time our immediately family has been together since Christmas nearly three years ago. I blink back my own tears, then say, 'Did you want to come inside, see our cool little apartment? The view is amazing.'

'That sounds wonderful, darling,' says Mum.

'Yes, please, love. I'm busting for the loo,' says Dad.

'Ron! *Goodness*,' says Mum, adding a tut. Dad just grins cheekily. God, I love my family. Cat takes Mum's carry-on from her, leading the way across the gravel driveway to our home in a Tuscan castle.

Chapter Eight

CAT

Tuscany

Jean-Luc and Josh just left with Mum and Dad. They're dropping them off at their accommodation and then heading to the location of Sarah's party. Josh has gone all out and Sarah is going to be so surprised——the good kind, I've assured her a thousand times. She can get so angsty about these things.

Though I'm one to talk.

'Hey,' she says from the doorway. Speak of the devil.

'Hello.'

'Just resting?' she asks. I pat the bed beside me and she comes over, slips off her shoes, and lies down. 'You okay?'

'I'm just brilliant,' I declare and we both chuckle.

'Look, tomorrow we'll go to Siena and find a new dress.'

'Or Jaelee might bring something that'll work,' I say.

'I thought you said you have totally different tastes.'

'Mmm, mostly.' I recall the elegant silk shift Jaelee lent me on our bus trip for my date with Jean-Luc in Rome.

She'd only just bought it during our brief stint in Florence but that's Jae, generous to a fault.

'Well, either way, we'll get the dress thing sorted—*and* the venue.'

I roll onto my side. 'I cannot believe those rooms.'

'I swear, Cat—and we can go online right now and I'll show you—when Mum first raised having the wedding here at the castle, the photos told a very different story. Most of them were of the great hall.'

'I believe you. I don't think you'd deliberately sabotage my wedding.'

'I thought of making it a themed wedding—tell everyone it's "Indiana Jones".'

'*I* was thinking toga party,' I say, 'You know, come dressed in your best bedsheet.'

We dissolve into giggles.

'Oh, my god!' she says, sitting up. 'I don't know why I didn't think of this earlier. What about the venue for my thing? Maybe we can swap out the party for the wedding—do my party at the castle. We could even swap the dates—bring the wedding forward two days.'

It's an incredibly generous offer—and it would also mean that Cécile and Louis would miss the wedding (a tempting bonus)—but I know how much thought and planning Josh has put into Sarah's birthday celebration. I've no doubt it would break his heart to change plans now, especially moving the party to one of those heinous rooms.

'Sez, that's lovely, really, but Josh … let's just say that you are absolutely going to *love* your birthday celebration—as is. So, no, we're not doing that, all right?'

She flops back onto the bed. 'Fine.'

'What?' I ask.

'*What* what?'

'What's the matter? It's not just the wedding, is it?'

'Yeah, no, well … yeah, it's the wedding stuff,' she says unconvincingly.

'Sez … come on. Any time one of us brings up your birthday, you get this odd look on your face.'

'What look?'

'A miserable look.'

'Oh. I thought I was hiding it better.' She props herself up again. 'You don't think that Josh … has he noticed?'

'Who knows you better than anyone?' I ask.

'You?'

'I mean, besides me.'

'Oh.'

'He has to have noticed, Sez.'

She buries her head in the pillow. 'I'm ruining this for him,' she says, her voice muffled.

'You're not ruining anything and it's not for Josh. It's for *you*. You usually like having a fuss made over you, *especially* on your birthday. So, what is it? What's going on?'

She peeks at me. 'It's something about the number.'

'Well, obvs, but why? Forty is not *old*. I'm mean, look at Mum. She's sixty-four and she's gorgeous. *You're* gorgeous.'

'I know.'

'And modest, so modest,' I tease.

It has the desired effect because she chortles at herself. 'I meant I know that forty's not old.'

'And?'

She sits up properly this time, crossing her legs and looking down at me. 'You know how I can sometimes get a little stuck in my own head?' 'A little' is an understatement but I nod. 'Well, that's been happening even more lately. It's hard to describe, but it's like there's something missing and a time crunch both at the same time.'

'What's missing? You love your life.'

'I do and I have no idea!'

Something occurs to me. 'Is it children?' Sarah has never wanted to be a parent but maybe that's changed.

She coughs out a laugh. 'Uh, no.' I guess not, then.

We're both quiet for a moment—Sarah no doubt contemplating the meaning of life, the universe, and everything, while I'm wondering how I can help my sister find her way out of this funk—and in time for what Josh has planned.

'Have you talked to Josh about this?' She shakes her head. 'So, he could be thinking that you're unhappy with him.' Her mouth gapes and she blinks a few times. 'That's not it, is it?' Oh, god, I hope not.

'No! I love Josh. He's … *no.*'

Bollocks, now I've got her even more wound up. 'Look, promise me you will talk to him—soon—before your birthday, Sez. He's gone all out and I know you're going to love it.'

'I will—talk to him, I mean.'

My phone buzzes on the nightstand. When I check it, there's a message from Jaelee.

About to take off. Will go straight to our accommodation and see you in the morning. J x

I tap out a reply.

Fly safe. Cat xxx

Another message pings back almost instantly.

And happy wedding week! It's going to be awesome! J x

I send a sticker back—cartoon me blowing a kiss—though I am not too sure how 'awesome' Jae will think everything is when I tell her about the venue.

'*Chérie.*' I swear, with that one simple word, Jean-Luc can make the rest of the world disappear. I've just finished getting ready for bed and he's beckoning me to join him at the glass doors to the balcony, his hand reaching for me.

I slip mine into his and he pulls me into an embrace, his chin resting on my head. One hand holds me firmly while the other cups my bum playfully, eliciting a smile. The naughty hand trails lightly up my back, shivers following in its wake, especially as his fingertips caress my neck. His hand comes to rest with a light touch under my chin and he pulls back slightly, tipping it up to him. His lips are soft on mine—familiar, yes, but even so, they send a ripple of electricity through me.

The kiss intensifies, our passion building, and I want him—*now*. He lifts me effortlessly, both hands now cupping my bum as I wrap my legs around his waist. He carries me to the bed and, one arm wrapped around me, holding me close, he lowers us onto it. His kisses assault my neck, my chest, and he pulls aside my camisole, his mouth finding my nipple. I sigh at the sensation, undoing his jeans and tugging at his cumbersome waistbands. Finally, he's free and when we're joined, we moan together at the exquisite pleasure.

'*Chérie*,' he says again, the word almost swallowed by my kiss. He straightens his arms, breaking the contact and looks at me, eyes wild with desire and his breath audible. 'I want to take my time with you,' he says, breathless.

'Next time,' I say, wrapping my legs around him tighter and moving my hips against him. He succumbs and sometime later, when our bodies are spent, sweat prickles our skin. 'You may need another shower, Catherine,' says my fiancé, smiling down at me cheekily.

'Worth it,' I say, 'especially if you join me.' I raise my eyebrows at him and he smacks a kiss on my lips.

———

'What? No fucking way.' Jaelee is nothing if not direct. 'Hold on, let me check my emails.' We're sitting on our balcony sipping tea and coffee, a beautiful Tuscan morning unfolding around us, the sun bright in the sky and a slight breeze ruffling the potted geraniums on the balcony. Jae and Alistair, her lovely Scottish boyfriend, joined us for morning tea a little while ago, and we're all sipping our hot drinks of choice. A plate of biscotti sits at the centre of the table—a spoil from our raid of the enoteca—but I am the only one eating them. They're simply too good to resist!

I've just told Jae about the options for the wedding venue and as she searches through emails on her phone, she dons one of her dogged Jaelee scowls. I sip my tea and catch Jean-Luc's eye. He seems amused. So does Alistair, whose mouth is twitching.

'So, how is your accommodation?' Jean-Luc asks him. Jaelee continues to frown at her phone, swiping and scrolling.

'It's nice. We found it on Airbnb, a little pensione just down the way. We were able to walk here, but we've rented a car for the trip.' They continue chatting about the town while I help myself to another piece of biscotti.

Sarah and Josh have gone for 'an exercise walk', which is (apparently) seeking out hills—plenty of those around here—and striding about to work up a sweat. They may be the only people I know who exercise when they're on holiday. But as someone who would rather stick a fork in my eye than work out, I declined the invitation to join them.

Jae holds her phone out to Jean-Luc, interrupting his conversation with Alistair. 'Can you read this for me?' she asks unnecessarily. 'I swear this says we can use the great hall for the wedding.' Jean-Luc reads the email, his eyes narrowing slightly in concentration. Italian *is* his fourth language after French, English, and German.

'Ahh,' he says sitting back against his chair. He signals for Jae to lean closer and shows her the screen. 'You see? This here' —he points— 'this word is "perhaps".'

'Perhaps?'

'*Oui.*'

'Really?'

'Yes.'

'Fuck. They're so different, those words in Spanish and Italian. Usually, they're more similar.'

'Jae, lovely, what *are* you talking about?'

'The word for "perhaps". I didn't … Shit. Sorry, Cat, this is on me.'

'So, you misread the email?' I ask. This is unlike Jaelee—she's usually on top of every detail.

'Uh, yeah.'

'But you had them translated, right? Your correspondence?' I ask, annoyance creeping into my tone.

'Well, you know …' She shrugs.

'You thought that knowing Spanish would be enough.' I sigh, now properly frustrated.

'Like I said, this one's on me and I will handle it. Jean-Luc,' she says, perhaps hoping to appeal to the groom while the bride skirts the brink of a tanty, 'I promise you will have a beautiful wedding, okay?'

He holds his hands out and shrugs. 'I would marry Catherine anywhere. It does not matter. Besides, she will already be wearing a bedsheet, so why not get married amongst the artefacts?' He sniggers softly, though not unkindly, and shares a look with Alistair who smiles back at him.

'All right you lot, enough with the joking. Jae, I have every faith in you, I do. And once we get the dress sorted and the venue … we can just enjoy the rest of the week.' Jean-Luc reaches for my hand, raising it to his lips and kissing it.

This. This is what I need to focus on. In a few days I will marry this incredible man and it shouldn't matter where it happens or what I am wearing.

It *shouldn't*, so why does it?

'Hey, guys,' says Sarah. She steps onto the balcony, followed by Josh, both glistening with sweat.

'Oh, I love this part,' I say leaping up from my chair. 'Jae and Alistair, this is my sister, Sarah, and her boyfriend, Josh.'

They smile and shake hands and Jae insists on hugging Sarah even though she begs off for being 'too sweaty'. 'It's *so* good to finally meet you,' Jae says. 'I feel like we've been email buddies for months now.'

'I know! I feel exactly the same way,' Sarah replies, grinning.

'Did you want to join us?' I ask.

'Shower first,' says Josh.

'Yeah, definitely—to both,' says Sarah. 'Shower, then joining you.'

'I'll go first?' asks Josh. She nods and he heads inside.

'So, you're coming wedding dress shopping with us today, right?' she says to Jae.

'Oh, yeah, for sure. But I did bring some dresses.'

'Okay, so I'll shower and get ready, we get Cat to try on your dresses and, if no joy, we collect Mum and head to Siena to shop.' It's fascinating watching the two most organised people I know ping off each other like this.

'Sounds good. I also need to figure out the venue,' says Jae with a grimace.

'Oh, yeah, that's uh ... we'll work it out. Dress first. I mean, she can get married anywhere, right, but she can't be naked.'

'Hello? I'm right here.'

Both heads spin in my direction as though they've only just realised I'm here.

'And?' asks my impertinent sister.

Jean-Luc and Alistair are openly chuckling now and this time when my fiancé reaches for my hand, I lift my chin. 'I'm going inside to try on Jae's dresses.' I push my chair back and retreat to our bedroom, laughter at my back.

I really do love each and every one of them—the buggers.

'Lastly, there's this,' says Jaelee. She's holding the brilliant blue silk shift she lent me the day I met Jean-Luc in Rome for our first date. We've already been through the other four options she brought. They all fit, as anticipated—we're still the same size—but they were a little too 'clubby' for my wedding day.

'It's beautiful,' says Sarah, running her fingers down the seam.

'Cat wore it on her first date with Jean-Luc,' says Jae to Sarah. 'I also brought these in case you decide to wear it,' she adds, rummaging through her large carry bag. She takes out a pair of silver strappy sandals. They're gorgeous and I love the dress, but I'm not sure how bridal it is.

Sarah glances my way, seeming to understand instantly, and says, 'Back-up?'

I nod and smile. 'Back-up. Perfect.' Not perfect, but Jae's expression is bordering on contrition and it's not her fault I left my wedding dress in an airport. 'Jae, thank you so much. I really do appreciate you bringing all these options.' She smiles one of those 'not smiles' and starts gathering the dresses, folding them haphazardly.

'How about I take that one?' asks Sarah.

'Sure, yeah,' says Jae. Sarah takes the blue dress from Jae before it gets bundled into the carry bag and hangs it in the wardrobe.

'And these.' Sarah places the sandals next to the box with my bridal shoes—satin Jimmy Choo, kitten-heeled sling-backs I bought online—second hand but never worn and only £100. You know what they say—one woman's unwanted gift from a former lover is another woman's treasure.

'Right, let's call Mum, tell her we're on our way, then

head to Siena!' I'm grateful for my sister's enthusiasm right now, especially as Jae, who is usually a powerhouse of organisation and gusto, seems deflated. Sarah disappears down the hall and moments later, I hear her on the phone with Mum.

'Jae?'

'Mmm.' She's still busying herself with the dresses.

I take the carry bag from her and place it on the floor, then sit on the bed. 'Come sit.' She joins me. 'Everything all right?'

'Yeah, I just … I feel like shit about the venue—like, *total* rookie mistake—*and* the dresses … I don't know what I was thinking. I mean, of course you're not going to wear black on your wedding day. You're Cat Parsons not Angelina Jolie.'

'Did she wear black? I thought she just let her kids scribble all over her dress when she married Brad Pitt.'

Jae snorts out a cynical laugh. 'I think you're right, but you know what I mean. You're feminine and pretty and you need to look … *ethereal* on your wedding day.'

'*Ethereal*? That's, uh … I'd just settle for stunningly beautiful.' We share a smile. 'Look, I think you've put a lot of pressure on yourself—you and Sarah both—'

'Are you talking about me?' Sarah enters the room, phone in hand.

'Talking about you, not to you,' I quip—one of our childhood barbs.

'Yeah, but what are you saying?' she asks.

'Just that you two have been amazing. Honestly, I couldn't have asked for better wedding planners.' Jae rolls her eyes, but I know it's because she's beating herself up. 'I mean it. You've saved me from so many hassles.'

'And caused some.'

'Jaelee, enough of that,' says Sarah. 'We've got a wedding dress to find and I told Mum we'd be there in ten minutes, so wallow later. You two, in the car now.' Another Parsons sister trait—breaking out 'bossy schoolteacher' mode as needed.

'Well, I guess I've been told,' Jae says to me.

Sarah goes over to the open glass doors. 'Guys, we're off!' There are murmurs from the balcony and Josh appears at the doorway to kiss Sarah goodbye. I push past them to get my own goodbye kiss.

'Have a good day, *chérie*,' says my soon-to-be-husband.

'You too.' I have a thought. 'Sorry, I haven't even asked what you're doing today?'

By now, Jae has joined us on the balcony. 'Yeah,' she says to Alistair. The men look almost apologetic.

'Jean-Luc?' I press.

'Pffft. *Désolé, mon amour*, but we are going wine tasting.'

I backhand him in the chest. 'Wine tasting? You're going wine tasting in Tuscany and I have to go shopping for a wedding dress with *Mum*?'

He shrugs and I growl at him, then break into a smile. I'm only *slightly* jealous of the day he has ahead of him.

'Excuse me!' says Sarah. 'We are going to *Siena* and it is amazing and we are going to have an incredible day. Besides, you can have all the Tuscan wine you want at lunch. Now, let's go.'

We say our goodbyes, Jae's including an instruction for Alistair to drive safely, then leave to collect our mother. And now that we're on our way, I really am excited about the day. We're going to Siena!

Chapter Nine

SARAH

Tuscany

The walled medieval cities south of Florence and north of Rome are incredible. I love San Gimignano, of course, with its soaring towers and unique skyline. It's also known for the best gelato in Italy, or so they say. Don't tell them, but I *have* had some pretty spectacular gelato in Venice and Rome—oh, *and* on the Cinque Terre.

There are other walled cities I adore too—Orvieto, renowned for its zebra-striped cathedral and Montepulciano for its brilliant food and wine—*especially* the wine—but my favourite of all has to be Siena.

Ah, Siena!

It's been a dozen or more years since I've been and when we arrive, it's clear that their 'shoulder season' would make any tourist bureau proud—it's *teeming* with tourists, even in October. As Mum and Jaelee jabber away in the back seat, I sense Cat getting increasingly frustrated with the search for a parking spot, something confirmed when I ease the four-wheel-drive into a tight spot and she sighs.

'Ready?' I say, smiling at her brightly.

'Absolutely.' I fear that with Cat's fluctuations between elated bride and could-become-a-Bridezilla-at-any-moment, we're dangerously close to the latter. Mum and Jaelee ease out of the back seat, careful not to hit the doors against the cars either side and Mum strides off purposefully to pay for parking.

'Hey.' Cat looks at me. 'You okay?'

'I'm fine. Let's just get on with it.'

I want to tease her with, 'That's the spirit,' but hold off. 'You're up and down today. Did you know that?'

'Yes. Sorry.' A few rows of parked cars away, Mum is frowning at the ticket machine and Jaelee joins her to help.

'Don't apologise, just tell me what you need. Pep talk? Tough love? Permission to whinge?' My last offer elicits a smile and she turns towards me.

'When we first had this idea—tagging along on your fortieth and getting married in Italy—it sounded so romantic and dreamy and … well … *perfect*.'

'It can still be all those things.'

'I know that—in here.' She taps the side of her head, like I do when I'm sharing the same sentiment. 'But in reality, it's intense and busy and all these issues keep popping up. Is it terrible that I just want everyone to sod off so we can have a quiet week together to celebrate—you, me, Jean-Luc, and Josh? I mean, I love everyone—you know I do—but …' She shrugs.

'No, it's not terrible. I've thought the same thing myself. Look, they're coming back so let's just have a fun day out, okay? We'll find you something perfect to wear for your wedding—'

'You are a lot more convinced of that than I am.'

'We will—and Siena is a *beautiful* city, Cat. You'll love it, I promise.'

Mum opens my car door and hands me the ticket. 'Come on girls, we're not here to sit around all day,' she says. I place the ticket on the dashboard and scrunch my nose at Cat, making her smile.

'Coming, Mum,' we sing-song together.

'Oh, I love Italy,' sighs Mum, leaning against the counter of a bar, an espresso in one hand. She takes a delicate sip.

'You certainly fit in, Mum,' I say. She does, actually. Mum has always dressed well but she also carries herself with a casual elegance—quite similar to many of the Italian women we've seen today, those that move fluidly through the crowds of gawking tourists, chins slightly elevated and with the occasional toss of glossy hair. (In a million years, I will never be like that.)

She'd even ordered our coffees with a surprisingly good Italian accent. '*Quattro caffè per favore,*' she said.

'Americano?' the man behind the counter asked.

Mum frowned slightly, then said, '*No, normale,*' as in, 'How rude of you to ask—we'll have regular espressos, thank you very much!' He nodded approvingly and a short time later, slid four tiny cups and saucers across the counter. To us, Mum stage-whispered, 'The guide from our last trip to Venice taught us that. The indignation really sells it—that way you get a *proper* coffee.' Our mum—International Coffee Snob.

She tips her head, finishing the shot, and says, 'Shall we?' Even Jaelee, who I sense is usually Queen Bee, hurriedly finishes hers and moments later, the four of us are standing on the footpath. I look about, getting my bearings. Again, it's been *years* since I've been here—and that was on a tour with fifty people following me around. But from the expectant expressions of my party, it's on me to lead this expedition.

'Sightseeing first or dress shopping?'

'Sightseeing,' says Cat right as Mum and Jaelee say, 'Dress shopping.' Great, so that settles nothing. Cat looks between us, her anxiousness evident—or is it frustration?

'How about this. We're really close to Piazza del Campo—we should see that before we do anything else. It's ... well, it's breathtaking, the heart of the city. You'll love it.' Two of three faces look unconvinced. 'This way ...' I start walking, expecting the others to fall in behind me, and we navigate the crowd in a close clump. 'And you've probably heard of the Palio, that famous horse race? It's run every year—twice, actually—and the *Contrade*—they're like neighbourhoods of the city—compete. Look.' I stop and point to a banner fluttering above us. 'That tells us what *Contrada* we're in.'

'Which one are we in?' asks Jaelee.

'Oh, uh ... I don't know. Most are animals of some kind—and one's a wave, I remember that.' I look up at the banner. 'An eagle?'

'Could be. You know you sound like a tour guide,' says Jaelee. God, I'm obviously being too didactic.

'Sarah was a tour manager all around Europe, remember?' says Cat.

'Oh, yeah, right,' Jaelee replies.

'It's very interesting, Sarah,' says Mum. Only I'm not sure that it is.

'Let's just go.' I stride off at a cracking pace, expecting the others to follow. As I walk, I realise that what came across in emails and video chats as 'direct', 'forthright', and 'all business' is just Jaelee's personality—she's like that in person too. I probably shouldn't take it personally—especially as she insisted on hugging me when we met, even though I was all sweaty.

A few turns later, I lead our party of four down a broad set of stairs and we emerge into the piazza. Even having been here many times before, I'm taken aback by the enormity of it. And its beauty. It really is breathtaking. 'So, they have a horse race here?' asks Mum. I'm not sure if I should continue my 'tour guide' commentary but Mum seems interested enough.

'Yes. So, they'll make a track around the perimeter of the piazza, laying down sand, because I guess it's better for the horses, and there's a huge crowd that watches, a lot of them from the middle of the track or from these buildings. There's also a pageant with the flag bearers from each *Contrada*.'

'Looks dangerous,' says Jaelee, casting her eyes around the piazza.

'Yeah. I've never been, but … some of those turns …'

'That's what I mean.'

'Do people die?' asks Cat. 'Do *horses* die?' she asks, clearly thinking that's worse.

This conversation has turned markedly morbid—hardly

where I'd hoped it would end up. 'Nope. No horses die and no people. It's run every time without incident and everyone lives happily ever after.' When I glance at Mum, she's smirking. It's not like I'll think they'll believe me—I'm just eager to change the subject.

'Hey, can you take a picture of me?' asks Jaelee. She adds, 'Please,' as she hands Cat her phone, then walks off and stands arms out and hip cocked like one of those models on *The Price Is Right*. Cat takes a few photos and gives Jaelee the nod.

'We should get a selfie too,' says Jaelee re-joining us. She holds her phone up to the four of us, but like Cat, she's quite small and her arm isn't long enough to fit us all in.

'Do you want me …?' I ask.

'Sure.' I take the photo—four smiling women filling up the entire frame. We could literally be anywhere. 'Okay. That's done. So, shopping?' she says.

Right, so incredible medieval square, lots to see, but we're done now. *Tourist*, I think unkindly. There are travellers and tourists in this world and Jaelee is definitely a tourist. Cat has her phone out and opens Google Maps where she's dropped pins for dress shops—mostly bridal, some not. She shows it to me and points to the nearest pin. 'Where's that from here?'

'As in, you literally have Google Maps open and you want *me* to direct you instead of her?'

'Yes.' She blinks at me. I look at the map again—I am particularly skilled at map reading—then lift my head seeking the best way out of the piazza. 'This way,' I say, sounding exactly like a tour guide. I should stop and buy one of those sticks with a pom-pom on top.

Wedding dress shopping in Italy—a Mecca of the fashion world—should be at least a *little* bit fun. But with a time-crunch and a picky bride (with a modest budget), it is so far from fun, I'd rather be at the gynaecologist. We're at the third atelier and have exhausted all the options in Cat's price range. Every dress is either too 'meringue' or too tight across the bust or too 'gapey' at the bust or too long—mostly too long, as Cat is a petite five-foot-one.

When we end up back on the cobbled streets, empty-handed for the third time, the collective frustration is palpable. I check my watch. It's coming on two and there must be more than a little 'hangriness' contributing to our tetchy vibe. 'Lunch?' I ask, brightly.

'Oh, thank god,' says Jaelee.

'That's an excellent idea, Sarah,' says Mum.

'So, what, I'll be wedding dress shopping with a food baby?' Bridezilla alert! Actually, that's not fair. I've seen glimpses of that (terrible) reality show and those women chuck full-on tanties because the napkins are coloured ecru and not eggshell.

'Catherine. I know we said we'd wait until after you found a dress, but we have to eat, darling. Just have something light, all right?' Thank god for Mum and her sense of reason.

'All right,' Cat agrees with a hefty dose of reticence.

I lead us away from the centre of town, knowing that if we get far enough from the hubbub, we'll find somewhere the locals frequent. Less than ten minutes later, we are seated outside a tiny *trattoria*, our knees practically touching as we crowd around a small square table. Our waiter is efficient and friendly in the way that Italian waiters are and he drops four menus on our table—in English—as he bustles past on his way to take an older couple's order.

'I'm having pasta,' declares Jaelee, her eyes widening as they scan the menu. 'No, gnocchi. And wine!' Cat throws her a look that I can't interpret.

'The sea bass for me,' says Mum.

'Mmm, that does sound good,' I say, though I am also eyeing up the pork with Chianti sauce.

Cat frowns. 'I guess I'll just have soup—and no bread.'

The waiter returns and Jaelee rattles off her order, along with Mum's and Cat's, then adds a carafe of white wine. She points at me. 'Did you decide?'

'The pork.'

'*El puerco*,' she says to the waiter. He looks confused.

'*Il maiale, per favore*,' says Mum. Wow, her Italian really is good. Go, Mum!

'Ahh, *sì*, the pork.' He collects the menus and disappears inside.

'Jae, you've got to stop speaking Spanish to the Italians,' says Cat.

'Why? He understood the other three dishes I ordered—*and* the wine.'

'You hope. If I end up with tripe because of you …' Jaelee rolls her eyes. A carafe and four glasses are deposited on the table and our waiter disappears again. I swear he's doing the job of four people.

'So, Catherine,' says Mum. 'You still haven't told us where you and Jean-Luc are going to live after you're married.'

Hah! You and Dad can get in line with the rest of us, I think, but I don't laugh because Mum's justified query has sent Cat into a tailspin. She looks like a goldfish who's been unceremoniously dumped onto the cobblestones.

I start pouring wine—generous filled-to-the-brim glasses of it. Jaelee accepts hers with a raised eyebrow, indicating that she's asked Cat the same question and is also none the wiser. We raise our glasses in a toast of solidarity and take big slugs while Cat flounders through a reply.

'Uh … we're still working out the details,' she says cryptically.

'Oh.' There are dozens of different 'Oh's that our mum emits, each with its distinctive flavour and this one says, 'I am judging you harshly'. Come to think of it, there are quite a few sub-varieties of the judgey 'Oh' too. Today's comes with a sizeable dose of incredulity.

'Well, you must know what will happen with Jane and the London flat?' asks Mum. A basket of plain white crusty bread appears on the table and despite her earlier declaration that bread was to be avoided at all costs because it induces food babies, Cat grabs a large piece, drizzles it with olive oil, and takes a generous bite.

'Mmm,' she says, her mouth full of bread. This is a risky move as Mum abhors poor table manners. 'We're still working that out too. For now, I will stay in London and …' she trails off, adding a shrug. Now it's Mum's turn to chug wine. At this rate, we'll need another carafe before the food arrives. Speaking of …

'More wine?' asks the waiter.

'Yes,' say four women at once. I make a promise to myself—when we get back to the castle, I will seek out my future brother-in-law and get the low-down on their living situation.

'Oh, Catherine. You look stunning.'

We're in the fifth and final bridal shop in Siena, having struck out again at the fourth. This is the tenth dress she's tried on and—thank god—it's perfect. I mean, *perfect*. She looks like a sexy Disney princess from the 1930s. The dress is in cream satin, cut on the bias so it skims over her curves. The off-the-shoulder cowl neckline makes her decolletage look amazing, but my favourite part is the fishtail train—so sexy.

'That's the one, Cat. It's *gorgeous*,' I say, relieved that she's (finally) found a replacement dress.

'And it'll go with your Jimmy Choos,' adds Jaelee.

'Oh, good point, Jaelee,' I say.

Cat swings from side to side, gazing at herself in the mirror.

'It is beautiful,' she says.

'What?' I ask, sensing her reticence. She eyes the hand-written tag that sits on a damask pouffe, its figures blaring, 'really expensive!' in Italian. Oh, right. It's *way* out of her price range. For some reason, Mum had insisted Cat try it on as soon as she found it on the rack. 'To get a sense of what we're looking for,' she'd said. But this is just cruel. It fits perfectly, it's a stunning design, and now Cat has to take it off and leave it behind.

Mum stands behind Cat and places her hands gently on her shoulders. 'Catherine, your father and I want to buy this for you—as a gift.' Oh, so Mum is *not* intent on torturing my sister—thank god!

'What? Oh, no, you don't have to do that.'

Mum smiles at Cat in the mirror. 'Darling, I wasn't there

to help you choose your first dress, and you haven't let your father and me pay for one *iota* of this wedding. *Please*. We want to do this for you.'

Cat's eyes glisten. 'Really? You're not just offering because we're out of options—*and* time?'

'No, nothing like that. I'd always intended to buy you whatever dress you wanted, and had we found anything suitable before now, I would have made the same offer.'

'Oh, Mum.'

'You really do look beautiful, Catherine. You're going to make a stunning bride.'

Several tears spill onto Cat's cheeks and she turns and hugs Mum. I love seeing them like this. Far too often, they are at odds with each other.

'Hey, can we get some more prosecco, please?' Jaelee asks the sales assistant. I suppose it's a fair request when Mum is about to spend €1300 in their shop. I've already had a glass, which I finished four dresses ago, but I suppose a half-glass top-up will be fine before I drive us back to Montespertoli. The sales assistant, a tall, willowy blonde woman with a full face of expertly applied makeup, obliges us with a broad smile, topping up our glasses in turn.

When we all have prosecco in hand, Jaelee raises her glass. 'To finding the perfect dress,' she says. 'Thank god!' adds Cat. 'I'll drink to that,' says Mum dryly, making me chuckle. *Karen Parsons, aren't you the comedian?* I muse. We clink glasses and drink.

Wedding dress

Now all we need to do is get the venue sorted. Oh, and the bride and groom need to decide where the matrimonial home will be—easy peasy, pudding pie. Right?

Chapter Ten

CAT

Tuscany

What an incredible day. Although, with most of it eaten up by dress shopping, we haven't seen as much of Siena as I'd hoped. We did fit in a quick visit to the Duomo right after lunch—but only the outside. Jaelee requested her usual 'take a picture of me' shots *and* we got some lovely shots all together with the cathedral in the background, a sweet elderly couple obliging us.

And Sarah was right—this city is beautiful. Maybe we can come back after the wedding—just me and Jean-Luc. With a destination wedding, we haven't planned a honeymoon as such, but some time alone after the festivities would be nice. Siena might just be perfect for that.

When we finish our prosecco, having taken our time now that our quest is complete, Mum slides her Amex across the counter and they hand over the carefully packed dress. Outside, we stroll happily through the hordes of tourists, heading towards the car. It's incredible how a sense of accomplishment can put a rose-coloured sheen on a crowd of tired, whiny tourists.

'Gelato!' I declare, spying a shop on the next corner.

'Oh, definitely,' says Sarah.

'Oh, god, yes,' says Jae.

'Really?' I ask her. The Jaelee I've travelled with rarely indulges in treats like gelato—*and* she's already eaten a huge plate of pasta today.

'We've earned it!' she declares.

'*Hell* yeah,' says Sarah. It occurs to me again how much pressure they must be under as my wedding planners—venue issues, the lost wedding dress debacle …

'My treat,' I add.

'Thank you, Catherine,' says Mum, 'that sounds lovely.' It's also the least I can do after Mum spent all those euros on my dress. I'm still reeling from the generosity.

Inside the gelato shop, we wait behind an antsy crowd, me trying to peek between the bodies at the selection of flavours. 'Lemon for me, darling,' says Mum. 'Just one scoop in a cup. And here,' she takes the dress from me and goes to wait outside.

'What are you having Sarah?' She's five inches taller than me, so she's got a better view of the display case.

'Mmm, one scoop of cherries and cream and one of dark chocolate—*amarena e cioccolato fondente*,' she says in a not-bad Italian accent. 'In a cone. I'll run hills tomorrow,' she adds, almost to herself. When I glance at her, she's frowning slightly. My sister is the fittest, healthiest person I know and I sometimes worry that she's too hard on herself those times she 'lets loose'. This certainly isn't the first time I've heard her plan her penance for 'overindulging'.

'Jae?' We're close to the front now and both have a much better view of the display cabinet.

'One scoop of pistachio in a cup.'

'Really?' I screw up my nose. 'All these flavours and you're going with that?'

'Yeah, what's wrong with pistachio? It's my favourite.'

'I love pistachios as much as the next person, but as an *ice cream* flavour? Blech.'

'Gelato,' says Sarah.

'Same difference,' I retort.

She starts explaining that there actually is a difference, but gives up when Jaelee talks over her. 'Well, what are you getting?'

I look along the length of the cabinet at all those glossy, swirly mounds of creamy goodness. 'Umm, chocolate, I think.'

'All these flavours and you're going with *that*? Might as well just have vanilla,' she teases.

'Oi.'

'Cat.' Sarah pokes me.

'What?' I toss her an annoyed look.

'It's your turn.' She points at the counter and when I turn around, a woman is waving at me to hurry up.

'Oh, sorry!' I rattle off the order in English, so I don't insult her with my murdered Italian, and in a couple of minutes we're outside, laden with gelato—two cups and two cones.

'Oh, my god,' says Sarah, one hand over her full mouth. Risky move with Karen Parsons right there ready to pounce on her bad manners. But lo! Mum seems to be in her own gelato heaven, revelling in the tartness of her scoop of *limone* with puckered lips.

'How's the pistachio?' I ask Jaelee.

'*Buonissimo*,' she replies smugly. It must be the only word she knows in Italian.

I concede with a smile then take a generous bite of my *cioccolato* and moan involuntarily. 'Oh, my god!' I say with my mouth full.

'Catherine, *please*,' says Karen Parsons, Etiquette Afficionado. Of *course*, she caught me out but not Sarah.

'Sorry, Mum.'

We eat as we walk, mostly in silence, and I soak in as much of Siena as I can, awed by the beauty of something as simple as a row of shopfronts with apartments overhead. I absolutely *must* return one day, only next time with my handsome husband in tow.

We make it to the car around 5:00pm and as Sarah navigates out of the carpark and through the winding streets surrounding Siena towards to the motorway, I lean my head against the headrest, content.

'Thank you so much for today,' I say to the others.

'It was fun,' says Jae, though she may just be saying that to be kind.

'You're welcome,' adds Sarah.

Mum clasps my shoulder from the back seat. 'It was our pleasure, darling.' I place my hand on top of hers and give it a squeeze. That's been the most surprising—and lovely—thing about today, a sort of turning point in my relationship with Mum.

The moment she offered to buy me the dress, I felt many things at once. Relief that we'd found the perfect replacement for my other dress (and not just something that would do). And gratitude, of course—what a generous and lovely gesture. But I also felt a twinge of guilt that I'd almost deprived her of such a special mother–daughter moment. I hadn't known until then how much it meant to her——*or* me.

Ours is a complicated relationship——it has been for most of my adult life. All those years ago, she must have thought my move to London would be temporary——that, like Sarah, I would stay for two or three years, then come home. But London became home. And over the last fifteen years, she's 'let slip' the not-so-occasional comment that she wishes I would visit Sydney more, or when I do visit, stay longer.

I've always handled what I thought was her disappointment in two ways——outwardly, I've brushed it off, made light, and inwardly … well, I usually bury those feelings as deep as possible so that on a day-to-day basis I don't have to think about how disappointed my mother is in my life choices.

But in that moment at the atelier earlier, I realised something. Mum isn't *disappointed* in me, she just misses me. I miss her too, if I'm honest. And Dad and Sarah. I love them all so much. But when you decide to live across the world from your immediate family, you can't dwell on that——it would make life impossible. Today, though, I felt the depth and breadth of just how much I love my mother. And it's curious that what began as a mini-disaster, ended with a joyous toast and a sort-of reconciliation in an Italian bridal atelier. Perhaps the fates, who I have been cursing under my breath these past few days, are actually smiling on us.

The low hum of the tires on the motorway lulls me into a sort-of meditative state as I watch out of the window. How fortunate I am. I am in Tuscany, staying in a castle, and spending time with my most favourite people in the world——here now or arriving shortly.

It *will* all work out. I have no doubt about that

now——the wedding, that is. Our decision about where to live looms, but I am an expert in burying feelings when I'd rather revel in reunions and celebrations for the foreseeable future. And after today's successes, I agree with Jean-Luc. It doesn't matter exactly where we get married——not when we're in this beautiful place with the people we love.

The people we love.

Ugh. Cécile will be here in a few days, Jean-Luc's sister. How on earth will I make peace with her? Is there even peace to be made? I know she's close to Vanessa, the perfect ex-wife, but why is she so resistant to forming a relationship with me? Why does she seem to hate me so much? I'm love-able! I am Cat Fricking Parsons and I am adored by many——beloved even!

Cécile's a tough nut.

I could try to find common ground with her——*again*. I do have something special for the girls to make up for them not being able to come for the wedding. That could be an in. Or maybe Cécile is a lost cause——maybe the whole Caron family is and I will forever be the woman who isn't good enough for Jean-Luc.

'Everything okay?' asks Sarah. I look over and she's glancing between me and the road. 'That was a pretty heavy sigh,' she says quietly.

I peek in the backseat. I'm not sure how much I want to share with Mum, but she's dozing. Jae is preoccupied with her phone, but she already knows about my tenuous relationship with Cécile. 'Just thinking about Jean-Luc's sister.'

'Oh right, *Cécile*,' Sarah says. 'She does anything to mess with you or your wedding and I will go major Sister Bear on her arse.'

'I'm sure it won't come to that.' Sarah scoffs. 'Actually …
I'm thinking I'll try to make peace with her.'

'Cat, this is *your* wedding. You don't need to make peace
with the bitchy sister.'

'Sarah's right,' says Jae.

'Mmm? Right about what?' Mum asks. Serves me right
for trying to have a sensitive conversation in a *car*.

'That the weather is supposed to be nice all week—sunny
and warm,' replies Sarah, deftly changing the subject.

'That is fortuitous, especially with your party being
outdoors.'

'Mum!'

'My party is outdoors?' asks Sarah.

'Well, yes, it's—'

'Mum! Stop talking please,' I say.

'Why?'

'Josh's plans are a surprise.'

'How was I supposed to know that? He never said.' I am
certain that Josh *did* say and I snort out an exasperated sigh.

———

Tonight, we're meeting up with Lou and Anders—just us
'young ones', as Dad calls us. He and Mum are having a
'quiet night in'. I *really* don't want to know what *that* entails.
Lou and Anders arrived in Tuscany just after lunchtime,
taking the afternoon to get the lay of Montespertoli and
settle into their pensione. I cannot *wait* to meet Anders properly—video calls aren't quite the same thing—and I just
know I'll adore him. Anyone who can make our Lou happy
is 'good people' in my book.

Jae has us booked in to a restaurant close to town——or, at least I hope she has. She may have inadvertently booked us in for indoor trampolining five towns away——she really must stop relying on Spanish to communicate with the Italians. We get it, Jae, they are both Latin languages. They're similar, of course, but what she may have mistaken for 'understanding' when we were travelling through Italy a few years ago, may have only been polite confusion. There's a big difference between ordering the wrong meal and planning the wrong wedding.

I take a quick shower——just a rinse, really, to refresh myself for dinner——and when I'm dried and wrapped up in my robe, I realise that Sarah must have had the same idea, as I hear the shower going at the other end of the apartment. Sometimes you just want to wash the day away, even if you did little more than walk the streets of a medieval city and try on wedding dresses.

I check the time. The guys will be back soon, along with Dad. I love that they included him in their outing today and he'll have been in his element——Dad *loves* wine tasting. He takes it quite seriously and even mentioned that he's been reading up——or is that 'tasting up'?——on Tuscan wines. He's particularly excited about 'Super Tuscans'. Sarah takes after Dad——she's quite knowledgeable when it comes to wine, whereas I just know if I like something or not. That's why she's the one who led the meeting with the vintner yesterday while I just sipped and savoured and nodded whenever anyone asked me something.

I hope the guys have had as good a day as we have.

Speaking of … there's the crunch on the gravel now. I'm contemplating what to wear for dinner when Jean-Luc comes into our room. He envelops me in a hug and kisses my neck, giving me shivers. 'You smell delicious, *chérie*.'

'Why, thank you. You smell like wine.' He pulls away and smiles down at me cheekily.

'Not too much, I hope. I was quite reserved.'

'Oh yes?'

'*Oui*. Your father, he is the expert and we ...' He commences a rather comical mime of swirling a glass, inhaling its bouquet, taking a sip, swishing it, then spitting. I giggle.

'So, the whole day?'

'Mmm ... *comme ci comme ça*. Alistair was very responsible ...'

'Well, I should hope so, as he was driving.'

'*Exactement*. But, for me, there was a little temptation at one of the wineries and ...' He purses his lips, then kisses the air. '*Incroyable*.'

'Did you buy any?'

'Ahh ... *oui*. But just one case.'

'What?' I laugh and shake my head. No doubt my dad egged him on.

'Your father also.'

'Uh-huh, I thought so.'

'But we do not have to take it. They will ship it to Paris.' Oh, right, home—*his* home. I nod, giving him a weak smile. 'And you? A successful day, *non*?' I'd texted him from the car that we'd found a dress. 'Can I see?'

He leans around me and starts unzipping the garment bag and I swat his hand. 'Oi.' He grins at me.

'It will be a surprise, *chérie*. I promise. So, we are getting an Uber at what time?' he asks, slipping his T-shirt over his head. He unzips his jeans and steps out of them, depositing both articles of clothing onto a nearby chair.

I take a second to appreciate the beautiful form that is my soon-to-be husband, then answer, 'Just before eight.' It was the earliest reservation Jae could get, as most Italian restaurants are barely open by 8:00pm.

Jean-Luc is most of the way into the en suite, when he leans out and says, 'Oh, and your father … he asked me today about where we will be living—together, when we are married …' My stomach clenches and as well as I know Jean-Luc, his expression is unreadable.

'Oh?'

'I told him we will decide soon, *n'est-ce pas*?'

'Oh, right, yes … of course. Actually, Mum brought it up today too,' I say, though I'm not sure why as it prompts Jean-Luc to emerge from the doorway. He comes to stand directly in front of me and peers down.

'Catherine … *chérie* … the more I ponder on this … my apartment … it is a home for us. It will belong just to us.' Oh, fuck. But what did I think was happening—that he's so laid back that he *wasn't* 'pondering', as he says, that he was content to let me ignore our situation until the decision was made for us by some twist of fate? Of course, he wouldn't do that—he's an intelligent man. Patient, yes, but there is only so long I can expect him to wait. We're getting married in a few days!

'Right,' I say quietly.

'You agree, then?' He smiles broadly. Oh, fuck, fuck, fuck. Have I just agreed to live in Paris?

'Sorry, I mean, you're right in that we need to make the decision. And soon.' He deflates a fraction and my stomach twists and turns so much, it must look like a Celtic knot in there.

'Soon, *mon amour*. It is not just your parents who are asking. Jane will need to know soon. And …'

'And what?' I whisper.

'*I* need to know.' I raise my hand to his cheek and he leans into it, then drops a kiss on my forehead and goes to shower.

So much for burying this decision down deep and holding off until after the celebrations. I guess the fates had something else in mind.

'Lou!'

'Cat!' It's like one of those vignettes at the end of *Love, Actually*, a tearful reunion of two friends who are close in their hearts but separated by an ocean and a continent.

She's taller than I remember, I think as she hugs me. 'And this is Anders,' she says, letting go. He steps forward and if *Lou* is tall, then Anders is a giant. He must be at least six-foot-five. He's also broad and looks remarkably like a lumber-jack—checked shirt and all. He leans down and gives me a hug.

'So nice to finally meet you,' he says.

'And you!'

When he releases me, I make the introductions—Jean-Luc, Josh, Sarah, and Alistair—and Jaelee steps up to hug Lou. They've only seen each other once since we all trav-elled together. Jae took a business trip to Vancouver, but that was a long time ago and this is the first time the three of us have been together in three years. It's a pity Dani couldn't get time off work——the four bus besties back together again.

After hugs and handshakes, we get seated around the large rectangular table. The restaurant is located, as many places in Tuscany are, on top of a hill overlooking a deep, lush valley, mostly hidden in the evening shadows. In the distance, lights twinkle along a ridge——Montespertoli. We're seated on the terrace, only they must have discovered the secret to keeping the mosquitoes away, as I have yet to see (or hear) one. It's a little chilly, but I've dressed for it, and the glow from the candles on the table lights our faces warmly. It's heaven.

The sommelier talks wine with Jean-Luc and Sarah and they order two bottles for the table——'Vermentino' is the varietal I don't recognise——and the waiter (aptly) waits patiently for our attention so he can tell us about the specials. My ears prick at truffle risotto, which they finish at the table *inside* a wheel of parmesan, and I stop listening——I'm definitely having that. Most of us order starters (a fennel and grapefruit salad for me), as well as a main dish, but none of us opt for the typical three courses——starter, pasta, then main. But I *may* have dessert.

Conversation down my end of the table turns to, 'So, how did you two meet?' with Sarah asking Lou and Anders.

Lou giggles. 'Oh, you know, usual thing——boy meets girl, boy saves vomiting cat … very romantic …' She and Anders glance at each other, both smiling.

'What?' Now Sarah's laughing.

'I know, right? I was looking after my neighbour's cat while she was on vacation and he got really sick, like, the day after she left! I woke up to the sound of him retching——possibly the worse sound in the world, by the way——and there was yarn-filled cat vomit everywhere, the poor thing. It was around four in the morning, so I found a twenty-four-hour vet online, bundled him up in a towel, and drove across town. Anders was the vet on duty.' She gazes at him dreamily. 'You were incredible with Mr Snuffles, hon.'

'Just doing my job, ma'am,' Anders replies playfully. Lou giggles some more and I'd swear she's blushing, though it's hard to tell in the candlelight. I love seeing her like this.

'Hold on, Mr Snuffles?' asks Josh drily.

'Yeah, you'd be surprised what some people call their pets,' replies Anders. 'And this cat is a Maine Coon who weighs nine kilos. He should be named something like Brutus or Rasputin or … Moose.'

'Moose! Ha, that's awesome,' says Josh.

'That may be the most Canadian thing I've ever heard—a cat called Moose,' says Sarah.

'Yeah, you may be right,' Anders says.

'So, you meet the vet and he's tall and handsome and capable …' says Sarah. Anders drops his chin to his chest, shaking his head. '…And then what?' she asks them both.

He sighs, then grins. 'Well, the cat needed to stay in for at least a day, so he could … you know … *pass* the rest of the yarn—but after I got him resting comfortably, I asked Lou out.' Lou beams at Anders.

'And is that allowed? Dating your patients?' teases Sarah.

'Definitely not. I have a strict "no bestiality" policy,' he deadpans.

'You know what I mean.' Sarah laughs.

'I do, and it's a first for me, but I was hardly going to let her leave without asking to see her again.' He reaches for Lou's hand.

'Oh!' says Lou, startling the rest of us. 'I forgot the worst part.'

'Is it having to go home and clean up cat vomit?' I ask.

'Well, yes, but no. It's even worse than that. By the time I got home—which was, like, just after nine, the Roomba had already run.'

There are groans from around the table. 'Okay, enough talk about cat vomit,' says Josh. 'I ordered the risotto.'

'Hah!' laughs Jaelee but I agree with Josh. I need that image out of my mind *immediately*. Thank god the sommelier has arrived with the wine.

Jean-Luc skips the tasting, 'I am sure they will be incredible,' he says and the sommelier does the rounds around the table, pouring the wine of choice for six of us, as Anders and Josh are having Peronis.

I sit back, looking around at our little party. Who would have thought that all those years ago when Lou, Jae, and I climbed aboard a bus in London about to embark on a two-week whirlwind tour of Europe, we'd end up here? Me reunited with Jean-Luc and about to marry my childhood sweetheart, Jae long over Paco, her ex, and living around the world with her new love, Alistair, a true 'digital nomad' running her own company, and Lou, divorced from Jackson and now loved-up with the gentle giant, Anders.

I wonder what we'd say to those three miserable women if we had the chance? 'It will be all right. Life will soon bring you great happiness, even if you cannot imagine it right at this moment. You are exactly where you need to be.'

Or some other 'bumper sticker' style wisdom.

We'd be right, though.

Chapter Eleven

SARAH

Tuscany

I wake luxuriously—not to the bleat of an alarm, not bolting out of bed to head to the gym before work—but slowly, stretching beneath the covers and sighing contentedly before opening my eyes. I've finally succumbed to the 'I'm on holidays' feeling. Bliss.

'Good morning, beautiful,' says Josh. I accept a kiss on my cheek, take a swig of water, then turn to get a proper one. There's nothing romantic about morning breath.

'Good morning.'

'You were smiling in your sleep,' he says.

'You were watching me.'

'Only for a few minutes.' I grin, wide awake now, and snuggle into the crook of his arm. 'Do you feel it too?' I ask.

'Feel what?' He twirls a loose curl around his finger and leans in for another kiss.

'That holiday feeling.'

'Oh, I feel it. Do you?' he asks, pressing his erection into my thigh.

I giggle. 'Oi,' I chastise, but I don't mean it and he knows that.

His lips are soft as they make their way down my neck and across my collar bone, and they hum against my skin as his deep chuckle turns to a sigh. When his hand trails slowly up my thigh and slips under my knickers, I gasp again as he caresses me. He's gentle at first—teasing me—but as I raise my hips, pushing against his hand, he expertly takes me to that magical place where I lose track of everything—where I am, *who* I am—and it's just sensation and wonder and …

I come back to the room, a little out of breath, and open my eyes to see him smiling down at me. 'God, you're beautiful,' he says.

'Thank you. Your turn,' I reply, pulling him on top of me.

'You two are up later than usual,' says Cat. She's making toast—her signature dish.

'Mmm?' I reply evasively as I flick on the kettle. She smiles smugly and I poke my tongue out at her—a sisterly way of saying, 'Shut up! You're having lots of sex too.'

'Oh, and happy birthday eve,' she adds.

'Um, thanks.'

'Jean-Luc's on the balcony,' she says to Josh. 'He's made coffee.'

'Oh, cool.' Josh grabs a mug from the cupboard and heads outside.

'So, how are you feeling?' asks Cat—with everything that's going on, it's the most loaded question ever.

'How are *you* feeling?' I retort. She looks up from the toaster, her puckered mouth sitting left of centre. 'That good, huh?'

She leans closer and whispers, 'Jean-Luc asked me again last night, right before dinner.'

'Asked you …?' Her eyes widen pointedly. 'Oh, right. *And*?' This disclosure reminds me that I've yet to pin her down on the subject—*or* Jean-Luc—and I wait with bated breath.

Instead of replying, Cat sighs and stares into the toaster. Like me, she prides herself on toasting bread to the perfect shade of brown but she's stalling.

'*And* I'm not sure,' she says eventually. 'Last night, he mentioned living in Paris again. And our marriage will be legal in France, so the logistics of me living there are …' Her hesitancy comes with a defeated shrug.

'Except you don't want to live there. And your marriage will be legal in the UK too.'

'I know …'

'And what about the other thing?' I ask. She pauses buttering toast and looks at me, a furrow between her brows. 'It's not just the city. How are you feeling about moving in together? Still worried about that?'

Her frown intensifies and she goes back to the toast. 'I don't know.'

I place my hand over hers and lean closer. 'Cat, it's wonderful, I promise. And you and Jean-Luc are close friends as well as lovers. That makes all the difference.' She nods and I sense she wants to drop it, so I do. I finish making my tea and head out to the balcony, aware that by discussing

Cat's issue, I've avoided a deeper probe into my angst about turning forty. Again.

My birthday will come regardless, as I have yet to develop the ability to stop the march of time. Besides, Lindsey and Nick are arriving today, so why not focus on that?

'Welcome to our castle,' I say with outstretched arms.

'Impressive. You've been here less than a week and you've already bought a castle.' Lindsey—her sense of humour's so dry, it's desiccated. She falls into my arms, hugging me tightly.

'Hey, Sez,' says Nick, leaning down to kiss my cheek.

'Come on, I want to show you the view,' I say, beckoning them to follow me. 'How are you guys feeling?' I ask, leading the way through the apartment to the balcony.

'Yeah, not too bad,' says Nick. 'We slept on the plane.'

'Well, you did,' Lins chides her husband. 'Whoa,' she says, taking in the view.

'Right?'

'This is gorgeous. Our room at the Airbnb has a view of the road.'

'Hey, guys. Welcome to our castle.' Josh joins us on the balcony and he and Nick shake hands, man-style. He kisses Lindsey's cheek.

'You perpetuating Sarah's delusion, or are you two selling up in Sydney and moving here?' she asks.

'A little of both,' Josh replies.

'It's pretty spectacular,' says Nick, leaning over the balcony. 'And it's a winery too, right?'

'Yep,' I reply. 'And it's good, the wine.'

'Well, yeah … I mean, Italy …' Nick says and we all murmur in agreement. 'So, we still on for today?'

'Yep,' replies Josh. 'As soon as the others get here, we're splitting up—men and women.'

'Can't wait! It's been ages since I've been to a buck's do!' says Nick, his eyes lit with playful glee.

'Cool your jets, babe,' says Lins. 'It's daytime and you're wearing purple. Doubt it's going to be anything like the ones you've been to back home.'

Nick shrugs, but Lins is right—no whisky bar, no strip club, no paint ball then a whisky bar and a strip club. The day that Josh and Alistair have planned starts with a soccer match—hence the purple. It's the team colour, apparently. Definitely not my cup of tea—kill me before making me watch a live soccer match, or a televised one for that matter—but Jean-Luc will like it.

Our girls' day out will be *much* more fun. Jae and I arranged it as a surprise for Cat. 'Hello!' Speak of the devil. She comes out to the balcony and greets Lins with a hug and accepts a kiss on the cheek from Nick.

'Looking as gorgeous as ever, Cat,' says Nick.

'Thank you!' she beams at him. 'I'm so glad you two are here.'

'Thanks for letting us gate crash your wedding,' says Lins.

'You're not gate crashing. You're family,' Cat replies and my heart nearly bursts at seeing my two best friends sharing a moment. 'You got in last night, right?'

'Yeah, around nine local time,' says Lins. 'But I totally crashed. It was hard to force my eyes open this morning.'

'Being out in the sunshine helps,' says Nick. 'And the

woman whose place we're staying at—I swear she must be about ninety—anyway, she made us these full-on coffees this morning—like rocket fuel. They definitely helped.'

Lins stifles a yawn. 'Sorry! I will rally, I promise.' I wrap an arm around her in a side hug.

Jean-Luc joins us, his longish hair damp from the shower. 'Bonjour, everyone.' I make the introductions, and Nick shakes his hand and congratulates him with a hearty (i.e. manly) pat on the back. Lins gets a kiss on each cheek and throws me a quick look that says, 'Ooh la la.' I suppose if I didn't think of Jean-Luc like a brother, I'd consider him hot too. But I do—the brother thing, not the hot thing.

'Hello!' Jaelee's voice echoes through the halls of the apartment. She and Alistair have picked up Lou and Anders and now we are ten. As soon as our parents arrive, we will be off. There's animated chatter and greetings, and Lins introduces herself and Nick to the newcomers. Cat seems excited about the day, chatting and smiling. She's doing a damned good job of hiding her uncertainty about the marital living situation even though I suspect it's bubbling below the surface. But by the time Mum and Dad arrive and we sort ourselves into two different vehicles—six men and six women—Cat is practically giddy.

Mum has offered to drive this time and, as she hates following directions 'from a machine', I sit up front with her so I can navigate. Lins and Lou sit directly behind us, and Jaelee and Cat, who are the tiniest of us, sit in the very back of the four-wheel drive in the 'kids' seats', as Jaelee called them.

'So, you're not telling me anything about where we're going?' asks Cat. A chorus of, 'No,' and in the mirror on the sun visor above my head, I catch her faux pout.

Our journey takes us from the winding back roads of Montespertoli onto the motorway and then off the motorway along more winding back roads. After an hour of driving, the warm Tuscan sun high in the late morning sky, Mum parks and we spill from the vehicle onto the gravel driveway of a sprawling resort, replete with rustic brick buildings with terracotta tiled roofs, and stone pathways lined with potted olive trees.

'We're moving!' Cat announces, playfully. We're not moving—we love our castle—but we will be spending the day here.

'*Buongiorno!*' A short, roundish man with thick grey hair, a ruddy complexion, and a broad smile waves to us from the front steps of the resort.

'*Buongiorno*,' we all reply together.

'*Benvenute*,' he says. 'Welcome. You are Caterina and her friends, *sì*?'

'*Sì*,' I reply. 'Hello, *mi chiamo* Sarah.' He nods, acknowledging that he knows who I am, which I should hope so after weeks of emailing each other—though his face is much rounder in real life than in the little thumbnail affixed to his emails. He shakes my hand with both of his, still smiling. 'And this is my sister, Catherine.'

'Ah, *la sposa*! The bride!' he declares, kissing her on each cheek. Cat grins at him. '*Lei è bellissima.*' Ordinarily, an older gentleman—a stranger no less—declaring how beautiful you are could be considered inappropriate—cringeworthy even—but *Signor* Fabbri is warm and endearing, and he beckons us to follow him around the side of a large, quintessentially Tuscan building.

We emerge onto a wide terrace that sits alongside a pool. 'Oh, my god,' says Cat. I catch Jaelee's eye and we grin. We knew she'd love it here—and wait until she finds out what we have planned!

'This place is *neat*,' says Lou. Cat wasn't joking about Lou's vernacular—it's straight out of the 1950s. Any moment now, she'll say 'phooey' or 'darn'.

'Come, come this way,' our host calls. He leads us past the neatly arranged sun loungers by the pool—oh, we are *so* going to lounge on those later—and into a long building. My eyes take a sec to adjust after the brilliant sunshine. 'Oh, my god!' says Cat again. We're in an art studio and around the perimeter of the room are large easels, each with a thick swath of paper clipped to it with large silver bull clips. On tall tables next to the easels are sets of charcoals.

'We're drawing?' Cat asks excitedly.

'*Life* drawing,' says Jaelee.

Cat bounces up and down. 'I've always wanted to do that!'

'Yes, you've mentioned it once or twice,' teases Jaelee drily.

'*Signorine*,' says our host—generous, considering our mean age is at least forty and two of us are married, 'please take a position.' We spread out around the room, each taking an easel and exchanging excited looks. A woman of around sixty enters. She's petite and elegant and I wonder if she's our model.

'This is Giulia. She is the teacher.' Giulia nods her head—no smile—then walks over to one of the tables and selects a piece of charcoal which she holds up, demonstrating the grip we should use. 'Loose, but firm,' she says. Right, so Giulia's no-nonsense and straight down to business. I pick up a piece of charcoal and mirror her grip.

Loose but firm? What the hell does that mean? That's like saying, 'light but heavy.'

'I leave you now. Lunch is later, on the terrace.' *Signor* Fabbri leaves, still smiling, his eyebrows raised as if to say, 'Have fun, ladies,' and when he closes the door behind him, Giulia clears her throat.

All eyes alight at once on her small form. 'The life drawing is like *life*, it is *fluid*,' she says, drawing out the word as she arcs the piece of charcoal in the air. 'Keep the charcoal moving on the paper. Smooth. Draw the *lines*. *Capito?* Understood?'

'*Sì*,' we say, six obedient students. 'Piero,' she calls out.

A tall, wide-shouldered man wearing a dark blue robe enters the studio from a door at the back of the room. The model.

He makes his way to the plinth in the centre of the studio, the patter of his bare feet the only sound in the room. *Oh. My. Fucking. God!* I think. He may just be the most handsome man I've ever seen—and my 'free pass' list includes Idris Elba and Henry Cavill. My eyes dart towards Cat and when hers meet mine, it's clear she's thinking the same thing. We stifle smirks and I'm suddenly fifteen instead of a day off forty.

'Hey,' whispers Lins. I look over and her eyes are as big as saucers. I snigger, my hand pressed to my mouth. How on earth am I going to get through the next hour without dissolving into giggles like the naughty kid at the back of class?

Piero slips out of the robe—holy fuck!—and arranges himself on the stool atop the plinth. I could literally hear a pin drop if someone were to accidentally drop one, but there's a moment of profound stillness as the six of us take in the entirety—and I mean *entirety*—of the natural wonder that is Piero, the nude model. Even Mum is a little flushed—perhaps because his penis is essentially staring right at her.

Giulia clears her throat again. This time, it says, 'Ladies! Pick your chins up off the floor, please. This man is a professional,' and we collectively 'hmm' and don serious expressions as we practise our loose but firm grips on our little black sticks.

'Choose the longest line you can see …' Oh, my god, I'm going to lose it. All I can think is that the longest line *Mum* can see is the shaft of his enormous penis. 'Watch the line of the body as you touch your charcoal to the page and follow that line as you draw.' Okay, I can do this. The longest line from my perspective is from the top of Piero's head, down his neck, along the outline of his muscular back and curving around at his bum. I keep my eye on Piero and allow my hand to follow on the paper. When I look at what I've drawn, it's half of an amoeba.

'Connect with the end of that line and draw the next one,' she says. I do, then scrutinise my two lines. If I squint, they *could* be the rear silhouette of a human being. Giulia continues to guide us and we continue to follow. She walks the room, giving instructions and the occasional praise, and when she gets to my easel, she purses her lips as her eyes rove my drawing. She nods a couple of times, then moves on. What does that mean? Am I an artistic savant or do I have the drawing skills of a three-year-old? Of course, it doesn't really matter. What matters is that this is incredibly fun—and from Cat's expression, she thinks so too.

'And, Piero, now change.' He stands and stretches his head from side to side and rolls his shoulders. My god, I could watch him do that all afternoon. Maybe we can slip him an extra hundred euros so he can do that by the pool while we lounge. *Sarah Parsons!* I chastise myself, *you are worse than those Buck's Do party-goers who pant and drool over the stripper!* Well, maybe not *worse* but certainly as bad.

Piero stays standing and adopts a more active pose, as though he's just thrown a discus or something. Apt really, as he does look like an ancient Olympian—all naked and athletic and ... The rustle of paper pulls me back to the task at hand and like the others, I flip my first drawing over the back of the easel and smooth out a fresh sheet ready to draw the longest line. This time, it's from the tip of the fingers on his left hand to those on his right, up and over the outline of his wavy hair. Once I have his outline drawn, I return to the muscles of his back, though when I draw them, they look like a wonky external rib cage. Giulia is at my side again. 'Take the side of the charcoal and shade like this,' she says, using one of my pieces to demonstrate. I do as she's done—well, to the best of my ability—and I *think* she may have cracked a slight smile at my efforts.

We continue for three more poses, each time, Giulia teaching us a new technique. By the time she says, '*Grazie*, Piero. *Puoi andare*,' and he slips his robe back on, I'm so absorbed in my drawing, I forget to get a final glimpse of that Roman God bum of his.

'Bye, Piero,' Cat calls out.

'Thank you. *Grazie*,' I say, shaking off my artistic stupor. The others say goodbye and thank you and, at the door, he turns with a wave and flashes us a broad smile that reveals perfect white teeth behind those full red lips. Crikey!

Giulia instructs us through the business of packing up and, before I know it, we are outside squinting at the midday sun. 'Well, that was, uh …' begins Mum. She shakes her head and giggles. Our mum—*giggling*!

The rest of us join in. 'Did you plan that?' asks Cat.

'You mean Piero?' I ask.

'Yes.' She leans in and lowers her voice. 'Was he supposed to be in lieu of a stripper?'

'No!'

'Honestly, Cat, we had no idea. We just booked a life drawing class,' says Jaelee.

'Well, if it wasn't you …' She turns her eyes skyward. 'Then thank *you*, fates.'

'Yes,' says Mum looking up, 'thank you very much for the eye candy.' Then she purrs—*purrs!*—then dissolves into more giggles.

'Mum!' I mock chastise.

'Oh, get over it, Sarah. I'm sixty-four, not *dead*.' Well, I guess I've been told!

Chapter Twelve

CAT

Tuscany

'What are you two whispering about?' Our lovely host—the rotund gentleman with the kind smile, not Giulia the scary drawing teacher—has just seated us for lunch on the terrace and Jae and Sarah are deep in conversation.

'Um, nothing,' says Sarah.

Jae's more forthcoming. 'Just catching Sarah up on negotiations about the venue.' Sarah nudges her with an elbow. 'What?'

'We're still in flux,' says Sarah, smiling at me brightly.

'Well, it's not a definite "no" regarding the great hall,' adds Jae. Sarah's lips tighten in frustration but I just shrug. At this stage, I have resigned myself to standing on a leopard skin rug while Jean-Luc and I exchange nuptials.

'*Signorine*, you are celebrating, so we begin with prosecco.' Brilliant. Bubbles are (almost) always a good idea—actually, I could have used a glass or two to get me through that drawing class. I had one eye on my drawings and one on Mum. It was hilarious watching her concentrate on getting the curve of that (impressive) penis just right.

All right, I also had one eye on our male model—but not just his penis, I promise. His body was incredible—like watching a Marvel movie up close. Who needs Captain America when there's Captain Tuscany? And I'm not sure I believe Sarah's assurance that he wasn't planned, but at least he didn't wave that penis in my face. I've been to enough hen parties to know that male strippers are not shy about wagging their willies about.

When we all have glasses in hand—a half-glass for Mum who's driving—Sarah raises hers. 'To my dear, darling, adorable little sister. I love you to the moon and back. Happy wedding week.'

'Aww, thank you, Sez.' Six glasses meet in the middle of the table in a round of clinks and we collectively sip. Oh, I really do love Italian bubbles and there will be *oodles* of it at the wedding.

A waiter arrives with an enormous antipasti platter—cheese, olives, cured meats, roasted peppers and aubergine. Oh my. I'm not sure what else is on the menu, but I could happily graze from this platter all afternoon. I load up a small plate and start munching.

'So, Cat, want to know what else we have planned for today?' asks Sarah.

I swallow. 'Well, lunch obvs. But there's something else? Oh, please tell me that it doesn't involve silly costumes and pink penis party hats.'

'*No*, nothing like that.' Sarah shakes her head at me.

'Well good because I've had my fill of penises for today.' Mum.

There's a beat of silence, then Lindsey pipes up. 'Now, Karen, do we really need to hear about your sex life over lunch?'

Sarah's eyes meet mine and we start sniggering. 'What? Oh, no I meant …' Mum shakes her head at herself, then joins in on the laughter, as do Lou and Jae. Lindsey winks at me. She may be my sister's bestie, but I'm also glad she's here. Anyone who can get Karen Parsons to have a good laugh at herself is gold in my book.

'So, what *are* we doing this afternoon?' I ask Sarah.

'Well, we had two options—horse riding …' I make a face. 'Exactly, so not that. The other option was lounging by the pool and getting massages.'

I sit up straighter. 'Are you being serious?'

'Yes.'

'That's brilliant.'

'I know.'

'No, I mean it.'

'I know you do and I agree. It's brilliant.'

'Sarah, don't be so immodest,' says Mum.

Sarah ignores her. 'Wait,' I say, 'I don't have my swimsuit.'

'It's in the car,' she says smugly, popping an olive into her mouth, her eyebrows raised at me.

'I love you.' Her expression softens.

'I love you, too,' she says, a hand over her mouth.

'And don't talk with your mouth full.' Oh, Karen. You can take the girl out of Sydney but you can never take the overbearing mother out of the girl.

'So, when does the witchy sister arrive?' asks Lou. She's on the lounger next to mine, peering at me over the top of her sunglasses.

'Oh, her. Jean-Luc said that we won't see Cécile and Louis until the wedding. Thank god.'

'Oh, well that's good, at least.'

'Mmm.'

'What's her deal, anyway?' asks Jae.

Mum and Lindsey are getting their massages in a cabana next to the pool; otherwise, I would shut this conversation down. Mum has strong feelings about how in-laws should behave and is horrified by the Carons' reception of her precious daughter—especially as Mum and Dad have embraced Jean-Luc as their son. And Josh. They are as quick to brag about their sons-in-law as they are about me and Sarah.

'I'm not sure. I think it's mostly driven by Jean-Luc's mum. And the family *loved* Vanessa.'

'Oh right, the ex-wife,' says Lou.

'Actually, make that *love*—present tense.'

'Do you think Vanessa's behind it? The hostility?' Jae asks.

'No. Perhaps. I don't know.'

'Does Jean-Luc still spend time with her?' asks Lou.

'Yeah, you said they're still friends,' adds Jae. 'When was the last time he saw her?'

'Um, hey …' says Sarah, 'maybe we should talk about something else.'

'It's all right, Sez.' To Jaelee, I say, 'Jean-Luc and Vanessa have lunch every few months or so.' She takes off her sunglasses and looks at me incredulously. 'Don't do that. He's very open about it and it's *lunch*, not dinner, not drinks.

It's in public and he always tells me when he's seeing her.' She shrugs and drops her glasses back onto the bridge of her nose.

'So, you think the witchy sister is in cahoots with the ex-wife?' Lou asks.

'I don't know if I'd say that—I've never even met Vanessa—but I do think Cécile is loyal to her no matter what. Never mind that she and Jean-Luc divorced more than a decade ago. *Amicably*.' All right, maybe this bothers me more than I've let myself believe.

'It sucks, Cat. I'm sorry,' says Jae.

'How do you get along with Alistair's family, Jaelee?' asks Lou.

'Great. They're awesome. Well, at first, I had a similar problem to Cat. Alistair's sister, Ainsley, was *not* a fan. Actually …' She swings her legs over the side of her lounger and faces us. '… It was *really* similar to what you're going through, Cat, 'cause Ainsley is close to Alistair's ex, Fiona.'

'Oh, that's right! I remember now,' says Lou.

'But, I mean, they'd only just broken up, like, a month before I got to Edinburgh, so maybe it is different …'

'But you're close now, right?' Lou asks.

'Yeah, for sure. We came to an understanding. And I get along with Fiona, too.'

'Wait, *what*?' I say. 'I don't think you've ever told me that part.'

Jae shrugs. 'It's no biggie. She and Alistair … I don't know, it's a bit like with Jean-Luc and Vanessa. Their breakup was on the cards for a long time before I came along, but they still care about each other. What?' She grins. 'Why are you looking at me like that? I'm not saying we're best friends or that we hang out all the time, but she comes to family events sometimes and we get along.'

'That's weird,' says Sarah.

'It is not!'

'It's a little weird,' says Lou.

'Fine.' Jae sits back, obviously miffed.

'Sorry, Jaelee,' says Lou. 'It's just that since the divorce, I haven't even *seen* Jackson's family—and his parents are still close with mine. It's just … I needed to have a clean break, I guess.'

'Well, yeah …' Jae says, her tone softening, 'that makes sense. I mean, your divorce … well, it was rough, Lou.'

'Absolutely. It makes perfect sense that you wanted a clean break,' I say. Lou nods as she chews on her straw.

'I think it all depends on the people and the circumstances,' says Sarah. 'And I'm sorry, Jaelee, you're right. If you and Fiona get along, then that's great. It must make it easier for Alistair.'

Jaelee nods. 'Well, yeah, I hope so. And I mean, I have an ex and he's married now and I've seen them a couple of times socially. That's been okay.' She's referring to Paco, who when I first met her, she had called 'the love of my life'. 'I think it comes down to being secure in your own relationship—knowing that you're with the right person—and not worrying too much about what everyone else is doing.'

'Is that how you feel about my situation?' I ask. 'That I shouldn't be worried about Vanessa?'

'But you're not *really* worried, right? You trust Jean-Luc.'

'Yes, of course.'

'Then your situation is different—it's not about the ex, it's about how his family perceives the ex. And they're not being fair to you. I mean, Alistair and I aren't even married and I'm considered part of the family. Christie, his mom—she and I are close. And same with his dad, Stuart. They say I'm like another daughter.'

Tears prick my eyes and I gulp. I know she's only trying to make me feel better, acknowledging that my feelings are justified, but it just makes me feel it more acutely—how much I'm missing out on. 'Hey,' says Jae, 'fuck, Cat, I'm sorry. I didn't mean to make you feel worse.'

I shake my head. 'I know you didn't. It's all right, and you know … everything you're saying, it's true. It's just, whenever I think about how much Jean-Luc is part of my family—and Josh—it breaks my heart a little that I'll never have that.'

'You have us,' says Lou, reaching over to take my hand. 'We can be your surrogate in-laws.' I smile at her weakly.

'Thank you, Lou.'

'Oh, totally,' says Jae. 'My mom already loves you from afar. She's always asking about you.'

'Really?' I grin. Jaelee's mum, Christina—Tina Tan—seems like hard work.

'Oh, yeah. She thinks you're a good influence on me.'

I laugh. 'Me? That's hilarious.'

'I'm pretty sure my mum thinks you're a *bad* influence on me,' says Lou.

I point a thumb in Lou's direction. 'See?' I ask Jae. 'Wait.' I turn and face Lou. 'Why does she think that?'

'Because you are a bad influence, Cat,' teases Sarah. 'You *look* like butter wouldn't melt in your mouth but …'

'Oi!' I say to Sarah. 'No, seriously, does she really think that?' I ask Lou again.

'Umm, yeah … and you, Jaelee. I think that *she* thinks

that if I hadn't have met you on our trip, then I would still be married to Jackson.' She grimaces at us.

'Bollocks, you would not,' I say.

'Well, *I* know that, of course. I guess she just wants someone to blame for the divorce.'

'She can blame your ex-husband,' hisses Jae. 'That would make more sense.' It would, Jae's right, and I know she's only ticked off because she has a soft spot for Lou. We all do. She's the best person I know and she doesn't deserve guilt trips from her mother for getting out of a bad marriage. I thought *our* mother was the Queen of Guilt Trips. Ha!

'Oh, I feel wonderful.' *Uncanny timing, Mum*, I think.

'Yeah? You have a good massage, Mum?' asks Sarah.

Mum arranges a towel on a sun lounger on the other side of Sarah. 'Oh absolutely. I can highly recommend Roberto's services.' His *services*? I swivel my head in both directions——yup, everyone else caught that too.

'Are you doing that on purpose now, Mrs Parsons?' asks Jaelee.

'I've told you to call me Karen, Jaelee.'

'Okay, *Karen*, are you doing that on purpose?'

'Doing what?' From her tone, Mum——who is now stretched out on the lounger——*is* playing with us. 'All I said was that Roberto's massage was excellent. He has great hands——very skilled.'

Sarah throws her head back and laughs and we all join in, even Mum. 'What's so funny?' asks Lindsey who's just returned from her massage.

'How was it?' I ask.

'Great. Maria——she has strong hands.'

'Oh, my god,' says Sarah, barely able to get the

words out.

'Why's that funny?' Lindsey looks between us, clearly baffled. 'Oh, never mind. I'm going to get us another round. Sarah, Cat, you're up.' She wanders away towards the pool-side bar.

'I get Roberto,' we both say at the same time.

I leap up. 'It's my wedding.'

'It's my fortieth,' she retorts.

I have an idea. 'Lou, want my spot with Maria?'

'Sure.' She gets up and slips into her flipflops.

'You're still gonna have to fight *me* for him,' says Jae from behind me.

I turn. 'What? That's not fair.'

She grins at me. 'All good—have the hot Italian man with the good hands. As you said, you're the bride.'

Just then, a rotund, balding, middle-aged man exits the cabana and walks alongside the pool towards the bar. 'Oh, look,' says Mum, 'there's Roberto.'

'Your turn, Sarah,' I say.

I stand at the partly ajar door to Sarah and Josh's room and tap lightly. 'Sez?'

'Come in. Just getting changed.'

When I enter, she's slipping into a pair of jeans and a long-sleeved top. We're dining in this evening, just the four of us, and 'dining in' at the apartment means eating outside on the balcony with the mosquitoes.

'Today was fun, hey?' she asks, stepping into her ballet flats.

'It was. Thank you again. Best hen party ever.' She grins

but her smile fades the moment she sees me.

'Are you okay?' she asks. 'You look a little … off.'

'Oh, I'm all right. Too much sun, maybe. I'm not used to it.' That's sort of the truth. It was 24°C today—practically a heatwave in England—and it's *October*.

She sits on the edge of the bed. 'Bullshit. Come sit.' I do, slumping onto the bed heavily. I stare at my hands, then hold out the left one, my eyes riveted to the ring on my third finger, *Grand-mère* Ellie's ring.

'Did you know that Vanessa used to wear this ring?' I ask.

'What? No. You said it was his grandmother's.'

'It was. Ellie, her name was. They were very close.'

'Who? Ellie and Vanessa?'

'No. Jean-Luc and his grandmother. He says she would have loved me.'

'Of course she would have.' I swallow the hard lump that's almost choking me. 'Hey, it doesn't matter that Vanessa wore it. He doesn't love her now. They're not married anymore.'

'I know. But part of me is jealous of her.'

'Well, that's understandable with how his family treats you.'

'Yes, but … that's not what I mean. I …' Her arm wraps around my shoulder and I lean into her. 'It's just … she got to meet Ellie, got to know her even, and I never will and …' Sarah's hand grasps my shoulder tightly. 'If I think about it too much … how Jean-Luc had to ask for this ring back … it makes me feel a little sick.'

'Well, then don't think about it.'

'Hah.' It's less of a laugh and more of a sardonic utterance.

'I'm serious. What good does it do?' I'm silent, knowing she's right. 'Zero, Cat. It does zero good, so you've got to stop it.' I nod. 'We could do, like, a cleansing ritual or something,' she says. I pull away and look at her. 'What?' She laughs. 'I know you're not really into all that—'

'Neither are you.'

'So? It can't hurt—and it may just help, the symbolism of it.'

I shake my head and shrug. 'All right, why not.'

'Awesome,' she says—a word she rarely used to say, but since she's been with Josh, says all the time. She gets up and retrieves her phone from her handbag and starts typing. 'I think you're supposed to use sage. I haven't seen any of that around the grounds but there's lots of lavender and rosemary.'

'Isn't it supposed to be dried?'

'Oh …' She reads something on the screen. 'You're right.' She looks up from her phone. 'How about we use the citronella candles?'

'You want to cleanse my engagement ring, passed down from my fiancé's deceased grandmother, with a citronella candle?'

'Like I said, it can't hurt. Besides, it's just symbolic. We could light a match and do it—doesn't matter how, just matters *that* you're doing it.'

'If you say so.'

'Come on. The guys will be back soon and we'll wanna be done before then.' She goes to leave the room but there's one thought that won't let me be.

'Sez?'

'Mmm?' She pauses at the door.

'Why don't they like me?' My voice cracks on 'like' and

in a millisecond my sister is across the room, kneeling in front of me as tears spill down my face.

'Hey … Oh, Cat.' She reaches up and envelops me in a big sisterly hug. 'Because they are fucking arseholes, okay? It has nothing to do with you. You are incredibly likeable—*loveable*. You're loveable, Cat, and Jean-Luc loves you more than anyone else in the world, and that's all you need to worry about, okay?' I sniff, a ragged sob escaping. She holds me tighter then pulls back and looks at me intently.

'You have me, and Mum and Dad, and the girls … you are so loved and you have so much family … you don't need them, okay?' I dip my head in a half-nod and wipe a finger under my runny nose. Sarah stands and snatches a handful of tissues from the box on the bedside table. 'Here.' She bobs down again. 'Cat, seriously, fuck them, okay? Fuck them and as soon as I get back to Sydney, I'm sending them a giant box of exploding glittery dicks.' I cough out a laugh and she smiles at me. 'No, I mean it. I'm talking extreme glitter bomb here. They'll be finding glitter in every nook and cranny for the rest of their miserable lives.' I snigger softly.

'Thank you.'

'You don't have to thank me. This is what big sisters are for.'

'Sending glitter bombs to shitty in-laws?'

'Sending glitter bombs in the shape of *dicks* to shitty in-laws.' We grin at each other. 'Now, go get cleaned up so we can cleanse the fuck out of that ring before the guys get back.'

'All right.' I sniff and wipe my nose. 'I love you, Sez.'

'I love you too. Now go.'

Chapter Thirteen

SARAH

Tuscany

Smudging an inherited engagement ring with citronella turned out to be just the panacea Cat needed. If only because by the time Alistair dropped off Josh and Jean-Luc, Cat and I were laughing so hard we were barely making any noise.

I blame Cat. All I did was light the candles. She was the one who came up with the incantation—a weird mishmash of childhood rhymes, a Lizzo song and I'm fairly certain she chucked in a line from *Hamilton*. We must have looked absurd, doing a sort-of funky liturgical dance around the balcony. Thank god the guys didn't catch us like that; it might have been enough for Jean-Luc to call off the wedding.

Instead, they find us sitting side by side facing the view and giggling uncontrollably.

'What's gotten into you two?' asks Josh an amused smile

on his face. He leans down for a kiss and when he gets close, he smells like sweat and red wine.

'Just, you know … girls' stuff.' He eyes me curiously.

'Hello, *chérie*,' says Jean-Luc. He plops a kiss on the top of Cat's head and I notice he's swaying a little and his eyes are unfocused.

'You guys have a good time?' I ask. Josh sits next to me at the end of the table and Jean-Luc sits across from Cat, reaching for her hand and clasping it in his.

'A wonderful day. Our team won. Hooray!'

'Hooray,' I echo, even though I have no idea who they were cheering for.

'And thank god we were wearing the right colour,' says Josh pulling at the hem of his (ghastly) purple T-shirt. I'd been unconvinced when he'd brought it home and put it on the 'pack for Italy' pile, but he'd assured me it was an essential part of the Buck's Day Out. He can burn it now.

'What's your team again, darling?'

'Fiorentina.' Cat nods as if the name means something to her.

'What else did you do?' I ask. Surely, they didn't spend the last seven hours at a soccer match. I know they *feel* like they go on forever, but they're only a couple of hours long, right?

'Game, then bar, then steak dinner,' says Josh.

'You're in Italy and you had a steak dinner?' I ask.

'Yeah. They eat steak here. There are, like, six steak houses right in the middle of Florence.'

'Huh, I had no idea.'

'And we had an *excellent* Barolo,' adds Jean-Luc.

'Two bottles of it, to be exact,' says Josh. 'I'm pretty sure

Alistair was bummed that he put his hand up for designated driver.'

'I'll give you the steak but drinking Barolo when you're in *Chianti* country?' I ask.

Josh shrugs and Jean-Luc extends his hands. 'I love all wine varietals equally.' He waves his hands in a large circle. '*Tous les vins*.' Yep, definitely drunk.

'So, you guys hungry?' I'm suddenly starving and when I look at my watch, it's obvious why. We ate lunch more than six hours ago.

'I could eat,' says Josh. Not surprising. He has a hollow leg, that one—he's constantly eating. I swear the grocery bill tripled when we moved in together.

'Jean-Luc?'

'Mmm, *peut-être*. What is there?'

'Um, you know, a bit of this, a bit of that.' I push my chair back from the table. 'Cat, you want something?' With 'food is love' as our unofficial family motto—thank you for that, Karen—and both Parsons sisters being expert emotional eaters, I'm anticipating a 'yes'.

'I'm ravenous.' See?

'Okay, be right back.'

'Can I have a beer?' Josh calls at my back as I cross the threshold into the kitchen.

'Of course you can have a beer, Josh. Just come and get it yourself.'

'Ugh …' It really must have been a big day for the guys. Josh is the least chauvinistic man I've ever met, let alone dated.

I open the fridge and start pulling out parcels of goodies. Two hands grab my bum. 'Jean-Luc, I told you, not while Josh and Cat are around.'

'Ha-ha.'

I straighten, my arms laden with food and Josh's breath is warm on my neck. 'You're very sexy, you know that?' he murmurs.

I turn and close the fridge door with my hip. 'Thank you,' I say, kissing him quickly on the cheek and shutting down any amorous overtures before he suggests a quickie in the kitchen.

'So, how was your day?' he asks. He opens the fridge and before I can answer, he shouts, 'Jean-Luc? Wanna beer?'

'*Oui!*'

'I'll have wine,' says Cat. 'White, please.'

'On it.'

Josh quickly fills the drink order while I unwrap the parcels and decant paper bags onto the counter, and with a glass of wine and a beer in hand, he says to me, 'Hold that thought.' He disappears out to the balcony and is back in moments, then hands me my wine. It's in a juice glass, as that's all the apartment has, but I like it— makes me feel like a local.

'Thanks.'

'Cheers.'

'Cheers.' He clinks the neck of the bottle against my glass and we sip. 'Mmm, delicious.' It's a Vermentino—not as fancy as the one we had the other night at dinner—but bright and fruity. If Greeks grow the best tomatoes in the world—and they do, trust me—then the Italians have cornered the market on delicious table wines.

To finish assembling our dinner, I commandeer the cutting board and arrange an antipasti platter. It's not quite as extensive as the one we had at lunch today, but each morsel will be delicious, as everything is from the *trattoria-*

slash-*enoteca*, my new favourite place. I add the finishing touches—some dried figs—and step back to assess my work.

'Looks amazing, babe. Want me to carry it?'

'Ah, yes please.' I grab forks, plates, and napkins and follow him outside.

He lays the platter on the table, then goes back for our drinks, and I take in this scene of pseudo domesticity—us seated on the balcony of our little Italian apartment, the sky turning a deep inky blue, stars twinkling, and a platter of delicious local fare for dinner—pure bliss.

As I pull my chair up to the table, a mosquito buzzes by—perhaps it didn't get the memo that this is now a bad-juju-free zone. I swat at it, a minor annoyance in an otherwise perfect moment, and sink back into my blissful state. This. This feeling is why Josh's present—our trip to Italy—is the most thoughtful one I've ever received.

Cat wipes crumbs of crusty bread from the corner of her mouth, smiling at something Jean-Luc has said about the soccer match—sorry, *football* match. She looks lovely in the soft light spilling from the apartment windows—happy. I really cannot understand why the Carons don't love her. She is generous and kind—*and* wickedly funny. Right on cue, she laughs loudly and Jean-Luc looks at her as though she is the most precious being on the planet. She is to me too—or at least, one of them. I swear if Cécile does one little thing to make Cat and Jean-Luc's wedding day anything less than perfect, I will have her guts for garters.

'Happy birthday,' says the deep, gravelly voice in my ear. It's going to be extremely difficult setting an alarm once we return to Sydney. I much prefer being woken gently by my sexy boyfriend.

I twist my torso, smiling as I feel the familiar 'pop' of the vertebrae in my mid back, and open my eyes. Josh is propped up on one elbow looking down at me. 'You're spoiling me, you know,' I say.

'I should hope so—it's your birthday.' Oh, right, *those* were the words I heard, the ones that stirred me from my sleep. It's my birthday. My *fortieth*.

'I meant the gentle wake up calls,' I say, not wanting to sour the moment.

'Maybe we can figure something out for back home.'

He nuzzles my neck and a ripple of pleasure makes its way through my body. As a warm feeling rises from between my legs, I push aside thoughts of sleep-ins and milestone birthdays, and lose myself in his touches. It's only when he presses his fingers to my mouth, reminding me not to cry out when I come that I mentally return to our room in the Tuscan castle.

I collapse against him, limp and spent. 'That was nice,' I say. The vibrations of his laughter jiggle me.

'I need to work on my execution if all you've got for me is "nice".'

'Execution is excellent—you're so good, I've lost my extensive vocabulary,' I say into his neck. More gentle laughter as he strokes my back. I push myself up, both arms straight, and peer down at him. 'I love you.'

'I love you too.' I kiss him, then push back the covers.

'Hey, where are you going?'

'Shower. Lots to do this morning.'

'Really? But it's your birthday.'

I pause at the door to the en suite. 'I know, babe, but I'm on wedding duties with Jaelee. We still *have* to figure out the venue. I swear, if I'd known all this time that Jaelee couldn't read Italian … What?' He looks a little crestfallen.

'Nothing.' He smiles but I don't believe it for one second. 'Tell me.'

'It's all good, just go have your shower.'

Fuck. I know there's some sort of party planned for me this evening, but maybe he had something else in mind, just the two of us. 'You sure?'

'I'm sure.' He doesn't sound it. 'Hey, you're still having lunch with your sister, right? And your friends?'

I'd forgotten about that. 'Um … yes, I think so. There's just so much going on this week, I've lost track.'

'That's saying something,' he jokes. He's right though—I'm Ms Clockwork when it comes to organisation—so I pay him the smile. 'Oh, and I do have something for you when you're done.'

'Someth— you didn't get me a present, did you?'

'I might have.'

I make my way back to the bed. 'But this trip is my present.'

'Well, yeah, but I wanted you to have something to open on your actual birthday.'

'I like presents,' I say softly.

'I know you do.' His characteristic grin returns and my heart flutters at the sight of it. Even after several years together, I still get overwhelmed by how heart-stoppingly gorgeous he is.

'Can I have it now?'

'Oh, so you're not in a rush anymore?' he teases.

I sit on the edge of the bed. 'I have time.'

He reaches up and kisses me, softly and rather sexily. Still, if he keeps doing that, Jaelee can figure out the wedding stuff by herself. He breaks the kiss and flings back the covers on his side of the bed, then crosses the room to his suitcase. I watch him go, of course I do. He's got a gorgeous body too, especially that pert, rounded bum.

'Close your eyes,' he says, laughter in his voice. Oops—I've been caught out perving on that bum. I close my eyes and smile to myself as I feel the bed shift beside me under his weight. 'Okay, you can open them now.'

He's holding out a card and a small flat gift box. I take the card first and open the envelope and slide it out. On the front of the card, the numbers four and zero shout up at me in gold glitter. There's even an exclamation point to make it as clear as possible—YOU ARE TURNING FORTY, SARAH! I open it.

To my beautiful Sarah,

Even at the salutation, I start to tear up.

I could never have imagined that booking a last-minute trip to Greece would mean I'd find the love of my life standing on a pier in Santorini. I think I loved you as soon as I saw you, only it took me a little while to figure that out. But I'm so glad I did. You were beautiful then. You're even more beautiful today – inside as much as out. I wanted a bigger life. You showed me how. My life with you is bigger and more wondrous than I ever could have imagined possible.

I hope your fortieth birthday is everything you dreamed it would be. I love you now and always. Happy birthday.

Love, Josh

I'm on the verge of ugly crying now, but instead I take a steadying breath and sniff. I look up and there are tears in his eyes too. 'Thank you,' I manage.

'Sure, babe,' he says, clasping my hand. 'And there's this. It's just … it's a little something.' He passes me the gift box, also covered in gold glitter.

'This is why I've been seeing flecks of gold on your clothes,' I say. 'I was wondering.'

He chuckles. 'Yeah. I kept it in a plastic bag but, you know …'

'Glitter finds a way.'

'Apparently.' I smile through my happy tears.

I slide the top of the box off and inside, nestled on a bed of crinkled gold tissue paper, is a framed watercolour of Santorini—just a sliver of the view with the bright blue dome of a church at its centre, hints of surrounding buildings in the curves of the lines and a windmill in the background. It's breathtaking.

'Oh, Josh.' My eyes drink in all the details and I check the artist's signature. It's not someone I know but I am already a huge fan. I lift my eyes to his. 'It's beautiful. I love it.' I lean over and press my lips to his. 'Thank you.'

'Sorry for the glitter.' We grin at each other and I shake my head.

'It's the gift that keeps on giving.' I look back down at the painting. 'I know exactly where I'm going to hang this.'

'Where are you thinking?'

'My side of the bed, just over my dresser, so I can see it when I wake up.'

'Sounds good.'

We regard each other and I wonder if he's doing the same thing as me, conjuring our meet cute—him the cute

American guy, me the Aussie chick, both of us on a dusty bus filled with locals and hoping we were going to the right marina to join our sailing trip.

We were the only ones to step off the bus at Vlychada Marina. 'Are you on the sailing trip?' I asked.

'Oh, thank god I'm in the right place,' he blurted. Then he apologised, saying that he'd spent the entire bus trip worrying he was on the wrong one.

We introduced ourselves, found our boat, and joined a group of people who became our floating family. It was the most extraordinary ten days of my life—literally life-changing, as Josh's card says. And not just for him, but for me too. I'd been so stuck before that trip. Josh helped me lift my head and fall back in love with life. Which is exactly why *he's* the love of *my* life.

'I should get in the shower,' I say, breaking the spell of reminiscing.

'Kiss me first.' I do. 'Now scoot.'

'Scoot? I didn't realise you were a grumpy neighbour from a 1950s TV show.' He may have lived in Australia for several years, but he's still a Midwestern boy at heart.

'Yeah, yeah.' He shakes his head, laughing at himself, and I head off to shower.

It's only as I stand under the hot stream of water that I think about what he wrote in my card. There amongst all those romantic and beautiful sentiments was, *'I hope your fortieth birthday is everything you dreamed it would be.'* And those are the words that run through my head as I shower, my stomach tying itself in knots.

How can Josh possibly know that all I've dreamed of over the past few months is to hold this birthday at bay? I haven't been honest with him about it. I've barely been honest with myself about it.

Because I thought I'd have it figured out by now, but here we are! The big 4-0. What the hell is this elusive bloody thing that's been niggling at me all these months, making me wonder what's missing from my life when I have *so* much?

I'm really hoping that a busy day of wedding planning will distract me but I know that at some point, I'm going to have to talk to Josh, tell him what's really going on. I just hope he doesn't think it's about him, this internal disquiet. It isn't. That's one thing I'm sure of.

———

'Let me do the talking,' says Jaelee.

'Are you sure that's wise?' I ask. She and I have just left the apartment and are making our way along the gravel driveway towards the main part of the castle.

'Ha-ha.'

'I'm not being funny. Bianca doesn't seem very agreeable.'

'Well, that's just because she hasn't met me yet. I'm better in person.' First, I'm not sure Jaelee has an accurate understanding of how intimidating she is in person. She may be a tiny human but I wouldn't cross her. And second, when the rest of us met Bianca a few days ago, she was all business and not a lot of warmth. Even the (uber charming) Jean-Luc could barely get her to crack a smile.

I'm here to support Jaelee but I wholeheartedly believe my (poor) sister and brother-in-law will either get married in a windowless room surrounded by dusty books or that grue-some room with all the dead animals. As we walk up a set of steps and through an archway, then emerge into the central courtyard, I have an idea. 'What if we ask about having it out here?' I say to Jaelee.

She looks around. The castle walls of irregular sandstone brick rise several storeys high on three sides of the courtyard and on the fourth side is a low outbuilding. Around the perimeter of the courtyard, potted topiaries and terracotta planters with tenacious geraniums and other unidentified greenery stand sentry. The paving is slightly irregular but that's nothing that Cat, an expert at walking in heels, couldn't manage.

'*Buongiorno.*' Bianca is standing in the doorway that leads into the great hall—the one she won't let us use. She has one hand on either handle of the double doors, as if she's a one-woman human shield—You shall not pass! She eyes us with an indecipherable look—perhaps because she's just caught us appraising her castle's courtyard.

'Good morning!' calls out Jaelee brightly. She walks over to Bianca, her hand outstretched. Bianca blinks at it a couple of times and, frowning, places her hand in Jaelee's. She pulls it back again almost instantly. A hand*touch*, rather than a hand*shake*. Jaelee's smile doesn't falter and I mentally award her a house point. If she can win over Bianca—literally the only person we've encountered on our trip who has been anything less than warm and friendly—she can have a whole bucket of them. And at the end of term, she can cash them in for a pizza party.

'*Grazie* for agreeing to meet us,' she says. At least she used one word in Italian. Bianca nods curtly, her mouth pressed into a firm line. 'I wondered if I could see the two rooms before we decide.'

Bianca tilts her head ever-so-slightly. Now *that's* an

expression I understand. It's the one I don when a fourteen-year-old tries to convince me that not doing her assignment because her parents took her on a surprise trip to the Gold Coast over the weekend—with two of her friends—is a reasonable excuse.

There's a pregnant moment of the two women regarding each other—Jaelee, eyes wide open with 'innocence' and Bianca wearing a stare that would make Maggie Smith proud. The moment ends with Bianca nodding, pushing open the doors to the great hall, and stepping aside. '*Va bene*,' she says unconvincingly.

We should have brought Jean-Luc. I *tried* to convince Jaelee, but she assured me she had this in hand. Though he is only a two-minute walk away and I'm contemplating running and fetching him—'Jean-Luc, come quick. Jaelee is microseconds from royally fucking this up' —when Jaelee breezes into the great hall and looks around.

'Oh, Bianca, this *room*. It's *incredible*.' I smile apologetically at the poor woman as I pass by and join Jaelee.

'The light, the *décor* …' Wow, she's really laying it on thick. She eventually turns back towards Bianca. 'Are you sure we can't use this for the wedding? I'd be happy to pay ten per cent above our agreed rate.' She is? I haven't heard her discuss this with Cat and Jean-Luc. Maybe she's planning on covering the difference herself. I hope she is. Even a small destination wedding has a sizeable cost, and my sister and Jean-Luc have paid for everything themselves, except Cat's new dress, which was a gift. And until now, Jaelee has stuck to the budget. God, if Bianca agrees, I really hope Jaelee's covering the difference.

'No, is not possible.' I expel a sigh I didn't realise I was holding in.

'Right,' says Jaelee, eyeing her opponent. It's almost as if I can *see* the machinations of her thoughts, the negotiation strategies playing across her face. 'May I see the other two rooms?' she asks sweetly.

I wait in the great hall, not daring to sit on any of the brocaded furniture, simply standing around, as Bianca takes Jaelee on a whirlwind tour of the library and the dead animal room. They return to me in less than five minutes, Jaelee catching my eye with an 'over my dead body' look.

'What about the courtyard?' I blurt. Bianca tilts her head, a confused frown on her face. 'The courtyard,' I say again pointing outside—with my (very limited) Italian I have no idea what the word is in her language.

A nod of understanding gets my hopes up, but they're immediately dashed when she says, 'No, is not possible.'

Jae snorts out a frustrated breath beside me. 'Bianca,' I say, 'I have to be honest. There has been a *big* miscommunication—and it's our fault ...' In my periphery, Jaelee's head snaps sharply in my direction but I continue. 'You see, my sister and her fiancé ... well, all of us, really ... we think this castle is *beautiful*. I mean, this room especially. But the other rooms—as special as they may be and they are *unique*—they are not quite right for a *wedding*, you see. They— sorry, *we* all want the wedding to be *romantic*, so we are really hoping there is some way we can use the courtyard, or some other part of the castle, so we can make the wedding really special.'

I've used my quotas of 'really' for the year, and I have no idea if her English skills allow her to interpret the pleading ramblings of a concerned big sister, but I watch her closely for any sign that I've broken through her stern insistence.

A small frown skuttles across her face and she bites her

top lip. She looks down at the floor—she's either trying to decipher what I've said or she's reconsidering. Her head lifts and her expression has softened considerably. 'There is another place,' she says, 'above the apartment.'

I break into a grin. 'You mean it?'

'*Sì*. Follow me, please.' She walks past us, out the double doors to the courtyard and turns right. Jaelee and I look at each other, then rush to catch up.

Chapter Fourteen

CAT

Tuscany

'Oh, good, you're back,' I say, meeting Jaelee and Sarah at the front door of the apartment.

'Wait till you see it, Cat. It's perfect,' says Sarah.

Jaelee follows up with, 'It's okay.'

I look between them—Jae's slightly sour expression and Sarah's elated one. 'I can take you up to see it now if you like,' says Sarah. 'Bianca has left it open for us.'

'Let's just say, security is lax for a reason,' adds Jae.

I really have no idea what to think, but there's a more pressing matter at hand. 'Presents first,' I say, grabbing Sarah's hand.

'What? No, you already wished me happy birthday. You don't need—'

'Don't be ridiculous. It's your birthday and you're spending the morning on wedding duties! It's time to take a break so we can spoil you.' She tuts as though receiving presents is a chore but she knows better—birthday presents are a big deal in our family. 'Besides, Jean-Luc went to the *enoteca* this morning for treats. And there's proper coffee.'

'Speaking of …' says Jae, making her way into the apartment.

'Wait, so are Mum and Dad here?' Sarah asks.

I shake my head. 'Golf,' we say together. Birthday presents may be a big deal in our family but a round of golf trumps all. 'Anyway, Dad says he wants to give you their present tonight. Come on.'

I tug at her hand, leading the way, and Sarah steps out onto the balcony to a chorus of 'happy birthday' in several different accents. She smiles shyly and I eye her curiously—she is definitely off her birthday game this morning. Josh says she hasn't even checked her emails or Facebook. No doubt there are dozens of birthday messages languishing unanswered.

She looks at the table where two presents sit, one from Jaelee and Alistair and one from us. There's also a cafeteria of freshly made coffee and a plate piled high with the chewy almond biscuits Sarah likes. All right, I like them too and I lean over and take one.

'Our present first.' Jae picks up a small gift bag and hands it to Sarah. 'It's just something small.'

'You didn't need to do this,' Sarah says.

'Ignore her,' I say right as Jaelee replies with, 'Of course we did, it's your fortieth!' I wonder if, like me, Jae catches Sarah's tiny wince at the mention of her age.

Sarah digs into the bag and takes out a small parcel of tissue paper. I already know what's inside but watch her face closely as she unwraps it. 'Oh, I love them.' She holds up a pair of silver earrings shaped like sunflowers.

'I figured. You stared at them for at least a minute in that shop window.' Jae bought them during our shopping expedition in Siena. 'I'm just going back for some souvenirs,' she'd lied before nipping in to buy them.

'They're so pretty. Thank you.' Sarah graciously accepts a hug from Jaelee and leans down to kiss Alistair on the cheek. 'And this is from you two?' she asks us rhetorically. I reply anyway with, 'Yes.'

'You do know that your presence is your present, right?' she says.

Now it's my turn to tut. I embellish it with an eye roll. 'Just open it.'

'*Fine*,' she says, feigning annoyance. Turning forty notwithstanding, there's now a glimmer in her eye and I cannot *wait* for her to open our gift. When I glance at Jean-Luc, he raises his eyebrows at me, his mouth stretched into a smile.

Leaving the gift box on the table, she unties the ribbon and opens it. Inside is a long, narrow, embossed leather box and when she takes it out, she looks at me inquisitively. I beam, thinking that I *may* just have out-gifted Sarah the Perfect Gift Giver. She opens the jewellery box and gasps. *Yes!* I think.

'Oh,' she says, 'these were Grandma's, right?'

'Yes. I had them restrung and that's a new clasp.'

She blinks at the string of pearls laying on a bed of black velvet, seemingly confused. 'But Grandma gave them to you,' she says, meeting my eye.

'I know, but … I wanted you to have them.'

'Oh, well, thank you. That's …' She smiles but something's off. 'Thank you, Cat—*and* Jean-Luc, sorry,' she adds hurriedly. Then she snaps the jewellery box shut and puts it back into the gift box. *What?* I'd expected tears—gushing happy Sarah tears—or a hug at the very least.

Oh, my god, she doesn't like it, I think. She doesn't like my thoughtful, beautiful gift and it's like a punch to the stomach.

'Coffee?' asks Jean-Luc brightly. I have a vague awareness of the replies as I try to come to terms with what's just happened.

'*Chérie,* coffee?' Jean-Luc's eyes are so filled with kindness—he just *knows*—but his empathy makes me feel even worse.

'Uh, sorry … I, uh, think I'll make myself a cup of tea.' I push past Jaelee and go into the kitchen and flick on the kettle. What the fuck is going on with my sister? I still have half a biscuit in my hand but my mouth is now bone dry and I toss it in the bin.

I feel his presence beside me, then those arms wrap around me and his chin rests on my head. '*Désolé, chérie,*' he whispers and I let the tears roll down my face.

'What do you think?' asks Sarah. She and Jaelee have brought us to a part of the castle we haven't seen before and I've shoved aside my hurt feelings to focus on our impending decision—the wedding venue. I look about the dusty space, an airy loft with high ceilings, archways demarcating 'rooms', and openings in the rendered brick walls where windows would ordinarily be. The floorboards look a thousand years old—that may be close to the truth—and it's directly above the apartment we're staying in.

'This is where they dry the grapes for their fortified

wines,' says Sarah. That would explain the large wooden racks tucked away into a corner and the wine barrels and other wine making accoutrement scattered about.

God, the light is incredible.

'Catherine?' Jean-Luc reaches for my hand and tilts his head silently asking, 'What do you think?'

'Mmm,' I utter noncommittally. 'So, how are you thinking we'd set it up?' I ask my wedding planners.

Jaelee immediately snaps into work mode—it's like a switch was flicked on her back. 'So, this space we're standing in would be for arrivals, pre-ceremony drinks, that kind of thing ...' She walks through an archway into the next 'room'. 'We'd set up this space with an aisle and chairs either side facing the window and you'd get married here.' She walks over to one of the windows, which has a similar view to the one we see from our balcony. 'Ceremony, I do, I do, blah, blah, blah,' she says, then she's off again through another archway. The three of us rush to catch up.

'Then in *here*, we'd set up for the reception. Use the wine barrels as tables—stand, have a drink, eat—along that wall, two wine barrels and some planks of wood becomes the bar, along *that* wall, we do the same for the buffet, we bring in the chairs from the ceremony and put them in groups around the perimeter so people can sit if they want and the whole place is pretty much one big dance floor. Bianca also said there's some portable lighting we can bring in.'

She stops moving and talking and pins us with an expectant look. 'Questions?'

'I have one. How on earth did you plan everything out already?' I ask.

She breaks into her trademarked million-watt smile. 'I'm a savant.'

'Clearly.'

'What do you think?' asks Sarah. 'It's perfect, isn't it?' I'm not sure it's *perfect* but it's certainly better than our other two options. 'And you did say "rustic", Cat,' adds Sarah. She's right about that, though …

'Catherine?' I look up at Jean-Luc, then around the cavernous space, picturing everything that Jae has laid out for us. Actually, it could be quite beautiful.

'What do you think, darling?' I ask Jean-Luc.

'I am happy if you are.'

I turn to Jaelee. 'From what you said before, you don't like it much.'

'Yeah, true, but I think we can make it work. Besides, it's not my wedding.'

'Sarah?'

'I think it will be *beautiful*, Cat. And no dead animals.' We grin at each other and I momentarily forget the hurt hanging between us.

I look back at Jean-Luc. 'I think we should have it here.' Out of the corner of my eye, I catch Sarah exhaling with relief. I suppose with the wedding only two days away we've been cutting it close. And I've (selfishly) relied on my two planners to bear that burden.

'Thank you, you two,' I say. 'Really.'

'No problem,' say Jaelee, matter-of-factly. 'Sarah, let's go tell Bianca. She's gonna need to get that cleaning crew in here tomorrow morning so we can set up in the afternoon.' Jaelee is efficient, I'll give her that.

Sarah smiles at me as she passes, grabbing my arm and giving it a squeeze. 'I'm so glad you like it, Cat. It's gonna be amazing.' When they leave, it's just me and my love.

I turn to him and he wraps his arms around my waist

and I latch my hands behind his neck. '*Tout va bien, chérie?*' I nod. 'Not long now and you will be my wife.'

'And you will be *mon mari*.' He smiles down at me, his beautiful green eyes creasing at the corners.

'Are you going to talk to Sarah?' he asks, breaking the spell of our mutual adoration. 'About the pearls?' he adds.

'I knew what you meant.' I rest my forehead on his chest and expel a heavy breath. 'I suppose I have to. I just ...' I lift my head. 'I really thought she'd love the pearls, but it was like I'd given her an Amazon voucher.'

'No, more like ... something painful. Something is not right with her, do you not think?'

'Yes. Yes, I do think. Maybe it's her hang-up about turning forty. Or maybe it's the stress of helping plan the wedding and everyone being here ... I mean, it's been lovely but it's also a lot.'

'It is a large week,' he says, meaning 'big week'.

'It is a large week,' I echo.

He presses his lips to mine and I succumb to the deliciousness of the kiss. When it turns into soft pecks and ends in a forehead kiss, I return to reality. I need to seek out my sister so we can have a difficult conversation. On her birthday. Bollocks.

'This place doesn't look like much, but this food is incredible,' says Jaelee, giving the *trattoria* a backhanded compliment as only she can do.

'So good,' agrees Lou, taking another bite of her bruschetta.

Sarah's picking at her burrata and tomatoes. 'Not

hungry, Sez?' I venture. By the time she and Jaelee returned from speaking with Bianca about the wedding venue, the others, including Mum and Dad, had shown up to the castle and the day's plans had got underway. Like yesterday, we've split into two groups—we women are lunching in the sunshine and then going to a nail salon a couple of towns away and the men are heading out for lunch, then off to set up for Sarah's party.

This means I still haven't talked to her properly yet.

'Um, not really.' She smiles.

'Well, a good thing too, because tonight—'

'Mum! Will you *please* stop talking about Sarah's party.'

'Surely she knows it's dinner, Catherine—'

'I mean it, Mum. It's Josh's surprise.'

Mum tuts and rolls her eyes and I'm reminded (not for the first time) how alike we all are, the Parsons women.

'It's okay, Cat. Josh did say not to fill up too much on lunch.'

'See?' says Mum, pinning me with one of her aggressive-aggressive looks.

'What evs,' I say under my breath.

'Oh, Catherine, must you talk like a twelve-year-old?'

'But that's *all* I know, Mum,' says Sarah. 'That it's dinner, so … you know … maybe …' says Sarah, signalling for Mum to shush. Even when things aren't quite right between us, she's still my biggest ally when it comes to Mum.

Lindsey chuckles softly throughout the whole conversation. She and Sarah have been best friends for years and Lindsey has been to a many a family gathering—she's like my parents' third daughter, only without the doses of motherly judgment—and she's well versed in our familial banter. Lou and Jaelee are markedly silent and it occurs to me that both have strained relationships with their mothers. I look across at Mum, who is feigning indifference at having been shushed by her daughters, and feel awash with guilt. I am so fortunate to have her here for my wedding and even though our relationship is sometimes complicated, she's here for me when I really need her.

'Sorry, Mum,' I say. It takes her by surprise, but I receive a grateful smile and she reaches across the table to give my hand a quick pat. I really do love my mother.

When we arrive at the nail salon, they're actually expecting us, which surprises me a little as Jaelee made the arrangements—ha-ha. I direct the seating arrangements to ensure that Sarah and I are together and across the way from the others so we can talk privately.

We select our polishes—colour for our toes and clear for our fingers—and relax into the massage chairs. I can't remember the last time we got mani-pedis together, but it would have been years ago in Sydney. I suppose if we lived in the same city, it would be something we did regularly.

Sarah fiddles with the controls of her chair, then moans as the chair starts pummelling her lower back. 'Feel good?' I ask unnecessarily. I select a more sedate rolling action for my chair as a woman pulls her rolling stool close to the foot spa and signals for me to lift one foot out of the hot bubbling water.

'Mmm,' says my sister. When I glance across, her eyes are closed.

'Looking forward to tonight?' I ask. Small talk. When

you're afraid to launch into serious stuff, start with small talk, right?

'Mmm?' she opens one eye, then closes it. 'I ... um ... yeah. I mean, I have no idea what it's going to be, but we're in *Tuscany* and Josh goes all out for this sort of thing, so yeah, it's gonna be great.' I know my sister better than I know anyone and even I can't tell if she's bullshitting.

The woman doing my pedicure taps my legs, signalling for me to swap. I do. 'Sez,' I say, speaking loud enough for her to hear me above the water jets. I look over at the others to see if they're listening in. They aren't. Mum's chatting to Lindsey and Lindsey's laughing at something she's said—I swear those two have a better mother–daughter relationship than Mum and I do—and Jaelee and Lou seem deep in a more serious conversation. All clear from an eavesdropping perspective, but now Sarah seems to have dozed off. 'Sez,' I repeat, louder this time.

'What?' she drawls, eyes still closed.

'I need to ask you something.'

She turns her head in my direction and opens her eyes. 'Sure.'

'Did I do the wrong thing this morning?'

'With the loft? For the wedding? No, I think it's perf—'

'No, not the loft. I love it. The loft is wonderful.' She smiles. 'I meant with the gift—with Grandma's pearls,' I say. Immediately after the words leave my mouth, a dark cloud scuttles across her face—just for a second but there's my answer.

'Oh, no, no, no, no. Nothing like that. No, they're lovely.' Methinks the lady doth protest way too fucking much.

'Well, you didn't seem particularly happy with them.'

'I said thank you.'

'Yes, but ... I put a lot of thought into your gift and it was like the pearls upset you or something.' As I've been talking, her expression has soured and something occurs to me, something that makes me feel like a right arsehole. 'Oh, Sez, I'm so sorry. Is it because you miss Grandma?'

She looks down at her hands where she's interlocking and unlocking her fingers in turn—her tell. I've struck a nerve. Bugger, I *am* an arsehole.

'No, it's not ... I mean, I *do*. I miss her and I know you must too, especially her not being here for your wedding, but ...' She's blinking back tears and I reach for one of her twitchy hands.

'Tell me.'

'Oh, Cat, I'm so sorry. They're such a beautiful present—*so* beautiful—and thoughtful, just as you said, *so* thoughtful. It's ... well ...' She closes her eyes again and takes a series of deep breaths, probably a good idea as she seems on the verge of a panic attack. I glance over at Mum and the others but they don't seem to have noticed. I run a thumb along the back of Sarah's hand in a soothing motion.

After a few steadying breaths, she opens her eyes and turns towards me again. 'You're gonna think I'm an idiot.'

'I won't because you're not an idiot. Just tell me.'

'Pearls are for ...'

She mumbles the second part of the sentence, so I don't catch it. 'Sorry?'

She sighs. 'Pearls are for old ladies, Cat. And everyone keeps telling me that forty isn't old ...'

Oh! The penny finally drops, then bounces on the floor and rolls into a corner where it spins and comes to a rest. My sister *is* an idiot. Of course, I don't say that.

'And I gave you something that's supposedly for old ladies.'

'Yeah, that's pretty much it.'

'Sez, they're *pearls*, not a crocheted toilet roll cover! Audrey Hepburn wore strands and strands of them in *Breakfast at Tiffany's* and she was only in her thirties—*and* she was totally gorgeous in that film. Actually, any film really—absolute stunner. And Marilyn Monroe wore pearls, Coco Chanel, Elizabeth Taylor ...'

She's nodding her way through my impromptu speech on the sexiness of pearls and I sense I'm close to convincing her when her mouth quirks and she asks, 'Is there anyone *alive* who wears them?'

'Yes!' I say, 'Rhianna, Lupita Nyong'o, Michelle Obama. Oh, I know! Sarah Jessica Fucking Parker.'

'I love her!' Sarah says right as Mum chides, 'Catherine! *Language*,' from across the room. Of *course* she heard that.

'Sorry, Mum.' I start sniggering and glance sideways at Sarah who's looking back at me, chin down and also laughing.

'You seem to know a lot about celebrities who wear pearls,' she says when our laughter dies.

'As I said, I put a lot of thought into the gift. To be honest, I considered the "old lady" thing myself—'

'Oh, *really*?'

'Yes, but when I got in touch with Nikole about my idea—you remember my friend, the jewellery designer ...?' She nods. 'Well, she thought it was brilliant—she *loves* pearls, says they're classic and beautiful. And *you* are classic and beautiful ...'

'Aww, thank you.'

'You are. A bit of an idiot sometimes ...'

'Hey!'

'I'm just repeating what you said.'

'I really am sorry I made you feel bad.'

'It's all right. I just …'

'No, I …' Her words trail off and we exchange a look that says everything words can't. Sisters——bound together by far deeper and longer lasting bonds than a misconception or misunderstanding can taint.

'Oh!' she says abruptly. 'I just had a thought.'

'Clearly.'

She ignores my sarcasm. 'The pearls——they can be your something borrowed. They'd be perfect with your new dress and they're mine now, so technically I can lend them to you.'

'I love it. Thank you.' She smiles. 'One last thing, though.'

'Mmm?'

'Even when you are Mum's age, you'll be a youthful sixty-something because you're you. I mean, look at Helen Mirren——she's in her mid-seventies and she's brilliant and bolshie and sexy as hell. You'll be just like her.'

'I don't know about th——'

'Sarah, I'm serious. A string of pearls shouldn't make you lose sight of yourself, your *real* self. The Adventure Chick, Sarah. The one with the gorgeous boyfriend who jets about the world and climbs mountains and … and whatever else you do.'

'I haven't exactly climbed a mount——'

'Doesn't matter,' I say, cutting her off again. 'You know what I mean. Just remember that no gift, no matter how you perceive it, should make you feel lesser than you are. All right?'

Sarah is quiet for a moment, finally uttering, 'Okay.'

'"Okay" is not good enough. Promise me.'

'I'll try.'

'There is no try. Only do.' She grins at me.

'Do the voice.'

'I'm not doing the voice.'

'Please.'

'Nope.'

'Come on.'

'There is no try. Only do,' I say in my (godawful) Yoda voice.

'Bahahaha.' Sarah is properly laughing now and I join in.

'What are you two talking about over there?' Mum calls out.

'Penises,' says Sarah, not missing a beat. Mum purses her lips—she's not impressed. 'Sorry, Mum, have you had your fill of penises today as well?'

At that, we all start laughing—me, Jae, Lou, Lindsey, even Mum. I hope when Sarah thinks back on her fortieth in years to come that this will be one of the memories that comes to mind.

Chapter Fifteen

SARAH

Tuscany

'So, I know it's dinner and it's outside …' I say to Josh as I stand at the wardrobe, flicking through my clothes.

'Hold on, who told you it was outside?' He's lying on the bed scrolling on his phone. Well, he was. Now I have his full attention.

'Who do you think?'

'Your mom.'

'Yep. Let's just say the CIA won't be calling her any time soon.'

'Mmm.'

'So … back to me. What should I be wearing? Is it dressy? Caz?'

He leaps up and comes over, wrapping his arms around my waist and nuzzling my neck. 'How about we skip it and stay here instead? Then you won't need to wear anything.' I turn within his embrace.

'Joshua, several little birdies have told me that you have gone to a lot of trouble for tonight. We're not skipping it.'

His storm-coloured eyes flash with lust and his brows lift. 'We could be a little late.'

I kiss him. God, I love those lips. 'What did you have in mind?' I murmur when we pull apart.

'The shower.'

'Oh, yes, brilliant idea.'

'And you won't need this …' He tugs at the hem of my top and pulls it over my head. 'Or this …' He reaches behind me and fumbles a little with my bra clasp, then slides the straps off my shoulders. His head dips, his lips caressing one breast, then the other and I close my eyes, luxuriating in the sensation.

'Or these …' he says softly, unbuttoning my jeans and unzipping them. I shimmy my hips as his hands run along my thighs, pushing my jeans to the floor. I step out of them. 'And you definitely won't need these.' He hooks a finger either side of my knickers and pulls them off. When I'm naked, he stands slowly and captures my mouth in another kiss. This one is urgent and hot, possessive even. His hands cup my bum, pulling me closer.

'I'm not sure I can wait,' he says, his mouth still against mine. 'C'mere.' His voice is gravelly and low and his pulls me to the edge of the bed where he frees his erection and beckons me to climb onto him.

I do, though I want to feel his skin against mine. I tug at his T-shirt and he whips it off over his head. Our eyes lock and we kiss again, our arms wrapped around each other as our hips rock in a shared rhythm. I lose myself completely in the feel of his body against mine, in the smell of his citrusy, masculine scent, in the guttural moans of pleasure he emits.

When we come back to the world, I pull him closer and bury my face in the curve of his neck, his soft curls tickling my forehead. 'I love you, Josh,' I whisper.

'I love you too. Happy birthday.'

I ease out of his embrace and lean back. 'Thank you.'

His eyes rove my face. 'You're so beautiful, do you know that?'

'Yeah, not bad for an old chick.' Oops, I've said it out loud.

His eyes narrow momentarily and he cocks his head. 'You don't believe that do you?' he asks.

'What? That I'm beautiful? Course, I do. I'm stunning.' When in doubt, self-deprecate.

'No, I mean what you said about your age,' he says, completely missing my (feeble) attempt at humour.

'Oh, no … no, all good.' I smile but I can tell he's not buying it.

He strokes the side of my face, frowning a little. 'One day, you *will* be an old woman …' I go to say something but he shakes his head and presses a finger to my lips. 'Let me finish my thought.'

'Okay.'

'One day—a very long time from now—you will reach an age that is objectively "old".'

'Well, I hope so.'

His mouth stretches into a smile. 'Yes, I hope so too. We both hope we'll have a long and healthy life together. Can I finish please?'

'Go ahead.'

He grins and shakes his head. 'I'm trying to be romantic.'

'You're doing an awesome job.'

Now he goes to say something, but instead he presses his lips together, smothering another smile. 'All I want to say is that it doesn't matter how old you are—or young,' he hastens to add, 'you will always be beautiful to me.'

'That's sweet. Thank you.'

'I mean it.' He jostles me to drive home his point and I only now realise he's still inside me. I climb off and sit beside him, taking his hand.

'I know you do. And thank you. I just …'

'What's going on?'

I meet his eye. 'It's nothing. It's just silly,' I assure him.

'You sure? You can tell me anything, you know that.'

'I know. It's all good.' He still doesn't seem to be buying it, but I don't want to have a maudlin conversation right before my birthday celebrations, whatever they may be. 'So,' I say standing and crossing back to the wardrobe. 'Any thoughts?'

'Your long floral dress. And your ankle boots,' he says.

I turn back towards him, intrigued. 'Okay … interesting.'

'And your denim jacket for later.'

'You've given this some thought.'

'I didn't realise I had but now that I think about it, every time I've imagined this night, that's what you've been wearing.'

'You *are* romantic, Joshua, you know that?'

'Yeah, but don't tell anyone. You'll ruin my alpha male reputation.' I snigger at that. He comes over and kisses me. 'First shower or second?' he asks.

'You go. I don't need to wash my hair or anything.'

'Okay.'

I watch him go into the en suite, then turn back to the

wardrobe and take out my long floral dress—bought when I was re-watching *Offspring* and inspired by Nina Proudman's boho-chic style—and my cropped denim jacket.

'Careful, the ground gets a little uneven here,' says Josh. The excitement intensifies as he leads me—*blindfolded*. We left the castle about a half-an-hour ago and I was allowed to see where we were going until the last few kilometres when Josh asked me to slip on my sleep mask. 'Okay, babe, nearly there.' When the car stopped, Mum, Dad, Cat, and Jean-Luc got out, calling, 'See you out there,' which intrigued me. Out where? Then Josh had come around to my side to help me out.

'Okay, just hold on a sec.' He moves behind me and places steadying hands on my shoulder. 'Okay, you can take the blindfold off now.'

I'm grinning as I slide the sleep mask off and when I see where we are and what Josh has done for my birthday, it's perfect—an absolute dream come true.

'Surprise,' shouts Mum—ironic as she has spent the past few days leaking details she wasn't supposed to. The others join in with 'Surprise' and 'Happy Birthday' and Cat claps and grins at me as I bask in love and the beauty of our surroundings.

We're in an olive grove under the boughs of two tall olive trees, their silvery grey leaves fluttering in the light breeze and late-afternoon sun dappling the alfresco scene. There is a long trestle table draped in a tablecloth patterned with tiny yellow flowers and at intervals along the table, there are jam jars filled with colourful posies and old-style, raffia-wrapped bottles have unlit candles protruding from their necks.

The table is *brimming* with food—antipasti platters, plates of melon wrapped in prosciutto, ceramic bowls filled with salads, loaves of rustic bread and bottles of olive oil for drizzling—no doubt from the grove we're in. And a small table off to the side proffers an impressive array of wine bottles—all with the same label. *Ah*, I think and when I lift my gaze, I realise I'm right. We're not just in an olive grove—this is a winery. Wowser. There's even music playing softly, though it's unclear where its coming from.

'Oh, Josh, it's amazing—just like that scene in *French Kiss.*' He snakes his arms around my waist, hugging me from behind.

'I'm glad you like it.'

'I love it so much. Thank you.' I turn to kiss him and stop short, my mouth falling open. 'Siobhan?! What?' I'm barely aware that Josh is chuckling as I pull from his embrace and throw my arms around our lovely Irish friend. She belts out one of her familiar laughs as she hugs me tightly. 'I thought you couldn't come,' I say, my voice muffled by her thick, curly tresses.

We pull back and grin at each other. 'Part of the surprise. I couldn't let your fortieth pass by without getting Joshivara back together,' she says, using the name she coined for the three of us when we met on Maui.

'Oh, my god.' I hug her again and we rock from side to side.

'Come on now. I want to meet the others,' she says. She knows Cat and Jean-Luc from our sailing trip to Croatia, and I am *so* glad she'll be here for the wedding, but she's yet to meet our parents or our other friends. She wanders over to the table to greet Cat and Jean-Luc and meet the others and I stay put, still reeling from the surprise of so many people I love all together in this incredible place.

'Happy?' asks Josh, his breath tickling my ear.

'Deliriously,' I say turning towards him. 'You've spoiled me—*again*.'

'You deserve it.' He leans down to give me a soft kiss.

'Oi, you two, enough of that. Get on over here, Sarah! Join your party.' Siobhan. Not surprisingly, she's has already made herself 'at home'. I approach the table, laughing, and Dad comes to greet me with a kiss on the cheek, even though we were just together in the car. 'Happy birthday, love.' He hands me a glass of white wine. 'Here, I think you'll like this one. It's bloody nice,' he adds conspiratorially.

'Thanks, Daddy.' We clink glasses and I take a sip. 'Mmm, that is *good*.'

'Told ya.' He gazes at me proudly and I'm overcome by how much that means to me. 'And listen, your mum and I have something special for you—your present—but first … Everyone,' he calls out to the group. The buzz of chatter dies down as Dad puts his arm around my shoulder and holds his glass aloft. 'Charge your glasses, please. I'd like to propose a toast.' There's frantic activity to get glasses filled and in hand and Dad waits patiently as he pulls me closer in a side hug.

'Firstly, thank you to Josh for arranging all of this. Karen and I couldn't wish for a better partner for our daughter and I get the sense that this is exactly what she would have planned herself—*if* you'd have let her.' There's a ripple of laughter. 'Now, some of you will know this, some of you are newer to the Parsons family, but Sarah was away for her twenty-first …' He looks at me. 'Where was it, love? Timbuktu or something,' he teases.

'Bali, Dad.'

'*Bali*, right. Anyway, intrepid is our daughter number one—always has been. So anyway, we didn't get to celebrate twenty-one with her and it turned out that for her thirtieth, Karen and I were away, so we missed that one too.' They were in Africa on safari and somehow didn't think it was a big deal to miss my *thirtieth birthday*—it was—but I don't mention that. 'Annnd … we've been waiting for a wedding …' He shrugs.

'Da-aad!'

He kisses the side of my head. 'Only joking, darling. One daughter getting married is enough drama for a lifetime, thank you very much.'

'Da-aad!' This one's from Cat.

'Oops, now I'm in trouble.' Dad mugs for the others and there's more laughter. 'Anyway, back to the business at hand. Here we are at Sarah's fortieth.' As Dad pauses for dramatic effect—*again*—my thoughts tumble over each other. Was it really *nineteen* years ago—nearly half a lifetime—that I went to Bali with my girlfriends for my twenty-first? In some ways, that feels like yesterday. In others, it feels like a millennia ago.

'Sarah …' Dad looks at me and I meet his eye. 'You are a wonderful woman. You're generous and clever and loving—and you've got your dad's sense of humour.' More titters of laughter and I smile at him, shaking my head. 'Seriously, though, love, you make your mum and me very proud every day.' He starts to tear up, reminding me where I get my soppiness from. 'We love you and we are *thrilled* to celebrate your special day with you.' He pulls me close and presses a kiss onto the side of my head. 'To Sarah,' he says, raising his glass higher.

'To Sarah,' everyone echoes.

'Happy birthday, love,' he says quietly, this time even more heartfelt.

'Thanks, Dad.'

'And this is for you.' He dips a hand into the inside pocket of his linen sports jacket and takes out an envelope. 'You don't have to open it now if you don't want to.'

'No, I do.'

Josh approaches. 'Great speech, Ron.'

'Ah, you know me. Any opportunity to show off. I'll leave you to it,' he says to me, before heading back to Mum.

'Present,' I say, holding up the envelope.

'Want me to take that?' Josh asks, indicating my glass.

'Thanks.' I open the envelope along the seam and take out a card that was obviously chosen by Mum. 'To our darling daughter who's turning 40,' it begins on the front. I skip the poetry written by someone at Hallmark and open the card. Dad has scrawled, 'Lots of love from Mum and Dad,' at the bottom, followed by two kisses and two hugs. I'll read the Hallmark stuff later—no doubt Mum will quiz me on it—but I'm more interested in the folded pieces of paper inside the card. 'Here,' I say to Josh, handing him the card.

I unfold the paper and read. 'Holy fuck-a-mole,' I say, eloquent as always.

'What? Show me.' I hold up the piece of paper. 'Mum and Dad have given me half-a-million frequent flier points.'

Josh's open-mouthed reaction makes me laugh. 'Holy fuck-a-mole is right. I guess when your Dad works for QANTAS for four decades …' he says, leaving the rest of the thought unsaid.

'So, where do ya wanna go first?' I waggle my eyebrows at him and he grins.

The bounteous platters and bowls of food are replenished by stealthy waitstaff and as the sun sets and the candles are lit, so are dozens of strings of fairy lights in the trees. My lovely late-afternoon party turns into something even more magical, like it's out of a fairy tale.

I'm reminded of the time, several years ago, when a silver fox named James surprised me with a rooftop picnic, including fairy lights and candles, to tell me he was falling in love with me. James passes through my thoughts from time to time, but I never regret my decision to end our romance. He is a wonderful man—just not the man for me.

I sit back against my chair, already having had my fill of the incredibly delicious food, and toy with the stem of my wine glass. Dad has poured me a Super Tuscan—essentially a Bordeaux-style wine made with Tuscan grapes—and it's delicious but I am pacing myself now, wanting to remember every detail of this incredible party.

I look down the table to where Josh is talking with Nick and Alistair and he throws back his head and belts out a loud laugh, almost as if he knows I'm watching the scene. God, I love him. I am grateful every day that the fates brought us together in Greece—even on the days he drives me mad by shouting at his video game or leaving his jocks on the floor next to the laundry basket. *It is literally right there—can't you make it the few extra centimetres?* I want to shout (but don't) because he puts up with my foibles too. And I am far from perfect. He's forever scooping used teabags out of the sink and putting them in the bin and when I'm reading, I will shush him if he tries to talk to me 'during a good bit'.

But my heart is swollen with love for him, as it often is, when I take in all that he's done to make my birthday special. My parents are here, my sister and brother-in-law, my bestie, one third of Joshivara! How he made that happen when Siobhan was a definite 'decline' is a minor miracle. Even having Jaelee and Lou and their partners here is lovely. With how special they are to Cat, they're like extended family now and it's perfect that they're part of this.

All my nearest and dearest here for a celebration in one of the most beautiful places in the world. Dad was right—it's exactly what I would have planned for myself had I thought of it. Sometimes I think Josh knows me better than I know myself.

'You're deep in thought there,' says Siobhan. She's been entertaining Mum with the story of how we all met and Mum has just excused herself to top up her Pellegrino—she's our skipper—so I have Siobhan to myself for the first time tonight.

I smile at my friend. I've missed her desperately, I realise now that the flesh-and-blood version is sitting before me. 'Just happy.' Her smile widens. 'So, tell me … you said you weren't able to come 'cause it's term time in Ireland.'

Siobhan is a teacher too, only she teaches at-risk youths so her work is a *thousand* times more intense than mine. *My* students are (mostly) adorable—they're all 'Yes, Miss' and 'Sorry, Miss'. Whereas Siobhan counts herself lucky if she goes a week without being called the C-word.

'I know, yes. At first, I *did* think there was no way I could get away, so I just told myself I had to get over it.'

'So, then how did you end up …?'

'Well,' she says, adding a vigorous hand gesture, 'the closer it got on the calendar, the more I started thinking, "Siobhan, you cannot possibly miss this. So, what if you just go down for the birthday party and the wedding?" You know, take a few days' leave for a *very important medical procedure* and make an extra-long weekend of it.' She grins cheekily and I grin back at her. It's impossible not to—her smiles should be trademarked, they're that powerful.

'So, *then* I chatted with Josh on WhatsApp and he totally corrupted me, encouraging me to lie to my school. "Oh, Siobhan, Sarah and Cat would love it. You *have* to come." So, last week, I booked a flight and here I am!'

I reach across and hug her tightly. 'I am so glad you did.' I sit back. 'And I hope you have a speedy recovery from …?'

'Oh, I haven't thought far ahead yet. Probably something gynaecological—even though my Head is a woman, she's the sort who'd be too squeamish to ask me anything more about it. I doubt she's ever touched her own vagina.' I start giggling.

'Oh, Siobhan—you're hilarious,' I say through my laughter.

She waves off my compliment. 'You know, I *nearly* brought a date.'

'Oh? You didn't tell me you were seeing anyone.' In truth, Siobhan could have been dating for the past year and I wouldn't have known. As close as we are when we're together, falling right back into that easy understanding and genuine affection for each other, she is terrible at keeping in touch—*terrible*! Josh and I can go months without hearing from her and suddenly there will be a long, newsy email in our inboxes. And she hates video calls—*hates* them.

'You should have brought him,' I say. 'He would have been most welcome.'

'First off, thank you. I knew that if I did want to bring a date, you wouldn't have minded. Second, he's a *she*.'

'Oh, wow. You're dating a woman.'

'I am.'

'And so …?' I have so many questions. When we met Siobhan on Maui, she was on her honeymoon *alone* having been left at the altar by (the eejit) Liam. And they'd been together for fourteen years!

'Well, her name is Keely and she's grand. Gorgeous, of course—I mean, *hello*—after Liam, I lifted my standards about a thousand per cent. And she's brilliant. I mean, actual proper brilliant—she's a surgeon.'

'Nice.'

'I know—finally dating a doctor, like Mammy always dreamed for me. Actually, that's how we met. Mammy was in hospital to have a hip replacement—long story, but she fell and it was bad and my sisters and I had to convince her that a hip replacement was better than a wheelchair. Anyway, Keely was her orthopaedic surgeon and she was brilliant with Mammy and at first, I thought that was all there was to it, you know—she's got this great bedside manner, she's lovely—but then when I took Mammy for a follow-up appointment, that's when I knew—I fancied her like mad. And I've never dated a woman before.' This I know. 'But I took a chance and asked her out and we've been seeing each other for about seven months now.'

'Wow, that's … I'm so happy for you, Siobhan. She sounds amazing.'

'She is. Can I, like, totally brag and show you a photo?'

'Yes! Yes, show me.' She rummages in her handbag,

which is slung on the back of her chair, and takes out her phone. She taps and scrolls, all with a lovesick smile on her face. 'Here, this is us at the Cliffs of Moher—we went for a mini-break a couple of months ago.'

In the photo, their faces are pressed together, their hair is whipping behind them in the wind, and their arms wrapped around each other's waists. Siobhan is quite a lot taller than the petite, redheaded Keely, so she's leaning down for the shot, and both are laughing—it's a gorgeous photo. 'The wind was intense,' says Siobhan. 'I had to hold on to her so she wouldn't blow away.'

I look up from the photo. 'She's beautiful. You're beautiful together. I can't wait to meet her,' I add.

'I so wish she could have come, but she's on call this weekend—you know, in case any pensioners have an emergency and need surgery.'

'I really love seeing you this happy,' I say.

'I can say the same about you.'

'Hi, Siobhan—sorry to interrupt but I haven't met you properly yet.' My bestie is suddenly beside me and I realise I've barely spoken to her since we arrived. 'I'm Lindsey, Sarah's friend from Sydney.' She holds out her hand to Siobhan.

'Oh, lovely to meet you.' Siobhan stands and wraps her arms around Lindsey, who returns the hug good-naturedly. 'Do you want my spot? I've been hogging the birthday girl and, besides, I haven't caught up with Josh properly yet.'

'Oh, thanks, that's kind of you.' Lindsey sits and Siobhan heads down to the other end of the table. 'Having a good time?' Lindsey asks me.

'It's amazing. I love it.' Moments later, there is raucous

laughter from Josh and Nick, and Lindsey and I look down the length of the table.

'God, that was fast.'

'It's the Siobhan factor. She's just that funny.'

She looks back at me. 'Even funnier than you?'

'Yes, definitely—mostly because half the time I make you laugh, it's unintentional.' She sniggers. 'See?'

'So, I wanted to give you your present.'

'Why does everyone insist on giving me presents after flying across the world to celebrate my birthday?'

'Oh, god. If you give me that "your presence is your present" BS, I'll vomit.' I press my lips together. 'So, can I give it to you now?'

'Yes, please.'

Out comes another envelope, which she's been hiding under the table on her lap. 'Here.'

I open it—another card, but this one doesn't say anything about my age and, if it's possible, I love my bestie even more. 'Read it later. It'll just make you cry. And me. I'll probably cry too.'

'Okay.' Lindsey isn't usually the sentimental type, but I'll respect her wishes. Inside the birthday card is a voucher to a day spa in the Blue Mountains.

'Ooh! Fancy!'

She chuckles. 'That's only part of it. We're going for the weekend, just you and me—it's the whole kit and caboodle. Oh, and Nick's watching Domino—that's his part of the present.'

'Cute! Boys' weekend at home.'

'Yeah, they can lounge around on the couch, watching sport and licking their balls.'

'Domino does like to do that,' I say, deadpan. 'The licking part.'

'Nick *wishes* he could do that—the licking part,' she retorts and we both roar with laughter. When the laughter dies, she looks at me with a soft smile, then leans across and kisses my cheek. 'Welcome to forty, Sez. You're gonna love it.'

We've always joked around about her being a whopping seven months older than me. But there's that word again—forty. And why is Lins so convinced that I'm going to love it? I mean, so far, it's been great—I've been lavished with presents, my lovely, thoughtful boyfriend has executed the perfect birthday party, *Siobhan's* here—an amazing surprise—but below the surface, it's still there, that elusive little bastard, my missing something.

What the hell *is* that?

Chapter Sixteen

CAT

Tuscany

It's the day before my wedding but also the morning after the night before.

Seriously, how much did I have to drink at Sarah's party?! I blink open my heavy lids and check my phone for the time. 6:09am. Gah! I do not need to be awake this early. I have a generous glug of water, close my eyes, rearranging the pillow so it better supports my neck, and try to relax. *Go away, headache*, I command. It continues to pound away, oblivious to my wishes. Go away, you sodding bloody bugger of a headache!

Why didn't I take my usual precautions last night? Headache tablets and lots of water before bed—*always*. Except when you roll up to the castle at 11:00pm having spent the last six hours eating, drinking, and being merry and you completely forget. Maybe this is a symptom of middle age—the forgetfulness *and* the hangover. And if *that's* the case, then maybe there's something to Sarah's angst about being forty.

Finally, I can feel myself drift along the cusp of sleep but a moment later, I land on the wrong side of it and my eyes spring open again. Bugger, bollocks, fuck, shit.

I slip out of bed, not wanting to wake Jean-Luc, and pad to the bathroom where I ferret around in my toiletries bag for headache tablets. I can't have forgotten para-bloody-cetamol, surely? Another look through the bag reveals that I have. *Argh!* I scream silently. Oops, my head does *not* like that. Sarah will have some. She's the most organised person I know—whenever she travels, she does two practice packs before her final one. She's like Amy Santiago from *Brooklyn 99* only more anal. I've never truly appreciated that level of fastidiousness until now.

I ease out of our room and tiptoe down to Josh and Sarah's room, then listen at the door to make sure they're not having sex. Silence. I turn the knob and peek in—both asleep. I open the door just enough for me to slip through and head straight for their en suite and close that door quietly. So far, I'm impressed with my stealthiness. Perhaps I missed my calling—I could have been a covert operative.

Sarah has a toiletries bag, a separate makeup kit, and a proper first aid kit—of course she does. I try to open the first aid kit—a plastic container with a latch—and the bloody thing is stuck. I'm now at the point where I've never wanted a headache tablet more in my life. 'Come on you bloody thing,' I whisper at it, my jaw clenched.

The latch finally releases, but I *may* have been a little heavy handed and medical supplies erupt from the kit and clatter onto the bathroom floor. I stand stock-still and stare at the door—maybe they didn't hear me. The doorknob turns and Sarah peers around the edge of the door. Bollocks. 'What the hell are you doing?' she asks, though not harshly and I inwardly applaud her restraint.

'I was trying not to wake you,' I whisper.

She frowns at me and looks at the detritus of my not-so-covert-after-all operation littering the floor. She reaches down and retrieves a packet of tablets. 'Here,' she says. 'You must really need these.'

'Sorry, Sez.'

She sniffles and shakes her head. 'Out, I need to pee.'

'Oh, right, sorry.'

Just as I'm through the door, she says, 'And go put the kettle on. I'm up now.' No-nonsense, big-sister mode.

'All right,' I whisper, but it's to a closed door.

I glance at the bed and Josh is still sleeping. I'm not sure how and I feel a pang of jealousy—I wish I could sleep through a great crashing sound. I leave and head to the kitchen and flick on the kettle.

A short while later, I'm sipping tea on the balcony of our castle, looking out over the valley, my headache starting to ease a little and I smile. I'm getting married tomorrow.

———

Sarah should have brought a clipboard with her—then she'd *really* look the part as she bosses us about doing her (wedding planning) bidding. She calls it 'being organised'. I call it 'being a drill sergeant'.

Unlike me, my sister managed to avoid a hangover despite fully participating in her birthday celebrations and being 'up with the sparrow's fart', as our dad likes to say. Turns out it's because, also unlike me, she downed two tablets and a bottle of water before bed. Josh and Jean-Luc are similarly unaffected and I am trying to not to hate them all—silently, of course. While my headache has eased, it's not completely gone and even though I have eaten a mountain of toast this morning, my stomach is still a little off.

We are a crew of seven—the four of us, Mum and Dad, and Jaelee. I felt sorry for Alistair, as he didn't sign up for wedding planning duties and ignoring Jaelee's protests of, 'He doesn't care,' I insisted he join the others who are spending the day in Montepulciano. It's the sort of name that's fun to say—Mont-e-pulll-chee-ah-nohhh—and, according to Sarah, it's an amazing town, so I am also moderately jealous of the day-trippers. *I am getting married tomorrow!* I remind myself. Hmm, yes, I should definitely focus on that.

'Right,' says Sarah, 'Jaelee and I have inspected the loft and it looks like there's still a lot to do.'

'There's still everything to do,' Jaelee says drily.

Sarah tosses her a look that says, 'I'm trying to manage expectations here.' Jaelee replies with a look of her own—'So am I!' Sarah clears her throat. 'So, Bianca sent the cleaning crew in yesterday—'

'But you can't tell,' Jae chimes in. I know my sister and she is incredibly patient, but it looks like she's about to lose it.

'And we will need to fix that. There's also setting up the space, as Bianca wasn't able to get anyone to help with that, like she'd thought.'

'Honestly, if she worked for me, I'd fire her,' mumbles Jae. I stifle a snigger.

'*Anyway*, I've asked for cleaning supplies and they'll be up in the loft, and Bianca has given us the key to the storeroom where the lights and chairs and other stuff are kept. Guys, Dad, you'll be with me, bringing everything up to the loft. Mum and Jaelee, you'll get started on the cleaning.'

Setting aside that Sarah's division of labour is very '1950s', I ask, 'Wait, what about me?' I don't *love* cleaning and setting up, but I am not just going to watch my nearest and dearest do all the work.

'Well, you don't want to mess up your manicure, and …' She hesitates as soon as she sees my piercing glare.

'My *manicure*? How precious do you think I am? Besides …' I hold up a hand. '… Clear polish, remember.'

'But it's your *wedding*, Cat. You shouldn't have to do all the grunt work. I thought you could go down to the *enoteca* and get us something for lunch.'

'I'm on sandwich duty?' I look about at the others and they all seem fine with the plan. Well, I'm not.

'More or less. And tea, coffee …'

'So, I'm also the tea lady.' Sarah sighs, her mouth twitching. I'm glad she finds this so amusing.

'There are some calls to make—final confirmations for the food, the flowers, the cake—that sort of thing,' offers Jaelee. Only, I don't speak Italian. Nor does she, of course, but I don't mention that.

'Um.'

'Well, what *do* you want to do, Catherine?' asks Mum impatiently.

'All right, I'll be the bloody tea lady. But I'm helping with the other stuff too. I don't want to be sitting around like Lady Muck while you lot work up a sweat.'

'Sounds good, love,' Dad says dismissively. 'Okay, Sarah, lead the way to the storeroom.' He must be over this conversation—everyone must because it's like there's an unspoken signal and the six of them erupt into activity.

'I'll head down to the *enoteca*,' I say to everyone and no one.

If my life were a film, this day would be the montage in the middle. There would be lively Italian folk music playing, the kind with a mandolin, violins, and an accordion—probably because that's what's bleating from Josh's portable speaker—and the camera would dip and swing between us, showing the progression of the space from a dusty loft into a dreamy wedding venue.

It would also capture Mum laughing as Dad pretends to dance with a broom, then takes her hand and twirls her, Sarah and Josh kissing every five seconds, and Jaelee frowning at her phone. In several shots, Jean-Luc would meet my eye across the room and just watch me, then smile and close his eyes like he couldn't believe he was going to marry me the next day.

All right, that's me—*I* am doing that.

Sometimes it hits me how incredibly lucky we were that night in Paris, how happenstance brought us together again. A few seconds either way and we would have missed each other, each remaining a fond memory.

But we did meet up. We did catch up. And we did fall (back) in love.

And he's brilliant and gentle and funny. He's also the sexiest man on the planet and I say that without prejudice. It's just a fact. He's so comfortable in his skin and with who he is and I find that an incredibly sexy trait. Not to mention how handsome he is and the way he *moves*—it's almost catlike it's so fluid. And when he runs his hands through his hair or looks at me intensely with those Kelly-green eyes, my lady parts stand to attention.

So, yes, as I've run up and down the stairs between the loft and the apartment, toting sandwiches and trays of tea and coffee, I've also indulged in several 'oh my god, I am marrying that incredible man tomorrow' moments.

I'm helping Sarah set out tableaux of pillar candles and sprigs of rosemary and lavender—it was her idea to raid the castle's gardens for greenery—when I notice Jean-Luc on the phone in the next room. He's speaking French and frowning. It could be a multitude of people on the other end of that call—an editor of one of the many magazines he writes for, his accountant, the woman in his building who collects his mail when he's away … but it's when he says, 'Cécile, *non, ce n'est pas possible*,' that my stomach clenches. Good god, what does she want now?

'Pffft,' he huffs in frustration as he rubs the back of his neck—uh-oh, not a good sign. '*Attends*,' he says and drops the phone to his side. He comes over to me.

'What's going on, darling?' I ask, mindful that Cécile is still on the line and can probably hear us. He lifts the phone and taps the 'mute' button. Still, I refrain from asking, 'What the hell's up with that bitch-faced dragon sister of yours?' and smile at him encouragingly, all bridal and magnanimous.

'Cécile and Louis, they were supposed to arrive today …' I knew this, of course. I've been hoping they'll go straight to their accommodation and I'll only have to endure Cécile's presence tomorrow when my entire support squad is by my side. 'But they have been delayed. Something about

Louis' work' —I seriously doubt that— 'and Cécile wants me to pick them up at the airport in the morning.'

'What? On your wedding day? Can't they just take a cab like Mum and Dad did?' I don't add that Cécile and her husband can most definitely afford it.

'This I suggest already.' He shakes his head and run his fingertips along his lips.

'Darling, it's more than a three-hour return trip. She must know this is big ask.' His eyes meet mine and I *know* he's conflicted. Sarah's hand lands on my shoulder in support. At least one of us has a decent, loving sister.

'What's going on?' Jaelee asks, inserting herself into the conversation.

'She's definitely on mute, right?' Sarah asks Jean-Luc. He nods. To Jaelee, she says, 'Jean-Luc's sister and her husband can't fly in today and she wants him to pick them up from the airport tomorrow morning.' I applaud her for not adding 'the unreasonable cow'.

'Um, no. Not happening. Gimme,' she says to Jean-Luc, holding out her hand.

He seems taken aback. 'You want my phone?'

'Yeah, let me talk to her. She speaks English, right?'

Jean-Luc's eyes narrow. I know that look—he's trying to figure out who he'd rather be on the wrong side of, his sister or Jaelee. He sighs and hands Jaelee the phone and we three watch, mesmerised, as she unmutes it and holds it to her ear.

'Hello, Cécile is it? This is Jaelee Tan, the wedding planner and one of Cat and Jean-Luc's closest friends. So, yeah, we already have a full itinerary for tomorrow morning—so much to do, *really* busy—and we can't *possibly* spare the groom for a three-hour drive into Florence. You'll need to take a cab. Oh, no, sorry, he's even busy right now—groom duties.' She trills out a faux laugh. 'You know how it is. Anyway, *really* looking forward to meeting you. We'll see you at the wedding. Bye now.'

She ends the call and hands the phone back to Jean-Luc. 'There you go.' She turns and strides away, saying to my dad, 'Ron, you are a master of stringing lights,' as she passes. I mean, she's right—Dad has done a brilliant job with the fairy lights, but she seems oblivious to the fact that she's left me, Sarah, and Jean-Luc utterly dumbstruck.

Sarah recovers her ability to speak before me. 'Well, that was masterful,' she says. 'So, if someone's being unreasonable, you just talk at them without taking a breath, then hang up.'

'She will not be happy,' says Jean-Luc, shaking his head.

'Then why are you grinning, darling?' I ask, my own mouth stretching wide.

He leans down and kisses me. 'Because my sister … I love her but *elle est peut-être une vache, non?*'

'Oh yes, indeed.' I think this may be the first time I've heard Jean-Luc speak ill of his sister and I'm not sure if it's good or bad that I like it.

'Everyone,' Jaelee calls out from underneath one of the archways. 'I think we are close to done. Sarah?'

Sarah consults the handwritten list she compiled after our change of venue and looks about the loft, literally checking off items. Moments later, she clutches the list to her chest. 'She's right, we're done,' she says. 'Well, sorry, the flowers arrive in the morning, so there's that—and the cake—oh, and the food but—'

'But what my co-wedding planner means to say is that, for today, we're done,' says Jaelee diplomatically. 'And it's *gotta* be Happy Hour.'

'Oh, absolutely,' says Mum. 'It must be five o'clock somewhere.'

'Here, Mum,' says Sarah, looking at her watch. 'It's five o'clock here——or close to.'

'Perfect,' says Mum and I suddenly realise how weary she looks. It has been an intense time since we all arrived, and Mum and Dad flew in a couple of days after us, so they may still be jetlagged. But they still showed up today and pitched in without complaint. Oh, I love my parents.

'Righteo,' says Dad, clapping his hands together. 'How about we get all the cleaning stuff out of here, then crack a beer on the balcony downstairs.'

'Wine is preferable, Ronald,' says Mum.

'Whatever you want, love,' he replies, landing a kiss on the side of her head.

'Catherine.' Jean-Luc's hand captures mine and brings it to his lips. I turn towards him. 'It is wonderful, *non?*'

'This place? Absolutely.'

'*Oui*, this place, but also … everything. Our friends, our family, being here … *you. C'est parfait.*'

He stoops to kiss me and oblivious to the others who are zipping about and packing up the space, I sink into the kiss, wrapping my arms tightly around him. 'Oi, you two. Honeymoon starts tomorrow,' shouts my dad from the other end of the loft.

'Da-aad,' Sarah and I say at the same time. I smile up at Jean-Luc and he's grinning. 'I love you,' I say.

'I love you, *chérie.*'

I get to marry him tomorrow, I think joyfully.

Chapter Seventeen

SARAH

Tuscany

My eyes spring open, then flick towards my phone on the bedside table. It's just after six and today is going to be full-on. If I can fall back asleep, I should snatch another hour or two. I close my eyes but tasks from my wedding preparation to-do list start flying around my head competing for attention. No good. I open my eyes again and look over at Josh. His back is to me and he's snuggled under the doona fast asleep.

My phone buzzes, alerting me to an incoming message. I check it—Jaelee.

You up?

I tap out a quick reply.

Yep.

Me too. Wide awake. Wanna do some yoga? Or go for a run?

Yoga or a run? Actually, a run would be great. Josh and I did a walk a couple of days ago, but with all the rich food and copious wine we've been consuming, I'm feeling a little blah.

Run. Meet you at the castle driveway in ten.

Cool.

I slip out of bed and gather my workout clothes and runners, then go into the en suite and quietly close the door. As I get changed and slather on some sunscreen, I start thinking through everything we need to do today before the guests start arriving for the wedding around five—this time in an orderly fashion, rather than random details dive-bombing my brain and stressing me out.

Despite the whole 'Italian–Spanish' thing, I really am glad to have Jaelee as my planning partner. She's no-nonsense and the way she handled Cécile yesterday—*wow*. I can be formidable when I need to be—and no one should dare mess with my sister—but that was just masterful, a lesson in passive-aggressive aggression. I definitely wouldn't want to fall on the wrong side of Jaelee.

I scoop my long curls into a ponytail, then regard myself in the mirror. 'I am forty,' I say softly. I press my fingertips to my cheekbones and lift the skin to where it would have sat ten years ago. Not that much of a difference. I frown, exaggerating the vertical lines between my brows. These are quite pronounced—a tool in the schoolteacher's arsenal.

Then I smile—big—and examine the lines that are begin-ning to frame my eyes. 'Crow's feet' the beauty companies call them. 'Laughter lines' says my dad. 'I love your mum's laughter lines. They remind me of all the times we've laughed together.'

Mum has played golf twice-a-week for at least twenty-five years. She's a sun lover from Sydney with laughter lines and all the other signs of being in your sixties when you spend a good portion of your life outside—and she's beauti-ful. Dad says so, of course, but objectively, my mum is a beautiful woman.

God, is *vanity* the reason I'm feeling out of sorts? Josh is eight years younger than me. Am I messed up about turning forty because I don't want to be that 'middle-aged woman with the hot, young boyfriend'? I frown again, but this time it's not deliberate and I drop my gaze and stare at the porce-lain sink.

No, I think, *this isn't vanity*. Besides 'beauty' has nothing to do with lines on your face—the presence or the absence of them. I know that. I *believe* that. And I take care of myself—I don't *feel* old. And Cat's right—you can be older and *still* be gorgeous and sexy. No, my internal disquiet is not about my face or my body. It's far deeper and I just need to figure it out—and soon.

It was all well and good to immerse myself in birthday celebrations, and the wedding preparations have been a good distraction too, but after today … Well, after today, I am going to have to figure out what's causing this.

I'm running late now and slip out of the bathroom, scribble a quick note for Josh, and go meet Jaelee at the end of the castle's driveway for our run.

'Huh,' says Jaelee, her eyes roving over the flower delivery. She starts poking around in the large flat boxes. 'No bouquet.'

'Really?' Now I start poking around, careful to avoid the business end of the roses. 'You're right.' She gives me a look that says, 'Duh.' 'I suppose we'll need to make one.'

'Do you know how to do that?'

'How to do what?' Mum has snuck up on us and we both start.

'Morning, Mum,' I say, and we swap cheek kisses.

'Good morning, girls.' I could be sixty and Mum will still refer to me as a 'girl'. 'What's the matter?'

'There's no bouquet,' says Jaelee. Mum frowns, then narrows her eyes at her. 'Not my fault, this time, I promise. I confirmed with the florist yesterday—*in English*.'

'Right, well, we'll just have to make one.'

'That's what we were saying,' says Jaelee, earning herself a pointed Karen Parsons look. 'So … yeah, um. Not *my* area …' She says, petering off under Mum's withering stare.

'Good thing I know what to do,' says Mum. 'Sarah, do you know where your father put that string he was using to hang the fairy lights?'

'Um, yes! Be right back.' It is a little more complicated than that, as I need to find Bianca to get the key for the storeroom. By the time I return to Mum and Jaelee, they have all the flowers laid out along the bar and are starting to fill the large pickling bottles Bianca has loaned us. They are laughing about something and I'm relieved that Jaelee is back in Mum's good books. It will make the day go much smoother if the two divas aren't at odds. Don't tell them I said that.

'Sarah, you and Jaelee keep working on the table arrangements and I'll start on the bouquet.' 'Table arrangements' is a little high-brow for posies in pickling bottles that will sit atop wine barrels, but okay.

We are elbows-deep in flowers when Josh makes an appearance, bearing a tray with three mugs—tea for me and Mum and coffee for Jaelee—and a plate of biscotti. 'Afternoon tea,' he calls out as he approaches.

'Perfect timing, babe,' I say, snagging the piece of biscotti with the most almonds.

He places the tray on the makeshift bar and scans the space. 'Wow, you guys have done a great job.' Jaelee looks up from her arrangement and flashes Josh a double-dimpled smile.

'And voila,' says Mum, holding aloft the bridal bouquet.

'Oh, Mum, that is beautiful.' For flowers, we went mostly with cabbage roses and greenery, and Mum has created a stunning bouquet in an array of peachy pinks.

She regards her work. 'Do you think Catherine will like it?' she asks.

'Yes, Mum, she'll love it.' She will—it's perfect for her rustic but refined wedding.

'Good. Right, now I just need to do the arrangement for the ceremony and anything left over can find a home in one of the smaller arrangements.' She lays the bouquet on the bar and starts selecting the tallest blooms for the ceremony arrangement, even though I didn't know until now that we needed one of those. Still, she's happy being needed and busy—a trait I have most definitely inherited from her—and with Jaelee starting to situate the finished arrangements around the space, I can take a quiet moment with Josh.

I hold my tea with one hand and his arm with the other and pull him towards the large 'window'—essentially an opening in the wall that looks out over the valley. 'Pretty huh?' I ask rhetorically.

'Oh definitely. Beautiful, actually.' When I look up at him, he's watching me, his compliment directed at me, not the view.

I bump him with my hip. 'Don't. I'm all dusty.'

He leans down and whispers in my ear. 'And sexy as hell.' This time when I peer at him, he has an eyebrow raised. 'Any chance we can sneak away for a bit before I head over to the resort?' He and Jean-Luc are getting ready at the resort where Mum and Dad are staying—they got Cat and Jean-Luc a room there for their wedding night.

'I don't think—'

'Cake's here!' shouts Jaelee, startling me. Some of the tea sloshes onto my hand and I flick it off, annoyed. I look over and she's holding out her phone, so the baker must have called.

'See you at the wedding,' says Josh quietly. He leans down for a quick kiss.

'Did you hear me?' asks Jaelee.

Josh smirks, his eyebrows raised, and leaves while I return to Jaelee and Mum. 'I think they heard you in Florence, dear,' says Mum, her eyes firmly fixed on the floral arrangement.

It would be easy to pile on but not wanting to stir the pot, I reply, 'Let's go down and meet them,' adding a cheery smile.

'Are you sure this is what Cat wanted?' I ask, eyeing the 'cake' curiously. The baker was lovely—not a word of English—but all smiles and Jaelee managed to understand 'refrigerate' before he drove away leaving me holding an enormous white box. We've brought it into the apartment and it's now opened on the small kitchen table. It's beautiful, but it's not exactly a cake—more like a stack of flaky pastry sheets with custard, cream, and fruit in between.

'*You* said that she wanted a traditional Italian wedding cake. This is what's considered traditional here in Tuscany. It's called a *millefoglie*.' I am *extremely* sceptical that this is what Cat meant.

'Hey, Sez,' says Cat from the doorway to the kitchen. I flip the lip on the cake box closed.

'Heyyy,' I say enthusiastically, 'what's up?'

She looks at me oddly. 'Why are you being weird? Oh, is that the cake?' She enters the kitchen as I place a flat palm on the lid of the box.

'It is, but it's bad luck to see the cake before the wedding.' Jaelee tuts. I deserve it. I've essentially pulled a wedding superstition out of my bum.

Cat gives me the odd look again. 'What? No, it isn't. Let me see.' She steps past me and lifts the lid of the box. All the air is sucked out of the room as my sister gasps. Cat eyes the 'cake' and Jaelee and I eye other. It's the first time I've seen even the slightest hint of panic in those brown eyes.

'It's …' A thousand years roll by. '… absolutely stunning.'

Jaelee and I expel sighs of relief and Cat tears her eyes

from the 'cake' and looks between us, then laughs. 'Did you think I wouldn't like it?'

'Sarah did.'

'You dag,' says Cat. 'It's exactly what I wanted.' She tuts at me and I'm too relieved to care that I'm the butt of the joke.

'We'd better get it in the fridge though,' says Jaelee. She lifts it carefully and I hold open the door as she slides it onto the middle shelf.

'Oh!' I look at Jaelee, panicked. 'What are we gonna put it on?' I ask. 'We can't serve it out of the box.' Or can we?

'This.' She crosses the short distance to the other side of the kitchen and holds up an ornate ceramic platter. It's large enough, though I'm not sure what farmers working the fields have to do with a wedding. Hmm, I suppose all but one horse will be covered by the 'cake'.

'Perfect,' says Cat, putting things into perspective. 'Now can I borrow you?' she says to me.

'Oh, right, yes. What's up?'

'My hair—well, maybe—that's what I wanted to get your thoughts on. Up or down?'

'Up, definitely,' I say right as Jaelee says, 'Down.'

Cat's eyes flick between us. 'Sorry, Jae,' she says. 'You're outnumbered. I'm going with up.'

'Then why did you ask?'

Cat shrugs. 'Just getting a sense check. Right, off to wash my hair.' She leaves and I notice a flicker of sourness cross Jaelee's face. She's probably used to her opinions having more sway.

'So, what time are the caterers coming?' I ask, trying to lighten the mood—well, *her* mood.

'Four. Let's finish with the flowers, then I'll head back to the Airbnb to get ready.'

'Sarah! Sarah!' Mum's voice rings out frantically. I pull the front door to the apartment shut with a bang and Jaelee and I rush to the staircase that leads to the loft. My parents are halfway up, Dad grimacing in pain and Mum looking stricken. 'There you are. I've been calling you for ages.'

'Sorry, Mum,' I say as I clamber up the steep stairs. 'Dad, what happened? Are you okay?'

'He's clearly not, Sarah.' Mum gets extra pissy when she's worried. 'He's twisted his ankle.'

'I'll get some ice,' Jaelee says.

'What happened?' I ask.

'Oh, you know, love. Just walking up the stairs, tripped and slid down several steps, then tried to right myself.'

I'm trying to remember my first aid—should we be taking his shoe off or leaving it on? 'Well, *do* something,' says Mum frantically. Karen Parsons—cool in a crisis except when that crisis is a hurt hubby. How to help someone with a twisted ankle suddenly pops into my head.

'Right, Dad, we're going to need to get you down into the apartment so we can take off your shoe and elevate your foot.'

'I've brought ice,' says Jaelee, breathless, from behind me.

'Great, ta. Bring it with you, 'cause we're going back to the apartment. Come on, Dad, I'll help you stand.' It's an awkward manoeuvre on a thousand-year-old staircase (okay, it may not be *that* old) but Mum and I help Dad up. We take it slow so we don't end up down the bottom, the three of us in a heap, and Jaelee goes on ahead to open the door for us.

Minutes later, Dad's shoe is off, his foot is resting on a chair, and I'm strapping it with a bandage from my first aid kit. When I've finished wrapping his ankle, I secure the bandage with a clip and rest Jaelee's homemade icepack on the injured joint.

'Here, darling,' says Mum, handing him two ibuprofen and a bottle of water.

'Thanks, love.'

Just then, Cat comes into the kitchen, wearing a bathrobe, her hair wrapped up in a towel. 'Oh, my god, Dad. What happened? Are you okay?'

Dad laughs in that self-deprecating way he has. 'Just a little tumble, love. Should be right soon.' He shifts slightly, then winces.

'If it's not broken,' says Jaelee. All heads swivel in her direction and she retorts defensively with, 'I'm just saying.'

'She's right,' says Mum. Jaelee is only voicing what the rest of us must be thinking, but it's a Saturday, only a few hours before Cat's wedding, and I'm sure that none of us want to head to the nearest emergency room.

'What about Anders?' says Cat. 'He could come and have a look, see if he thinks it's broken.'

'Isn't he a vet?' asks Jaelee.

'As in a veterinarian?' asks Mum, incredulous.

'Well, yes, but he's the closest we've got to a doctor. If he thinks it's just a sprain, then …' Cat trails off then looks to me for support.

'I think it's a good idea.' I'm not a hundred per cent on board, but there's a time crunch and if we can avoid a trip to hospital then it's worth a shot.

'He's on his way,' says Jaelee, tapping her phone to end a call. Wow, she works fast.

'All right,' says Mum, seemingly relieved. 'Jaelee, let's you and I finish in the loft. Sarah, you stay here with your father. Catherine, you … you go back to being a bride.' I'm not sure why Mum doesn't want to stay here with Dad while we wait for Anders, but maybe it's because it'll be too stressful for her and she needs to keep busy. She and Jaelee leave.

Cat gives Dad a kiss on the cheek. 'I hope you're okay, Daddy,' she says to him quietly.

'I'm sure it's nothing love,' he says reassuringly, flashing a hopeful smile. Cat doesn't say anything more but throws a look of concern my way as she departs the kitchen. I press my lips together—no use reassuring her when I have no idea how bad it is.

'Can I get you something, Dad?' I ask when it's just the two of us. 'Cup of tea?'

'A nip of Scotch would be great,' he jokes.

'Not sure we have any of that. And if you *do* need to go to hospital, then …'

'You're right love.' He blows out a heavy sigh. 'A cup of tea would be great.' I turn on the kettle and take out a mug and a teabag, then decide I'll have one too and grab a second mug. 'I feel like a right idiot,' says Dad.

'What? No, Dad, it was just an accident.'

'Yeah, but on my daughter's wedding day and I'm supposed to walk her down the aisle …'

'Even if you're on crutches, Dad, the aisle's only ten feet long. It'll be okay.'

The kettle boils and I pour water over the teabags, then

look over at Dad. 'How are you feeling? The ibuprofen kicking in yet?'

'Oh, yes, definitely.' I'm not sure I believe him. I think he's putting on a brave face—that or something else is up. I finish making the tea—strong and milky, no sugar, the way we both take it—and set the mugs on the table.

'Thank you, love.'

'Of course.' He takes his and we sip in silence. If something *is* up with Dad, keeping quiet is the best way to get it out of him.

'You know,' he says after a minute or two, 'sometimes it hits me—the ageing thing.' See?

'How do you mean?'

'Like falling today. I'm not as steady on my feet as I once was and I can't do as much either. I mean, I *can*—I can spend a whole day in the backyard or the shed working on a project—but I'll be feeling it for days to come. The body isn't what it used to be, that's for sure. And my spatial aware-ness has gone to shit—always bumping into things.'

'More so than usual?' If I inherited my predilection for organisation from Mum, then my clumsiness comes from Dad. 'If that's a sign of ageing, I must be ancient.'

He chuckles softly. 'What was it that we used to say? That you were a ...'

'Disaster waiting to happen,' I say, finishing the thought with him.

'Still,' he says, smiling warmly at me, 'it's better than the alternative.'

'What is?'

'Getting older.'

'What's the alternative?'

'What do ya reckon?' Oh, he means death.

'Oh, yeah, definitely.'

'And how are you?' he asks, seemingly a non sequitur.

'Me? I'm fine. Why? What do you mean?'

His eyes narrow slightly and his expression softens. 'Daughter number one, I know you and Cat think I'm one of those oblivious dads who has no idea what's going on, but I'm not. And something is up with you.'

'I was just thinking the same about you—before you told me about the ageing stuff,' I say with a smile.

'See? Another thing you get from me—we're both open books.'

'Yeah.'

'So, what's going on in your book?' he prods.

'Oh, you know, freaking out about turning forty, a general feeling of restlessness—the usual.'

He frowns. 'Forty isn't an age to freak out about, love.'

'So everyone keeps telling me.'

'It isn't. Today aside—and okay, the odd day here and there—most of the time I don't *feel* old and I'm close to seventy.'

'You're sixty-six, Dad.'

'That's what I said—close to seventy.' I roll my eyes. 'Hey, it's two years closer to seventy than it is to sixty.'

'Okay, I'll give you that. Continue.'

'But they're all just numbers, love. We're here, we live—and none of us know for how long—then we're not here. Life's both short and long. Short enough that you can't faff about waiting for it to begin and long enough that you can always start fresh, make a different decision, do something else. Is that what's going on with you? You want to make a big change?'

'No … no, it's not that. I love my life. I love Josh, my

232

friends, you all——my *job*. I love all the little things that make up my life. I don't want to *change* it as such … I just … I just feel like there's something missing, something I haven't done yet, and any time I get close to figuring out what it is … I can't quite …'

'It's not kids, is it?' he asks. 'Have you changed your mind?'

'No. Cat asked me the same thing.'

'Right, well, it's a logical question, I suppose.'

'For someone my age.'

'Yes,' he says. *And* we're back on the 'forty' thing again. We both sip more tea, each contemplating my not-quite-a-dilemma.

After a while, Dad says, 'You know what your Grandma Joan used to say …' Grandma Joan was Dad's mum, the one who gave her pearls to Cat. She died after a long illness when Cat and I were in our early twenties. Even though we knew it was coming, it was absolutely devastating because we loved our grandmother fiercely. She was tiny——only four-foot-eleven——but had a huge heart and even after living in Australia for more than forty years, she still had a broad Yorkshire accent. Grandma is the reason I began my love affair with tea——or 'a proper brew' as she'd call it——at the precocious age of seven.

'I remember a lot of things Grandma used to say. I still hear her voice in my head telling me, "There's no sense in worrying about things that haven't happened yet",' I say with my (appalling) Yorkshire accent. Dad chuckles again. 'That the one you mean?'

'Well, no. I mean, yes, that's always good to remember, but I meant the one about getting out of your own way——that when you're tying yourself up in knots, to stop wallowing and lift your head.'

'Oh, that's a good one.'

'My mum was a wise woman.'

'I miss Grandma.'

'I do too, love.'

We're quiet again, then I break the silence with. 'Okay, back to me now. How the hell do I get out of my own way?'

He chuckles softly, then says, 'You know something you used to talk about all the time, but I haven't heard you mention in years?' I wrack my brain and come up empty. 'You wanted to go to Africa——to teach.'

'Oh, my god, you're right.' My mind starts somersaulting, thoughts zipping around and connecting and it suddenly hits me. The letter I wrote to myself when I was a teenager, this obsession that something's missing from my life, the dread of hitting a milestone that, like Dad said, is just a number, an arbitrary marker of time. 'Aunty Tessa's school,' I say quietly. How had I forgotten? I hadn't just wanted to follow in her footsteps as an adventurer——I'd wanted to go to Africa and teach in her school!

Maybe I'd hidden it from myself, that long ago promise I'd made, because of how painful it is to think of her incredible life cut so short. Dad must be feeling it too, as his eyes gloss with unshed tears. 'Sorry, Dad,' I say, leaning over to grab his hand.

'It's all right love. Another one gone but in no way forgotten. In any case, have a think about it. Maybe that's your missing piece.' Not only my missing piece, but it's quite likely the reason that the number itself feels so … *hefty*. Forty is only three years off the age Tessa was when she died.

I get up and wrap my arms tightly around my Dad and he pats my back gently. 'Thanks, Dad. I love you.'

'I love you, too, daughter number one. And you know you can always come to me when you're on the horns of a dead llama.'

His deliberate malapropism does the trick and gets me laughing just as a booming Canadian voice calls out, 'Hello?' I release Dad from the hug and go to meet Anders at the front door.

Chapter Eighteen

CAT

Tuscany

Anders' visit has revealed two things. First, before he was a veterinarian, he was a paramedic and I cannot exaggerate how much that little nugget of information set Mum at ease. Her expression practically screamed, 'Hooray, he's had medical training—for humans!' Then she fawned over him, offering him everything from a cup of tea to her third born. Thank god I snuck in at number two.

The second thing is that he doesn't think Dad has broken his ankle, or any part of his foot. He has checked Dad for concussion, re-done Sarah's strapping, and says to stay off it as much as possible and that if the pain gets worse, not better, then we should get an X-ray tomorrow, just in case.

'I think you're all set,' he says to Dad, rising to his full 'mountain man' height. Lou, who has watched on adoringly, gazes up at him, love and pride radiating from her face.

'We really can't thank you enough, Anders. I don't know

what we would have done if we didn't have a medical professional in the family,' says Mum. See? She's only known him five minutes and now he's part of the family.

'Honestly, it was nothing, Mrs Parsons. Just happy to be of assistance.' Hang on, is Mum *blushing*?

'Oh, none of that "Mrs" nonsense. I'm just Karen.' Just Karen?! I chance a glance at Sarah even though I'm very close to laughing and this may send me over the edge. Yup. Her lips have all but disappeared between her teeth and her eyes are wide, telegraphing, 'OMG, MUM!' I stifle a snigger and Dad taps my leg with the back of his hand. All three of us are in on it now.

'Well, we should get going, let you all get ready,' says Lou.

'See you at five,' adds Anders.

Mum sees them out and I can't hold it any longer. I start shaking with laughter and soon Sarah has joined in. 'Girls,' stage whispers Dad, 'stop it.' But that just makes us laugh even more.

'What's so funny?' says Mum, now back in the kitchen.

'Er, nothing, Mum,' says Sarah. 'So, is there much more to do upstairs?' she asks.

'All done. Jaelee has gone back to her accommodation to get ready. She said you're to meet the caterer at four and show them where to set up.'

'Roger that,' says Sarah earning her a tut.

'Ronald, we should go.'

'Right. Of course, love.' He flattens both hands on the table and pushes himself to standing.

'How is it, Dad?' I ask as he carefully transfers his weight to his left foot.

He nods, a small frown on his face. 'It's not too bad.'

'Well, here, let me help you out to the car,' says Mum.

Sarah and I make room so they can shuffle out of the kitchen, into the hallway, then out the front door. We stand on the gravel watching Mum get Dad situated in the car, Sarah in a set of dusty workout clothes and me in my dressing gown.

'Well, don't stand out here in your dressing gown, Catherine. Good god,' says Mum as she rounds the front of the car to the driver's side.

'Bye, Mum,' I say, ignoring her. 'See you in a couple of hours.'

'Smile and wave,' says my sister to me quietly. 'Just smile and wave.' We do and they go and then it's just me and Sarah.

'Right,' she says, 'shower for me, then let's get you fully bridal.'

'I'm getting married today,' I say, suddenly struck by how surreal it feels.

'Yes, you are, little sis, and it is going to be magical.' She hooks her arm in mine and we go back inside.

'Okay, you can look now.' Sarah has always been a dab hand at makeup. I'm pretty good at it but she's next level so she was the obvious choice for doing my bridal makeup. I swivel on the stool to face the mirror above the dressing table and peer at my reflection.

'Oh, my god, my skin looks like porcelain!'

She chuckles next to me, well chuffed with herself. 'Well, I had a good canvas, and *this*,' she says holding up her favourite 'blur' product.

'You've done a beautiful job, Sez, thank you.' My makeup is subtle and natural-looking, bringing out my hazel eyes and highlighting the apples of my cheeks. My lips are a velvety rose and no doubt I will need to reapply a dozen times, but I *love* the colour choice.

'You're welcome, sis.' Her eyes flick to her phone resting on the dressing table. 'I'll quickly do my makeup, you do your hair, then you can help me with mine.' Sarah's the makeup aficionado, but I'm the hair guru so I'm DIY-ing.

Just then, there's a knock at the door. 'Caterers,' we say together and Sarah goes to let them in. Only it's not them.

'Hi, we couldn't wait, so we're early.'

'Well, *Lou* couldn't wait …'

'Hey!' she says to Jaelee.

'In here,' I call out. An instant later, my bus besties appear in the doorway, each looking extra glam in their own special way. Lou is wearing a flowing maxi dress in a soft peach, her blonde bob in beachy waves, and Jae is wearing a cocktail dress in fuchsia, her hair a pin-straight sheet of black down her back.

'*Hiii!*' drawls Lou, crossing the room and leaning down to envelop me in a massive hug.

'Hi, lovely,' I reply, my voice muffled by her shoulder.

'I know we're, like, *way* early but I got so excited.' She steps back and peers down at me. 'Wow, you look *super* pretty,' she says.

'Sarah—genius with a makeup brush.'

'On that …' says Sarah who's lingering in the doorway.

'Go,' I say, waving her away.

'I thought you'd be dressed by now,' says Jae.

'It's only four.' She shrugs.

'No, no, no—everyone will wait for the bride,' says Lou.

'Besides, you don't want to sit around in your wedding dress—you put it on at the very last minute.' As she's the only one here who's actually been married, I'll be taking her advice.

'Now, what did you decide for your hair?' she asks.

'Up. Actually, I was just about to——' I'm interrupted by another knock at the door. 'Now, *that* must be the caterers.'

Jaelee leaps up. 'I'll handle it,' she says. 'I've got it, Sarah,' she calls out down the hallway.

'Okay,' Sarah calls back.

The chatter of voices echoes down the hallway and just as I'm about to start on my up-do, Jae appears at the bedroom door holding a gold giftbox with a red bow on top. 'This is for you,' she says, crossing to deposit it on the dressing table.

'Oh, thank you. So, it wasn't the caterers?'

'Oh no, they're here too. I'm gonna go supervise.' She closes the bedroom door behind her, leaving me and Lou in relative quiet, the sounds of muffled voices and foot traffic receding into the background. I open the small white envelop affixed to the box—a bottle of my favourite champagne—and slide out the card.

So sorry I can't be there. Happy wedding day! Lots of love to you both, Mich xoxoxo

'Aww, that's so sweet,' says Lou, reading over my shoulder. It *is* sweet—it also makes me miss Mich even more. I so wish she could be here.

'Mich is one of my besties,' I say, leaning the card against the box.

'I remember you saying. She teaches at the same school as you, right?'

'Yes—she's my partner in crime.'

'Okay, I'm intrigued.'

'Well,' I say with a smile, 'she's very clever and an excellent teacher, but she's also extremely naughty.' Lou grins. 'For instance, in our staff meetings—which are *so* deathly dull, they could practically put you into a coma—we pretend to "take notes" but, really, we're writing to each other—whole conversations without saying a word. The hardest thing is not to laugh, which Mich is very good at and I'm terrible at, so she's constantly getting me into trouble.'

'How come she's not here?'

'She had hoped to come—although that meant flying into Florence last night and flying back out again tomorrow, which she was totally willing to do, but her mum's not been well lately and now she's in hospital. Mich didn't want to leave London … just in case …' I'm unable to say the rest of the thought aloud.

'Oh, I'm so sorry to hear that.'

'Me too, and no matter how much I wish she were here, I'm glad she's with her mum.'

'Mmm, for sure.' We're both quiet for a moment, me thinking how fortunate I am that my parents are in good health—*and* here with me—but the mood has turned gloomy and I'm getting married in an hour. Lou must sense that a change of subject is needed because she claps her hands together and says, 'So, are you getting excited?'

'Absolutely,' I say, taking her cue to move on from unhappy thoughts. 'I get to *marry* Jean-Luc today!'

'I'm so excited for you, Cat. And to think, I was there are

the beginning—well, not the *beginning* beginning, but the second beginning, the Paris one.'

'You were a very important part of that, Lou. You even captured our first kiss.' Lou had snuck a photograph of us kissing after our date in Rome.

She shakes her head. 'I still don't know whether to be proud of that or embarrassed.'

'No! I love that you did that.' I place both hands over my heart. 'Was it a little creepy? Who's to say?'

'Yeah, yeah …' We dissolve into laughter.

'Right—now, my hair.' I stand and turn my head upside down, gathering my tresses loosely in one hand.

'Oh, I'm distracting you. I'll go help Jaelee.'

'You're not distracting me,' I say, upside-down. 'I like having you here.' I right myself, then sit and take a hair tie from the dressing table to secure my loose ponytail. I look at Lou in the mirror. 'Is it weird that mixed in with the excitement is this odd sort-of nervous surrealness?'

'Nope. Totally normal. At least, it was for me when I married Jackson.' Bugger, we've gone from ailing parents to ex-husbands.

'Sorry, Lou, we don't have to talk about—'

'I don't mind, honestly. We were happy together back then so those are good memories. Just know, it's going to be a blur. Before you know it, the guests will be leaving and you and Jean-Luc will collapse into bed exhausted. So savour it as much as you can. Try to remember the little moments.'

'Thank you, Lou. I will.' I tilt my head to the side. 'You know, I've heard that before—the "no sex on the wedding night" thing, but it's *Jean-Luc*, Lou, and he's so sex—'

'La la la,' she cries out, clapping her hands over her ears.

I laugh. 'All right, I won't say anything more.' She drops

her hands and I go back to my hair, pinning locks from my ponytail into a pile of loose waves.

'I will say this, though,' she says, 'my wedding day started at six in the morning, so that may have had something to do with it.'

'Six?'

'Yeah. There was me, my mum, three bridesmaids, a flower girl, and Jackson's mum all getting ready at my parents' house and we had to be at the church by eleven, so the hair and makeup people arrived at six-thirty. Then after the ceremony, it was the photos in the park, then the reception—and that went for *hours*. So, by the time we got to the hotel that night, I'd been in wedding mode for, like, fifteen hours.'

'No wonder sex was the last thing on your mind.'

'Right?' She pauses, then adds, 'We made up for it the next morning though.' She bursts out laughing.

'Lou!' It's the most lascivious comment I've ever heard her make and now I'm again laughing.

There's a sharp double tap on the bedroom door, then Jaelee walks in. 'Food's under control.' She plops down on the bed.

'Thank you, Jae.'

'No problem. And, by the way, you're gonna *love* the menu.'

'I have no doubt.' I take a dab of styling product, rub it between my palms, and start pulling tendrils from my up-do to frame my face.

'Especially, 'cause you raved about the food when we went there for dinner,' she adds casually.

'Wait, what?' I spin around to face her. 'That place with the risotto in the parmesan wheel?'

'Yep, and speaking of the risotto, guess what one of the dishes is?'

'Are you being serious?'

'Yep.'

'But I thought you booked the caterer ages ago.'

'I did. But I also wanted to check it out before the wedding. If the restaurant sucked, I would have found some-place else. You've gotta have great food at your *wedding*.'

'True,' I reply. 'Thank you, *really*.' She shrugs—all part of the (free) service, I suppose. 'And neither of you tell Jean-Luc this, but I am *so* looking forward to that risotto.'

Jaelee smirks. 'Not the dancing or the cake?'

'Or the *vows*?' asks Lou.

'Actually, those too. And the prosecco!' Jae's dimples flash and Lou tuts and shakes her head. I turn back towards the mirror and lift a hand mirror to see the back of my hair.

Jaelee leaps up. 'Here, there's just one …' She smooths out some of the hair between my nape and the hair tie, then reaches around me to grab a hairpin, which she secures. She looks at me in the mirror and rests her hands on my shoulders. 'Perfect.'

'Thank you.'

'Right. Thirty minutes and counting,' she says, back in wedding planner mode. 'I'm guessing you don't need help with your lingerie so …'

'No, been doing that by myself since I was three.'

'And Sarah's helping you with the dress?' asks Lou.

'That's right.'

'Well, then that's our cue,' says Jae. 'Next time we see you, you'll be walking down the aisle.' My stomach flutters with nerves at her words and I remember what Lou said—to savour every moment. I wonder if she meant savouring the nervousness as well.

They leave, Lou throwing a proud Mama Lou look over her shoulder on the way out, and soon I am alone again, the bride to be.

I start adorning myself with jewellery, each piece with its own significance. A simple gold bracelet my parents gave me when I graduated from university, diamanté drop earrings—a find from Camden Market bought especially for today—and Grandma's pearls. That's my something old, something new, and something borrowed ... what's my something blue? Hmm. I'm not typically a superstitious person, but something blue wouldn't go amiss right now. Maybe it would quell these rising nerves. I cast my eyes about the room as though the perfect blue item will pop and say hello. Just then, the door opens and Sarah peeks in. 'Hey,' she says.

'Hello.' She merges into the room, fully dressed and looking divine. 'Wowser, you look incredible.'

'Thank you.' She does a little shoulder shimmy then spins.

I stand. 'No, I mean it. That dress was pretty on the hanger, but ... I have no other words.' It's a tea-length dress in rose-gold silk chiffon, nipped at the waist, with a wide bateau neckline and capped sleeves, and she's towering over me in three-inch rose-gold sandals. Sarah grins at me. 'Oh, you wanted me to put your hair up,' I say. 'We still have time.'

'We don't really—besides, it's not often my curls behave themselves and I was thinking I would wear it down. What do ya reckon?'

'I reckon,' I say, bunging on my Aussie accent, 'that I loike it, I loike it a lot.'

'It's different, I loike it,' she retorts, and we spend a good thirty seconds in 'Kath and Kim' mode, nodding at each other and making faces like total dags.

'Okay, enough of that,' she says, suddenly all business. 'Let's get you into this dress.'

'Right.' I whip off my dressing gown.

'Jesus. I didn't realise I'd get dinner and a show!'

'Don't be a prude, Sarah. They're just boobs.' I take out the uplift bra that matches the seamless knickers I'm wearing, do up the clasp, and slip the straps over my shoulders.

'Wow, your boobs look great in that.'

'Um, hello, I know. That's why I'm putting up with the fact that it feels like a vice.'

'Ready?' she says, taking my dress off the hanger. 'Arms up or step in?'

'Step in, I think.'

'Right. Hang on.' She takes the duvet off the bed and lays it on the floor, then carefully drapes the dress on top so I can step into it. I do and she pulls it up to my chest. 'Hold it against you and I'll do up the buttons.' The dress is secured by two dozen tiny pearl buttons and I'm a little impatient with how long it's taking to do them up. If we *don't* have sex tonight, it will only be because of all these buttons! I imagine myself asleep, still wearing my dress, and laugh.

'What's so funny?' Sarah asks.

'Just thinking that Jean-Luc had better not drink too much tonight or I'm going to be stuck in this thing till morning.'

'Hah! Hilarious. Like that time Jane Fonda went to that awards ceremony but couldn't get out of her dress by herself. Remember? She posted a photo of herself wearing it at breakfast the next morning.'

'Maybe you should come with us to the resort after the wedding.'

'Uh, yeah, I'm not doing that. You and Jean-Luc are gonna have to figure that one out on your own. All done.' She pats my shoulders then slowly turns me around and looks me up and down. 'Talk about wowser.'

'Really?'

'Come on, Cat, you know you look great in this dress. Right, now, shoes.' She crosses the room and retrieves my Jimmy Choos, then kneels and helps me step into them and does up the buckles. 'Okay, *now* you're done.' She stands then takes a step back and gazes at me. 'You really do look amazing, Cat.'

'I wish there was a full-length mirror in here.'

'Oh, duh, I'm such an idiot—there's one on the back of our bedroom door. Come on.'

She's out our bedroom door in a shot and I follow, the clack of our heels on the tile floor reverberating through the apartment. I peek in at the caterers as we pass the kitchen and they are buzzing about. The older woman shoots me a smile and a nod of approval, which I graciously accept with a shrug of my shoulders. I step into Sarah and Josh's room and when she closes the door, I finally get to see my full bridal self—dress, shoes, and jewellery on, and hair and makeup done.

'Oh,' I say. It's both me and a sexy-princess version of me, a version I've never seen before.

'Told ya.' We lock eyes in the mirror and exchange smiles.

'I'm so glad you're here, Sez. I wouldn't want to do this with anyone else by my side.'

'I'd give you a big hug, but we're both kind of fragile right now,' she says, her eyes slick with unshed tears.

'Literally and figuratively,' I say softly.

'Yeah.'

I suddenly remember that one niggling detail. 'Oh, I meant to ask,' I say, turning towards her, 'any chance you have something blue? That's the only thing I'm missing.'

'Something … *oh*, the something *blue*. Um …' She looks about her room the same way I'd looked about mine a little while ago. 'Actually … wait here a sec.' She disappears into her en suite and returns holding up a bottle of blue nail polish. 'What about this?'

'Umm …'

'Well, we don't have to do all your nails—we could do like in *Drop Dead Diva*—you know, where she just paints her pinkie nail for good luck.' I screw up my nose. 'Sorry, I haven't really got a better idea.'

I press my lips together. 'Ah, fuck it, let's do it.'

'Really?'

'Do it before I talk myself out of it.'

Sarah leads me over to her dressing table and places my hand flat on the surface—an extreme care measure—then paints my right pinkie nail blue before doing her own. 'Now we're the blue pinkie sisters,' she says holding up her finger.

Just then the front door opens. 'Sarah,' Josh calls out.

'In here.'

'Just you, though. I'm already in my dress,' I say loudly.

Josh's head pokes into the room. 'Hi, it's just me.'

Sarah beams at him. 'Hi, babe. Come on in.' He does, going straight to Sarah. 'Wow, you look amazing.'

'*You* look amazing.' He presses his lips lightly to hers,

leaving her lipstick intact. '*Both* of you look amazing,' he adds.

'Why thank you, brother dear,' I say.

'Are Mum and Dad here yet?' asks Sarah.

'Soon. They were right behind us when we left the resort. I'm gonna head up to the loft—keep the nervous groom company—and I guess we'll see you up there.'

'Wait, is he really nervous?' I ask, feeling a surge of my own nerves coursing through me.

'The good kind,' he says gently. 'Excited nerves.'

'Are you sure?' And are my nerves the 'good kind' or abject terror?

Josh grabs both my hands in his. 'Positive. He's excited, that's all. No cold feet. Just can't wait to marry you. Okay?' I nod. 'And you really do look beautiful, Cat,' he says. He drops a featherlight kiss on my cheek, pats me on the arm, and departs with a wink at Sarah, making her all swoony.

'He's a good egg, is your Josh,' I say.

'I know,' she says with a sigh.

I glance at the clock—ten minutes to five—and expel a long slow breath.

'Girls?' Mum calls from the front door.

'In here!' shouts Sarah.

Mum comes into the room, stopping short as she catches sight of us. 'Oh, girls ... oh my ...' She presses her lips together, looking like she might cry at any second. 'Ronald, Ronald come quickly and see.' Sarah and I share an 'aww, bless' look.

'Coming, love.' Dad hobbles into the room and, like Mum, stops short when he sees us. 'Well, isn't that a sight to behold? Look at my beautiful girls.' All right, now *I'm* dangerously close to tears—but I won't cry because I don't want to mess up Sarah's painstakingly applied makeup. 'Karen, you get in there with the girls, let me take a picture.'

He takes his phone from his suit pocket and Mum steps between us and we wrap our arms around each other and Dad takes a thousand photographs before Sarah says, 'Okay, Dad, now let me get some with you, Mum, and Cat.'

Dad brushes a tear from under his eye and smiles. Sarah uses her phone for the photographs, something I'm grateful for as hers is the latest model and I think the last time Dad upgraded his, Obama was in office.

It's only as Dad steps into place that I realise he's wearing sandals—well, 'mandals' as Sarah calls them—man sandals, those ones like Fred Flintstone wears. It's not that I mind—certainly understandable considering he must be in a lot of pain, but I'm shocked that Mum allowed him outside their room like that.

'Just try not to get your father's sandals in the photo, Sarah,' says Mum. *Right on cue*, I think. We smile, Sarah takes the photographs, and then it's time.

It's time for us to go to my wedding.

'Right, do you have everything, love?' asks Dad.

Sarah lifts her satin clutch—also in rose gold—and says, 'Maid of Honour kit.'

'Oh, the bouquet!' says Mum, disappearing down the hallway. 'I left it in the kitchen,' she calls out. She soon returns holding a stunning bouquet of roses and greenery. 'Here you are, darling.'

'Oh, Mum. It's beautiful. And Sarah said you made it.'

'Well, those floristry classes had to pay off some time,' she says modestly. Sometimes, she surprises me.

'I love it, thank you.'

'Right, so Sarah, you and your mum will go first and we'll bring up the rear.'

'Okay, Dad.' Sarah reaches for Mum's hand.

'Good god, Sarah, do you have one blue fingernail?'

'Yep, and so does Cat.' Mum frowns at me over her shoulder and huffs out a sigh. And sometimes Mum doesn't surprise me in the least.

We're just outside the front door, me walking Dad more so than the other way around, and I notice three latecomers coming up the castle's driveway.

'Oh, you go on ahead, we'll follow,' says Mum, her passive-aggressive politeness telegraphing how impolite she thinks it is to arrive late to a wedding. 'Can't have you arriving after the bride,' she adds for good measure.

As they walk by, Cécile gives me a taut, smug smile, Louis waves sheepishly then quickens his pace, and it only occurs to me after she's passed by, that the third person in their party is Vanessa, Jean-Luc's ex-wife.

'Well, fuck,' I say out loud.

Chapter Nineteen

SARAH

Tuscany

When I spin around, my sister's face is contorted—confusion mixed with fury, is my best guess. 'Cat? You okay?'

'Catherine—*language*,' says Mum.

'Cat?' I ask again. Dad and I exchange worried looks.

'That's …' Cat shakes her head as though she can't believe her eyes. 'That woman—she's Jean-Luc's ex-wife.'

'Vanessa?' I ask unnecessarily. I turn back around and see Cécile, Louis and—OH. MY. GOD!—Jean-Luc's ex-wife disappear up the staircase to the loft. What the actual …? There's no *way* Jean-Luc would have invited her, even if they are on good terms. He knows there's a *big* difference between Cat accepting the occasional lunch date with Vanessa and his ex-wife ATTENDING THEIR WEDDING! This had to be Cécile's doing. That cow.

'Let's go back inside,' I say, taking charge. Mum fumbles her ardent disagreement, indicating that she's just as flummoxed as Cat, and I usher my family inside the apartment and into Cat and Jean-Luc's bedroom. Cat immediately starts pacing, her kitten heels click-clacking loudly.

'Catherine, it's all right, darling, we'll sort this out,' says Mum. Only, how are we going to do that exactly? This isn't one of those enormous weddings where you can bury—so to speak—the exes in the back row. There's barely even a back row!

Cat looks like she's on the verge of tears or about to tear someone's head off. Maybe both. And Dad looks completely helpless. *Think, Sarah,* I tell myself. Jean-Luc must know by now. And his sister has pulled this stunt—he'll have to be the one to fix things.

'I'll be right back,' I say.

'Where are you going?' asks Mum.

'I'm going to talk to the groom.' Cat's eyes lift to mine and it's clear now that she's closer to crying than chucking a tanty. 'Do not cry. You'll ruin your makeup.' Of course, I don't really care about her makeup, but it does the trick and she presses her lips together while blinking back tears. 'Everyone stay put,' I command as I leave. But really, where are they going to go?

I head out the door, along the gravel driveway—as fast as I can because I'm on tiptoes so I don't shred my satin-clad heels—then up the stairs to the loft. At the top, I almost crash into Lou and Jaelee.

'We were just coming to find you,' says Lou. 'Jean-Luc's ex-wife is here.'

'I know,' I say, wincing. 'And so does Cat.'

'Well, fuck,' says Jaelee.

'That's what she said. Wait, how do you know that's Vanessa?' I ask them.

They share a loaded look. 'Cat Facebook stalked her when we were on our trip together,' says Jaelee.

'And you'd never forget a woman who looks like *that*,' adds Lou.

We peek through the archway into the next room and seated right at the back is a Halle Berry look-alike. 'Right,' I say. Cécile whispers something to Vanessa then looks right at me and smiles sweetly. Only it isn't sweet. It's cruel and I'm positive she knows that.

'Which one of us is going to deal with the witchy sister?' asks Lou, her voice an octave lower than usual. 'This *must* be her doing.'

There's a moment of contemplation and I assume, like me, the others are conjuring heinous punishments for 'witchy sister' Cécile. I snap out of my wrathful reverie. 'Okay, we'll deal with her later, but right now I need to talk to Jean-Luc. Where is he?'

'He and Josh are in the room at the end, waiting for my signal,' says Jaelee.

I look through two archways into the furthest room where we've set up for the reception, but I can't see him or Josh. 'So, he doesn't know yet?'

'As soon as we realised, we came to find you.'

'Oh, my god. Okay. I'll go tell him and see what he wants to do.'

I set off, my heeled sandals loud on the ancient wooden floors and as I pass into the next room where all the guests and the celebrant are waiting, their heads turn in unison. Fuck, I hadn't thought that far ahead. 'Uh, hi everyone. Just a little delay. Nothing to worry about. Just, uh … sit back, chillax …' I inwardly roll my eyes at myself—*chillax*? Have we suddenly been transported to 1995? 'Uh … be right with

you.' I don't want to stick around long enough to field questions—this isn't a press conference—but I do catch Lindsey's eye and with a cock of her head she asks if she can do
anything. I shake my head 'no' and continue into the next
room where I run into Josh.

He saves me as I stumble. 'Hey, what's going on?'

I look over at Jean-Luc, who's waiting by the window,
and grab Josh's hand. 'Come with me.'

As I approach him, Jean-Luc's eyes search mine—confusion and worry playing out behind them. 'Is it Catherine?
Her feet are cold?' he asks.

'No, she's madly in love with you and can't wait to marry
you.'

He's visibly relieved for a sec but then a frown appears.
'But what then?' How on EARTH do I tell him that thirty
feet away, his ex-wife is waiting to watch him marry my
sister?

Oh, fuck it, I think. 'Your ex-wife is in the next room.
Cécile brought her.'

His reaction would be comical if this were a movie and
not real life—disbelief tinged with 'ha-ha, very funny'
accompanied by a snort of laughter and then stillness, his
eyes locked on mine, and finally realisation. '*No*,' he says in
an intense whisper.

'Yes.'

'Fuck,' says Josh.

'Yes to that as well.'

Jean-Luc's eyes are roving the floorboards as though they
have the answer to this dilemma. He blows out one of those
French sighs, the ones like a raspberry. 'I will—— I will take
care of this.'

I want to ask how, but he's off before I can form the

word, and Josh and I follow him into the next room. '*Bonsoir*, everyone, *pardon* but we will need just a moment of your patience. Nothing is wrong, but we will commence *bientôt*—as soon as possible.' He smiles, then reaches down and grabs Cécile's hand, tugging on it until she stands.

Vanessa stands too and Jean-Luc pauses then leans across and with a tight smile, kisses her on both cheeks, his expression fraught. He turns and drags Cécile by her hand into the reception room. Josh and I step back to let them pass and Jean-Luc takes her over to the window where they have a hushed but heated conversation in French. I only understand every tenth or twelfth word, but when Cécile shrugs and crosses her arms across her chest, I want to bitch slap her into oblivion. I hadn't known I was capable of such violent thoughts until now.

'*Pardon*,' says a soft voice behind us. I turn and there she is, the Halle Berry look-alike.

'Hello,' I say, a sharp edge to my voice.

'I … I think I will leave,' she says.

'Good idea.'

She recoils as though I've smacked her. 'I … *je suis désolée* … Cécile, she convinced me that …' She pauses, taking a breath. 'I now see that Jean-Luc did not know … this was very stupid.' At least she seems contrite, but I'm not quite ready to let her off the hook.

'And *cruel*. My sister saw you. She knows you're here.'

'*Je comprends*. I am sorry. I will go.' So, the ex-wife is not heinous, just misguided—or gullible. How on earth did Cécile convince her this was a good idea? I thought Vanessa was supposed to be intelligent.

'*Mon chou*,' she calls out—an endearment that's hard to hear—and Jean-Luc looks up from his conversation with

Cécile. He throws his sister a harsh look, then rushes over. He remains silent, a vein pulsing at his jawline. Vanessa rattles off what I am assuming is a heartfelt apology about how stupid she'd been listening to Cécile. Then she leans over and they repeat the rigid cheek kisses and she goes to leave.

Cécile is there in a shot, pulling on her arm and imploring Jean-Luc to stop her from going. '*Non*,' he says to her emphatically and in English he adds, 'I will speak to you later. This is …' he seems to battle to find the word, then '… inexcusable. *Désolé*, Vanessa, but I agree, you must go.'

Vanessa nods then leaves. Like mine earlier, her footsteps echo on the floorboards as every one of the wedding guests watches her departure. I notice that Louis drops his head and shakes it—hopefully he's as appalled by his wife's behaviour as the rest of us. '*Tu es un idiot, petit frère*,' hisses Cécile. Well, I know what that means.

'Hey! Back off,' I say, glaring at her. She scoffs at me.

'Sarah,' says Jean-Luc, placing a hand on my arm.

'*This* is the family you want to marry into,' Cécile says to him.

'Yes. I am proud that they are my family, unlike how I feel about you at the moment.'

Well, that stung. She has no words and her eyes tear up. She swallows heavily as the siblings glare at each other. '*C'est si blessant*,' she says, her voice catching.

Jean-Luc's expression softens slightly. 'Cécile … I love you but I am very angry. And you will need to apologise to Catherine.' She shakes her hair back and lifts her chin, the stubborn cow. 'I mean it, or I will ask you to leave.'

Her eyes narrow, then she snorts out a sigh and swipes at

an errant tear. '*D'accord*,' she says, though I don't believe for a heartbeat that she'll apologise to Cat.

Jean-Luc nods, clearly relieved, then steps past her and with a bright smile, he addresses everyone who is waiting—our friends, the celebrant, and Louis. 'Just one more moment, please. I must go and get the bride.' He jogs across the loft and disappears down the stairs.

Cécile's eyes flick towards mine and I give her my best schoolteacher glare until she scurries away back to her seat.

'Well, that was …' says Josh, placing his hand on my shoulder. I turn and give him a quick hug.

'That *was* …' I tip my head up for a kiss. 'Thank you for not having a shitty family.'

'Thank *you* for not having a shitty family.'

'Right. I've gotta go. I'm back on Maid of Honour duties.' I turn and he lightly slaps my bum. 'Hey,' I say over my shoulder. He winks at me and we grin at each other. Oh, I love that man.

Jaelee and Lou meet me at the top of the stairs. 'That was intense,' says Lou.

'You should have seen it from up close.'

'So, Jean-Luc's gone to get Cat?' asks Jaelee.

'Yeah.'

'But that's bad luck,' says Lou. She looks almost as worried about the bad juju as she did about Vanessa being here for the wedding.

'I think we've already crossed that bridge, Lou,' says Jaelee.

'I guess.'

'Look, I've gotta go, but maybe you could break out the bubbles for everyone … you know, while they wait? And talk to the celebrant?'

'On it,' says Jaelee, leaving me with Lou.

'It's going to be okay,' I say to her.

'Poor Cat.'

'I know. Look I should ...'

'Go—sorry.'

I navigate the steep stairs in my three-inch heels as quickly as I dare, not wanting to be the second member of the family to topple down them. When I get to the bottom, I spy Jean-Luc and Vanessa at the end of the castle's driveway embroiled in what looks like an intense conversation.

'Oh, for fuck's fucking sake.' If I thought the stairs were tough to navigate, how in the hell am I supposed to handle this? That's a hell of a detour you've made, Jean-Luc! I have a thought and do my tiptoe trot back to the apartment. Maybe until we sort this mess out, I should switch to my flipflops. 'Dad!' I call out. He stands as I enter Cat and Jean-Luc's bedroom.

'What is it, love?'

Cat looks on the verge of tears again, so that's my priority—assuaging the bride's fears. 'Vanessa's left. Jean-Luc told Cécile off. Jaelee is pouring bubbles for the guests and this will all be sorted out soon, I promise.'

'All right,' she says feebly.

'Cat. I *promise*, okay?' She nods and Mum watches her worriedly, stroking her hand. 'Dad, can I borrow you for a sec?' I ask.

'Sure, love.' He hobbles over and I lead him out to the stoop.

'Look,' I say softly, indicating the end of the driveway where Vanessa and Jean-Luc are still talking.

'Oh dear.'

A taxi pulls up moments later and Vanessa climbs in.

'Oh, thank god.' When she closes the door and it pulls away, Jean-Luc stares after it, then drops his head and shakes it. 'I think he might need a fatherly pep talk.'

'I think you might be right, love,' Dad says. 'Be right back.'

Dad makes slow progress down the driveway and when he reaches Jean-Luc, he places a hand on his arm and Jean-Luc turns. I can't hear what he's saying, but I've benefitted from one of Dad's pep talks many times over the years—even just today—and it's not long before a smile appears on my brother-in-law's face. They hug—man-style, with back slaps—and start walking back towards me.

'See you up there, son,' says Dad and my heart nearly melts at 'son' as he slips past me and into the apartment.

'Wait, I need to talk to her,' says Jean-Luc.

Now that Vanessa's gone and this wedding is back on track, all I can think of is Lou's warning about 'bad luck'. But this isn't my call. 'Hang on.' I click-clack back to the bedroom. 'Cat, Jean-Luc is at the front door. He wants to talk to you.'

She looks up, her face radiating love. 'Did he really send Vanessa away?'

Well, he did—*after* she made the decision for herself—but I'm not telling Cat that. It will remain a secret till the day I die. 'Yes.'

'And he told Cécile off?'

'Oh, yeah! And he told her he was proud to be joining our family—*and* that she owes you an apology.' Cat's expression sours. 'It's okay. She's not coming anywhere near you without one of us by your side.'

Cat nods then scrunches her nose in contemplation. 'Actually, after all this … I sort of … I want to *arrive* at my wedding—does that make sense? I don't want him to see me in here like this. I just want to be the bride.'

'Totally get it. I'll go tell him.'

I turn to leave. 'But tell him that I love him more than anything and I can't wait to marry him,' she calls out loudly.

'I love you too, *chérie*,' Jean-Luc's voice echoes along the hallway.

'See you upstairs,' she shouts.

'*D'accord, mon amour.*'

'Oh, for god's sake,' I mutter to myself, re-joining Jean-Luc at the front door. 'So, we good?'

He grins then plants a kiss on my cheek. '*Oui.*'

'Well, then get the hell outta here. We'll be five minutes behind you.' He jogs back to the bottom of the staircase to the loft and disappears. I return to the bedroom, where Mum is smoothing down Cat's dress and fussing with her hair.

'Right, you've chewed off all your lipstick, so let's re-apply,' I say, retrieving the tube from my clutch. Cat lifts her chin obediently and stretches her lips wide. In several swoops of colour, she's perfection again.

'So, shall we get this road on the show?' says Dad, another of his favourite malapropisms.

Cat grins at him. 'I'm ready, Daddy.'

We reform our bridal procession of four and head down the hallway past the kitchen, stepping out onto the driveway for take two. I swear to god, if anything else goes wrong, then maybe the universe is trying to tell us something.

Chapter Twenty

CAT

Tuscany

Arriving at my own wedding must be the most surreal, most beautiful moment of my life.

We climb the stairs to the loft slowly, as Dad's ankle is still very sore. Close to the top, strains of Etta James' 'At Last' reach my ears. I'm so glad I chose this song to arrive to. It's not only perfect for Jean-Luc and me, with our love story spanning decades, but with all the hitches this past week, it has even more meaning now.

As Mum and Sarah continue walking towards the assembled guests, Dad pauses at the top of the stairs. 'You ready, love?' he asks quietly.

I nod and smile up at him and he kisses the top of my head, then offers his elbow which I take. Mum and Sarah walk the short aisle, Mum taking her seat in the front row and Sarah standing next to a tall, elegantly dressed man who must be the celebrant. Just out of view, Jean-Luc will be waiting and my heart races at the thought of seeing him, of *marrying* him.

The celebrant signals to our guests that they should stand, and they do, turning around to face us as we cross under the archway into next the room. The beaming smiles that greet us make my heart swell. Jaelee and Alistair——Jae filming our arrival as planned——Lou and Anders, Siobhan, Lindsey and Nick, and Jane. She grins at me and I return it. Even Louis has a smile for me but I don't dare look past him to Cécile. Nothing is going to ruin this moment for me, especially my witchy sister-in-law.

We reach the aisle and my eyes finally meet Jean-Luc's. A gasp escapes——he's so handsome in his charcoal suit and lilac dress shirt, and the warm, golden light of the late afternoon sun spills through the large window, setting him aglow. His hand reaches for his heart and he closes his eyes for a second, as though he's overcome with emotion. I know just how he feels.

Dad and I walk side by side and at the end of the aisle, he kisses my cheek and takes his seat next to Mum. I cross to Jean-Luc and face him and take his outstretched hand. 'My god, Catherine, you are exquisite,' he whispers. Tears prick my eyes and I don't trust my voice enough to reply.

In my periphery, the celebrant signals to the DJ-slash-bartender to fade the music and Etta's voice slowly quietens. He then steps forward, facing our guests, and flashes us a benevolent smile. Even though Jaelee assured me she's booked a celebrant who speaks English, I am fully prepared for this entire ceremony to be conducted in Italian——her track record being what it is——but not even that could dampen the joy residing in every cell of my body.

'Ladies and gentlemen,' begins the celebrant and Jean-

Luc and I tear our eyes from each other's to look at him. 'I am Giuseppe and I welcome you, family and friends, to the nuptials for Caterina and Gianluca. What an afternoon to be married—*meraviglioso!*'

'There's a lot of … *amore* … in this room. Yes, *love*,' says the celebrant, his tone more serious now. 'And when two people come together in matrimony, they become a family and *you*' —he indicates our loved ones— 'also join as one *famiglia*.' It's a lovely sentiment, though I am not sure how it will sit with Cécile. 'Now, Caterina and Gianluca, you have asked to say some words before you make your vows. Caterina, please, you say now your words to Gianluca.'

Even though going first is what I wanted—I was terrified that by the time Jean-Luc finished speaking, I'd be a blubbering mess and unable to say a word—my mouth is suddenly dry and everything I've written—and *rehearsed*—has flown out of my head. I turn towards Sarah and she steps forward to take my bouquet. 'Help!' I telegraph with my eyes.

She takes the flowers from my shaking hand, then reaches down and clasps it tightly. She gives me one of her big sisterly looks, one that says, 'Breathe. You've got this.' I breathe, close my eyes momentarily, then open them and turns towards my love. The words reappear and I begin.

'Jean-Luc … my darling … who could have foreseen all those years ago that my best friend, a bookish intellectual with a quick wit and a mop of quintessential noughties hair …' —laughter from our loved ones— 'would be the one to teach me what it is to love—that love is vibrant and joyful, that it's part friendship, part passion, part compassion, and part hope. I am so grateful that we met again as adults—it was only by chance but I believe with every part of me that it was meant to be.'

I got through it! I grin at him and he smiles back at me, his glistening eyes filled with warmth.

'Gianluca.' He glances at the celebrant, then locks eyes again with me.

'Catherine,' he says, 'sometimes when I look at you, I see glimpses of the girl I fell in love with so long ago. It's in the toss of your head when you laugh, the frown you make when you are concentrating, how you wrinkle your nose when you do not like something.' More gentle laughter from our loved ones. 'These things—perhaps small to someone else—are just a few of the million reasons I love you. Being with you as you are now, a woman, it is like the world has opened up to me again. My life has become more enriched, more joyous … just *more* with you in it. You are the love of my life and I cannot wait to live the rest of it with you.'

'Aww,' says Lou—likely involuntarily as she's a sucker for romance. I am too, to be honest. My heart is already full and we haven't even got to the vows yet.

'*Bellissimo*,' says our celebrant. 'And now Caterina and Gianluca will take their vows. Some of these vows will be familiar and some are a little … er … untraditional but I am a modern man, this is a modern couple, they write their own vows, so *everybody* is happy.' Clearly a pro, he mugs for the crowd who laugh again—so far, our wedding is hilarious—then says to me, 'Caterina, please repeat after me. I, Caterina, take you Gianluca to be my husband.'

'I, Catherine, take you Jean-Luc to be my husband.' *This is really happening!* I think and as I parrot the celebrant and make promises to my love, I try to imbue every word with its truest meaning.

'I will love you, respect you, and be kind to you. I will forgive you for being fallible, ask for forgiveness when I've done you wrong, and assume best intentions when we disagree. I will champion you and your successes, be your advocate and stand by your side, and be your support when you need to lean on me. I will respect and cherish your independence, your completeness as your own person, but will proudly call you my husband. Throughout our marriage, I will aim to honour all in you that makes you *you*, while always striving to be my best self.'

'And now you make the rest of your vows,' says the celebrant. Until this point, these are the vows that Jean-Luc and I wrote together, but the next part is where I've added my own and again, I'm going from memory.

'Jean-Luc, I promise to make you toast and tea whenever you are sick, and never to step foot in your kitchen otherwise.' He raises his eyebrows, his mouth quirking. 'I will continue to brag—loudly—about your professional successes because I am so, so proud of you and I'm in awe of all you accomplish. I promise not to cut my hair short, because I know you like it long—and to be honest, it's also because I look terrible with short hair. I tried it once in my early teens when I became obsessed with Natalie Imbruglia. It was not good.' He chuckles at that and Sarah laughs loudly behind me.

'I will look after you, the same way you look after me, and I promise to laugh with you, travel the world with you, dance with you to 90s music in the lounge, and play backgammon on wet Sunday afternoons, even though I prefer gin rummy. I promise to love you—now and for all my days.' Lou lets out another 'aww' and when I look over at her, she's running her fingertips under her eyes.

'And Gianluca, please repeat after me.' I look back at my nearly-husband. 'I Gianluca take you Caterina to be my wife.' As Jean-Luc repeats our shared vows, I listen intently, letting the cadence and pitch of his voice wash over me as he says the most beautiful things. Then it's his turn for the part he wrote himself.

'Catherine, I promise to embrace your family as my own, forever grateful to have another sister, a new brother, and another mother and father.' I glance at Mum seeing the tears streaming down her face. She sniffles politely and smiles at me through her tears. 'I promise to have grand adventures with you—that we will travel, we will try new things, that we will embrace what excites us and maybe terrifies us, *non?*' he adds cheekily. I just know he's talking about skydiving and that is a big fat '*non*' from me! I tilt my head so he knows I'm onto him. 'I promise that we will make a beautiful home together, a sanctuary where we can be ourselves—and just *be.*' At that last thought, my breath catches. Home. Is he envisioning his apartment in Paris when he speaks of home? Oh, my god, how have I let this indecision go on so long? How has *he?*

I push the thought aside as his grasp on my hands tightens and his gaze intensifies. 'And just like you, I promise to love you—now and for all my days.'

We smile at each other, both through the blur of tears. 'Gianluca and Caterina are exchanging rings.' The celebrant looks expectantly at Josh, who digs into his suit pocket. The celebrant takes them and gives mine to Jean-Luc and his to me. 'It is nice to put them on together, I think,' he says to us. 'One, two, three, go!' he adds and Jean-Luc and I both laugh, then slide the rings onto each other's finger. Mine is a simple and delicate gold band that complements my engagement ring beautifully and Jean-Luc's is platinum with an onyx inlay.

'And now that you have made your vows and exchanged your rings, you are married! *Puoi baciare la sposa*! It's time to kiss your bride.'

Jean-Luc scoops me up in an embrace, dips me, then kisses me to the cheers and claps of our loved ones. When he rights me again, we grin at each other and I land another kiss on his lips. Grinning, we turn to face everyone and he raises our joined hands as though in victory. We did it. We bloody well got married.

The hugs and kisses come fast and thick and I'm soon swept up in well-wishing and congratulations.

'Great dress!' says Jane hugging me tightly. When she releases me, I do a little shimmy to show it off. 'I think I like this one even better than the first. You look ridiculously hot for a bride.'

I grin at her. 'Aww, thank you.'

'And stop with the false modesty. Very unbecoming.' I stifle a snigger, my lips pressed together. She glances over at Jean-Luc. 'Actually, you two may be the hottest bridal couple I've ever seen.'

I follow her eyeline and take in the beautiful man that I've just married—swoon!—then turn back to Jane. 'I'm so glad you could come. I mean, I know we see each other every day, but it means the world to me that you're here.'

'Wouldn't miss it.'

'And look, I know we owe you a decision—'

She holds up a hand and smiles at me. 'All good, lovely. We'll figure it out.' She's being far kinder—and more patient—than I deserve. 'Right, now I'm going to congratulate your handsome hubby.'

'Save me a dance later?' She and I have spent *many* hours on the dance floor together.

'Oh, you know it.' She kisses my cheeks and steps away.

Louis, one of the last to congratulate me, is shy when he steps forward. '*Félicitations*, Catherine,' he says, kissing me on both cheeks. '*Bienvenue dans la famille.*' If only. Louis married into the Caron family—like I just have—but unlike me, he is both welcomed and loved. It could be because he's French, or because he and Cécile have given Jean-Luc's parents grandchildren, or maybe it's because they were relieved *someone* wanted to marry that acerbic cow.

This is your wedding, *Cat. Be nice*, I tell myself.

'*Merci, mon frère.*' At that, he smiles before stepping aside to congratulate my husband. 'My husband'—it's only been a few minutes and I am already in love with those two words.

Alistair and Jae are last and when Jae steps up, she says, 'Great job!'

I laugh. 'Thank you, Miss Wedding Planner.'

'And congratulations,' she says, throwing her arms around my neck. I return the hug and when she steps back, she holds up her phone. 'Oh, and I just checked and I got the whole thing on video.'

'Oh, thank you, Jae.' Sure, it was our plan, but I worried that she'd miss the ceremony because she was too busy filming it.

'Oh, no trouble at all. I filmed you walking in, then set up the tripod on that barrel over there.'

'You clever thing.' This earns me a double-dimpled grin.

'I took some terrific photographs too, Cat,' says Alistair as he hugs me. 'You're going to love them, I promise.'

'Oh, you are a darling. I was barely even aware of you, you were so stealthy. Thank you.'

'An absolute pleasure. It's not every day I get to be a wedding photographer.'

'On that,' says Jaelee. 'I'm going to get you a celebratory glass of prosecco. Then you've got about ten minutes before we head out to the vineyard for pictures. We want don't want to miss the last of the sunlight.'

With Sarah on Maid of Honour duties now that the wedding has started, Jae has taken over logistics and like I always knew she would, she runs a tight ship. Josh will be taking most of the wedding photographs with his digital SLR, but Alistair is also a decent amateur photographer and between them, I have no doubt we will have an array of beautiful images of our day.

Sarah's laugh catches my attention and when I look over, she's chatting with Lindsey. I cast my eyes about and everyone is in such a joyful mood, my heart is singing right now. 'Catherine.' The voice is quiet and deep and it startles me. I spin in its direction and there she is——Cécile.

'Hello, Cécile.' She leans forward and I endure her Sahara-dry cheek kisses.

'Congratulations,' she says, though her cold eyes could turn a grown man into stone.

'Thank you.' I won't bother speaking French to her, even though I certainly know enough to have this conversation. She'd only scoff at my accent and make me feel like utter crap——*more* like utter crap, that is. She's the sort of woman whose very presence can suck the life out of you——like a Dementor in designer clothes. She looks about the loft and there it is, that supercilious sneer. Never mind that we were supposed to be married in the great hall. I won't bother explaining that either.

'Cat, can I borrow you for sec,' says my sister. She whisks me away, her arm hooked around mine, before I can politely excuse myself. 'What did Sister Bitchface want?' she asks, steering me in the direction of the bar. Jaelee is already there and turns right as I approach, a flute of prosecco in each hand.

'Here you go,' she says.

Sarah takes a flute off the bar and holds it up. 'To the best rustic-chic wedding in Tuscany.' We clink glasses and I take a sip—delicious but I'll need to pace myself. There are photographs, then the celebrations—food, wine, dancing, the cake!—and at some point, I'm supposed to sign the paperwork.

'Jae, where's the celebrant? Aren't I supposed to sign something to make it official?'

'Lots of time for that. I invited him to stay. The more the merrier, right? Besides, we need to get you guys outside for pictures.' She signals across the room to Alistair.

He heads over. 'Are we about ready?' he asks.

'Definitely. You good to round up Josh and Jean-Luc?'

'Aye, no problem.' Before he goes, he takes her glass from her and has a sip. 'Delicious. Should I bring a bottle down to the vineyard?

'Ooh, great idea!' says Sarah. She turns to the guy behind the bar and requests a bottle and some clean glasses, which Alistair takes from him.

'Meet you outside in five minutes,' he says, giving Jae a quick kiss.

'Jaelee,' says Sarah when he's gone, 'he is *such* a darling.'

'Yeah, he is,' she acknowledges.

'And hot.'

They both snigger. 'Yeah, he *definitely* is.'

'I mean, I think Josh is, of course, but Alistair's like a male model,' says Sarah.

'I brought that up *one* time and he laughed for a good solid minute. It's a shame——he'd make a killing.'

As they continue talking about Alistair's non-existent modelling career, I look over at Jean-Luc who's in a lively conversation with Anders and Lou. He laughs, hand to chest, and I won't say so to the others but *he* is the most handsome man in the room. Possibly in any room anywhere.

'Okay,' says Jae. 'The appetisers should be out soon so I'm just going to check on the caterers. You two drink up and meet me at the bottom of the stairs, okay?'

Sarah salutes her and Jae makes a 'that was weird' face then strides off in her impossibly high heels. We watch her cross the space, smiling and stopping to say hello to everyone. Well, everyone except Cécile and Louis, who are on their own in the corner. Cécile——all tight-lipped and glowering——grasps a full glass of prosecco and Louis talks at her, a false smile plastered on his face, while she conspicuously ignores him. Poor Louis.

'That was a beautiful ceremony,' Sarah says. 'I barely kept it together.'

I turn towards my sister. 'Oh, my god, me too. I was listening——you know, really wanting to be in the moment, but there was also part of me that just wanted to get through it all without turning into a blubbering mess.'

'Like Mum.'

'She wasn't that bad.'

'Haven't you noticed that she's not here right now?'

I glance about. It's not like there's a cast of thousands up here in the loft—how did I miss that Mum is missing? 'Oh, my god, you're right. Where is she?'

'She asked if she could freshen up in the apartment. She's gone to redo her makeup.'

'Aww, bless. That's so sweet.'

'I'd be down there with her if it weren't for the funny parts—Natalie Imbruglia!' she says chuckling. 'Oh, god, how bad was that haircut? You looked like a twelve-year-old boy.' She laughs now—*at* me.

'You finished?' I ask drily.

She stops laughing. 'Come on,' she says, downing the last sip of prosecco. 'We should go—don't want to piss Jaelee off.' She takes my hand and we head towards the stairs. 'Oh, and I loved the part of Jean-Luc's vows—what he said about a home. That was *really* beautiful,' she says.

'It was,' I say, as we pass Cécile and she narrows her eyes at me.

Tomorrow, after the festivities, when I'm properly alone with my husband for the first time, he will no doubt want to have that conversation. That *dreaded* conversation. I owe it to him, of course, to discuss it properly, to unpack and unpick why it's causing me such torment. And I owe it to Jane—poor love.

But until then, I must shove aside all thoughts of where we're going to live and simply relish every moment of my wedding. Well, except the witchy sister. If only I could shove *her* aside and right out the nearest window. Though I do have a contingency plan if she doesn't play nicely.

Chapter Twenty-One

SARAH

Tuscany

The late afternoon sun is simply beautiful as we round the castle walls and make our way out into the vineyard. 'Magic hour' photographers call it and I can see why.

'I scouted about earlier,' says Josh, 'and I think we should head over this way for the first series of shots.'

Cat lays a hand on my arm. 'First series?' she says to me quietly. 'Did we inadvertently hire a Helmut Newton wannabe for our wedding?'

'Technically, you didn't hire anyone,' I tease.

'I know. And I really appreciate it—Josh, you, Jae, Mum. We couldn't have done this without you.'

'I was only teasing,' I say.

'I know. But I mean it.'

'You're welcome. Now come on.' We set off, Cat with one hand in mine and the other holding up the fishtail of her dress, carefully picking our way across the uneven ground in our (collectively) seven-hundred-dollars-worth of shoes.

'How much further?' Cat calls out to Josh a couple of minutes later.

He surveys the scene. 'Actually, here's good.'

'Thank god,' she says under her breath as Josh starts fiddling with his camera. Jean-Luc has been bringing up the rear with Alistair, and he snakes an arm around Cat's waist whispering something in her ear in French. I step away. I caught enough of it to be embarrassed.

Josh lifts his head and catches my eye and sends a wink my way. Soon, the photo shoot begins in earnest with him directing Cat and Jean-Luc into place, then through a series of poses. Meanwhile, Alistair makes short work of the cork in the prosecco bottle and pours for me, Jaelee, and himself. We clink glasses, then sip.

'We couldn't have ordered better lighting,' I say, taking in the wonder of the sky, its sunset hues both familiar *and* unique. One shot that Josh just took—Cat and Jean-Luc gazing at each other in profile and silhouetted against an orange sky—will no doubt be a favourite for years to come.

'Oh, didn't you know? I called ahead,' says Jaelee.

I chuckle. 'When I was touring, we used to take credit for everything—tongue in cheek, of course—but, you know, "We hope you're enjoying the beautiful sunset we ordered" —that sort of thing.'

'My Mom's birthday is on New Year's Eve,' she says. 'Every year, I tell her I've organised some fireworks for her.' We laugh.

'My guess is that Tina believes you,' says Alistair.

He and Jaelee share a look, his mouth contorting in

amusement. To me, she says, 'My mom's a little ... intense,' right as Alistair says, 'narcissistic.' I look between them and Jaelee feigns outrage, then giggles. Having organised this wedding with her via email and video chats over the past few months, then spending the week with her, this is a side I haven't really seen before—she's almost *girlish*.

Eventually, it's time for Josh and me to join the bride and groom and Josh hands over his camera to Alistair. I *may* be a little tipsy as I take my place next to the others, so I take extra care not to trip in my heels or let them sink into the ground. Once we're all in position, Josh's firm hand on my waist keeping me from stumbling over a divot or into a hole, Alistair takes several shots. 'Smile,' he says again and again—though he needn't really bother. I'm a couple of proseccos in, two of my favourite people just got married, and we're in Tuscany! I'm probably grinning like the Joker.

'Got room for two more?'

'Daddy!' Yes, even though Cat is thirty-eight, she still occasionally calls him 'Daddy'. Okay, I do too.

He and Mum are standing at the edge of the vineyard, Dad with a Peroni in hand and Mum holding a flute half-filled with prosecco. 'Hey, you two,' says Josh, 'perfect timing.' He looks past them. 'No Louis and Cécile?' he asks.

I catch the not-so-surreptitious roll of Cat's eyes as she walks over to Mum and steals a sip of prosecco. 'Yeah, no,' says Dad, 'it didn't seem like they were too keen.'

'That makes two of us,' murmurs Cat and Mum tuts at her.

'But it's time for family photos,' says Josh. He looks at me helplessly.

'I will go,' says Jean-Luc.

'No, darling, stay. We can get some photographs of you, me, Mum, and Dad,' says Cat.

'I'll go,' I say. 'Maybe I can make them change their mind.'

'Are you sure, Sarah?' asks Jean-Luc.

'Yeah, for sure. All good,' I say, volunteering to walk into Medusa's lair—tipsy and in heels. Not only do I have to convince Cécile to get her skinny French arse down to the vineyard, I have to do it without bitch slapping her smug mug for trying to ruin my sister's wedding. Well, I acted in high school. I was the lead in the school musical, even though my voice is only okay and the dance teacher I had when I was four asked Mum to find me an activity 'more suited to my talents'. Surely, I was cast because my acting talent made up for my shortcomings in the other two 'threats'—*right*?

I pick my way back down the rows of grapevines, now seriously considering popping on the Havaianas for the rest of the wedding. When I make it back to the loft, there's a general hubbub of cheer, the small but lively group of guests drinking from flutes or beer bottles and snacking on prosciutto and cheese—the lucky buggers.

Cécile and Louis are next to the large window near where Cat and Jean-Luc exchanged vows and Cécile is looking out—unmistakably at the photo shoot. '*Bonsoir*,' I say cheerily as I approach. 'We haven't officially met yet.' This is technically accurate considering our only interaction so far is me telling her off right before the ceremony. Under her steely gaze, I soldier on. 'I'm Sarah, Cat's sister.'

'*Enchanté*,' says Louis, stepping forward and landing three perfectly executed cheek kisses—three! I like him already.

Cécile eyes me coldly. '*Enchantée*,' she says, though no cheek kisses and not even a hint of a smile. *Do not bitch slap her, Sarah*, I remind myself.

'Um, so, we're taking family photos down in the vineyard,' I say, pretending that I didn't just catch her spying on us, 'and we'd love for the two of you to join us.'

'Your parents already asked us,' she says. '*Mais, non, merci.*'

I'll 'mais, non, merci' you in a moment, I think. I catch Louis' eye and he seems extremely uncomfortable—uncomfortable and unwilling to do anything to convince Cécile otherwise. Maybe I was too quick to like him after all.

I reckon there's two ways I can play this—well, probably more but only two that I can think of at this moment. I can placate Cécile and try to get her onside, appealing to her inner human (which must be in there somewhere) or …

'Well, Cécile, the thing is, this is a *family* occasion and, like it or not, you and Louis and Alice and Abigail' —I mention their daughters' names, even pronouncing Alice as 'Ah-leese', for added effect— 'are *family* now. Just like Cat is now part of the Caron family.' She winces almost imperceptibly at that but, to her credit, she maintains eye contact. 'And, as it is a *family* occasion and we're about to take the *family* photos' —I'm really laying it on now— 'your presence is required in the vineyard *tout de suite*.' I flash a broad smile—one that says, 'Do not mess with me—I am the Maid of frigging Honour.' 'Then, after that, you can continue to sulk the night away like a spoiled child. How does that sound?'

There's a flash of anger behind those green eyes but she raises her eyebrows—a surrender of sorts—and nods sharply. '*D'accord*.' Louis visibly relaxes beside her and I refrain from doing a victory dance. '*Ouvre la voie*,' she says, indicating that they will follow.

Several minutes later, there are surprised expressions all around as I lead Louis and Cécile towards the others. Jean-Luc greets his sister as though she hasn't been a petulant cow, then Alistair directs us all into position and calls out, 'Smile!' for the umpteenth time. He takes several shots and I have no idea if Cécile is smiling or not, but at least we have evidence that she and Louis were at the wedding. And if she continues to be a pill, we can edit her out 'in post'.

'And Karen and I have very fond memories of our fifteen-year-old daughter *begging* us to let her "best friend"' —Dad does the air quotes— 'stay the night.'

'We *were* just friends!' Cat protests.

'We realised that, love, which is why we said yes.'

'But I had to sleep in the guest room,' says Jean-Luc.

'Well, we were understanding, Jean-Luc, not stupid.' There is laughter all around, including from my newly minted brother-in-law. Well, mostly, as a glance at Cécile reveals that she is less than amused with Dad's anecdote-filled 'Father of the Bride' speech.

'In any case, you and Cat were as thick as thieves that year and you became part of our family. We loved you back then. We love you now. We're thrilled that you two found each other again and Karen and I would officially like to welcome you to the family.' Dad raises his glass of wine and toasts, 'To Jean-Luc.'

'To Jean-Luc,' we echo. Josh slips an arm around my waist and I lean into him as I sip my prosecco, revelling in the warmth of familial love.

'And now, I believe I am handing over to my eldest daughter, Sarah.'

Oh, right, my turn. As all eyes land on me, I step away from Josh and collect my thoughts. Maid of Honour-slash-wedding planner duties have kept me busy until now, even with Jaelee doing most of the heavy lifting since the wedding started, but after the toasts, I am slipping off these shoes, piling up a plate from that delicious looking buffet, and letting loose. Well, as loose as one should get at their sister's wedding when one is forty.

'Firstly, I just want to say how lovely it is to have you all here. As Giuseppe, our celebrant, said' —I motion towards him and, smiling, he dips his head in acknowledgement— 'there is a lot of love in this room ...' I say this without irony as, even though her behaviour has been atrocious, *surely* Cécile loves her brother. '... with both family and those who we've chosen as our family along the way. Jean-Luc, like Dad said, you became part of ours all those years ago. I remember that you were a bright, thoughtful boy with a sharp wit and a gentle heart. It's no surprise that you've grown into the man you have and I am *so* thankful to have you as my brother.'

I'm toasting through the blur of tears now and I'm not the only one as Jean-Luc wipes under one eye. 'Cat, you are my closest person, my bestie, my partner-in-a-thousand-crimes—'

'And the rest,' heckles Dad. Mum nudges him with the back of her hand.

'And the rest, Dad, yes, thank you. Anyway, Cat, I love

you, I am very happy for you both, and I am *so* glad we could be here with you to share this joyous occasion. To Cat and Jean-Luc.'

'To Cat and Jean-Luc,' everyone echoes.

'And now I think we're eating ...?' I look at Jaelee to confirm and she nods. 'Hooray! Everyone grab a plate—there is *plenty* of food—and whatever you do, do *not* miss the truffle risotto. It's divine!' Saying there is plenty of food is an understatement, as I'm certain there's enough for each guest to have brought two guests. I get the sense that we'll be eating leftovers until we fly home.

Fuck. How can a single thought ambush you like that, obliterating all joy in its path? In a couple of days, we'll leave Tuscany and head back to Sydney while Cat and Jean-Luc fly to ... well, despite my best intentions, I have no idea where. I just know that it won't be Sydney. *This* is the hardest part of living across the world from my sister and best friend. And it happens every time we see each other—that tipping point in the trip when it is close to saying goodbye and I can no longer ignore that it's looming.

'Hey,' says a soft American voice in my ear. 'You look a little ...' I shake my head, hoping a head jiggle will fix everything, and smile up at him.

'I'm fine.'

'I'm not buying it.'

'Oh.'

'What's up?'

'It's nothing.'

Josh is onto me—it's in the tilt of his head and the intensity of his gaze. 'I ... it just hit me all of the sudden that we're coming to the end of the trip.'

His shoulders drop. 'Oh, right, of course.' He sighs.

'Yeah, that's always rough.' He's quiet for a sec—perhaps thinking about all the times we travelled together then had to say goodbye. Our relationship wasn't long-distance for very long—less than a year—but it was still hard to be apart. 'Hey …' His fingers brush my neck as his thumb strokes my cheek—both sensations send shivers down my spine. 'Let's not think about that now, okay? This is a celebration.'

I nod at him. He's right—now's not the time to dwell on goodbyes. There is only tonight and this beautiful celebration. 'Come on,' he says grabbing my hand, 'before your dad eats all the risotto.'

'I love you, sister,' says Cat, slinging her arm around my shoulder.

'I love you too.' I scrutinise the bride as she bops in time to the music—yep, definitely approaching tipsy. 'Hey, have you eaten anything?' I ask.

She shrugs. 'I had a crostini.'

'Gee, a whole crostini? C'mon. We're getting you some food.' I take her hand and walk her over to the buffet where Siobhan is loading up a plate.

'Hello, lovelies,' says our gorgeous Irish friend. 'Cat, you have thrown a truly specular wedding. Just beautiful.'

'Ohhh, *thank* you, Siobhan,' she replies—as though she was the one who planned everything. She starts eyeing the buffet and I let it slide.

'I so wish Keely could have come,' Siobhan continues. 'I desperately want you two to meet her. When are you coming back our way, Sarah?'

'Oh, uh … probably next year some time.'

'Well, you must promise to come to Dublin and you can absolutely stay with me—ooh! By then, you might be staying with *us*.' She waggles her eyebrows.

'We'd love that, Siobhan.' I feel a little guilty. Josh and I met Siobhan in Hawaii a couple of years back and she'd invited us then to come visit but, even though we've been to the UK a couple of times, we've never crossed the Irish Sea. And I've always wanted to go to Ireland too. Maybe we *will* get there next time we're in the northern hemisphere.

'What are you having?' Cat peers curiously at Siobhan's plate.

'Well, I confess I've already tried some of everything but this is my favourite—the aubergine.'

'Oh, yum!' Cat takes a plate and serves herself a generous spoonful of roasted eggplant in a red sauce. Yikes. Maybe a buffet was a bad idea. Maybe anything with a sauce was a bad idea. It smells good though and I serve up some for myself while keeping a watchful eye on the slight tilt of Cat's plate. I will cry if she spills anything on that exquisite dress.

'We've been rubbish about visiting too,' says Cat through a mouthful. 'Sorry, Siobhan. Ireland's definitely on the list though.'

'Oh, not to worry. It's life, isn't it? It gets in the way of good intentions. I mean how many times have I said I'd love to pop over to London for a weekend …' She shrugs.

'You're always welcome.'

'But I'll have to be quick.'

'What's that?' Cat stops eating and places her fork on her plate. 'Quick?'

'Because you're moving to Paris,' says Siobhan. Uh-oh.

Cat puts her plate down and delicately wipes at the corners of her mouth with a napkin before laying it on her plate. I watch every movement unsure of what I can—or should—say to reroute this conversation. Cat looks up at Siobhan and even I can't read her expression—guilt, shame, fury?

'Uh … actually, we're still deciding about that—where we're going to live.'

'Oh. But I thought … it's just that I was talking to Jean-Luc's sister earlier and she said you were moving to Paris.'

There's a moment in which Cat is perfectly still, a myriad of thoughts playing out across her face and I am torn between staying by her side and marching right over to Cécile and bitch slapping her after all.

'Sorry?' says Cat.

'Oh, have I got that wrong?' asks Siobhan. 'I'm sorry. I've upset you now.'

'No … I …'

'It's okay, Siobhan. Cécile probably just got her wires crossed,' I say, leaping into the conversation.

'She must have,' says Cat, though I know she doesn't believe that for a second. 'If you'll excuse me?' Cat strides off.

'Well, fuck,' says Siobhan, 'I've only gone and stuck my big foot in my big fat mouth.'

'No! It's not … it's not your fault. I promise. It's just … it's been a little contentious is all and Cécile … well, she's a prize bitch. She knows that a decision hasn't been made yet and I think she's just trying to stir up trouble.'

'Oh, for fuck's sake. What sort of person does something like that at their brother's wedding?'

'Exactly. Look, I should …'

'Oh, sorry. Done it again, going on and on … Go, go after her!'

I leave Siobhan at the buffet and follow Cat, catching Jaelee's eye as I go. With a jerk of my head, I signal for her to join me and she does, covering the space between us surprisingly quickly for someone in five-inch stilettos.

'What's happening?' she asks, falling into step beside me.

'Cécile. She's stirring up trouble.'

'Oh, the Paris thing?'

'Yeah, how'd you know that?' I ask.

As we near the stairs, Lindsey approaches. 'What's going on with Cat?'

'Cécile,' says Jaelee without breaking stride. 'She's telling people Cat's moving to Paris.'

'But that's still undecided, isn't it?' ask Lins.

'Yep,' replies Jaelee. 'She's a piece of work.'

Before we descend the stairs, I cast an eye back over the reception searching for the offending sister. Shocker—she's watching us. I'm tempted to do that finger gesture you see in movies—'*I'm* watching *you*, Cécile'—but I doubt she'd care. My gaze flicks over to Jean-Luc who has his back to us and is laughing at something Alistair has said. I don't want to upset him—I'll only bring him into this is if all else fails.

'Sarah, come on,' says Jaelee, who—somehow—is already halfway down the stairs. How the hell does she walk in those things? I follow her and Lins and moments later, we stop at the bottom of the stairs, looking both ways along the gravel driveway. It's past sunset now, but there's enough moonlight to see that it's empty.

'She's probably inside the apartment,' I say, heading off.

The others follow but our search is fruitless, our voices echoing through the empty apartment.

'Would she go back to the vineyard?' asks Lins.

'Hmm, I don't think so. Not in the dark,' I reply. 'She must be in the castle courtyard.' I hope I'm right as it's the only other place I can think of. We make our way there, me in the lead and cursing my choice of footwear for the umpteenth time tonight.

The moonlight casts deep shadows across the courtyard but against the far wall, I make out the silvery silhouette of my sister sitting on a bench—and she's not alone. Bianca? I wave to the others to follow and we traverse the courtyard. Cat and Bianca look up as we approach, their conversation halting, and Cat carefully dabs a linen handkerchief under her lower lashes.

'Hey,' I say.

'Hello.'

'I will leave you,' Bianca says, scurrying away before any of us can say anything.

'Thank you,' Cat calls after her.

'*Buona serata*,' says Bianca. She closes the double doors to the great hall.

'Are you okay?' I sit on the bench next to Cat.

She sighs and sniffles. 'Did I mess up my makeup?' She turns her face towards me so I can inspect it, though in the moonlight it's difficult to see.

'You're still gorgeous,' replies Jaelee.

'Cat, if you want, I'll go and ask Cécile and Louis to leave,' offers Lins.

'Tempting,' say Cat. 'But that will probably make it worse.'

'Hmm, maybe.' Lins seems to be champing at the bit to send Cécile packing—we're in total agreement there.

'Honestly, why does nothing anyone says sink into that thick skull of hers?' asks Cat. 'I mean, Jae, you've told her off. Sarah, you have. *Jean-Luc* has. How does she go through life being this much of a bitch? It's my fucking wedding day. Can't she just be decent for five fucking minutes? What's it going to take?'

'We could sic Mum on her,' I suggest.

'Last resort,' says Cat.

'That's what I was thinking about Jean-Luc,' I reply.

'Does he …?' Cat's eyes widen.

'No,' I say, hurrying to reassure her. 'I don't think he's noticed you're gone yet, but he will, Cat. You've got to come back to your reception.'

'I know.' She stands and smooths down her dress, sighing loudly in resignation. 'Come on. We still have to cut the cake and I'll be damned if I'm going to let that woman stop me from dancing at my own fucking wedding.'

'There's my gal,' says Jaelee.

We're walking across the courtyard when something occurs to me. 'Hey, what were you and Bianca talking about?' I ask.

'Family.' She gestures for us to follow her down the steps and when we're out of earshot, she stops. 'Apparently, she lost both her parents recently.'

We all reply at once.

'Oh, god,' says Jaelee.

'That's so sad,' says Lindsey.

'Oh no, what happened?' I ask.

'Her mum died a few months ago—a heart attack—and her dad was so heartbroken that he died a few weeks later. Totally healthy, just a broken heart.' I lift my hand to my mouth in shock.

'That's terrible,' adds Jaelee and Lindsey's lips flatten into a line. None of us have lost even one parent. I can't imagine losing both Mum and Dad in the space of a few weeks.

'*And*,' says Cat, 'her mother's favourite room …'

'Ohhh,' says Jaelee, just as it also occurs to me. 'The great hall.'

'Yes.'

'That's why she didn't want you to use it,' says Lins.

'She said it was too soon. She couldn't bear it. And that broke *my* heart,' she says, raising a hand to her chest.

'Is that why you were crying when we arrived?' I ask.

She nods. 'By the time I got down here, I'd worked myself into quite a lather and I was pacing the courtyard when Bianca came out. She asked what was wrong and I started on this whole tirade about Cécile … When I mentioned that she was family … that's when Bianca asked me to come and sit. She said that family can be difficult but that I should make peace.'

'She hasn't met Cécile,' quips Jaelee.

Cat smiles. 'True. But she and her dad clashed—a lot—and now he's gone.' We're all quiet for a moment.

'I suppose you never really know the pain that some people are hiding,' says Lins.

'Do you mean Cécile?' asks Jaelee.

'No, Bianca. Though there must be *something* going on with that woman,' replies Lins.

'Mmm,' I say, though I'm dubious there's a legitimate reason for her behaviour. I genuinely believe Cécile's just a horrible person.

'*Anyway*,' says Cat, 'we should get back before my handsome hubby misses me.'

'But how do you want to play this?' I ask. 'With Cécile?'

'How about instead of Mum, we sic Dad on her,' Cat suggests.

'What? I'm confused. Sic *Dad* on her?' Our dad is the most jovial, sweetest man on the planet.

'Yes. Give her a hefty dose of the Ronald Parsons charm. If she still hates us after that, then she can go fuck herself.'

Lindsey and Jaelee laugh. 'I'm not sure she hates all of us, Cat,' I say. 'Pretty sure it's just you.'

'Ha-ha, you're hilarious.'

'Catherine?' Jean-Luc is standing at the bottom of the staircase that leads up to the loft. 'Everything is all right?' he asks.

She steps forward. 'Yes, darling, everything is perfect. Shall we go cut the cake?'

In the weak light, confusion flashes across his face but he breaks into a smile, then offers his arm and they head back upstairs.

'You know,' says Jaelee to us quietly, 'I attended the second wedding of a Real Housewife back in Miami—it was filmed and everything—and *that* wedding had less drama than this one.'

'Ooh, I love those shows,' says Lins. 'They're my guilty pleasure. Come on, we're switching to liquor and you're gonna tell me everything.'

I follow Lins and Jaelee up the stairs as they chat excitedly. I couldn't give a flying fuck about the Real Housewives. I'm just relieved we've averted yet another crisis. I glance at my dress watch—8:17pm. We just need to get through the next few hours. 'Get through'——surely that's not the ideal way to feel about celebrating your sister's wedding, apt as it may be.

But with operation 'Ron Parsons, Charmer' about to launch, Cat's going to need her Maid of Honour on high alert. This could turn into Real Housewives——or Real Bitchy Sisters-in-Law——in a heartbeat.

Chapter Twenty-Two

CAT

Tuscany

I love my dad.

I love the rest of my family too, of course, but as soon as Sarah had a quick word in his ear about Cécile, Dad lifted his concerned gaze and scanned the loft, pinpointing Cécile and Louis. Then he strolled over, broad grin on his face, and leant in for a cheek kiss before she even knew what was happening. I've been watching them from the bar as Jean-Luc and I await the arrival of the *millefoglie*.

'Have I told you how beautiful you are, *chérie*?' my husband murmurs low in my ear, sending shivers of delight through me. I tear my eyes from his witchy sister and peer up at him from beneath my lashes.

'*Moi?*' I ask with faux modesty, a hand placed delicately on my chest. 'Not in the past hour.'

He stares into my eyes. 'You are beautiful—*exquise*. I cannot wait to make love to you later.' He grasps my waist with one hand, pulling me close, and kisses me in a way that tells me he doesn't care who's watching. Oh, my. I am in full swoon mode now and for a second, I contemplate slipping out of my own wedding—again. Only this time for a much better reason than talking myself out of a violent act.

And even though I've known Jean-Luc more than half my life, he can still make my lady parts stand to attention with just a glance. Speaking of … down girls. My dad is *right over there*.

Hmm, *also* speaking of …

Jean-Luc turns towards the bar, asking the bartender for a glass of Chianti, and I redirect my gaze towards the odd trio of my dad and my in-laws. Louis is full-on laughing as Dad regales them with one of his stories, gesticulating wildly. A lifetime of Dad's tales has taught me that they are *mostly* true, with the sort of embellishments that make them memorable. 'Why let the truth get in the way of a good story?' he always says. But with his hyperbolised anecdotes and their accompanying gestures, Dad is often the life of the party. Like he is now.

I watch Cécile closely as she listens to Dad. Oh, my god. Was that the semblance of smile I just saw? *Mais, non, ce n'est pas possible*! Honestly, when I suggested that we send Dad over to charm the beastly cow, I wasn't sure if (even) *he* could make a dent in that armour of hers. It can't be normal for someone to detest their brother's girlfriend—now *wife*—as much as she detests me.

I do have one more tactic up my sleeve—something special for my nieces. When Cécile made the (ridiculous) decision not to bring the girls to the wedding, I bought them charm bracelets, each with two charms to start them off. Both bracelets have a small silver disc inscribed with an 'A' for Abigail and Alice, then a pair of ballet slippers for

Abigail, who's been dancing since she was three, and a star for Alice, who at four is precociously fascinated by astronomy. They're gift-wrapped and tucked behind the bar. I've just been waiting for the right time to give them to Cécile and Louis. Of course, with all her antics—bringing Vanessa, having to be strongarmed into taking family photographs, then telling Siobhan (and god knows who else) that I am moving to Paris—there hasn't *been* a right time.

'Oh, my god,' says Sarah, who has stealthily appeared by my side—uncharacteristic for her. 'It might actually be working.' She's watching the trio in the next room and right as I look over, Cécile touches Dad on the forearm. Sarah's eyes fly to mine. 'Oh, wow. He's good. He's really, *really* good. So, you still going ahead with the presents for the girls?' she asks.

'Maybe I don't need to,' I reply. 'Though what am I going to do with two monogrammed charm bracelets? I suppose we could give them to the girls at Christmas.' I glance over at Jean-Luc to see what he thinks, but he's disappeared. I've been so fixated on his sister, I didn't even see him walk away.

'I think you should do it now,' says Sarah, pulling my attention back to the matter at hand. 'Go talk to her while Dad's got her warmed up.'

'Eww.'

'Not like that, Cat. Gross.'

'You're the one who said it.' She tuts. 'You really think I should do it now?'

'When else? You're cutting the cake soon. For anyone who doesn't want to hang around at a wedding, that's the cue to leave.'

'Hmm, I suppose.'

She disappears around the back of the bar and returns with the small boxes. 'Go——before you talk yourself out of it.'

I draw a deep breath and take the gifts from Sarah then walk purposefully across the room. I am a woman on a mission——a potentially dangerous, but necessary, mission. 'Cécile,' I say slipping the boxes behind my back. 'I wondered if I might have a moment.' The tepid smile she was sporting disappears the instant she sets eyes on me and her entire countenance sours.

'Louis,' says Dad, 'how about we top up these drinks.' Dad holds up an empty wine glass to punctuate his point.

'Uh, yes, of course.' They slip away, Dad catching my eye as he leaves and sending me a look of solidarity. As I said, I love my dad and just knowing he's on my side gives me a little boost of confidence.

'Shall we sit?' I ask Cécile.

Eyeing me curiously, she nods then moves to a pair of chairs that look out the nearest window. Sitting side by side wasn't exactly what I had in mind but I sit next to my sister-in-law, setting the gifts in my lap, and peer out at the inky outlines of conifers and a sky peppered with stars. 'It's beautiful here,' I say without thinking.

When I realise it's an odd start to our conversation, I turn towards her but she's watching the view too. She nods again——a chink perhaps, a way in. My mind suddenly floods with dozens of fleeting memories of our time together over the past couple of years. Jean-Luc and I have visited their home in Lyon——mostly to see our nieces——but have never been invited to stay over. We always book an Airbnb somewhere close and our visits are only ever for a night or two.

And of course, I've seen her at the familial home——on

the outskirts of Lyon. We *have* stayed there while visiting Jean-Luc's parents, but it is a cold house. And I don't mean the temperature, although in the dead of winter it's freezing. I mean that the Carons may love each other, but theirs isn't the sort of home where that love is evident, where it permeates the air like it does at my parents' home. It's more of a house, a dwelling where the inhabitants happen to be related. And Jean-Luc's parents only ever speak French, even when he first brought me home and they knew I could barely understand a word.

I am certain that in their minds I am a massive downgrade from the beautiful, accomplished, and sophisticated Vanessa.

Just seeing her today … my stomach clenches at the image of her walking into my wedding.

But there's something else. A flicker of anger warms my centre, its flames licking and growing as I sit next to a silent Cécile. How dare she. How dare she try to derail my wedding by bringing Vanessa. How dare she sit here in silence when she has so much to apologise for. Unlike the anger and hurt I've previously felt at her hands, this is fury—it's potent and mature and intelligent and I now know just what to say to her.

'Cécile …' I watch her as I wait for her to meet my eye. A vein pulses at her jawline, a tell shared by her brother when he's upset or angry, and she eventually turns to look at me, her expression hard. 'I want to be very clear. I know that you and I will never be friends and we will never be sisters. But, like it or not, Jean-Luc and I are married now and you and I are part of the same family. I'm not going anywhere, so you have a choice—you can make every family occasion a living nightmare for us both for the rest of our lives, or we can come to some sort of accord. We don't have to like each other, we just need to be civil——for Jean-Luc.'

Her eyes narrow as they return to the view. That's fine. At least she looked me in the eye as I proposed the terms of familial peace. Part of me still wants to shake that smug look off her face, but take the wins when they come, right?

'You know, I love your brother more than anyone in the world and I will do everything I can to make him happy.'

'Except move to France,' she spits.

'What?' My head snaps in her direction, her words surprising me. Is *that* what all this is about? 'I …' My voice falters.

'You see? You love my brother *so much* but you won't deign to live in his home country.'

'It's not that. I love France.' *Do* I? I don't often speak without thinking, but this time … have I misspoken?

Cécile looks at me, her eyebrows raised. She doesn't believe me either. 'I know that to you, my brother and I are not close, but that is just a comparison——*your* comparison. You and your sister, you are like giggly schoolgirls together.' She catches my frown. 'It is fine. That is how you are but, in my family, love does not look like that. But it does not mean it is not there. You have never understood that. That is clear.'

She looks away again leaving me to chew on her words. And they sting because they are steeped in a deep-rooted truth. Unwittingly or not, I *have* compared the Carons to our family——how they are with each other versus how we are together——and I have made the arrogant assumption that we have more love in our family than they do in theirs.

'And you do not "love France", as you say,' she continues, 'so … you will take Jean-Luc away——to England, perhaps *en*

Australie … C'est si simple.' She shrugs as though this is a fore-gone conclusion. *Her* conclusion, and quite obviously, their parents' as well.

So it *is* just as I've imagined. They genuinely believe I'm going to steal their much-loved brother and son and they will never see him again.

But that's ridiculous! In no scenario I've imagined about our life together have I thought Jean-Luc would cut ties from his family. Not once. Family is *the most important* part of life. I would never ask Jean-Luc to give his up—*never.*

'Cécile …' Her chin lifts slightly, but she won't look at me. 'Cécile, *please* …' She meets my eye. 'You know how important family is to me, right?' Her gaze falls away momentarily but when she looks at me again, she nods. '*Why* would I want to take that away from the person I love most in the world?'

A crease forms between her brows. 'I …' Her gaze falls again, this time to her lap where she's set her empty glass.

As all my experiences with the Carons converge into one prickly, miserable memory, I have a telling realisation. While I've experienced my hesitancy to move to Paris as some sort of *pull* from England, and London specifically, it may have more to do with feeling *repelled* by France. There's the tenu-ous, often fraught relationship with his family, yes, but that's only part of it. There are also Jean-Luc's friends, who seem to tolerate me at best, the seemingly endless comparisons with Vanessa (even if many are self-imposed), and this constant feeling of being 'other'.

And all this has obviously fed the fractured relationship I have with his family and very likely hurt Jean-Luc.

Well, fuck.

I don't have the level of French to convey this to Cécile

and even if she's fluent enough in English to comprehend (which I suspect she is), there's no way I trust her to empathise or even understand. Layered beneath this hesitancy is the irony that I'd intended to have it out with her, yet it's her words that have led to this realisation. I may not like her and I can't say I enjoy feeling this way about myself—particularly at my wedding—but at least I've had a break-through of sorts.

And sometime in the next few days—very possibly tomorrow—I'll need to find a way to explain this to my husband.

'Here,' I say to Cécile, holding out the gift boxes. I want to wrap up this conversation so I can get back to the wedding celebrations. She frowns at the boxes, clearly confused, but takes them with her free hand. 'They're charm bracelets. For the girls. Sarah and I had them when we were little—Dad travelled a lot for work and he'd always bring us a charm from wherever he'd been. Anyway … I just adore your girls, Cécile, and I wanted them to have something special, something they can add to as they grow up.'

She blinks away her confusion and her expression softens a little—but just a little. 'Uh …'

'Everything is okay?' Jean-Luc asks, startling us both. I look up at him, catching his concern, then hurriedly stand. I have an out.

'Yes, just giving Cécile our gifts for Alice and Abigail—the bracelets,' I add, as I wrapped them before he saw them and I'm not sure if he remembers what they were.

'Of course,' he smiles but it doesn't reach his eyes. My poor darling—this consternation between Cécile and me … it must be so hard for him. I look to her for support. Odd, I know, but I'm hoping she will assuage his concerns, so he can properly enjoy the rest of the wedding.

And then a miracle occurs—Cécile *smiles*. She holds up the boxes. 'Ah, *oui*, Catherine just gave me these for the children. I am sure they will love them.'

I exhale in relief. It's not a full-on peace accord—I doubt I'm in line for the Nobel Prize or anything—but it's something, a teeny, tiny olive branch. And I suppose we have a lifetime to build upon that kernel.

'*D'accord*,' says Jean-Luc smiling brightly. He must sense it too—this turning point. 'Because it is time, *chérie*—the cake.'

'Oh! Yes, the cake. Come on Cécile, you won't want to miss this. It's a *millefoglie*. That's layers of—'

'*Oui, je sais*,' she says cutting me off. Right, I see. *Baby steps, Cat, baby steps*, I tell myself.

Jean-Luc takes my hand, kisses it and leads me into the next room. 'Ladies and gentlemen,' he calls out. Our DJ-slash-bartender twigs—and the music fades, then stops. 'May I present my beautiful and amazing and wonderful wife, Catherine.' Aww, that is so lovely. It also indicates how much he's had to drink. Jean-Luc rarely calls attention to himself like this. *Perhaps our marital lovemaking* will *need to wait until tomorrow*, I think, chuckling to myself. And thank god Sarah made me eat something earlier, or I'd be in the same boat.

'Now it is time to cut the cake—well, as you can see, it is a *millefoglie*, not so much a cake, but a traditional Tuscan pastry and if it is half as sweet as my beautiful wife is, then it will taste delicious!' My mind flies straight to something lascivious and Dad's 'ahem' and Sarah's wide eyes indicate that I'm not the only one. Maybe it's just the Parsons who have dirty minds. I scan the gathered group and there are a couple of sideways glances, so it's not just us. I focus my attention on Lou—there's no way *she* immediately thought of cunnilingus. Her attentive smile reveals that I'm right.

'So, no need for more waiting,' says Jean-Luc. 'Catherine …' He signals that I should cosy up to him and we both take hold of the knife and cut through the layers of flaky pastry, custard, cream, and fruit, making a right mess of it. But no one seems to care. There are cheers and clapping and flashes of light and before I know it, one of the caterers has whisked it away to serve up.

'Now, one more thing while we are all here like this together,' he says. 'A thank you. A thank you to all of you for coming to Tuscany. It means *so* much to us both that you are here.' It's the first time he's spoken for us as my husband and I'm overcome with emotion, glad it's him and not me who's speaking. 'And thank you also to Jaelee, Sarah, and my new mother-in-law, Karen, for planning this beautiful wedding. We …' He pauses, emotion strangling his voice. 'It has been perfect in every way.' Well, that's a little hyperbolic, but all right, darling. 'Anyway, thank you. There is still a lot to eat, to drink. And dancing!' he declares, grinning.

Jean-Luc is an incredibly sexy dancer and it suddenly occurs to me that I've yet to dance with my husband! Through more cheers and clapping, the music starts playing again. And at the first few notes of 'Get Lucky' by Daft Punk—one of my faves *and* a song we danced to in Switzerland a couple of years ago when we were falling back in love—I grab his hand and pull him onto the dance floor. 'Don't you want to eat some cake?' he shouts over the music.

I shake my head and waggle my eyebrows as I start to move my shoulders in time to the music. 'Ah,' he says, grinning down at me. He slips his hands around my waist, nestling them at the small of my back, as we come together and dance in perfect harmony. My lady parts jump to high alert again, only this time, I don't tell them to heel. Instead, I drape my arms over his shoulders and, forgetting that we're surrounded by our loved ones, dance with my beautiful, loving, and extremely sexy husband.

Chapter Twenty-Three

SARAH

Tuscany

'Here you go,' says Josh, my Havaianas swinging from his fingers.

'Oh, thank god.' I pad over to him in my bare feet, the soles blackened from the ancient wooden floors. 'Thank you, babe.' He earns a kiss for his troubles, then I slip them on.

'Sarah, I'm taking these downstairs,' says Dad, holding a box of wedding presents.

'Okay, Dad. They can go in Cat and Jean-Luc's room.'

'Righteo.' They'd said 'no presents' on the invitations but no one actually shows up at a wedding without one—well, except Cécile and Louis, the tacky in-laws. It seems that Cat did make a dent in Cécile's six-inch emotional armour with their little chat before the cake cutting, but as I predicted they left soon afterwards. After today, I'm hoping to go the rest of my life without ever encountering the witchy sister again. Though Abigail and

Alice sound fun and I've always wanted nieces—even nieces
'once removed' could be worth tolerating a little Cécile time.
If she'd even allow that—she probably hates me by association.

'Everything okay?' asks Josh.

'What? Oh, sorry—just thinking about Cécile.'

'Here, let me.' He takes over covering the *millefoglie* with
plastic wrap. We made a decent effort considering it would
have served a much larger wedding, but I'm not sure we
should bother saving it—surely that pastry will get even
soggier by tomorrow. 'So, you think that they'll be okay
now?'

'Sorry?'

He stops swathing the pastry in plastic. 'Hey, why don't
you head down, take a shower, and I'll finish up.'

'Oh, no, I'm fine—just a little tired.'

'That's what I mean. We're nearly done anyway.'

On cue, Mum brings over the last of the flower arrangements. 'Are these still going to the local hospital, Sarah?' she
asks.

'Um, yes. Bianca said she'd arrange a pickup tomorrow
but I'll check with her in the morning. Oh, not this.' I
retrieve Cat's bouquet from the bar.

'Now what are you going to do with that? You can't
bring it back to Australia.'

'I know, Mum. I just thought it might be nice for Cat to
have it until we leave. I'll put it in her room.'

Mum waves a hand at me indicating she doesn't care
and it's only now that I really see *her* exhaustion. I check my
watch—11:48pm. No wonder. It's been a long, full,
emotional day and it's late.

I cast my eyes about the space. We've worked efficiently since the guests trickled out, clearing up under the glare of industrial lighting which casts a cold blueish glow over the loft. The leftovers have been packed up and cleared away, with many of them now residing in the fridge downstairs and the rest sent home with the caterers—they'd protested but what were *we* going to do with a mountain of food? We're leaving soon. The unopened wine has been consolidated and will be collected by the vintner in the morning, and Cat and Jean-Luc will receive a final bill for the alcohol. The sound system was packed up and put into the bartender's boot almost as soon as the bride and groom departed, which was about an hour ago. And now it's just us and the dregs of the *millefoglie*.

'I think that's everything,' I say.

'Thank god,' says Mum wearily. It's uncharacteristic of her—she never shies away from hard work—and I give her a sideways hug.

'Ready to go, love?' asks Dad who's returned from the apartment. Mum only had a couple of celebratory proseccos, so she's the skipper.

'Absolutely.' Josh and I follow them out, him carrying the soggy pastry. At the bottom of the staircase, I turn the large grey switch from '*acceso*' to '*spento*' and the loft descends into darkness. We say goodnight to my parents, and by the time Josh has made room in the fridge for the *millefoglie*, I am lying supine on our bed, my filthy feet dangling over the edge.

'Did you wanna get in the shower?' he asks, crawling onto the bed next to me.

'Is that a proposition?' I flop a hand onto his chest and lazily run it up and down, 'Because this is the level of energy

I have right now. I could definitely lie here while you do all the work, but there's no way I'm up for shower sex.'

He chuckles softly. 'I was actually thinking how much you'll hate yourself in the morning if you get into bed sweaty from dancing *and* with blackened feet.'

'Oh, right.'

'But while you're in there, I'll consider your generous offer of sex.' I lift my weary hand and flick him with it. 'Ow.'

'That didn't hurt, you wuss.'

'Come on,' he cajoles and I roll over and sit up on the edge of the bed. He crawls up behind me and, kneeling on the bed, unzips my dress, pressing his lips to the curve of my neck.

'Joshua.'

'You taste salty,' he says. It does feel nice, his micro kisses along the line of my shoulder but he's right. I need a shower.

'Okay, I'm up.' I stand abruptly, slide the dress off my shoulders and when it falls to the floor in a pool of rose-gold chiffon, I step out of it and walk to the bathroom. The shower does feel good—*invigorating* even. Maybe I *am* up for a little post-wedding sex.

Only when I finish my ablutions and return to the bedroom, my dress is draped over a chair and Josh is fast asleep on top of the covers—dress shirt and shoes and socks off, trousers on. He is so sexy, *so* handsome. And that's on top of being my someone. Sometimes when I look at him, I pinch myself that we found each other.

'Josh,' I whisper. I undo his belt and his trousers and start sliding them down his legs.

'Mmm, tomorrow morning,' he murmurs. 'I promise … all kinds of sexy time.'

I smile to myself and tug the trousers over his feet. 'Get under the covers,' I say. Sleepily, he does and when I get back from the kitchen with two small bottles of water for our bedside tables, he is well and truly out. I climb into bed and scooch close so I can press a kiss to his cheek. 'I love you,' I whisper, even though he can't hear me.

I wake, blinking a few times and see Josh smiling down at me. 'Good morning,' he says. He drops a kiss onto my forehead and I stretch luxuriously under the covers.

'What time is it?' I ask, stifling a yawn.

'Time for tea.' He points to the bedside table and there sits a steaming mug of tea.

'Oh, I *love* you.' I rearrange my pillow against the bedhead and prop myself up, then reach for it and take a generous swig. Ah, tea—the panacea for late nights and overindulgence and quite often, emotional turmoil. Fortunately, it's only the first two I need to salve this morning. I'm not quite awake enough for a deep dive into the latter.

Josh sits on the edge of the bed and watches me. 'Sleep well?'

'Yes, actually. Totally out cold.'

'Good. You obviously needed it.' He reaches for one of my wayward curls and wraps it around his finger, twirling it softly.

As he moves closer, I realise he smells of cologne and deodorant and that the hair at his nape is wet. 'How long have you been up?'

'About an hour and a half. I figured you wouldn't want to sleep much later, so I brought you the tea.'

I have no idea where my phone is—probably in my satin clutch, its battery life ebbing away—but my watch is within reach. I check it. 'Oh, my god, it's after nine already,' I say, bolting upright.

He chuckles. 'Like I said, you must have needed the sleep. Hey …' I look at him, frowning. 'You are totally entitled to a sleep in, okay? It's been an intense week.'

I flop back against the pillow. 'You're right. Thank you. And for the tea.'

'You're welcome. So … what do you want to do today? We've got the whole day to ourselves,' he says, eyebrows raised.

'Ah, that's right!' I sip my tea and start thinking of all the things we *could* do today—just me and Josh in Tuscany!

'Well, we do have one thing later, but it's not till five.'

'Oh, right—that,' I reply.

'You don't wanna go?' Jaelee has planned for us all to meet at the resort for a final poolside goodbye before we go our separate ways. It's been lovely meeting Cat's friends—Jaelee and Alistair and Lou and Anders—and it will be the last time we see Siobhan or Jane for a while, but part of me wants to beg off and have a quiet night in.

'Um …'

'I get it. It's been a lot of socialising.' Josh is one of the few people who truly understands that I'm an extroverted introvert. Sure, I can be the life of the party, but after a while I just want some time alone—or with my closest people—to recharge. An intimate dinner party is heaven. A week of dinners and parties and day-drinking and eating out—even in *Tuscany*—has started to wear thin.

'How 'bout we go, we see everyone, and we leave early.'

'Really?'

'Yeah, for sure. I mean, we've still got tomorrow with Cat and Jean-Luc' —a pang of sadness at saying goodbye to them rips through me, but I bat it away— 'and we'll see your parents and Nick and Lindsey at home, so …'

'So, we spend some quality time with Siobhan—'

'Joshivara back together again,' he interjects.

'Exactly.' I grin at him. 'And we hang out with the others a bit, then call it a night.'

'Sounds like a game plan.' He leans in for a quick kiss.

'So, what do *you* want to do today?' I ask. I'm only just realising that for most of the week, we've explored the region separately—him off with the groom and me off with the bride.

'Well …' He takes one of my hands. 'How about, 'cause it's just the two of us, we head down to that winery on the other side of town. They do picnic hampers and we can have lunch in the vineyard.'

'But didn't you go there the other day with the guys?'

'Yeah.' He grins at me again. 'That's how I know about the picnics. Besides, I was there with the *guys*, not my gorgeous girlfriend.'

'That's me.'

'That is one hundred per cent you.'

'It does sound nice.'

'You're not sick of Tuscan food and wine yet?'

'Impossible,' I say. 'It's like Greek food. I could happily encamp here for the rest of my life and live solely off olives, cheese, and cured meat.'

'And bread.'

'Oh, my god, the bread. And the wine!'

'Yeah, even a wine troglodyte like me knows it's good.'

'You're not a wine troglodyte anymore,' I say. 'Not after all those times you've been wine tasting with Dad.'

'You mean, the wine tasting *lessons*? The ones where I have to take notes?'

I grin. 'He can get a little didactic.'

'Must be where you get it from,' he teases, smiling back.

'Hey!'

'The *teaching* ... you're a teacher, that's all I meant.' I give him a side-eye. 'I swear.'

'That's mediocre back-pedalling at best.' He grins at me and I sip more tea. 'Hey, don't suppose you'd wanna go for a run before we head out? I'm feeling kinda blah and want to move my bod.'

'Oh, I'll move your bod,' he says, leaning closer to kiss my neck.

'Mmm, I like that.' I carefully place my tea on the bedside table, only half-drunk, and reach for Josh. He kicks off his shoes, flings the covers off me, and crawls on top of me. 'Hell-o there,' I say, breathily. He dips his head to kiss me, his full lips soft against mine, teasing, and the touch of his other hand on my breast, his thumb rubbing the nipple, sends a wave of pleasure over me.

'You're wearing too much,' he says, his lips trailing along my jawline. I pull my top off over my head as he makes short work of my knickers. His hands roam my body, his touch warm as he caresses my breasts, trails lightly down my stomach, then reaches around to firmly cup my bum.

It's heaven but ... 'Now *you* are wearing too much,' I say, impatient to have him naked, his skin against mine. I tug at the hem of his T-shirt and he reaches for it, pulling it over his head one-handed. I glance down at his taught torso. Hot.

SANDY BARKER

It's also my second-favourite outfit of his—just jeans and a bare torso. My absolute favourite is him naked. 'Jeans,' I gasp. 'Off. Now.'

He rolls onto his side of the bed, sliding his jeans and jocks down his legs and kicking them over the edge of the bed. He lies back, one hand supporting his head and I prop myself up again to take in the glorious sight of my gorgeous boyfriend, wearing only a lascivious expression and sporting an erection.

'Come here,' he says, his voice gravelly. He tugs at my hand and I slide over to him, then onto him, stretching my body the length of him, pressing against his erection. He closes his eyes, a guttural growl of pleasure blended with a sigh. I'm hungry to taste him and our mouths come together. The kiss is messy and passionate, our teeth clashing, our tongues exploring each other's mouths, our lips bruising. I'm flooded with desire from the taste of him, the smell of his skin, the touch of his hands, the feel of his chest rubbing against my breasts, my nipples hard from the pressure. And when I can't stand it any longer, I lift my hips so he can enter me.

'Oh,' we cry together, the sheer pleasure of being joined—of being alone in this apartment—evoked in one syllable. We move together, our eyes locked. 'You're so sexy, Sarah,' he says. And I *feel* sexy, his glorious touches sending me over the edge and I'm conscious of nothing but the delicious sensation that rises through my body from my core. I cry out again, pleasure rippling through me and making me shudder. I return to the room slowly and open my eyes to see my lover smiling. He's close, I can tell. 'Your turn,' I say, picking up the rhythm, and I watch him intently as he closes his eyes and his climax takes hold. God, he's so sexy.

Eventually, we both still and he opens his eyes. We grin at each other.

I crawl up beside him, snuggling in the crook of his arm and his fingertips lazily drift across my shoulder as mine caress his chest. 'Makes a difference when we don't have to be quiet, huh?' I ask.

His chest shakes with laughter. 'I hadn't really thought about it, but yeah.' He kisses the top of my head. 'So, still wanna go for that run?'

'Nope.'

'Really?'

'Why don't we just stay here all morning?' I look up at him, catching the surprised expression on his face.

'We haven't done that in a while.'

I think back over the past few months and try to remember the last time we stayed in bed all morning, talking and making love. I have a vague memory of a rainy Sunday, but it was too long ago to remember the specifics. 'Then we're overdue.'

His expression shifts. 'I love you, Sarah,' he says, a shallow crease forming between his brows.

The emotional heft of his words bring tears to my eyes. 'I love you, too, Josh.'

He studies my face for a sec. 'So, you're not ... you're not having doubts?'

What?! I prop myself up on my elbow. 'What do you mean? Doubts about what?'

His gaze falls away and the crease between his brows deepens. 'Never mind.'

'Josh, no ... what? Please tell me.' I sit up now and peer down at him. 'What do you mean?'

'It's just ...' I rest a hand lightly on his shoulder, wanting the connection—*needing* it. What on earth is going on with him? Now *he* sits up, resting against the bedhead and pulling the covers over his nakedness. Uh-oh, that's my move, my protective move when being naked feels figurative as much as literal. My stomach curdles.

'Josh, please … you're scaring me.'

He looks at me now, his expression clouded by a myriad of emotions and none of them good. 'It's just that over the past few months … in the lead up to this trip …' He huffs out a ragged sigh. 'You've been a little … I don't know … distracted—unhappy even.'

Now I'm frowning as I scour my memories again, only this time it's for instances of 'distraction' and 'unhappiness'. And then it hits me. I've done an utterly shitty job of hiding this undercurrent of unease about turning forty and my poor boyfriend has been stewing over this for *months*—worried the whole time that it's about him, about *us*.

But what did I expect? Both Cat and Lins have mentioned it and Josh knows me as well as they do—better in some ways.

'Josh—'

'I just wondered if it was me,' he says, adding fuel to this awful fire. 'If you're dissatisfied with me, with our relationship.' Oh, god, I was right and I'm a terrible person. How the fuck have I let this go on so long?

'Josh, *no*, no! I promise, this has absolutely nothing to do with you—with *us*. You are *perfect*.' He cocks his head, clearly doubtful. 'Well, not that you're perfect … you're as human as the rest of us but … fuck! I just mean that you're perfect for me. *We* are perfect *together*. This is …' I spot the sheen of tears in his eyes and my heart breaks that I've unwittingly hurt him so much.

I grab his hand. I must make him understand. 'Josh, babe ... I am *so* sorry that you've been worried about this. But I love you. I love our life together. I *love* it. It's everything I never knew I always wanted,' I say, hoping to bring some levity to this conversation. It doesn't. 'And this shit that's been going on with me ... it's hard to explain, and believe me, I've tried—with Cat, with Lins, even my dad—but it's about *me*—'

'Wait, what?' Oh, shit. I'm totally fucking this up. 'You haven't been able to tell *me* what's going on but you can tell your sister and your best friend—and even your *dad?* Well, that's awesome. That's just fucking awesome.'

He shoves the covers aside and climbs out of the bed, retrieving his jocks and jeans from the floor and roughly stepping into them. 'I'm supposed to be your *partner*, Sarah. We're supposed to be able to share these things—work them out together.' The sound of his zipper emphasises his anger—his completely justified anger. Why did I think that keeping this from him—this distraction, as he so rightly pegged it—was a good idea? It shouldn't have mattered that it was difficult to convey. I should have found a way.

He grabs his T-shirt from the end of the bed and slips into it. 'Josh ... please ... can I explain?'

He glares down at me. 'I don't know, Sarah. Apparently, you've had months to figure out how to explain, but here we are.' He looks around the room and spying his phone on his bedside table, takes it and shoves it into his front jeans pocket.

'Are you leaving?' I ask, though him hurriedly dressing should have been my first clue.

'I'm ... I'm not *leaving*. I'm going for a walk. I need ... I just need to be anywhere else right now.'

313

Tears splash onto my cheeks as I watch him walk out of our bedroom, leaving the door wide open. The front door to the apartment slams behind him, the sound reverberating against the tiled floors.

'Well, fuck,' I say to the empty room.

Chapter Twenty-Four

CAT

Tuscany

'May I join you?'

I glance over my shoulder coquettishly and nod at my husband. He slips out of his briefs and steps into the shower, his hands immediately roving over my slick skin. I lean back against him, the hot water sluicing off our bodies as his lips nibble at my neck. A firm hand skirts my stomach, sliding lower and making me gasp. I arch my back, pressing my hands against the white tiles to steady myself.

He turns me around, the spray from the shower now running down my back, then lifts me, both hands cupping my bum. I encircle him with my legs as he holds me against the tiles, the coolness of them a shock after the steamy water. We kiss—urgent, our tongues entangled—then he enters me. It's sexy and intense—*harried* and a vast contrast to the slow and sensual lovemaking of last night.

His mouth breaks from mine and we're both gasping. His lips find my neck again and as he comes, he emits a guttural sound that permeates my skin and resonates through my body. I am close and he picks up the pace again. I cling to him, arms wrapped tightly around his shoulders, legs around his waist. I feel the pinch of his fingers grasping me. I feel him inside me, hot water cascading over me, coolness at my back and all these sensations at once send me over the edge.

We part just enough to make eye contact, our eyes saying multitudes—love, desire, longing, acceptance. He leans close and kisses me softly, teasing my lips with his. 'You are so beautiful, Catherine,' he murmurs.

I take in the wet locks of hair adorning his forehead and cheeks, his beautiful green eyes, flecked with gold and brown, his proud brow line, high cheekbones, and full mouth, his Gallic nose. I take in every detail of my beautiful husband's face. 'So are you,' I say.

He drops his chin, smiling shyly and endearing himself to me even more—if that's possible. Then we disentangle ourselves, finish showering, and start our first full day as a married couple with a sumptuous late breakfast on our private veranda.

'So, what would you like to do today?' he asks, sipping his black coffee. The detritus of our meal lies across the table in front of us—we were both ravenous, as neither of us had much to eat yesterday, despite the resplendent buffet—and I sit back, full and contented.

I have a fleeting thought of a day trip into Siena and dismiss it. 'Is it silly that I just want to read a book by the pool?'

He shakes his head, smiling. '*Non, pas du tout.* As you have said, it is a large week. We should take the whole afternoon for relaxing before the guests arrive.' He's referring to the gathering Jae has organised here later this afternoon—a happy hour of sorts and the last time we'll all be together.

My gaze shifts to the nearly full glass of prosecco in front of me. It must be warm now and, as I watch the last few lazy bubbles make their way to the top of the glass, I feel a pang of sadness that it's nearly time for goodbyes. I already know it will be hardest to say goodbye to Sarah. As I sometimes do, I wish she'd just move back to London. That was only ever in the realm of possibility the year she was dating James, the London-based art dealer. Of course, she was also dating Josh at the time. And no amount of selfish longing that my sister will move back to London could ever trump how happy I am that she's found her 'someone', as she says.

I reach for Jean-Luc's hand. 'Thank you—for understanding.' He lifts my hand to his lips, pressing a soft kiss onto the knuckles.

'Of course, *chérie*,' he says, 'I need some peaceful time too. And I thought perhaps we could …' He hesitates and shrugs.

'Perhaps we could what?'

He gives me one of those looks, one that bores into my soul. The copious amount of bread I've just consumed curdles in my stomach as I realise what 'perhaps' means. How long did I think we'd merrily carry on, putting off the discussion about our living situation? Still, the morning after our wedding seems a little too soon. I'm not ready—mentally, logistically, *emotionally*. But from his expression, he knows that I know what he means.

'Let's get changed for poolside relaxing,' I say brightly,

SANDY BARKER

postponing the inevitable. If I'm going to have a difficult conversation, maybe it will be less difficult under the brilliant blue of a Tuscan sky.

'*D'accord*.' He gives me a tight smile, his lips invisible, and gets up abruptly from the table, his chair scraping against the stone pavement. The sound is harsh to my ears, perhaps a harbinger of what's in my immediate future.

I hope Sarah's having a better morning than me.

'Hello, love.' Dad. He stands next to my sun lounger, plunging me into shade, and looks down at me.

'Hi, Dad.' I invert my Kindle on my chest. 'What are you two up to today?'

'We're squeezing in a round of golf,' he replies.

'Oh, really? Three days is too long to go without?' I tease.

'Exactly,' he says, missing my sarcasm. 'But we might be a little late to your do tonight, love.'

'Oh, that's all right. As long as you can pop in at some point and say your goodbyes.'

'*There* you are, Ronald.' Mum. 'Hello, Catherine. Where's Jean-Luc?' God, not even twenty-four hours married and we're already expected to be joined at the hip.

'Hello, Mum. He's in the room. He had to make a couple of phone calls——work, I think.'

Mum purses her lips on the word 'work'. Ah-hah! Even her beloved son-in-law, who until yesterday could do no wrong, can't escape the Karen Parsons Judgment Train. Choo-choo, all aboard. At least I no longer have to ride it alone. 'Right. Well, we're off. Your father's got us a one o'clock tee time—though we didn't bring our clubs, of course, so we have to rent and last time …' She shakes her head at the horror of rented golf clubs.

'I'm sure they'll be fine, love. It's supposed to be a very nice course—even better than the last one,' says Dad, his excitement obvious.

Mum harumphs, unconvinced. 'Anyway, I'm afraid that means we'll be a little late to your gathering.'

'It's all right, Mum. Dad said.'

'Well, have a lovely afternoon. Enjoy the first day of your honeymoon,' she adds brightly. 'Honeymoon' is a bit of a stretch, considering we've only got one more night in Tuscany and tomorrow evening we fly back to London.

'Thanks, Mum. Enjoy your round of golf.' Dad drops a kiss onto the top of my hat before they head off towards the car park. I watch them go, catching Dad pat Mum on the bum and her swatting his hand away. They really do have a good marriage—yin and yang, they are, and still madly in love, even though they are vastly different people.

'Was that your parents?'

Jean-Luc sits on the lounger next to mine, placing his phone on the table between us. 'Yes. They're playing golf today.'

'No vacation from golf, even when they are on vacation.'

'Exactly. If they ever build a golf course on Antarctica, I think they'd fly there just to play a round.' He smiles, then settles in. 'So, how were your phone calls? Any interesting assignments coming up?' He's got a series of interviews in Edinburgh next week about Scottish independence—he'll be staying with Jae and Alistair—but after that, I'm not sure what else is on his calendar.

'Er … the calls … they were not for work.'

'Oh?' If not work, then he must have been speaking to his family. 'Is everything all right?'

'Pfft. I do not know, Catherine. It seems that we are behaving like the ostrich, *non?*'

My stomach curdles again. My straightforward husband is being cryptic and that can only mean one thing—he was speaking to his mother and she pressed the issue of our living situation. God, I wish everyone would just stay the hell out of it. Only, that's not fair. They're our loved ones. They care about us and the fact that even Sarah has asked about it means their concern is normal—annoying, but normal. Time to stop being an ostrich, I suppose.

'Do you want to talk here?' I ask. 'Or in our room?' Mum and Dad secured us an extra late check out, so we can stay until our farewell event. Actually, I suspect they've had to pay for an extra night, which is very sweet of them.

He lifts his gaze and scans the pool area, frowning slightly—though that could be from the sun. There are less than a dozen people scattered about—some on sun loungers, some in the pool, and one couple sits at a poolside table, sipping wine and playing cards. No one is within earshot, and who knows what languages they speak anyway. Essentially, we have the privacy we need for a difficult conversation. Only, it feels like the bright midday sun might be too incongruous with the subject matter.

'Let's go to our room,' he says.

'Of course,' I say, standing and gathering my things. I only have one thing to say—'I don't want to move to Paris'—but they may just be the hardest words I've ever had to utter. As we walk in silence back to our room, carrying a bubble of tension with us, I go from a curdled stomach to waves of nausea. As soon as the door is unlocked, I run for the bathroom and slam the door, making it just in time to vomit up my honeymoon brunch.

'Catherine, *chérie* … are you all right?' Jean-Luc taps lightly on the bathroom door as I kneel on the cool tiles waiting to see if another wave is coming.

'I'm all right,' I say, my voice strangled.

'Can I come in?'

'No! No, sorry … just … may I have a moment pl—' I don't get the rest of the word out before I'm heaving again into the toilet. God—I've either totally overeaten or I'm more worried about this conversation than I could have foreseen. Eventually convinced there's nothing left to bring up, I wipe my mouth with toilet paper and stand and flush the toilet. I go to the sink and peer at myself in the mirror, and the pallor of my skin is concerning.

'Catherine?' Jean-Luc's worry carries through the wooden door.

'Be right there,' I say. I rinse my mouth, then splash some water on my face and pat it dry with a hand towel. I look at my reflection again and take a deep breath. I do feel better—no longer nauseous—and there's no point in putting this conversation off any longer. I owe it to Jean-Luc. In fact, it's overdue, my confession.

Confession. Is that what's coming? I suppose it is. I confess that I have pretended everything is fine and perfect when really, I am terrified.

Because what if we come to an impasse? What if we can't make a decision that we can both live with? My heart starts racing at the thought, one I've buried for months, and my breathing becomes shallow. I don't want to vomit again, so I try to control my breath the way that Sarah does when she feels a panic attack coming on. As I breathe slowly and audibly, Lou's voice echoes through my mind. 'Be brave. Feel the fear and do it anyway.' Strangely, it's calming. I take one last slow breath and quietly tell myself, 'Be brave,' before leaving the bathroom to talk to my love.

'You are afraid,' he says matter-of-factly after listening to me ramble on for several minutes.

'I … sort of. I don't think I'm explaining myself very well.'

'You are afraid that you will never assimilate into a Parisian lifestyle.'

'Uh … no. If I'm afraid—and yes, there is some deep-seated fear amongst everything else—it's that I can't make you understand.'

'Understand what exactly?' Just that question tells me I am botching this. That and the deep crease between his eyebrows.

I take a breath and mentally regroup. 'I am not afraid that I won't assimilate into the Parisian lifestyle. There is a lot that I love about being in Paris. It's a beautiful, *beautiful* city. I love the art and the architecture. I love walking the streets and waking late and sipping enormous milky coffees at tiny cafés. I love your apartment—'

'*Our* apartment. It is ours now, Catherine.'

'Our apartment. I *love* it—I really do—but it doesn't matter how much I love Paris … I …'

'*Quoi?*' he prods.

'It will never love me back.'

He barks out a laugh and it stings as much as if he'd slapped me. Jean-Luc has never derided me before. We are

322

on uncharted ground. 'Why is that funny?' I ask, my voice wavering.

'*Désolé*—sorry, Catherine, that was unfair. But a city cannot love you. How can a city love you?'

'All right, I get it. It's a strange thing to say but that's how I feel when I'm there. Like a visitor at best and an interloper at worst.' A frown scuttles across his face. 'Interloper' must be a 'look-up word', an English word he is not familiar with. 'Interloper,' I say, 'like an intruder.'

He shakes his head in disbelief. 'But *non*—'

'But yes! I get it—you're blind to it, but it doesn't mean it's not real. It just means that you're oblivious—oblivious to the sideways glances and the tuts and smug scoffs. And I'm not just talking about the woman at the neighbourhood shop—though she's no charmer, that's for sure—I'm talking about the people we socialise with, your *friends*.' He expels a frustrated sigh but I can't close Pandora's box now. Besides, these truths would worm their way out eventually. 'How can you not have realised that any time we get together with your friends, they'll converse with me in English for a minute or two, then switch to rapid-fire French—talking across me and excluding me from the conversation?'

'But your French … it has improved vastly. You must understand these conversations by now.'

'Must I? I mean, sure, I can understand half of what's said, but I'm not fluent yet. Not even close. By the time I've figured out how to respond, how to contribute to the conversation—conjugating the verbs, assigning the right fricking article—the moment has passed and they're onto something else. Not one of them tries to include me.'

A look of concentration settles on his face, as though he's

running through the dozens of conversations I've been excluded from. 'I wish you'd read *Almost French* like I asked you to,' I say, referring to the memoir I first read in the early-00s but re-read a few months ago. It's about an Australian woman—a journalist—who falls in love with a Frenchman and moves to Paris to be with him. Even after *years* of living there, of becoming fluent in French, of making friends and immersing herself in the culture, of becoming a *citizen*, she will only ever be *almost* French. It's clear from his expression that he's forgotten. 'That book,' I say. 'The one with the Australian woman.'

'Ah, *oui*,' he says in recognition, 'but I do not need a book to understand my wife.'

'It seems that perhaps you do!' I say, my pitch rising along with my volume. 'And it's far worse with your family!' I add emphatically. 'They go out of their *way* to exclude me. How am I supposed to make a home in France when even my in-laws don't want me there?' The tears arrive, as they often do when I'm frustrated and angry, but these are tears of sadness too, of hurt and rejection.

And now we're at the crux of it. Jean-Luc's family may live in Lyon, nearly five hundred kilometres from Paris, but their emotional reach negates that distance and if I *did* move to France, I'd be seeing a lot more of them than I do now. And not only do they openly dislike me, they use my 'non-Frenchness' like a weapon. Cécile calling me 'simple' and 'shrill' in an overheard conversation is just the tip of the iceberg—especially when she cranked up her tactics to eleven, trying to derail our wedding. Even with the fragile peace we've established, she and I still have a very long way to go and that's if she doesn't recant her not-quite apology.

'Catherine ...' he says, his eyes pained. I know he just

wants to make things right but when he says, '*Ça ira*,' I see red.

'Don't placate, me, Jean-Luc. It will not be *fine*—not for a long time and maybe not ever. I just cannot see giving up my home in London—my job, my friends, my *life*—to walk into the lion's den dressed head-to-toe in meat like Lady frigging Gaga.' His confusion is almost amusing—he tilts his head, then shakes it, his eyes narrowing and lips pursing. 'You know, because she wore that meat dress to the MTV Awards.' His head shaking becomes head swinging and as it ricochets from side to side, he sucks his breath in through his teeth, stifling a grin.

'Never mind,' I say, half-a-second from dissolving into laughter. 'I just mean that I want to live somewhere that feels like home. Like London does.'

He looks at me, serious again. 'And you don't want the same thing for me?'

Tears prick my eyes. Of *course* I want him to live somewhere that feels like home. I never want him to feel as displaced as I would if I lived in Paris. 'Yes! Of course, I do. But you love London, don't you? It seems like you do.' I say, grasping. Because London is my home. It's where my heart sings and I feel most like myself. 'Fuck,' I say to myself, the stark realisation hitting hard. London is to me what Paris is to Jean-Luc.

'What?'

'We're the fish and the cat.'

'I do not understand.'

'My name aside, we're the *fish* and the *cat*. They can fall in love, but where do they live? The fish can't live on land and the cat can't live in the sea. So ...'

'I see. But Catherine, what did you think would happen?

About a home for us? Did you presume' —he means *assume*— 'that we would live separately and visit one another?'

'I don't know. Maybe …'

'But that is a child's belief, *non*?'

'Is it? Thank you very much for that condescending assessment.'

He snorts out a breath and bites his upper lip. 'You are my wife. I am your husband. I want us to have a home together.'

'I want that too.' Now, right as the words come out, I realise I *do* want to make a home with him, that I'm no longer afraid that he'll decide I'm not enough or that he'll tire of me, that living together will ruin what we have. Ironically, I'm fairly certain it was Vanessa's appearance at our wedding—*and* him sending her away—that started tipping the scales.

'But not in Paris.'

'This seems like it's come as a surprise to you and that … *baffles* me,' I say. 'You *had* to know that this is how I feel. On *some* level you had to know.'

'You seem very certain that I am knowing all these things.'

'Yes! Because you are the clever one, the worldly one. You're the one who has everything figured out in life.'

He laughs, but it lacks even a trace of humour. '*Non*. It is not as you say. I have as many uncertainties as you.'

'All right, let me ask you this—if you were so uncertain about this—about our living situation—then why did you *marry* me before we had it all sorted?'

'Because *I* am afraid!' he shouts. He stills, his eyes filling with tears, and holds back a ragged sob. 'I am afraid, my love.'

'What? Why?'

He nods. '*C'est vrai.* I am afraid I cannot make you happy. That you will not want to make a life with me. That you will live in your flat with Jane and I will be a visitor, an *interloper.*'

'No! No, I … I don't want that. I love living with Jane, but that time … that's over.' As the words leave my mouth, they consolidate my truth and the next part comes easily. 'I do want a life with you. I want us to sleep in the same bed as much as possible and yes, I know you travel for work all the time, but the rest of the nights …'

'But not in Paris.'

'Please stop saying that. I know——I get it now. Paris is your home. It's where you are most yourself.'

'Yes. And no.'

'What?' I ask again. We're both crying now and I sniffle and drag a knuckle under my nose.

'Catherine, *you* are my home.' A sob escapes as he rushes to me and gathers me in his arms. 'You are my home, *chérie,*' he says, his lips buried in my hair. I cling to him, hating myself for not noticing this enormous fear he's been carrying around. Another sob racks my body and he tightens his embrace. We stand like that for many moments, eventually stepping back and regarding each other. His face is tear-stained, his nose red, and I must look the same.

'There is one thing I have thought about,' he says quietly, taking my hands in his. 'Perhaps it is a good compromise, a way for the fish and the cat to live together——although I am not sure about being a fish …' I smile at his weak humour.

'We could find an apartment together in London for most of the year ...' My breath catches in my throat. 'And perhaps for the summer, we live in Paris ...' He shrugs, his eyes so filled with hope and his words so thoughtful, that my heart aches. 'When you are not teaching—like a vacation.'

Relief floods my body. A compromise. A perfect—extremely generous on his part—compromise.

'Oh, my god ... Jean-Luc—darling, that is ... I think it's *perfect*,' I say, sighing out the last word.

'Really? I was so unsure. I thought that perhaps Paris was, how do you say, off the table entirely.'

'No. I really do love it there and I want to learn to love *your* Paris, to improve my French. I do want to make it a home, of sorts ... just ...'

'*Je comprends*. I think your connection to London ... it is more intense than I have imagined. We will make a wonderful home there.' I smile at him. 'And when I am not in Paris, I can rent out my apartment.'

'Of course! I can even help with that.'

'And Jane?' he asks.

'She'll understand, I promise. And we'll give her plenty of notice so she can find a new flatmate.'

'*Parfait*.' We smile at each other.

'Oh, and one more thing ...' I say.

He lifts a finger to my cheek and wipes away a tear, then leans down for a soft kiss. '*Oui, n'importe quoi, ma chérie.* Anything.'

'It's just ...' His lips move to my jaw, then my neck.

'Mmm?'

'If we're going to live in your apartment—'

'*Our* apartment.'

'Right. Our apartment ...' God, it's hard to concentrate

when the touch of his mouth has my body on high alert, but I must get this out. 'It's just that … in the summer …'

He pulls back abruptly and grins at me. 'We will get air conditioning.'

'Oh, thank god! Wait, how did you know that's——'

'Because you are not exactly subtle, Catherine.'

'Right. Yes. Sorry about that. You know me, typical whinging pom.'

He laughs softly. 'It is charming.'

'I seriously doubt that.'

'I think you interrupted me before, Mrs Caron …' he says, sliding his hand down my thigh. He gathers the hem of my dress and pulls it up to my waist. Even though I'm not officially taking his name, I do like the sound of 'Mrs Caron', especially coming from my sexy French husband——my sexy French husband who's going to live with me in London.

So the fish and the cat *can* live together after all.

Chapter Twenty-Five

SARAH

Tuscany

I'm sure it's not the 'done thing' to bother your sister when she's essentially on her honeymoon, but Josh has been gone a few hours now and he's not answering his phone—I'm starting to worry. I fire off a text.

Sorry! Can you please call me? Sort of urgent :(

Since he left, I have showered and dressed, met with Bianca about getting the flowers to the hospital, and have cleaned up the apartment—not that it was especially messy, but every dish is washed and put away and I've even cleaned the outdoor table and swept the balcony. I'm now onto my preliminary pack, though no amount of rolling my clothes and zipping them into packing cubes is soothing the rising panic.

I stare at my phone, which is annoyingly silent on the bedside table, and plop onto the bed. 'Please come back,

Josh,' I say aloud. I'm hoping that by the time he does, I'll have figured out how to explain the unfettered longing inside me—one that has *nothing* to do with Josh and our relationship, or my career, or my family and friends. A longing that I now believe is about a promise I made myself twenty years ago.

The front door of the apartment opens, abruptly ending my angst, and when Josh appears in the doorway of our room, a feeble smile on his face, I rush to him and fall into his arms. The sobs immediately follow, a release of sorts. As irrational as it may be, there was a small part of me that worried he wouldn't come back—*at all*. 'Hey, hey ...' he says, his hands running up and down my back.

'I'm so sorry,' I say into his shirt.

'It's okay. I'm not really mad, not anymore—it's just ...' He sighs. 'Hey, can we sit?'

I nod, then step back and wipe under my eyes, sniffling. He takes one of my hands and leads me to the bed and we sit side by side. I reach for a handful of tissues and blow my nose. 'How was your walk?' I ask.

'Yeah, you know, lots of hills. I got a bit lost, to be honest.'

'Hah!' I laugh, the harsh sound echoing around the room. 'Sorry.'

'Nah, it is funny. Even with Google Maps, I still got myself turned around. At one point, I was walking in the wrong direction for a good twenty minutes. It's only when I came to the winery I was talking about earlier that I realised.' We chuckle softly at his expense, then he takes a deep breath. 'Look, Sarah, I've known for a while that something wasn't quite right—with you—and if I'm completely honest, I thought that it might have been about me. About us. That maybe you were having doubts and—'

'No! I promise, it's not that. I love you.'

'I know that. At least, my head knows but sometimes I couldn't convince my heart, so I just ignored it. I should have asked you before what was going on. But I was just too scared. I'm sorry.'

'Josh, you have nothing to apologise for. *I'm* the one who should have said something—even though I've barely had the words to explain it to myself. But I should have known you'd twig that something wasn't right, that you've been worrying all this time … *I'm* sorry.'

He nods and looks at me, his steel-grey eyes stormy but filled with love. 'Why were you able to talk to everyone but me?'

'That's a fair question—it is—but I don't know the answer.' He looks down at the floor, frowning. 'I don't think that's anything to worry about though,' I add hurriedly. 'Just a little disconnect. No relationship is perfect all of the time.' I'm right, aren't I? He looks back at me, still frowning. Oh, god.

'Look, before I met you, I was determined to stay single—remember?'

'Of course, I remember,' I say quietly, the tears threatening to return. It had been a massive bone of contention—and a source of pain and doubt—for the better part of a year. I don't know that I will *ever* forget that.

'Well, this is one of the reasons.'

'What? What do you mean?' The budding nerves blossom into full-on terror—have we inadvertently crashed into an insurmountable problem?

He gets up and wanders over to the window and scowls

out at the view. 'This feeling—this *doubt*. I hate wondering if we're okay, if we're still on the same page. Because once I realised that I did want to be in a relationship—with *you*—then I got all these ideas about what it would be, how we would be together. And this … *thing*—whatever it is that you're going through—it's really thrown me for a loop.'

'I hadn't realised. But I know that now and I'm really sorry.'

'And that's just it. *I* couldn't be honest with *you* about any of this. That's not how a relationship should be.'

'What are you saying, Josh?' I ask, my voice strangled. 'Do you want to break up?' I barely get the words out. My heartbeat pounds in my ears, a thudding roar, and this bright, vast, open room suddenly seems to close in on me.

Josh's eyes fly to mine. 'What? No!' He's across the room in a shot, kneeling before me and taking my hands in his.

'Are you sure?'

'Yes, I'm sure. I just … I don't want us to *ever* be in this situation again. That's all.'

I half sigh, half sob. 'Oh, thank god.'

'See? I've even fucked this up.'

'No, no, you haven't. No more than me, anyway.'

'We need to be *way* better at communicating.'

'Way better,' I agree. I exhale, long and slow, more controlled this time.

'Did you really think that that's what I was saying? The breaking up thing?' he asks.

'I don't know. Yes. I guess.'

'Can we rewind, do you think?'

'Rewind. What do you mean?'

'To before we had this stupid fight.'

'Okay,' I say, unsure where he's going.

'Sarah, I've noticed that you have had something on your mind for the past few months. Is it about me or our relationship?'

'No,' I say shaking my head earnestly. 'I think it's about Africa.'

He blinks at me. 'Wow, really? Africa?' I nod. 'That's like … possibly the last thing I imagined you saying.'

'I should explain.'

'That would be good,' he says with smiling eyes, the corners of his mouth upturned slightly.

'Well, you remember when you told me about this trip—at Lins and Nick's?' I ask rhetorically.

'Yes,' he replies anyway and I shake my head at him.

'Well, it was weird that day hearing the number forty and connecting it with me.'

'Yeah, you seemed a little …'

'Freaked out. I was freaked out.'

'Was it the number itself or just hitting the milestone?' he asks.

'Well, I thought at first it was the number—and at times, it *has* been about that. I mean, *forty* is halfway to *eighty* and—'

'But you're gonna live *way* past ninety, that's for sure,' he interjects.

'Well, we don't know that—no one knows know how long they have, but that's a whole other thing and can I please just make my point?' I widen my eyes so he knows I'm only half-serious.

'Please continue. No doubt, sometime in the next hour, we'll get to your point.'

I respond to his teasing with a dramatic sigh, then continue. 'So, yes, sometimes it was about the number—and of course, Cat goes and gives me Grandma's pearls so *that* didn't help and ... never mind,' I say, cutting myself off. I do not need to revisit the 'I'm old' tangent. 'Anyway, so the day after you told me about Italy, I went looking for this letter I wrote to myself when I was around nineteen or twenty—'

'Hey, I wrote one of those,' he says.

'Really?'

'Yeah,' he laughs, 'don't sound so surprised. It was for a class in college.'

'Mine was for a class too.'

'You know what mine said, at the end?' he asks. 'Live a big life.'

'Oh, wow. That's ... that's the trip to Greece—living a bigger life.'

'Yeah. I re-read the letter right before I booked that trip.'

'You never told me that,' I say.

He shrugs. 'It never came up. So what did *your* letter say? "Go to Africa"?'

I chuckle. 'Not exactly. But it was a reminder about someone who meant the world to me at the time. Aunty Tessa.' He tilts his head, inviting me to tell him more. 'One of Dad's best friends—just this incredible woman and she was brave and adventurous ... I wanted to be like her.'

'You are,' he says softly.

'Getting there.'

'Hey, you're Adventure Chick, remember.' He captures my hand in his, squeezing it, and I give a weak smile in return. 'And you said "was",' he adds quietly.

'Breast cancer. Aged forty-three.'

'Ahhh,' he says as though thoughts are sliding into place.

'Yeah, exactly. So, the Africa connection ... Tessa built a

school there. Well, she was partway through building a school there when she …'

'And you want to go there to teach.'

'I do. Thank you for getting that straight off the bat—especially as it took me ages to figure it out.'

'Like four months?' he asks with a slight smile.

'Like four months, yeah. It was only when I was talking to Dad yesterday and he mentioned it … I think I'd buried that promise to her—to *me*—because it was too painful. Also, I think maybe Tessa's age when she died …'

'Only three years older than you.' The kindness in his eyes, the understanding—*this* is why he's my person.

'Exactly. I think that was a big part of it—of all this.' He nods. 'You would have loved her.'

'I don't doubt it.' He smiles at me warmly. 'So,' he says, 'when are you thinking? And for how long?'

'Well, I don't know exactly … *soon*? I mean, I have to ask the school, of course, but if they say yes, I can take long service leave. I've got, like, *months* owed to me. Oh! I could teach for a whole term! Oh, my god, that's perfect. I could finish out this school year, then go in January. I mean, that's the hottest month of the year, but still, it would be good to start the school year with the students. Oh, this is gonna be amazing!' I start bouncing up and down, clapping my hands just under my chin. I may be forty, but I can still get as excited as a child about to go to Disneyland.

'I have so many more questions,' he says, laughing. 'But I'm really excited for you, Sarah. It sounds awesome.' He wraps me up in his arms and we hug tightly.

I pull back. 'Hey, have you ever been to Africa?' I ask. 'Would you want to come with me?'

'I would love to go to Africa with you—even if it's just

for part of the time. And are we talking a specific country or the entire continent?' he teases.

'South Africa—Cape Town.'

'Okay. Well, that's a start.'

'Oh, and we can go to a game park! One of those parks with rescue animals——' Just then, my phone bleeps with a message and I look at it, seeing Cat's name on the screen.

'Did you want to read that?' he asks.

'I'd better. I sent her a message earlier saying it was urgent.'

'I'll give you some privacy, then,' he says standing.

'You don't need——'

'It's okay. Oh, hey,' he says, 'instead of going out, how about a picnic here in the vineyard—make a dent in some of those leftovers?'

'Sounds perfect. Thank you.'

'I'll start getting stuff together.' Before he goes, he leans down and kisses me—softly and sweetly—and when he closes the bedroom door quietly behind him, I sigh. So much turmoil, so much pain and misunderstanding … if only we'd just *talked* to each other. I'll never try and hide something like this again. Even if I don't know exactly what 'it' is at the time, I'll be sure to tell Josh that something's going on.

I pick up the phone and call Cat. When she appears on the screen, she looks a little peaky. 'Hi, are you okay?' I ask.

'Yes, just been quite a morning.'

'Oh, were you hungover?' As Maid of Honour, I'd tried my best to ensure she'd stayed hydrated and had enough to eat to combat the free-flowing prosecco, but maybe I'd failed.

'No, I don't think so. I felt fine when I woke up ... just a little sick after brunch.'

'Oh, well that's a shitty way to start your honeymoon.'

She laughs softly. 'It's funny that everyone keeps calling it that. We go home tomorrow.' Sadness clouds her expression.

'Yeah.' We're both quiet for a sec and no doubt—like me—she's contemplating the goodbyes to come.

'Sorry, you said there was something urgent. Is everything all right?' she asks.

I fill her in on my tumultuous morning—every topsy-turvy detail (except the sex part—she's always been squeamish about my sex life)—and end on a happy note with my Africa plans.

'Oh, Sez, that sounds brilliant. And Aunty Tessa would have loved that.'

'Thanks,' I say with a wide smile, my heart full. 'I think so too.'

'Sooo ... I have news as well.'

'Oh, really?' I say, feigning indifference. I don't want to put any more pressure on her, but she *really* needs to sort out the whole living situation.

'Yes. Jean-Luc is going to keep his flat in Paris—'

'Oh?' I'm pretty sure this isn't what Cat had hoped for.

'No, no, it's a good thing, I promise.' She goes on to explain what they've decided, including a weird tangent about a cat and a fish, but the gist is that they're both content with their decision.

'That sounds a lot more feasible than a long-distance marriage,' I say.

'Mmm, quite,' she replies.

'God, how good are we, eh? Here we are in romantic

Tuscany, celebrating these incredible milestones with our gorgeous men and we've both had massive arguments.'

'Love is messy, I suppose.'

'Yeah,' I agree—that one syllable conveying so much.

She smiles brightly. 'Anyway, it's all sorted now. I'm even hoping Cécile and I can find a way to make peace—properly, I mean.'

'After all the shit she pulled—'

'Yes, yes, all right,' she says, interrupting. 'I know it was bad, but I can't keep wallowing. I've got to at least *try* with Jean-Luc's family. Perhaps agreeing to live in France for part of the year will mean they hate me a little less. It's a start, anyway.'

'At least Louis likes you. *And* your nieces.'

'Actually, that's been my plan all along. Infiltrate the Carons via the children.'

'Hah! Love it. So, what have you got on for the rest of the day?' I ask.

'Massages, I hope. Jean-Luc's just gone to reception to see if they can fit us in.'

'Oooh, jealous.'

'What about you two?'

'Josh is making us a picnic from the leftovers, then we're heading into the vineyard here at the castle.'

'Oh, that's lovely.'

'Gotta make the most of our last full day in Tuscany.'

'Right,' she says quietly. She's frowning again and all I can think is, *Please don't say it!* But then she says it. 'I'm going to miss you.' My eyes mist, blurring her face, and I bite my lip and blink back the tears. 'Soz,' she says, shorthand for 'sorry'. I shrug. 'Oh!' she exclaims, jolting me from imminent melancholy. 'I forgot to tell you. Guess what Mum and Dad gave us for our wedding present.'

'What?'

'Half-a-million frequent flier points!'

'Like me!'

'Exactly. We should plan a trip together—all four of us—somewhere tropical.'

'The Maldives!'

'I hadn't thought about the Maldives.'

'I have,' I say, 'they're halfway.'

'Between …?'

'Between the UK and Sydney. It's perfect. None of us have been there before and we've probably got enough points for flights and accommodation. But after I get back from South Africa, okay?'

'And when's that?'

'I have no idea—Easter time maybe? *Logistics*, Cat! So much to figure out but I'll keep you posted.'

She turns around, smiles, then turns back to the camera. 'Jean-Luc is back. It's massage time.' She makes the 'squee' face.

'Well, enjoy and we'll see you in a few hours for happy hour.'

'All right. Enjoy your picnic!'

'Love you.'

'Love you too,' she says, ending the call.

'Da-aad, enough with the toasts,' I cry. I'm only half joking. Even when they're slightly embarrassing, Dad's toasts are always from the heart.

Our farewell gathering is in full swing, Jaelee having arranged an area for us that's both poolside and close to the resort's bar and, until Dad stood on a chair and called for our attention, joyful chatter and laughter permeated the early autumn evening. For an event I'd wanted to skip, it's actually been a lot of fun.

'I won't take up too much time, love, I promise,' he says to me. 'Now come over here—both my girls. Come on.' Cat and I exchange an 'uh-oh' look, then move through the loose knot of loved ones to stand either side of Dad. He rests one hand on my shoulder and the other on Cat's head. 'You really are short, aren't you, love?' he says peering down at her. Cat shakes her head in amusement. I am *so* grateful that Dad's keeping it light—the goodbyes are *just there*, lurking in the shadows and they are absolute buggers.

'I just wanted to say, on behalf of Karen and myself, that we are very proud of our two beautiful daughters.' Oh, god, that's not light, Dad—that's gonna make me cry—for the third time today! Where's the jokey-teasing toast where everyone laughs and rolls their eyes?

'Catherine,' he says, 'congratulations again on marrying the love of your life. We are thrilled for you both and no rush, love, but I would like to be a grandad while I'm still young enough to pick them up.'

I laugh along with everyone else while Cat chastises him with, 'Dad!'

'Don't blame me, love. Your mother wrote that line.'

'Ronald! I absolutely did not!'

'Oops, now I'm in trouble with two Parsons women,' he says to the rest of us. Mum tuts at him over the laughter, a surreptitious smile on the verge of breaking free. I sense that she's dreading the goodbyes too and sometimes it's easier to joke around than dwell on the sad things.

And poor Cat. I know I laughed along—as I said, sometimes it's easier to joke—but she's barely been married twenty-four hours and the 'baby talk' has already started. I'm not even sure she and Jean-Luc want kids. She's mentioned it a few times, but in that abstract, hypothetical way. They've hardly started picking out baby names!

'And Sarah …' Oh, god, here we go. *Please say something funny, Dad*, I will him. 'You've hit a major milestone this week, love …' Something funny—please! 'And your mum and I are very proud of the woman you are.' Not funny, not funny. I really don't want to cry. This will be the last time my immediate family is together for who knows how long and I may not be able to stop. I conjure the funniest memory I can think of under pressure—me waiting in a hotel room in Hawaii for Josh—naked on the bed—and in walks the bellboy *then* Josh. 'And we're so pleased about your plans to work at Tessa's school.' There's the sheen of tears in his eyes as he smiles down at me. Nope. Caught naked by a bellboy isn't even make a dent. 'She'd be really proud of you too, love,' he adds quietly.

Well, here they come! I blink back tears as I dig into my handbag for a tissue. 'And one last thing—a big thanks to you, Jaelee. You've probably heard that quite a bit this week, but I know that *all* my girls—Karen included—couldn't have put all this together without you. So, thank you, love.' The focus off me—thank god—I look over at Jaelee who seems (uncharacteristically) humble, her cheeks flushing as she smiles shyly.

'Right!' says Dad, clapping his hands together. 'No use hanging about like a shag on a rock. I reckon we'll do the rounds and say our goodbyes, then let you young people carry on.' He jumps spryly off the chair and the hubbub of conversation starts up again as he turns and hugs me. My tears are flowing freely now—shocker, I know.

'Tessa really would be proud, love,' he says, releasing me from the hug.

'I know, Dad.'

'And I'm really glad you figured out your one thing.'

'My one thing?'

'Yeah, you know, like in the movie, *City Slickers*.' I look at him blankly. We watched it together as a family when Cat and I were kids but all I remember is the baby cow called Norman. 'Don't you remember?' I shake my head. 'Curly, the old cowboy, tells Billy Crystal that there's only one thing in life that's important—and that he has to figure out his one thing.'

'Oh, right.'

'I'm not explaining myself very well.' This is where I get it from—my tendency to talk in circles and elicit confusion. Ironic, really, considering I'm an excellent teacher (if I do say so myself). But when it comes to explaining my emotions or my thoughts or philosophies … I often tie myself up in knots. Still, I do get where Dad is coming from.

'You've explained it perfectly, Dad. I just needed to figure out what was missing and I did.'

'And you did!' He hugs me again.

'Thanks for the nudge in the right direction,' I say, my voice muffled by the hug.

'Of course, love.' He steps back. 'So, we'll see you back in Sydney.'

'Yep.'

'You two travel safely.'

343

'Will do, Dad. Love you.'

'Love you too.'

He smiles, then turns towards Cat who already has tears in her eyes. God knows how hard this will be on her—at least I get to see Mum and Dad whenever I want.

'Sarah.' It's Mum.

I reach down and grasp her hand and she smiles at me. 'Looking forward to Venice?' I ask. They're heading there tomorrow for a week's holiday, probably a welcomed change from the hustle and bustle of the past week. She nods, and her smile turns bittersweet. 'Just hard to say goodbye, isn't it?'

She blinks a few times. 'I'm not as sentimental as your father, but yes. You know, when you girls moved to London all those years ago … that was very hard on me. It was on your father too, but I felt like part of my heart had been ripped out.'

'Oh, Mum.' I squeeze her arm as a tear escapes and she swipes it away.

'Oh, I'm just being silly.' She tosses her head and blinks a few times. 'Anyway, I love that you're close by and most of the time, the pain of missing Catherine, it's down here.' She places a hand flat on her lower chest. Well, I definitely understand that—I use the same coping mechanism. 'And spending time with her here in Italy … well, it's been wonderful but it's brought all that to the surface and …' She swallows.

'Mum, have you told Cat any of this?'

She shakes her head. 'I don't trust myself. I'll probably end up a blubbering mess.'

'That's okay, Mum. No one here is going to think any less of you. You should tell her.'

344

She sniffles. 'I suppose you're right.' She eyes me curiously. 'And when did you get to be so wise, Sarah?'

'Don't you remember? As soon as the clock strikes twelve on your fortieth birthday, it's like this veil is lifted and you suddenly know all the secrets of the universe.'

She tuts and rolls her eyes, then smiles—exactly the reaction I hoped for, because with her calm and collected façade in place, she may just be ready to tell her youngest daughter how much she misses her.

Just then, something catches Mum's eye and her expression does a one-eighty. 'Sarah, isn't that …?'

I follow her line of sight and, yes, it *is* in fact … 'Piero,' I half whisper. Our Roman god-like life-drawing model is at the bar chatting up a very pretty (and very lucky) woman.

'Mmm, he nearly looks as good in clothes as he looks out of them.'

'Mum!' I say, my attention swinging back to her.

She presses her lips firmly together, their edges slightly curled up and raises her eyebrows at me. 'Sixty-four,' she whispers, 'not dead.'

We both dissolve into giggles—possibly the only time I've giggled with my mum. When the giggles subside, she kisses my cheek and without saying another word, goes to wait her turn to say goodbye to Cat. It could be a long wait—Dad's goodbye is lasting longer than one of Cher's farewell tours.

Familiar arms snake their way around my waist. 'You having a good time?' asks Josh.

I lean against him, laying my hands over his, and breathe in his delicious aftershave, the one I gave him for Christmas last year. He smells of sandalwood and spices. As we sway together gently, I cast my eyes over our motley crew—old friends and new, and family—imprinting the image on my mind. No doubt there are dozens, maybe hundreds, of photos that were taken this week but I want to remember this night exactly as it is.

The delight on people's faces, the cackle of Siobhan's laughter as she tosses her black tresses, the glances Anders sneaks at Lou, obviously in love with her, Lindsey chatting conspiratorially with Jane, kindred pragmatists amongst the rest us, Dad doing the rounds, having endeared himself to everyone here, Jaelee balancing on five-inch heels, her expression softening every time she sees Alistair, Jean-Luc catching my eye and smiling, and finally, Cat and Mum sharing a special mother–daughter moment. It's perfect.

'Yes,' I say, answering Josh's question, 'but I'm ready.'

'Ready?'

I turn inside his embrace, clasping my hands behind his neck and look up into his beautiful grey eyes. 'Ready to go home.'

'Lots to look forward to.'

'Yeah.' I nod, grinning. 'Oh! I forgot to tell you—I can't believe this totally slipped my mind—but Cat and I are thinking we should all go to the Maldives.'

'All?' He cocks his head, then his eyes lift to scan the people gathered around us.

'Just us four,' I say quietly. 'They got frequent flier points from Mum and Dad too—that was their wedding present—so we just need to find a time when we can all go.'

His eyes drop to meet mine. 'That sounds amazing.'

'After Cape Town, though.'

'Obviously.'

'Or maybe before—depends on how quickly I can get that organised.'

'Definitely.'

'Are you teasing me?'

'Always.' He smiles, then dips his head, capturing my lips in a rather sexy kiss.

'All right, you two, enough of that. At least wait till your mum and I leave the party.'

'Ugh, Da-aad!'

He bellows out a laugh then shouts, 'Goodnight, everyone,' and grabs Mum's hand and they leave the party to a chorus of 'goodnight'.

That's the first goodbye done but it was also the easiest.

Chapter Twenty-Six

CAT

Tuscany

Goodbyes are wretched things … and here come a slew of them.

At least Dad's speech got me laughing—well, sort of. A few married colleagues had warned me that the topic of babies would come up this week. I'd forgotten, but Dad's words were a stark reminder that at thirty-eight, Jean-Luc and I will need to decide soon-ish if we want to be parents. But one major life decision at a time—we only sorted our living situation five minutes ago. And Jane—lovely Jane—was so understanding when we broke the news to her earlier. She's even promised to help us look for somewhere in Docklands so we're still in the same borough.

'Cat, come here, love,' says Dad, holding his arms out wide. I step into his embrace and try not to dissolve into tears. He's not tall, my dad, but neither am I, and his hugs have always felt like the safest place in the world to be. 'Only partly kidding about the grandchild thing,' he says. I lean back and give him one of my schoolteacher looks. He grins at me, making me smile.

'You're very naughty, Dad,' I say. 'We've only just got married.'

'Yes, love, but you're pushing forty and I know you young people think you have all the time in the world—'

'So, first I'm old and now I'm young?'

'Exactly.'

We regard one another for a moment. As has been true each time I say goodbye to my parents, this one will hurt acutely for some time, then eventually dull into an ache that becomes part of my emotional landscape. Living across the world from my immediate family is the hardest part of calling London home. But it is home and now I'm going to share it with my new husband.

'Are you excited about Venice, Dad?' I ask.

'Ah, you know me, love. I'm happy if your mum's happy and she's been talking about going back for a while now.'

'But it's *Venice*.' *I* wouldn't mind an extra week away in one of the world's most romantic cities but I'm due back at school in a couple of days.

'I'm sure it will be great. Best pizza in the world!' He waggles his eyebrows.

'I won't tell the entire city of Naples that.'

He sighs. 'We're doing that thing, aren't we?'

'Where we just talk rubbish until it's time to say goodbye? Yes, we are.'

'I miss you, love.' I suddenly can't speak—a lump the size of a pizza has lodged in my throat—so I just nod. 'It's been *wonderful* being here with you and you have to promise to come home soon, okay?' Even after living in London for fifteen years, Dad still refers to Sydney as my 'home'.

I manage to squeak out, 'I will,' before he hugs me again, quickly and tightly, then steps away, clearing his throat and putting on a show of saying cheery goodbyes to the others.

I blow my nose as Mum steps up, almost shy. 'Hello, Mum.'

'Hello, darling.'

It appears she has something to say—and not just 'goodbye'—but is having trouble getting the words out. After a moment, I reach for her hand. 'I know, Mum. Me too.' A sob takes hold as tears stream from her eyes and she embraces me tightly.

'I really do love you, you know,' she says. 'And I *miss* you—*so* much,' she adds, barely above a whisper.

'I miss you too, Mum.'

She pulls away and places her hands on my shoulders, then composes herself, smiling tautly. 'Enjoy the rest of your stay.'

'I will.'

She takes a deep breath, sighing it out. 'See you, then.' She pats my shoulders and goes.

Our parents say quick goodbyes to our friends, Dad in his typical jovial way and Mum even more reserved than usual. Then Dad tosses in a final dig at Sarah and Josh for snogging in public (again) and they're gone. I stare after them for a moment and feel Sarah beside me. 'That sucked,' she says.

'Yes. I feel like escaping back to the castle so I can have a good cry in private.'

'We can head off soon if you like. No need to prolong these goodbyes any longer if you're not up to it.'

I lean into her and she wraps an arm around my shoulder. 'Am I a shitty person if that's exactly what I'd like to do?'

'No. You're not. And if you like, you can blame it on me. Tell everyone that, as I'm now forty, it's nearly my bedtime.' She glances at her watch. 'Actually …'

'It's not even eight.'

'Exactly.'

'If we lived here, we'd just be heading out for an early dinner.'

'I seriously do not know how the Italians do it.'

'Siesta,' I say.

'Yeah, yeah … even so … I only bust out a nap in extreme circumstances. I doubt it'd ever become part of my daily routine—even if I did live here.'

'Oh, hey, did you see that Piero's here?' she asks.

'Pier— Oh, really? Where?'

I look around and right as she says, 'At the bar,' I spot him.

'Oh, my god.'

'I know, right.' We stare openly at him as the blonde he's with laughs, flicks her long hair over one shoulder, then licks her lips. 'I think he's in there,' I say.

'I think he could be in anywhere he wanted.'

'Ewww, Sarah!'

'What?' she says, laughing. 'Don't be such a prude!'

'I'm not a pr—'

'Catherine, *chérie* …'

'Hello, husband,' I say, looking up into his gorgeous green eyes and hoping like hell he didn't catch *any* of that conversation.

'Hello, wife.' We stare at each other intently.

'Do you two want to be alone?' teases Sarah.

'Actually …' He drawls, punctuating his words with a half-shrug. 'I'm exhausted. And you must be as well,' he says to me. 'Should we …' he jerks his head, indicating that he wants to leave.

'Oh, thank god—*yes*,' I say. 'Let's bid *adieu* and head the Merc.' Confusion mars his perfect face.

'Head the Mercedes home,' says Sarah, addressing his unasked question.

'Ahhh,' he says, dropping a peck onto my lips, 'one week with your sister and you become all Aussie again.'

'What's wrong with that?'

'*Rien*, my love.' He smiles cheekily then turns to the others and announces that we are heading back to the castle soon.

There's a collective disappointed 'aww' from our friends followed by a frenzy of activity—Josh offering to retrieve our bags from reception and call an Uber, hugs, tears, laughter, promises, and half-whispered words, spoken through tears or feigned cheerfulness—farewells that will need to tide us over till next time.

'Anders is wonderful, Lou,' I say. 'I'm so happy for you.'

'He's a sweetheart. I'm very lucky.'

'He's the lucky one, Lou. And make sure you give us plenty of notice so we can come to Canada for the wedding,' I say. I leave her open-mouthed and wide-eyed, squeezing her hand one last time, before seeking out Jaelee.

'Hey, girl,' she says.

I hug her tightly and after a moment's hesitation, she returns it. 'Will I see you before you fly south for the winter?' I ask when we step apart.

'Hmm, doubtful. But it'll go fast. It always does.' She's

right. Their stints of living in the tropics seem to fly by and before we know it, she and Alistair are back in the UK.

'Thank you again for everything, Jae.'

'You've said that at least a dozen times already.' She tempers her words with a one-dimpled smile.

'Well, let's make it a baker's dozen and call it good.'

'Deal.' She hugs me again——short and sharp this time——then turns and goes before I become a blubbering mess——or maybe she's worried that she will. Being with Alistair has softened the edges on my prickly friend and I love her all the more for it.

'Cat, you gorgeous woman!' From a rigid hug from Jaelee into the ample bosom of Siobhan. I laugh as she smothers me with her own unique brand of Siobhan love. 'Now,' she says, holding me at arm's distance by my shoulders and staring down at me, 'you absolutely *must* promise to come see me in Dublin.'

'I promise. *We* promise.'

'Good. Because I want you to meet Keely and I want to show you about, and we'll go to all the best places and we'll even do the touristy bits. Do you like Guinness? Never mind if you don't——rite of passage for all visitors. And the view from the top of the factory is grand. You'll love it.' She hugs me again. 'Oh, I am so happy for ye.' She rocks me from side to side and I cling on for dear life. 'Right, now I'll let you go,' she says, literally letting me go.

'Thank you so much for coming. We've loved having you here.'

'Wouldn't have missed it.' She smiles at me, her eyes twinkling, then lifts her head and scans our group. 'Where's that handsome husband of yours?' She leaves before I can answer and no doubt is about to smother Jean-Luc in another effusive goodbye.

I get hugs from Lindsey and Nick and from Anders and Alistair—his comes with a promise to FaceTime as soon as they get to Bali in a few weeks—and then it's time to go. Waving to our friends, we four make our way out of the resort—Josh and Jean-Luc with our luggage in hand—and find our ride.

It's quiet during the seven-minute ride from the resort to the castle. No doubt my sister, brother-in-law, and husband are as exhausted as I am—physically and emotionally wrung out from the most intense and wonderful week of my life.

I lean my head against the window and cast my eyes across the expanse of the sky, now a deep blue punctuated with dozens of stars, then along the silhouettes of the tall, skinny conifers that dot the hilltops, my gaze landing on the warm glow from houses nestled in the valleys.

It's so beautiful here.

'Are you sure you have everything?' Sarah asks. She's just completed her third round of 'final checks' before we hand over the key to the castle apartment.

'Definitely.'

'Says the woman who left her wedding dress in Italy.'

'Ouch. That's not nice.'

'Sorry.'

She makes a move towards the bedroom she and Josh have inhabited for the past week. 'Sarah. You've checked it three times. We need to go.' Jean-Luc and Josh are already in the rental car, our luggage stowed safely in the boot.

She pauses and looks at me. 'I hate this part.'

'So you're stalling.' She nods. 'Come on.' I grab hold of her hand and gently pull her across the threshold.

'All good, Sarah?' Josh calls from the car window.

'Yeah. Be right there.'

Bianca is waiting at the bottom of the steps leading up to the castle and we walk along the crunchy gravel driveway to meet her. '*Buongiorno*,' I say. A glimmer of a smile alights on her face, then disappears.

'*Buongiorno*. Did you enjoy your stay?' Two nights ago, she shared her deepest sorrows with me but none of that vulnerability is visible now. Perhaps she's embarrassed.

'Oh, totally,' says Sarah. 'You have a beautiful castle—and we loved the apartment. It's so serene here.'

The memory of the killer wasp pops into my head and I stifle a laugh. Sarah glances sideways at me, shushing me. 'And thank you for all your help with the wedding,' I say hurriedly. Bianca nods curtly and that small smile appears again. 'And, please, whatever you can salvage from the leftovers ... the food ...'

Another nod. 'I will look and maybe take some to the ...' She seems to struggle for the word in English. '... *la casa di riposo*—' She gestures. 'Older people, where they live ...'

'Oh,' I say, twigging. 'That's perfect—*perfetto*.' May as well toss in one of the ten Italian words I know and it really is *perfetto* that the food won't go to waste. *And* she's already taken the flowers to the nearest hospital. 'Thank you,' I say, smiling at her brightly.

'*Grazie*,' says Sarah.

'Yes, *grazie*.' Part of me wants to hug her, this quiet

woman who lost both her parents not long ago. But I sense that she'd hate that. 'Oh, and here.' I hand her the enormous key to the apartment and she nods again.

'Well, bye,' says Sarah, our cue to leave. I raise my hand in a wave—another nod in reply—and we walk back down the driveway and climb into the car—me in the front with Jean-Luc, who's driving, and Sarah in the back.

'*D'accord?*' asks Jean-Luc.

Now it's my turn to nod, as I don't trust my voice, and he puts the car into gear and reverses out of the driveway. I watch our castle home out the windscreen, then we change directions and in moments, the enormous structure disappears, swallowed by leafy trees and dappled sunlight.

The hardest farewell is now only a few hours away and the mood in the car is contemplative—or perhaps that's just me. I look over my shoulder and Josh has his earbuds in—listening to a podcast or something—and Sarah is watching out the window. She must sense my gaze because she looks at me and smiles sadly. I return the smile then continue watching out the windscreen.

The Tuscan countryside as we descend the hills around Montespertoli is so beautiful, with its rolling hills, a patchwork of green and straw-coloured grass, and stands of those tall, skinny fir trees. And after this past week, it will forever hold a special place in my heart.

I'm married. I'm married to my first and only true love and just the thought fills me to brimming with joy.

'Oh, god. Pull over. Jean-Luc, *please* pull over.'

The car veers off the road, bouncing along the rough verge before coming to an abrupt stop. I fling open the door and retch onto the dusty ground. Jean-Luc unlatches my seatbelt so I have more mobility and I turn in my seat and empty my stomach while he rubs my back soothingly.

'Oh, Cat,' says Sarah, her voice permeating my nausea. 'Do you think it was something you ate?'

As I breathe slowly, in through my nose and out through my mouth, finding my equilibrium, I cast my mind back to last night. After returning to the castle, we'd all been so shattered and were so over wine and rich food, I'd made a giant plate of buttered toast, and we'd sat on the balcony watching the starry sky, sipping coffee and tea and talking about nothing in particular until we headed off to bed around nine.

And I'd had exactly the same for breakfast—toast and tea. Jean-Luc hands me a bottle of water and I take a swig to rinse my mouth, spitting it out onto the ground, then sit back against the seat and take a small sip.

He rubs my leg gently and when I glance at him, his face is etched in concern. 'I'm all right,' I say, sending a reassuring smile across the car.

'You are sure?' he asks, right as Sarah asks, 'Are you really okay?'

'Yes, absolutely. Probably just car sick. The roads are very windy.'

Sarah emits an unconvinced 'mmm' from the back seat and Josh reaches for one of my shoulders and pats it. I breathe out a long slow breath, then take another sip of water. My stomach has settled now, so I close the door and put my seatbelt on. 'All good, darling,' I say. 'We can go now.'

He frowns, but puts the car into gear, looks over his shoulder, and pulls back onto the road. When we're on our way again, he reaches for my hand and brings it to his lips, then rests it on his thigh, covered by his own.

———————

'I hate this part,' says Sarah, looking between the three of us.

I've been dreading it too, each increment of time over the past day-and-a-half inching us closer to this moment. We've returned the rental car, checked in to our respective flights, and have dragged out this goodbye so long, our dad would be proud—but there are only so many airport espressos you can stomach. Especially with the current state of mine.

As it's easier than saying goodbye to my sister, I start with Josh, standing on tippy toes to reach up for a hug. He envelops me and for a second, my feet leave the ground, making me laugh. He puts me down and releases me. 'Thank you for everything—for being a wonderful brother-in-law and Best Man and …' My voice falters and here they come, the tears.

'Hey, no need to cry,' he says. 'I know I am immensely missable but …' He winks at me. 'Besides, aren't we all going to the Maldives together?'

'Apparently,' I say, adding a sniffle. 'I love you,' I say throwing my arms around his waist.

He pats my back. 'Love you too.'

I step back abruptly before I start boo-hooing and reach into my jeans pocket for a tissue but come up empty. Sarah shoves a small packet into my hands—expert crier, always prepared. She and Jean-Luc have said their goodbyes and now we all swap places.

'Fucking goodbyes,' she says. 'They suck a million dog's balls.'

I chuckle and we smile sadly at each other, each through tears, then she encircles me in a fierce hug. The sobs start—no sense is trying to control them now—and as our embrace shudders with them, I couldn't tell you where mine end and hers begin.

All I know is that it breaks my heart every time we have to say goodbye.

Eventually, our crying subsides, and we pull apart to wipe our eyes and blow our noses. When I look at Sarah, her carefully applied makeup is now smeared across her face and adorns a wad of sodden tissues. No doubt, I look the same.

Why did we even bother with makeup this morning? Blind optimism? Gross stupidity? The Parsons sisters are *criers*. We should have been gifted shares in Kleenex rather than frequent flier points—we'd both be retired by fifty!

The giggle starts deep within me and bubbles up, bursting out and now I'm a tear-stained woman, standing in an airport, laughing maniacally. Sarah starts laughing too, wiping away her errant tears and we share the joke, even though I'm not certain she knows what the joke is—or that I do, for that matter.

'Uh, what's so funny?' asks Josh.

'I have no idea,' replies Sarah through laughter.

'Ohh-kay …' he replies.

'*Chérie?*'

Sarah and I continue giggling a few moments more—I wonder if she's enjoying the release as much as I am—but eventually the laughter dies. She grabs both my hands. 'Love you, dear darling adorable little sister.'

'Love you back, dear darling adorable older sister.'

She pulls me in, plants a kiss on my cheek, then turns and calls out, 'Bye,' over her shoulder. Josh raises a hand, then rushes to catch up to her. I sigh and wipe my nose again.

'Catherine, come here.' My husband wraps me up in his arms, his chin resting on my head and holds me, his fingers gently stroking my back. I'm emotionally spent, so there are no more tears, but I wish I could just crawl into bed and snuggle up with my handsome hubby and forget about the world for a while. Instead, we need to get on a plane now.

'Are you all right?' he asks, his voice soft.

'Yes,' I reply. Because I am all right. I am more than all right. I am loved, I am appreciated, I am supported, and I am about to embark on the biggest adventure of my life with the man I love.

'Then let's go.'

Eight months later

CAT

London

Sarah's face appears on my phone screen. We've woken her—and Josh—but with good reason.

'So? Am I an aunt or an uncle?' she asks. I chuckle softly as Josh appears next to her.

'You're an uncle!' I reply, playing along.

'A boy!' she exclaims. To Josh, she says, 'We have a nephew!'

'I know, babe, I heard.'

Jean-Luc leans in, our son swaddled and sleeping in his arms, and holds him up to the camera.

'Ohhh.' Sarah starts sobbing and through her tears, manages, 'He's beautiful.'

Jean-Luc and I grin at each other. 'We think so also,' he says, looking back at Sarah.

'So, does he have a name yet?' asks Josh.

'Oh, yes! He's called Sebastian.'

'Sebastian,' wails Sarah. 'I love it.'

'So, are we calling him Seb or Bash or Bastian?' asks Josh.

'Seb?' I screw up my nose and look pointedly at my brother-in-law. 'We are not calling him any of those—we're calling him *Sebastian*,' I say.

'Got it.' Josh's mouth quirks, but I know he'll honour our wishes.

'And does he have a middle name?' asks Sarah, her eyes wide and slick with tears.

I glance at Jean-Luc. This is still undecided. I'm not in love with the name Ronald, even though I adore my dad, and Jean-Luc's father's name is Ralph—pronounced 'Rafe' like Ralph Fiennes, which I don't mind, but if we lumber our poor child with R-A-L-P-H, he'll be forever correcting people about its pronunciation.

Even so, I've argued with my husband that it would be a wonderful way to honour his family and perhaps even endear me to them—at least a little. It's been a less-than-optimal familial journey since our wedding—some family occasions just shy of something out of a soap opera. But I have it on good authority that producing a grandson will win me some much-needed brownie points and I wouldn't mind capitalising on that. Catherine Parsons Caron, beloved daughter-in-law and mother of Sebastian Ralph Parsons Caron. It's a bit of a mouthful, I agree—maybe we won't end up giving him a middle name after all.

'We have not decided yet,' says Jean-Luc with a diplomatic smile. He steps away and starts gently pacing the hospital room, cradling his son and cooing at him adoringly. I've heard many new parents describe this feeling as their heart bursting with love—but that's not quite right for me. It's surreal and beautiful and perfect and terrifying. And he may not have been planned, but Sebastian is everything I never knew I always wanted, as Sarah would say.

My heart isn't bursting. It's brimming—with love, joy, and excitement about our future.

'Ca-at, hell-ooo.' Oops—I've been so wrapped up in motherly joy, I've abandoned the conversation.

'Sorry.'

'No apologies needed, *Mum*,' she says, beaming at me.

Mum—god. *Mum*. I add it to my growing list of surreal moments—the 'firsts' that are coming fast and thick. No doubt, they will continue to come, each little milestone marking its point in my life.

I'm a mother now.

'So,' she says, 'we'll let you go—go bask in the gloriousness of your new son—but we love you. We love you all and we'll talk to you soon, okay?'

'All right. Speak soon.'

'Well, sort of soon, because we're flying back from Cape Town tomorrow but I'll message you when we get home and we've unpacked and, you know …'

'Yes, I know,' I say with a smile. My sister can't function after a trip until everything is unpacked, washed, sorted, and put away. 'Oh! Before we let you go, did you see Lou's news on Facebook?'

'Yes! Anders proposed! That's so lovely.'

'Yeah, that's awesome,' adds Josh.

'It is,' I reply. 'We're calling them next—and Jae and Alistair after that.'

'Ooh, maybe another destination wedding,' Sarah says, waggling her eyebrows.

I laugh. 'I'm sure Jae would love that. Maybe she should expand her business—officially become a destination wedding planner.' She smiles, then wipes her bleary eyes. 'We should let you go,' I say—it *is* the middle of the night. Jean-Luc brings our son back into frame and raises a tiny hand to wave at them.

'Bye Sebastian, we love you,' she coos at him, even though his eyes are closed.

'Fly safely,' I say.

'We will! Oh!' she says, startling me. I glance at Sebastian but he's still fast asleep. 'The Maldives! I've got that at the top of my to-do list. We should book something for your anniversary.'

'Sez, we just had a baby.'

'Yeah, and …? He's a Parsons *and* a Caron—the kid's gonna be a traveller, Cat. Might as well start him early.'

'We haven't even brought him home from the hospital yet!'

'Never too soon …'

I roll my eyes at her. 'We'll think about it.'

'Okay,' she says, frowning slightly.

'Bye, Cat,' says Josh. 'And, Jean-Luc, congrats, man.'

'*Merci*,' says my grinning husband.

'Bye,' says Sarah, waving. 'Bye from Aunty Sarah, Sebastian. I love you. Bye …'

We end the call and I place the phone on my lap and look up at Jean-Luc. 'What do you think?' I ask.

'I think we need to get him his passports *tout de suite, n'est-ce pas*?'

I grin at him. 'I meant his *name*, silly.'

Jean-Luc shrugs then looks down at our son. 'What do you think, Sebastian?' He leans in close as though he's listening, then lifts his head. 'He says "Ralph" but we spell it the British way—R-A-F-E.'

'I love it.'

'He is already wise, our son.'

'Takes after his papa.'

Those intense green eyes lock onto mine and he leans down and kisses me—a proper kiss, the kind that usually leads to lovemaking, though there will be less of that in the foreseeable future. And just as I start to lose myself in the sensation of my husband's kiss, Sebastian emits a mewling cry.

Jean-Luc steps back, stroking his face and making soothing shushing sounds, as his tiny balled fists wave in the air. 'I think he might be hungry,' I say.

'I think you may be right, Mama,' he says, handing me Sebastian.

Mama. My heart may just burst.

Acknowledgments

It's mind-blowing to be writing the acknowledgments for my seventh book and the fifth and final in the Holiday Romance series, especially as the first in the series, *One Summer in Santorini*, was only published three years ago.

I started this series by telling a simple boy-meets-girl story from my own life. I went to Santorini, a shell of my former self, heart-broken and cynical about love, and I met the love of my life. It was all very 'Insta Love', though Instagram didn't exist at the time, but a lengthy long-distance relationship and sixteen years later, we're still together and our little meet-cute has sparked a whole series and a cast of characters I've grown to love almost as much as my real-life loved ones.

I have so enjoyed writing Sarah, Cat, and Jaelee, as well as their family, friends, and love interests. They've made me laugh out loud, they've made me ugly cry, and sometimes, they have frustrated the hell out of me as they've done whatever they've pleased while I – their creator – have been left to write them out of the fictional corners they've painted themselves into. It's bittersweet to say goodbye to the gang, but I do with love and assuredness that they all got their (much deserved) happily ever afters.

I love being an author. It is literally a dream come true and I am so grateful to those who support me, my writing, and my career – my dream.

To Ben, the cute American boy who has morphed into my very own silver fox, thank you for knowing exactly how I like my tea, for bringing me a glass of pinot at the end of a long day of writing or editing, for letting me read aloud the messages sent by my readers, and for being my sounding board and coming up with some of my cleverest lines. Thank you, mostly, for steadfastly supporting me as I follow my dream and believing in it as much as I do.

To my sister, Vic, you're the best sister and muse an author could ever ask for. Thank you for being an inspiration – not just for the character of Cat but because of your tenacity, your loyalty, and your selflessness. You are a wonder to me and the best little sis I could ever have asked for. It's obvious why you're one of my dearest friends.

Mum, Dad, and Gail, you are seriously the BEST parents ever – supportive, generous, loving, and some of the best people I know. To the rest of my loved ones – my family by birth and those I've adopted along the way (whether you've wanted me to or not), thank you for being part of my heart's rich tapestry. I can only do what I do – in all aspects of life – because I have emotional ports scattered far and wide. I'm fortunate that so many places in the world feel like home – just because you're there.

Jennie Rothwell, my editor extraordinaire, this is our third book together and I'm so grateful for your insightful feedback. Working with you has honed and elevated my writing and I really appreciate the care you give to my work. Thank you also to the rest of the incredibly hard-working team at One More Chapter – Charlotte Ledger, Bethan Morgan, Emma Petfield, and Sara Roberts.

As always, an enormous thank you to my brilliant agent, Lina Langlee of The North Literary Agency. You were there at the very beginning of this series and have helped guide me through (can you believe it?) five books! I feel so fortunate to have you in my corner – I couldn't (and wouldn't) do this without you. YOU ARE THE BEST!

A huge thank you to Jenna Lo Bianco, fellow author and Melbournite, for so generously giving your time to provide an Italian edit, ensuring that the locations, culture, and language were accurately depicted. I can't wait to see your brilliant book babies fly – it is only a matter of time, I am sure of it. Thank you also to my (wonderful) brother-in-law, Mark (Brother Bear), for reviewing *mon français mediocre* and ensuring it was correct.

As always, I am grateful to my fellow authors (massive understatement). Being a part of the writing community, and especially the Romance writing community, is a privilege and an honour and I am constantly in awe of how generous you all are *and* of your incredible work, which is an inspiration to me. A special thank you to the volunteers who run our associations, the Romance Novelists Association (UK) and the Romance Writers Association (AU), for continuing to support and elevate the Romance genre. And to my fellow #AusWrites-ers and #6amAusWriters – I love our exchanges on social media and (sometimes – not often enough) getting to see you in person.

A special shout out to my fellow Renegades and writerly besties, Andie Newton, Nina Kwiatkowski (Kaye), and Fiona

Leitch. Our daily catch-ups keep me sane and I am in awe of your incredible talent and brilliant writing. You are so dear to me and I cannot wait till we're all together (one day).

I am also a (grateful) member of the wonderful Facebook community, Chick Lit and Prosecco. I love engaging with you and especially appreciate your support for my cover reveals and publication days, and for inviting me onto your blogs. A special thank you to the dazzling Chick in Charge (and fantastic author), Anita Faulkner, for your bright spirit and unwavering support, and to community SUPER-STARS, Sue and Ian (mwah).

Thank you also to the reading and reviewing community – the bloggers, podcasters, and reviewers who generously share their thoughts on reading and books. We (literally) couldn't do this without you. A special shout out to Veronica and Darren of Australian Book Lovers, Hayley Walsh of Write Words Podcast, and Dani Vee of Words & Nerds, and to Rachel Gilbey for always assembling such great blog tours.

And lastly, dear reader, thank *you*. Thank you for coming on this fun and fabulous journey with me. I hope you had a blast! I certainly did.

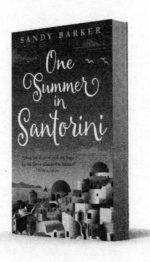

There was something in the air that night…

Sarah has had enough of men. It's time to rekindle her first
true love – travel – so she books a sailing trip around the
Greek islands with a group of strangers.

The very last thing Sarah wants is to meet someone new, but
then a gorgeous American man boards her yacht… And
when she also encounters a handsome silver fox who
promises her the world, she realises that trouble really does
come in twos.

Will Sarah dive into a holiday fling or stick to her plan to
steer clear of men, continue her love affair with feta and find
her own way after all?

Note to self: don't sleep with your flatmate after a curry and three bottles of wine … especially if he's secretly in love with you and wants you to meet his mum.

Cat Parsons is on the run. She doesn't *do* relationships. After ten years of singlehood even the hint of the 'L' word is enough to get her packing her bags and booking herself onto a two-week holiday.

A European bus tour feels like a stroke of genius to dodge awkward conversations at home. But little does Cat realise that the first stop will be Paris, the city of love itself.

Will she find a new way of looking at it?

How far would *you* go in the name of love?

Sarah Parsons has a choice ahead of her. After the trip of a lifetime she's somehow returned home with *two* handsome men wanting to whisk her away into the sunset.

Pulled in two directions across the globe, it's making life trickier than it sounds. Her gorgeous American, Josh, wants to meet her in Hawaii for a holiday to remember.

Meanwhile silver fox James plans to wine and dine her in London.

It's a lot to handle for an Aussie girl who had totally sworn off men…

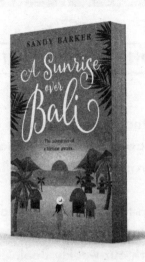

Home is where the heart is . . .

When Jaelee Tan leaves her high-flying PR job in Miami for a sabbatical in Bali, the last thing she expects is for it to become permanent. But when her boss demands the trip be cut short, Jae does the only thing she can think of and quits on the spot.

With two months in Bali, a new group of friends and the gorgeous scenery and beaches, Jae is determined to make the most of her new-found freedom. And when she locks eyes with hunky Scot, Alistair, Jae wonders if she'll lose her heart to more than just a Balinese sunrise.

'A gorgeous escapist romance'
Emma Robinson

YOUR NUMBER ONE STOP

ONE MORE CHAPTER

FOR PAGETURNING BOOKS

One More Chapter is an
award-winning global
division of HarperCollins.

Sign up to our newsletter to get our
latest eBook deals and stay up to date
with our weekly Book Club!
<u>Subscribe here.</u>

Meet the team at
<u>www.onemorechapter.com</u>

Follow us!

 <u>@OneMoreChapter_</u>
 <u>@OneMoreChapter</u>
 <u>@onemorechapterhc</u>

Do you write unputdownable fiction?
We love to hear from new voices.
Find out how to submit your novel at
<u>www.onemorechapter.com/submissions</u>